James Fagan is an English language teacher, stand-up comedian (his failures and family providing much of the material), avid reader and a big fan of the sess. He's lived the sad existence of an unpublished author for 31 years, but like a reverse genie in a bottle, as you pick up and hold this piece of him, you have already granted one of his wishes. If James has two more wishes coming his way he would like them to be: a) to never again have to write a biography in the 3rd person (thanks publishers), b) to open up a Japanese-style naked bathing house in inner city Dublin.

This book and collection are dedicated to my wonderful family, my lovely and loving partner, and my amazing friends. For all the laughter, inspiration, patience, forgiveness, and love, I dedicate this book to you. They have made this book possible in that they have allowed me to write for the sheer love of it, without any want or right to seek my fortune in writing. For when it comes to family, friends, and love, I am among the richest people in the world. If becoming financially rich has even the smallest possibility of distancing myself from these amazing people – then fuck the imaginary money. But if, somehow, this book does make a miracle amount, let's say – anything beyond €50,000 net – then I have two other goals in life: to use any miracle-money to open up Ireland's first ever Korean-Japanese inspired naked bathing house, run at cost, to provide a space where we can let our hair down and take our nakedness back from a world that criminalizes and censors its honest representation while feeding us a force-fed diet of contorted 'perfect' bodies. My second goal is to fund a Rory Gallagher tribute film which would consist entirely of live performances, where any live performance without video would be given over to an animation studio (looking at you – Cartoon Saloon).

James Fagan

SMALL DOSES

AUSTIN MACAULEY PUBLISHERS™

LONDON * CAMBRIDGE * NEW YORK * SHARJAH

Copyright © James Fagan 2024

The right of James Fagan to be identified as author of this work has been asserted by the author in accordance with sections 77 and 78 of the Copyright, Designs and Patents Act 1988.

All rights reserved. No part of this publication may be reproduced, stored in a retrieval system, or transmitted in any form or by any means, electronic, mechanical, photocopying, recording, or otherwise, without the prior permission of the publishers.

Any person who commits any unauthorised act in relation to this publication may be liable to criminal prosecution and civil claims for damages.

This is a work of fiction. Names, characters, businesses, places, events, locales, and incidents are either the products of the author's imagination or used in a fictitious manner. Any resemblance to actual persons, living or dead, or actual events is purely coincidental.

A CIP catalogue record for this title is available from the British Library.

ISBN 9781035809493 (Paperback)
ISBN 9781035809509 (ePub e-book)

www.austinmacauley.co.uk

First Published 2024
Austin Macauley Publishers Ltd®
1 Canada Square
Canary Wharf
London
E14 5AA

Special thanks for early draft proofreads and feedback go to my brilliantly mad uncle Les Coogan, my wonderfully amazing friend Aileen Parnell, and my one-in-a-billion dad, David Fagan. When my father returned my first draft he said: 'it's good son, not nearly as bad as I expected. I can see you making it as an author 10 years from now, give or take a year'. Thanks dad, knowing you, I couldn't have asked for more promising praise than that. Special thanks as well go to Jerry Doyle for a random act of kindness given to me out of the blue.

Table of Contents

Part 1 — 11
   The Difference a Teacher Can Make — 13

Intermission — 73
   Half-Pipe — 75
   Blessington Basin — 85
   Scrubbing Rocks — 87
   Prologue to Jamie's Lucid Dream Diary — 88
   What's That? — 94
   Flies and Windows — 95
   Tommy's Rambles — 98
   Satellite — 119
   A Letter to A Godchild — 121
   Spending Too Much Time on My Phone (Again) — 133
   Passing by Your House — 134
   A Poem for Walt Whitman's Atoms — 141
   The Vegan Haikus — 143
   Talking Shit and Backflips — 145

Part 2 — 159
   Tightrope Thursday — 161
   Pre-Drinks Before Free Drinks — 168
   One for the Road — 181

Stripping for Strangers	*186*
The Morning After	*197*
Filling In	*201*
And Leaving Out	*205*
Saturday	*216*
Sunday	*221*
Monday	*224*
And Monday	*227*
And Monday	*230*
And Still Bloody Monday	*239*
Tuesday	*247*
And Tuesday	*253*
Wednesday and Thursday	*261*
Court Day	*266*
Friday	*275*
You Can't Escape Shakespeare	*285*
If I Can Have an Afterword with You	**301**

Part 1

The Difference a Teacher Can Make

In my 3rd year of secondary school, my English teacher of two and a half years, Mr Mulch, was changed for a new teacher, Mr Watchem, and that little change helped to make the person I am today. It wasn't that old Mr Mulch, the auld rascal, retired. No, he remains, to me, the only public-school teacher I've even known to be fired—and not for his crimes against us, which were many, but he was fired after a media frenzy declared him a 'pimp.' My oldest friend still carries a newspaper article—'Local Teacher Charged for Pimping' as proof that at least some of our school day stories aren't entirely fabricated. Of course, you should always take your newspaper articles with a bucket of salt. My own understanding of the case is this: It turned out that our old boring English teacher had a habit of sleeping with sex-workers, taking secret videos of the encounters, and then refusing to pay them on the grounds that he would otherwise release the footage and thus reveal the woman's profession to her family and friends. Well, eventually our old Mr Mulch tried this with a woman who must have called his bluff. I don't know what stigma she has since been subjected to, but I imagine she came off on the better end of the ordeal. Mr Mulch was disgraced, fired, and is currently in the no-man's land of our judicial system, circling there perpetually as far as I know.

If you knew him you would hardly believe the whole thing. I mean, Mr Mulch stood for me as a sort of godly representation of boredom. Like the Grim Reaper whose various guises are always made to convey a sense of death, or Cupid's statues which go for innocent love and the not so subtle reminder that with love comes babies, (which was at least true once upon a time). Everything about this man was dull, withered, grey, boring, dull. Boredom in body, flesh, voice and tastes. Boredom in spirit and jokes, the most boring man I've ever known.

It was as if the power of every airport and catholic church service I have ever witnessed resided within him. He dressed in the same dull clothes every day, and, as far as his students could tell, lived as if he were already dead. His voice caused me to look up a word for it—soporific—something that induces sleep, so at least he taught me that, as well as the valuable lesson that even the most boring among us can surprise you. Whenever I, or one of my friends from school, bump into one of our old teachers we always ask if they had suspected anything, and they inevitably tell us that they were just as shocked as anyone. It seems you can get away with a lot of mischief simply by being too dull to warrant notice, god only knows what Michael Martin gets up.

It's from Mr Mulch that I've become convinced that it must have been a mixture of bad teachers and/or bad parents which have ingrained in so many of us the feelings of guilt and secrecy which come from enjoying ourselves; from being happy, as a dull teacher encourages no smiles from their unhappy prisoners, and so to smile means to be up to mischief, to laugh becomes a telltale for trouble, and when happiness becomes suspected and attacked it becomes guilty too. We had to make what little guilty-fun we could to survive that class. Among my other teachers, the good, the bad and the terrifying, not one had their absence met with such a universal outcry of joy than poor old Mr Mulch. The only prayers I remember making were for the absence of Mr Mulch, and his absences coincided with those prayers just enough to keep me in the faith for nearly 20 years.

And yet; I laugh now to think that the whole time he was putting classes to sleep he was likely dreaming of the next free go he could squeeze out of some poor hard-working woman, for they must have been incredibly hard working to go through the motions with such a man. Only once did I get to observe him outside of a classroom, and that was when I was taken to the greyhound track by my family, and there I happened to see him, sitting there by himself, sipping the one beer all night and, I suppose, gambling his money away. Perhaps he actually did pay the sex-workers when he won on the dogs and only resorted to blackmail when he had a particularly unlucky run, whatever the case, good riddance, because our English classes during his reign were beyond miserable.

We discussed books as if they were bricks, poetry as if it were drying paint, and we handed each essay and assignment to him with dread. As a teacher, he fixated on easy to correct grammar and punctuation mistakes and returned every white page smeared in his murderous red. The best you could hope for was to be given back a piece of writing with minimal molestation. There was no encouragement, no comment on creativity or originality, all he cared for was

English without mistake, and in this way his boredom spread through us and in us like an anaesthetic. He sucked all the joy and enthusiasm out of the subject worse than any vampire could, for vampires are at least meant to gain something from sucking the life from others, Mr Mulch was more like a zombie, who slowly and without any sign of self-benefit gnawed away our enthusiasm for English day-by-day as each mark of his red pen chipped a little more away of our living prose and promise.

If he had not been arrested for 'pimping,' it's possible that literature would have been forever tainted and inaccessible to me. It's a tragedy that a child's ability to grasp a subject is so much determined by the relationship of student and teacher, and for all that our teachers are rarely respected (or inspected).

In any case, our school was scandalised by the whole ordeal, which may have been the reason why we ended up with an English English teacher. I, for one, like to imagine our school principal ordering the very finest of English teachers from the mother country of this ubiquitous language. But what mattered was that he was the very best English teacher I could ever have imagined, as if, like a pendulum, he was every bit as good as old Mr Mulch had been bad. For a start there was his name, Mr Watchem, a name so suitable for the profession that I'm rather surprised Charles Dickens never made use of it.

I remember him as a serious young man for the most part, and he could also be a little stern and dry. For example, he came in every day in black slacks, black shoes and a white long-sleeved shirt, so his clothes were as fixed as ours—only we were stuck with a uniform. He did, however, have what seemed to be an endless supply of interesting cufflinks. I remember red and yellow referee cards, cufflinks made from old English coins, even a Doctor Who inspired pair unless my fancy deceives me. But, more than anything else, I remember that he loved his subject, and I hope he loves it still, for his enthusiasm is what blew off the dead dust left behind from our previous teacher and finally gave me back a love of poetry and stories. So thank you sir, beyond this blur of fiction and non-fiction, I thank you sincerely.

Anyway, perhaps I would have forgotten the first time I met Mr Watchem if it weren't for the essay he had us write: *What single word would you use to describe yourself? Justify your answer in 2-4 pages.* It's a long time since I was faced with that question, but to the best of my memory here is what my answer looked like:

~~Happy~~
~~Optimist~~
~~Realist~~
~~Argumentative~~
~~Bookworm~~
~~Moody~~
~~Easy~~
~~Normal~~
~~Funny~~
~~Inconsistent~~
~~Irregular~~

The list continued until I lost the will to live and began staring blankly at my page. Everyone else was writing furiously around me as I tried to imagine what words they had used. Maybe they couldn't find the right word and they had settled, maybe there was no right word, maybe that was the whole idea? What word would *you* choose? (_____?). But no matter what angle I used to try and pry open the question I just couldn't decide on what to write. Then I made another mistake in looking up, and I saw clearly that Mr Watchem was watching me. That ended me. A familiar sinking feeling took hold, one that always seems to start in my stomach and then gets pushed towards my head. This sick feeling continued to pass back and forth between head and gut until Watchem announced we had one minute left. Finally a shred of inspiration hit me and I put something down on the page without furiously crossing it out:

Indecisive: I must be indecisive (Please see above!).

When I went to hand it up with the rest, wanting nothing more than to leave that class and forget it ever happened, Mr Watchem asked if I could stay behind for a minute. He *was* watching me, and that sinking feeling started to move down into my legs and cause them to shake. As it turned out though, Watchem put me at my ease.

"I think you overthought it," he said with a friendly smile, glancing at my mess of a page. I stayed silent. "Although it's a funny answer. Mm… What's your name again? You forgot to write it on your essay."

"martin, sir."

"Well, listen Martin, there's 2 points to this essay, the first and most important is for me to get a grasp on this class's writing and grammar, to know what I need to go over before getting you lot ready for the junior cert, the 2nd point is to help me remember all your names by learning a bit about you. So, can you write me another essay tonight?"

"yes sir," I said, "but what should I write about?"

"You can write about anything, anything you want," he said. If I wasn't so shy I might have replied—I can write about anything well enough, but I can never choose anything to write about, but my face must have relayed the message for me, for after a moment he continued:

"Ok, finish the essay you started, explain why you're indecisive in 2-4 pages, and if you can't do that, just write about a hobby you enjoy, ok?"

"ok, thanks sir," I said, and left the class in a fog of thoughts.

Here is a reimagining of that 2nd essay, to the best of my memory:

Why I am indecisive. And a hobby I enjoy:

When I was very young everyone thought that I had a speech impediment, and the more I learnt to speak the more pronounced the problem became. It was so bad that I couldn't even say my own name, instead I went around calling myself 'marmim' instead of Martin. My parents still bring it up as a funny story that I was known as Mumbling Martin, or just plain Mumbles, on account of my funny speech. Most of my earliest memories come from this time. Perhaps the worst of them is having to repeat again and again the same words and phrases as my parents while they tried to hide their worry and anxiety. Everyone learns to speak, it's a fact that we take for granted, and which makes the experience of learning to speak so beautifully relaxed.

I often wonder that if everything were taught in the same inevitable way as speaking how much easier things would be, for we get to learn this incredibly complex skill and massive body of knowledge with perfect patience and complete confidence. But, having said that, because it is so taken for granted it completely erodes our core beliefs and speaks to our worst fears when it doesn't work out that way. I'm sure my parents allowed some time to pass before becoming too worried, after all, no child is perfect and mistakes are to be expected, but sooner or later they had to face up to the fact that things weren't working out with me; that I wasn't working within the norm. My speech was terrible, and it was only getting worse.

It's impossible to remember exactly what I went through, and, in any case, it's in the past and the facts forgotten and obscured, but I do remember how I *felt* during all this, or at least I can't remember this period without feeling: The feeling of sinking, of the frustration of having to repeat myself so much, the teasing from my siblings and new school mates. I remember wondering why I was the only child going to two schools—my normal primary school and what I later learnt were speech therapy sessions twice a week. More than anything else, I remember being observed, and corrected, and found wanting.

I remember the speech therapist quiet well as a nice woman with long black hair who would get me to play game after game, and who had a much easier time hiding any anxiety that she might have had over my lack of progress. Professional patience, or just plain paid-for patience, no matter, for in any case my obscure memories of her still bring a smile to my face. My family and friends, on the other hand, increasingly made me feel like I was being scrutinised all the time, so that I became withdrawn and reluctant to speak at all for fear of being corrected and made to repeat what I had just said. It must be hell on earth for those who grow up with a disability, because if the disability doesn't shatter your confidence, been constantly watched will, or, to put it correctly, a disability, in what we consider to be a developed society, and within a reasonably well-off family, is often no real disability to the individual in question, but creates a disability in everyone else to treat that person, well, just like everyone else, (or, I might phrase it thus—A disability hinders your right and liberty to be treated equally, because most of us suffer already from too much anxiety to handle anything adequately which doesn't belong to our limited and limiting sense of reality. Although, in reality, this last part was likely not part of my original essay, but reality is only as limiting as we would have it—and anyway, reality, like all things, has its expiry date), anyway.

This went on for a few years, and every remedy was tried and tested to either get me to speak properly or discover the source of the problem. It must be said that my parents, despite accidentally instilling in me a hatred and fear of being corrected, did everything within their power and a good deal beyond to help me. In the meantime, I went through life with this growing nagging feeling that there was something wrong with me, and I became ever more reluctant to open my mouth. True, I learnt to read and write at a normal enough pace, and this must have been some relief to my family, but it's hard to get on in this world if no one can understand you when you're talking. Eventually my parents took me to someone who figured out the problem—I had a strong and unusually deep build-up of fluid in my ears which was preventing me from hearing clearly.

It wasn't that I couldn't *speak* properly, I just couldn't *hear* properly. It all sounds too simple to be true, but there it was. A few weeks of eardrops later and the barrier that separated me from the world was dissolved as my ears were put to right. Only I didn't consider them better at the time. True, I could now tell the difference between an M and an N, a T and a C, and so on, and my speech finally began to improve, but for the first time I could hear with the sharpness and volume of everyone else, and for someone living life with the volume set to 6, say, 10 became unbearable. I don't mean to say I had super hearing, instead I had a super sensitivity to sound. I became so used to hearing the world through hidden fluid that I was like a raw nerve without it. So as I was finally learning to speak properly and please my parents, I became increasingly troubled by certain noises. Chief among them is the sound of hard brushes against rough surfaces like concrete. If a motorised street cleaner or some dust peddler was nearby I normally went hysterical at the sound, and even now I'm liable to block up at least one ear and wince. And it wasn't just certain pitches that got to me, any loud noise was bound to freak me out.

This sensitivity to loud noises not only kept me away from live music and street cleaners, but it also effected what my dad was hoping to be a solid football career, and as much as I enjoyed kicking a ball around with my dad, the screaming and frenzy of a football match was too much. Any match I saw or took part in left me too confused and frustrated to follow along, and with my growing hatred of being corrected and feeling scrutinised all the time I had one of the quickest football careers in history. My brother, Shay, only a year and a half younger than me, became the most promising football player in the family, securing a bond and a burden with our father that I'll never have. And so whenever our father took us out to practise, or took my brother out to play a match, it was never long before I had nested myself up a tree, out of sight, happy and free.

But despite my sensitivity to loud or piercing noises, and a few missed opportunities here and there, I was coming along, even if I was growing to be a bit odd. My parents joke that during this time I went from Mumbling Martin into Martin the Martian, but I was now an acceptable oddity. My confidence was shattered from the double blow of being constantly corrected *and* finding out that the whole thing was due to my hearing rather than my ability to speak. I learnt from an earlier age than most that your parents don't always know what's best (even when they're trying their best). Still, I was getting over myself well enough. That was until I succumbed to shingles at 7 years of age. Not something that normally affects young children, but I got it and remained hospital bound for weeks. I still remember, with embarrassment, the temper-tantrums I threw over the frequent injections I was required to take and the misery of it all, but it was in hospital, where there were no longer any trees to escape to, that my dad handed me a new bridge to connect us; it was in hospital that I started to seriously enjoy the boredom-relief and escape of books.

Books not only suited the hospital in terms of keeping me quiet and docile, but they suited the grumpy awkward child that I had become. I continued to take criticism and scrutiny very badly, and while my speech was improving, I still had a tendency to slur and mumble. But in my head there was no one to correct my own inner voice, and so when I read there was no stumbling, no trepidation, no scrutiny; just freedom and solitude, a *guided* solitude—books—a space to be alone without being lonely, a journey of someone else's words brought to life by your own inner voice, my silent, sweet, uncorrectable inner voice. Books soon became my number one pastime, and these days I think books are to be credited with restoring some degree of my self-confidence. I still struggle with the idea of being watched and corrected, and I think that also goes some way to explain why I'm indecisive, but, perhaps it is also why I love books.

Fin

This is the essay I handed up to Watchem, and while I was worried over how personal it was, he had nothing but kind words to say about it. In fact, he thanked me for sharing such a personal story with him, and he did so sincerely. So, for better and worse, that 'thank you for sharing' is somewhat responsible for what follows, but I owe him far more than that. In the following year Watchem set up our school's first debating club, which I went for and thrived in. It helped to grow my confidence and gave me an environment where I could make new friends. And so, it's to Watchem that this story is dedicated to, and to anyone else who has kept enough of their enthusiasm to rekindle or awaken the enthusiasm of others, and if we ever meet again sir, it'll be my honour to buy you a pint.

Hooked

Towards the end of 5th year, when we were handed the itinerary for Maynooth University's open day, I scrolled through it with my usual flippant disinterest—'Economics,' easy-peasy. 'English,' god no, 'History,' wishy-washy, 'Anthropology...' what the hell's *'Anthropology?'* The brochure described it as 'the study of humankind in all its aspects' which tickled my curiosity, 'maybe' I thought. It seems I had taken the first bite, now it was up to the lecturer, Dr Kurt Carey, to reel me in. Dr Carey did so by throwing the widest intellectual net possible, which, given the subject, was wide beyond belief. My recollections of that introductory seminar always rotate around the following:

"Social anthropology, the study of man, is of course also interested in the behaviour of our nearest cousins; Chimpanzees and Bonobos. Chimpanzees and their aggressive behaviour have gotten most of the attention, but it's only in recent years that we are focusing on bonobos, which resemble chimpanzees very much, but with a couple of key differences—females are the dominant members, and they resolve the majority of their disputes with sex and orgies...

"here we are interested in all human behaviour, one fascinating study taking place at the moment is to observe human behaviour in elevators. What happens if someone enters a packed lift and faces the people there rather than turning to face the door. In anthropology we encourage students to break social rules such as these to better...

"We seek to understand our own culture by studying other cultures, so we spend a great deal of time studying cultures and societies from all over the world..."

"Anthropology's main research tool is ethnography, which is studying people in their own environment over an extended period of time, usually between 6 months to 2 years. After completing my BA in anthropology I spent 1 year living among a group of people in Papua New Guinea, literally living in a forest eating insects..."

I left the seminar with no clearer understanding of what anthropology is, but my appetite was whetted. The subject seemed such a mix of sociology, psychology, zoology and history that I found it hard to resist, for its very vagueness appealed to me, for I am vagueness made flesh. Yes. St. Martin, the patron saint of vagueness. (You can go to saint Anthony when you know what you're looking for, and pray to me when you don't even know that much). It also helped that Dr Carey was a very charismatic fisher. He had the voice, gender and appearance that would have guaranteed him an easy and respectable career in Irish politics, but, since he was an anthropologist as opposed to a politician, he had far more interesting stories to tell, or at least that he could tell openly.

His combination of charisma, height, serious stature, deep voice and a seemingly unlimited pool of interesting stories and anecdotes made Carey one of the best open-day fishers in the student fishing business, and I was hooked. But I can't place all the blame on Dr Carey, it only makes sense that the vaguest of people would fall into the vaguest of subjects. And more to the point, we were as good as a school of fish because, for most of us, college seemed our only possible option, so that Dr Carey's net was a net within a net within a net within a net, thrown not towards an open sea so much as a fish farm.

The only other memorable incident that happened over the course of the day was this; in my absentmindedness, I accidently gave a black eye to another fish while exploring the campus. I was making the dangerous combination of walking and stretching when a woman's face met my elbow as she was turning her head. I apologised fervently, but she laughed it off and we went our separate ways— my face growing red as hers started to bruise. I would later be told that the black eye which later developed caused her a good deal of explaining and annoyance, and was the most memorable incident of her own open day.

At the train station I met back up with Mark and a couple of other friends from our school, and we spent the journey back to Broombridge discussing which lectures we attended and which we found interesting. I was the only one among them to attend the one on anthropology, and so I surprised them when I declared my intention to study it, as I could only explain in the vaguest possible terms what studying anthropology might entail.

"I don't know," I was giving up, "you study culture and people, the social rules people take for granted, and if you do a masters you get to travel and study some out-there group of people who are still living in forests or something, what's not to like?" My friends seemed unconvinced.

"What job would you get out of it?" Mark asked.

"I don't know, what are you planning to get out of studying English? Sure everyone can speak English, you don't need college for that."

"Well, if you want a job as a writer, editor, journalist, teacher, critic, I'm pretty sure a degree in English is going to help," Mark replied.

"Yeah right," said I, trying to keep the attention off myself, "imagine your CV when you finish—I studied English; I can read, write and speak better English than anyone else!—what good is that when every CV is going to be proof-read into perfect English anyway?"

Mark laughed, "well, when you can finally explain to us what anthropology is, I'll be able to put you down properly." He got me there.

Anthropology, anthropology, anthropology. Bonobos having orgies, forest-dwelling tribes, eating insects, staring at people in elevators. I could think of little else during the next few weeks. But when I told my parents that I would apply for an Arts degree in Maynooth, with the intention of studying anthropology, they weren't convinced.

"What job would you get out of it?" My father, Richard Penny, asked.

"I don't know," I said, again getting exasperated, but at least by now I had done a little more research about it. "Some charities seem to hire anthropologists, they send them off somewhere to see how their money could best be used to benefit people, you can get research jobs too. But I guess if I kept at it I could become a lecturer... or something."

My dad shook his head. "Charities pay pittance son, except for the corrupt ones, but they only pay their top people well, and you have to give up your morals." My mam, Maggie, seemed to hold no strong opinions on the topic as long as at least one of her children graduated from college, but, happy enough to back up her husband, she added:

"I would love for you to be a lecturer, but you can lecture on anything, can't you? Maybe you should study something more practical, like English?"

"Study English!" I jumped. "I have a library card for that. Look, I know I love to read, and I always do ok in English at school, but I can do that in my own time, when else am I going to have the chance to study something like anthropology? Isn't college about trying new things?" I pleaded.

But my parents just looked at each other, in truth they had no idea what college was for besides helping you to secure a good job. In their day college was for the wealthy and free, or at least for people who liked school, and their schooling was spent getting constantly hit and humiliated by their miserable catholic teachers, who I suppose were passing on the lessons they received from their own miserable catholic parents. The miserable history of miserable old Ireland—first we were subjugated by the English, then by the church, and now we hardly know what we're subjected by. My parents barely made it out of school alive, and so college was supposed to be our frontier, our own land of discovery, the next step, the next toss towards the future by the Penny family. Throw a penny and make a wish, then swim-swim-swim my ignorant fish. All my parents knew about college was that my uncle had gone, obtained his BA, and got a great job out of it. My sister, Kate, had gone to college too, but she dropped out, and while she was making it as something of a freelance artist, it remains clear in our family that my parents, if they had their way, would have seen her graduate. How could I or they know that since the time of my uncle colleges have been gleefully flooding the market with degrees and leaving us fish lost in a sea of forever-shrinking opportunities. But I, lost in my own way, continued:

"Sure look at Kate—great at art, studied art, dropped out… I got through school without losing my love of books, and even that was a close call, I don't want to give college a go at destroying that." Finally my father shrugged, "It's your future Martin, but college is expensive, and we just want to make sure it's going to be worth it for you. Plus, I'm sure Kate learnt a few useful things before dropping out."

"Sure, well, as I said, I'd have to study anthropology by doing an Arts degree, which means I have to study 3 subjects in my first year and finish by studying 2 subjects, so I won't just be studying anthropology."

"What else are you planning to study then?" My mother asked.

"Economics anyway, it's easy enough in school and the open day lecture was easy to follow, I don't know what my third subject will be yet, but they give you a few weeks of attending different lectures to decide." The word 'economics' had a magical effect on my dad, and he nodded approvingly. "Well, at least that's a practical subject, you might even get into marketing and advertising," he smiled. My mam nodded, 'hopefully this one graduates' she must have thought.

Having finally made a decision regarding college, I settled into my final year of what I felt to be State-sponsored, State-enforced, and State-couldn't-care-less imprisonment—for a passive and indifferent prisoner is how I often felt in school. But the teachers, in their turn, began to treat us differently: Nearly adults and unlikely ever to return, the teachers behaved a little more freely themselves, for even prison guards are confined in their own way and enjoy loosening up when they can. Our economics teacher, in particular, surprised us all by opening up a class by looking conspiratorially at us before saying:

"In the final year I always ask my class one question, because I want to know if there's a good answer, even though these days I have to be careful about which classes I ask." We grew silent and attentive. Mr Fogerty was the oldest teacher we had, and he rarely spoke of anything beyond his subject. Old Mr Fogerty. He must have been teaching economics for over 40 years, and his interest in the subject certainly wasn't the compound kind, but more of the diminishing returns. To be fair, I imagine that so slowly did the age gap between himself and his students increase that he only noticed—perhaps as he was getting into his late thirties—that it was getting harder and harder to connect with his pupils.

"Every popular reference point he had to bridge the gap between himself and us had been worn away and destroyed by the passing of time. This must be the curse of teaching; you keep getting older as the students become comparatively younger, and so you become less and less connected with their world until you eventually become a living fossil, and Mr Fogerty was the oldest living fossil in our school. However he was known outside of the school, to us, he was only an old economics teacher, living within a fog so thick that even the economics he taught us would prove to be outdated. The class were all ears. It had been a long time since Mr Fogerty had last tried to engage us in anything non-economical. In full possession of the floor, he asked us:

"What have black people ever done?"

The class was silent, we could never have expected this. Mr Fogerty continued: "I mean, they've been in touch with civilisation for hundreds of years, but their continent's a mess. They've never seemed to civilise themselves, and so we gave civilisation to them, but since then, what have they done? Inside and outside of Africa, accomplished black people are the exception, never the rule, why?" Our long silence was broken by Tommy, one of our celebrated class-clowns:

"Sir, Jesus was black."

"NO HE WASN'T!" Fogerty barked back, "he was middle-eastern, not black."

Another boy tried, "they do deadly at the Olympics sir, in a lot of sports we can't catch 'em."

"Yes, they run fast, but only because they're running away from our knowledge," Mr Fogerty said, provoking a terrible shock-laugh, the complicit laugh of Ireland's lingering racism, a laugh despite ourselves. We didn't know it, but Mr Fogerty had heard it all before, and had sharpened his rebuttals throughout the decades.

"What else?" He challenged.

"Alexander Dumas was black sir," said Dan, one of our early-enlightened ones, and the envy of myself.

"Yes, yes," Mr Fogerty nodded, "a great writer, but an exception, and he was only half-black, I believe. What else?"

"Phil Lynott," threw one.

"The same," answered Mr Fogerty.

"Jimi Hendrix," said another, and "Bob Marley," shouted one.

"EXCEPTIONS," shouted Mr Fogerty.

A silence.

Finally Tommy came in again "they're great with computers sir."

"What?" Mr Fogerty hadn't heard this one before.

"Yeah sir, they make computers, they always work with computers, every call-centre is full of em, and they run a lot of casinos sir."

"You're thinking of Indians," Fogerty said, igniting an explosion of laughter at Tommy's expense. Fogerty shook his head and decided it was time to end it.

"Right…," he said when silence was returning as we wiped the tears from our eyes as little ripples still erupted here and there, "Right, well, if anyone has a proper answer, I'd love to hear it—"

"Music sir," interrupted Dan. "Besides Phil Lynott and Jimi Hendrix, they have Stevie Wonder, Prince and Michael Jackson, and my dad says that everything Elvis ever sang he stole from black people."

"Phhh," Mr Fogerty shook his head, "they have no Beethoven, no Pavarotti, no Mozart, no Beatles. NEXT." Silence again, Mr Fogerty looked like he was done anyway, but in my mind I answered him as follows: 'Sir, jazz is better than classical. We have no John and Alice Coltrane, no Miles Davis, no Charles Mingus, and we stole our rock and roll from their blues.' No, I said no such thing, and words not said should remain dead. Anyway, I stand by what I didn't say, but I'm ashamed to say that on the day I said nothing, and Mr Fogerty had it all his own way, and he continued:

"I'm not saying anything bad against them, mind, but it's a puzzle. Ireland was as poor and as mistreated as Africa. That's what makes it such a puzzle. We too were colonised, divided, robbed, starved and kicked about like dogs. The English also painted us as an inferior race. 'No blacks, no dogs, no Irish' they used to say. But we've never been short of writers, inventors, scientists; the land of priests and scholars, and now the land of the Celtic Tiger, why is there such a difference then? Well…? If you find an answer let me know."

That class, which must have been in 2007, stuck with me. It gave me another nudge towards anthropology as I was hoping I would find an answer for him there, but it also serves to remind me of the outdated foggy nets we're still swimming through. It's too easy today to say that North Americans or Australians are racist (meaning *we* are not), but let's not kid ourselves. Regarding Mr Fogerty, I imagine him as a typical old Irish racist, but a good teacher nonetheless. Although he did get an awful lot of things wrong—he was a staunch believer in our miraculous Celtic Tiger for one, and made no prediction of it being shot, run over, and buried at the public's expense. I might as well add that 'The Celtic Tiger,' for those unfamiliar, was a period of time in Ireland when our TVs got bigger and bigger (while weighing less and less), but somehow our public hospitals, schools and transport systems remained the same only grew more expensive.

(No, I don't understand it either, but apparently it was a good thing). Mr Fogerty also spent most of his off-topic rants trying to convince us all to invest in banks, and economics was supposed to be his subject. Well, we're all blind in our own way I suppose. But that was it, the final nudge, I want home that day feeling a little ashamed and dirty, and determined to find in anthropology an answer to Mr Fogerty's racism, at least that was the plan.

A Parting Gift Given

As we came closer towards the last day of school I felt there was one thing I needed to do: I was determined to buy Mr Watchem a present. I had given presents to teachers before back in primary school, but always they were given through me, not by me. But just once I wanted to give something myself. And so I went into town and bought for Mr Watchem a pair of Guinness cufflinks. I showed them to my closest friends and they admired them and said it was a good idea. But throughout our last week of school I couldn't bring myself to give them. I felt too shy, too nervous. The idea, as it got closer to becoming a reality, now seemed too ridiculous—'giving a teacher a pair of cufflinks!' But, on the last day, before our final English class, I confessed my fears to Tommy, our class-clown, my hero. Tommy listened, laughed, and, when the class began, stood up and said:

"Sir, Martin has something to give you, a deadly present sir."

"Do you Martin?" Watchem asked me with a smile. Suddenly all eyes were on me and I found myself in motion as the blood rushed to my cheeks. I took out the box of cufflinks and presented them to Watchem, saying "it's just these sir, thought you'd like them… add to your collection." Watchem opened the box, laughed, admired them, and showed them to the class, saying:

"They're fantastic! You know, it's funny, you buy a nice pair of cufflinks for yourself and suddenly you come to have a collection, but no one's ever bought me Guinness cufflinks before. These are excellent Martin, I won't forget this." I awkwardly nodded and walked back to my seat, mumbling as I went "you're welcome."

"Thank you Martin" Watchem repeated, "They're great," then, putting them on, he got on with the class, giving us a final review before our exams, and my heart raced the whole time as I stared at Tommy with hate and gratitude.

When the class ended Watchem gave me a pat on the arm and thanked me again, saying as he did so "I know you'll do well for yourself." I thanked him for everything and left, my face tomato red and my nerves in a spaghetti knot. Never did I hate and love Tommy so much, but if it weren't for him, my worst self would have got the better of me. 'Well' I thought, 'that's it, hopefully I'll see Watchem again someday, when I'm old enough to buy the man a pint and talk to him without becoming a red-faced fool.' And that was 'school days over' as my dad would sing.

During the summer I managed to obtain a job in a cornershop near where I lived. I got the job because, on the morning of the interview, I had to step over Gardai tape just to get in. It seemed there had been a stabbing there the day before. The job helped to further settle my parents regarding my decision to study anthropology as now I could begin to pay my own way towards it. Everything seemed to be coming together. I was a happy fish.

First Year of College

I walked the 20 minutes from my parents' house to Broombridge train station and stood under the fire-blackened shelter for the little protection it provided when, looking down, I saw a rat lean over my right shoe, paws on leather, to drink up a little puddle-water. I smiled, 'no one will believe me' I thought. The rat finished its drink and casually ran off as the train came in. I sat down and stared out the window. At the next stop Mark came aboard and sat beside me.

"Well, how's things Martie?" Mark asked.

"Grand, yeah. the Summer assignments are starting to pile up...not much news."

"Fair enough. Can you explain what anthropology is yet?" He ribbed.

"Yeah, yeah," I smiled, "I'm getting there." We were nearly finished our first year at Maynooth and even then I could only explain anthropology thus—It's the study of humankind through the lens of culture using ethnography, or long-term participant-observation, as its research tool—but I knew Mark too well for that, he would insist on an explanation of 'culture' and I was still grappling with that one myself.

"And how's English going?" I deflected.

"Grand, lots of reading. Reading *Dubliners* at the moment."

"I've read that," I said.

"Yeah, but it's a different thing to studying it."

"Go on then."

"Well... do you remember the last story, *The Dead*?"

I thought back. "Yeah, the guy dancing with a woman at some party, then becoming real gloom and melancholy when his wife or girlfriend gets stuck thinking about some dead guy she used to know. Apparently they used part of that story for the speech at Father Jack's funeral."

"Yeah," said Mark.

"Well?"

"Well, do you remember back when they're at the party and enjoying themselves? At one stage Joyce writes about the door being left open and a chill wind entering the room, well, you learn to watch out for little things like that, the first sign of 'the dead' entering the story, like a ghost. Perhaps the chill is what sets your man's wife on thinking about her dead ex. It's a nice insight, especially since Joyce was famous for being cryptic not giving the reader too much information."

"Yeah," I agreed, I thought back, I remembered the chilly draft alright, or convinced myself that I remembered it, and I had to admit that the allusion had escaped me. I nodded and said "yeah" again respectfully, but then my mind threw me a bone to cudgel one back as I'm not at all agreeable to being lectured to on

Joyce by someone reading their first work by said author while being hand-held and led along through the work of a man who loved nothing more than trolling academics.

"Your right, I missed that, but you're wrong about one thing. The first allusion of the dead, of what's to come, of the memory that haunts you're man and his wife, the first allusion to all that comes from the title of the story, doesn't it? Not the chilly draft." Mark laughed.

"You should have taken English."

"Hmm."

"Why didn't you anyway? You read enough."

"Well, two things stopped me. One is, as fascinating as your *Dubliners* insight is, I don't like the idea of studying a book, of re-reading it, I've never re-read a book outside of school, there's too much I want to read for that, like, all that time we spent in school on *Macbeth*! *MacbethMacbethMacbeth*—I became sick to death of reading *Macbeth*, so much so that I haven't read any Shakespeare since. And that's the second thing, I feel we were saved when we got Watchem, but that school has given me such a hatred for things, things like Irish, maths, French, I don't want to risk ruining English too, sure if old Mr Mulch had remained our teacher I'd probably hate English today. And anyway, haha, if studying English means re-reading the same books I've already read then I'm glad I didn't do it..."

"Alright... Fair enough," said Mark. "God, remember Mulch, the dirty old codger. I wonder if he was ever sentenced in the end."

"Who knows, but god I'm glad they got rid of him. Anyway, did you read *A Portrait of an Artist*?" I forced.

"No, not yet."

"There's a great quote in that one, something like 'Ireland's the pig that eats her young,' and 'Ireland's history is a net I'm trying to escape from'."

"It makes sense," said Mark, "sure his books were censored here for years."

"Yeah, but it still makes sense, that's the problem, a hundred years later and it still makes sense. Anthropology, and my third subject, Classical Studies, they're showing me what a net I've been living in."

"Jaysus, we're getting serious now," Mark said. He looked at me now, now serious Martin. "What nets are you talking about?" He asked.

"It's mad," I sighed, "but when we started here I was still praying to god most nights. I'd still pop my head into an odd church. And... I felt proud about it, even though I kept it to myself. But, what nonsense. I'm 19, nearly through my first year of college, and it's hitting me that it's all nonsense. And the Catholic religion's only part of the net."

"Well, I agree religion's a load of shite," Mark said, "I didn't know you were particularly religious though, but what's knocked it out of ya?"

"Everything," I answered. "In Classical Studies all I seem to learn is the original material the Christians took and repackaged as their own, and then the other material they didn't like they just swept under the carpet. Eventually that hidden-way material came back and inspired people to think outside of the papal box, you know, the whole Renaissance, but the Church resisted it the whole way. And none of it makes sense anymore. Why would god allow so much history to take place before making himself known? And in any case, you wouldn't believe how open minded ancient pagans were. I mean, it makes sense to me now, if you believe in a handful of gods and you meet someone who believes in a different handful you're probably not going to fight about it. Ancient Greeks, Romans, Celts, Germans, Egyptians, they killed each other, but not over religion. And in anthropology it's one part of the globe after another that never even had a chance to learn about god except from missionaries whose diseases wiped out half their population, and they were succeeded or preceded by racist colonisers who enslaved the other half.

"And early anthropology was such racist shit-show, but it was racism backed up by religion and pseudo-science and paid for by colonisers. It's crazy, and it hit me, why wasn't there a native American Jesus? A Papua New Guinian Jesus, a Japanese Jesus, an Eskimo Jesus? They say Jesus could walk on water, so why didn't he make a round trip? And he could raise people from the dead, but instead of raising an army of followers and Gospel spreaders he couldn't get together enough people to play a decent football match. I was raised to believe that the almighty god could only have one son, only one, but chose to send him down when one side of the world knew nothing of the other side. None of it makes sense. He waited tens of thousands of years of allowing people to worship whatever they fancied, but couldn't wait another two thousand years for the invention of television and the internet. But... until recently, I really believed it all... or I think I did." I sighed and scratched my head while Mark sat in a bemused silence. I suppose he wanted to laugh, he wanted to make fun, but I somehow went from wanting to show off what I knew of Joyce to letting out the pressure that had been building inside me. Poor manners on my part. After a silence he tried:

"Well, college has done you a lot of good so far." I laughed.

"Yeah, sorry, it's just weird. I came into college a little guarded, thinking, well, 'college won't make an atheist out of me.' And I saw all the old priests going about their business around the campus and thought I'd be alright. But I wasn't. And I'm glad college has knocked most of that shite out of me, but I guess I'm just waiting for it to put some sense back in… What about you anyway, is college knocking your wits about?"

"No" Mark laughed. "But I'm enjoying English, plenty of reading and discussing, I'm sure it'll stand to me someday."

"You mean when you start writing?" I asked.

"Haha, maybe, someday. But man, forget the academic side and god and all that shite, college is supposed to be about the craic, are we having pints tonight or what?" Mark asked.

"Yeah shit, I forgot to say, I'm meeting up with a girl from my anthropology class, Clodagh, the one I nearly knocked out with my elbow, you remember?"

"I remember the story," said Mark.

"Well, she's bringing a friend with her and she asked me to bring one too."

"That's more like it!" cheered Mark.

I filled him in on the details as our conversation pulled into Maynooth's station. The two of us walked through the turnstiles and out over the bridge, along the water and past the shops we walked. Maynooth. We separated as both of us went to our first lecture of the day. I had anthropology 101 with Dr Carey on Malinowski and all the people he didn't sleep with. As per usual I left the lecture as confused as ever, but one incident stood out, as Dr Carey had asked:

"What's the first thing they teach you in school?" A hundred answers were given and rejected. Reading? Writing? Saying the alphabet? No. Getting up when you hear a bell? No. Respecting a teacher? No. Answer your name in a roll-call? No. Eventually, out of pure exasperation, Dr Carey threw us the answer—"the first thing they teach you is to sit still, for hours. Think about it, little children, a large group of them, sitting still for hours and hours. Not only is that something that has to be taught, but we label children as suffering a mental disability if they can't do it." I played with that conversation as I walked about, it seemed like an anti-climactic answer, but, being honest, I was more annoyed that I hadn't been able to figure it out.

Economics next. This lecturer's lectures consisted of too much PowerPoint, but, if you asked him a question, he had all the patience and knowledge in the world to answer you. But the crazy thing was the class. I couldn't believe it, but I felt like I was back in secondary school. His lectures were filled with paper-plane throwing idiots, people playing Pokemon ROMs on their laptops, people shouting, joking, laughing, turning the lecture into a classic public school doss-class. They award 10% of the overall grade for attendance, and that alone seems to keep the class full of people wishing to be elsewhere, why do colleges do this? Why would you award 10% of an overall academic grade to so-called 'attendance?'

As if to be physically present in itself should be awarded? It can only be because colleges are becoming less centres for education and more focused on profits and business. No 3rd level institution should award points for attendance, for attendance is not attention. Anyway, I had my final lecture in Classical Studies, and spent most of my time making quick glances at a woman I sometimes smiled at, and who sometimes returned my smile, but for the life of me I couldn't bring myself up to talk to her. Instead, I distracted myself by writing a shitty little love poem.

Well, I thought, I was still only 19 and desperately inexperienced when it came to women, and, in any case, I had made friends with one woman from anthropology and would be drinking with her and a friend of hers after. Maybe a little practise with them would give me the bravery needed to talk to my classical muse. No harm practising love's arrows on harmless sparrows I argued, Catullus said otherwise, but nothing can knock a coward's justification for his own cowardly actions.

Lecturing done, no work, and on top of my reading I happily went to the student bar to meet up with Clodagh and her friend, Kinky. Clodagh had recognised me in our first week of anthropology as the one who left her with a black eye and, teasingly, she wasn't going to let me forget it. Actually, Clodagh would go on to tell me that she was happy for the connection when she found that her friend, Kinky, was barely attending any lectures and she found herself awkwardly without a friend. It seems I proved an easy friend to make, 'a little quiet and strange, but polite, compliant even, although he always seems busy' is how she apparently described me to Kinky, 'compliant' fits. As for the rest, who isn't 'quiet' and 'strange' until you get to know them? It came as a surprise to Clodagh then when, the week before, Kinky told her that she was interested in me, and she was happy enough to set us up. Clodagh I was too shy for anyway. So she agreed to organise a drink for us, as long as I brought a friend of my own.

"Well, how are ya Martin?" Clodagh huggingly asked when she saw me.

"I'm grand yeah," I said, awkwardly hugging back.

"Do you remember Kinky at all? Believe it or not she's in our class."

"Yeah" I lied, "but I don't think we've talked before. How's things... Kinky?"

"Grand, yeah," she said.

"So," I tried "your name can't really be Kinky, can it?"

"No," Kinky laughed. "My name's Kitty, but I call myself Kinky for short."

"I see," said I, "but..."

Clodagh, seeing it coming I'm sure, interrupted: "Well! Let's get some drinks in."

"Right so," said I, "what will yas have?" I ordered a round and we sat down to a table as me and Clodagh tried to catch Kinky up on everything she missed from the lectures, which gave me a welcomed chance to try and wrap my head around them myself. When we were nearing the end of our first round Mark showed up. I jumped up and made the introductions, and Mark, laughing and smiling away, asked what we would have at the bar. The women gave their orders and I, still out of my seat, said I'd join him (to warn him) and give him a hand. As we got to the queue Mark opened: "they seem nice, do you got dibs on any?"

"No," I said, "I don't think so. But I'm telling you one thing now Mark, I've had a few drinks with Clodagh, and she's dead sound, but she's never, never, bought me a round back. And any of her female friends I've drank with have been the same." I shook my head and repeated, "they'll never return a round, or I'll marry the first one that does."

"You're joking," Mark said, "do they think you're rich?"

"Are *you* joking, I've a job in a corner shop for fuck's sake, and she's she's on a grant. No one that works is rich."

"Right so, I'll get this round to save your pockets, but I won't be getting them another. Thanks for the heads up, they want equality but they forget to pay equally!"

"Not all women man, my sister's never been like that,". The two of us came back to the table with a table of drinks.

"Cheers," said Clodagh clinking glasses. "Cheers" we said.

After another round and getting fed up Clodagh asked Mark if he fancied a game on the pool table. "Sure," he said and the two of them walked off with Clodagh giving Kinky a sly wink.

Me and Kinky sat awkwardly making small talk when her phone buzzed, checking it she saw a message from Clodagh—*I told u he's shy, make a move!*

She smiled and put her phone away.

"Everything alright," I asked.

"Yeah, grand... so, have you broken any hearts on campus yet?"

"N-no" I cracked. "No, to tell you the truth, going to an all-boys primary and secondary school hasn't given me a lot of confidence for all of that."

"You mean you haven't had any girlfriends?"

"I had a few yeah... but nothing substantial. Kissing behind the shops, getting handsy in the park, that sort of thing" I sighed, Kinky laughed, I continued:

"I nearly went all the way with a girl in a bar who was convinced I looked the image of Sid Vicious, but, I got too drunk and ended up getting sick in the jacks and thrown out of the place," Kinky laughed some more.

"And my last girlfriend," I continued, "broke up with me after 2 weeks by text because I was off on a family holiday to Portugal and I guess she thought I'd be having too much fun without her, to be honest, I should have seen it coming, the entire time we were going out she kept telling me how she wanted to become a nun." At this Kinky was nearly double-overed in laughing.

"At least your honest," she finally said, "I don't think I've ever met someone so honest," she laughed.

"You can thank alcohol for that," I smiled, which must have been the case, for my head was beginning to swim, and I felt I had said far too much, but it was strange, the more openly I spoke, the more Kinky laughed, and the more she laughed the better she seemed. Now it seemed her very eyes were smiling on me. So, taking another sip of desperate courage I continued:

"No, to be honest, I've been so terrified of saying it here, of having people know it, that... I'm, well, inexperienced... No, I haven't been able to break any hearts yet."

"You could try mine," Kinky whispered, leaning in, and my whole world seemed to shift under her little shuffle, until I leaned in too, and eyes were closed and lips met lips in a dark-drunk bliss and 'surely' I thought 'college was made for this!' In drunk-slow time we made out and made little the world around us as the world dissolved. Until Clodagh, returning to the table, desperately cleared her throat to clear the room of what she would later describe as a 'desperate scene.' And I snapped back with a jolt, but Kinky kept my hand in hers and it gave me something, something to take the embarrassment away from Clodagh and Mark and their smiling faces, a couple of stupid smiling faces that should have drowned in the pool table. But I didn't care, hand in her hand I didn't care, and I skipped off to the bar a new man to go and get another round, no longer giving a fuck for how many I paid for.

The next day me and Kinky had agreed to meet for coffee. The weather being nice we took our coffees to go and found a quiet bench to sit and sip, sippity sit, slipperilly sippity sit and oh god I wanted to sip from her lips.

"Thanks, I need this," said Kinky.

"Hangover?" I asked while somehow calming myself.

"*Yeah.* you don't have one?"

"I never get them," I said, no lie.

"What?"

"Never… I think I burn off the alcohol too fast, plus I rarely drink more than three or four."

"Well, we'll fix that," she laughed. "Listen," she said now and I tried to listen. "I like you, you like me, right?"

"Yeah" I lied, or half-lied, I had no idea what I liked to be honest, but I knew what I wanted. "I like you too."

"So we're going out then?"

"Yeah," said I, confused, "sorry… I just assumed we were, yeah," Kinky laughed.

"You shouldn't assume," she said, "or you'll make an ass of 'u' and 'me.'"

"What?" I asked.

"Nothing," Kinky laughed. "But… There's one thing. You said you're a virgin right," I tensed, "and, well, I guess I got a reputation for rushing into things. And I actually like you," she laughed, nervously, "so, basically, I want us to take a month, starting from yesterday, before we sleep together."

"Sure," I said, "sure," filling the silence. "If that's what you want, but, for me, besides feeling awkward about it, I don't feel strongly about being a virgin… it is what it is, but, I'm not looking for a big deal to be made about it."

"But, it *is* a big deal. Well… Maybe not for men so much, but when it actually happens I think you'll feel differently. Besides, a month would be good for me too, I've never cared for anyone well enough to want to go out with them for a month without sex. You should feel special! And we can still do plenty in the meantime, they don't call me 'Kinky for short' for nothing. I'd give you a handjob right now if my head wasn't banging."

"Thanks," I laughed as the penny dropped. "Sure, one month, starting from yesterday," I smiled. "I can do that, and I suppose it'll keep us focused on the exams."

Kinky smiled and we sipped our coffee while I tried to let go of sipping what I had really wanted to sip. We spent the rest of our coffee date talking exams and assignments. It was nearing the end of the term, the mad season. But soon we would break for Summer, and, I smiled, 'this Summer… I'll finally get to have sex this Summer.' Wait 3 minutes for the coffee to cool, and 30 days to sip the brew. I sipped my bitter coffee and sighed, 'why did I get a stupid coffee anyway,' I thought, 'I much prefer tea.'

Second Year of College

With the Summer over I walked the 20 minutes from my parents' house to Broombridge station. No rats this time. It's weird, but a rat leans on my shoe once and a part of my brain expected him back there every day, and every day I was disappointed he didn't show. Rats. It reminds me of the time I saw a fox running through someone's garden, and I don't think I've ever passed that garden again without looking for that fox. Anyway, I smiled at my wandering thoughts as they made way for the train and, getting on, I took out my book, careful to hide its cover from the nosy passengers my brain supplied. I wasn't long reading it when Mark made me jump out of my skin with a—

"Well Martie, how's things, ready for 2nd year?"

"Alright Mark. Yeah, ready as I'll ever be," I said, flustered, and putting my book away as fast as I could. "You gave me heart attack," I said.

"I can see that," Mark laughed and sat. "What ya reading anyway?"

"Well… to tell the truth, it's called *Instant Confidence*," I said, clandestinely showing him the cover. "My dad gave it to me when he was finished with it, figured why not."

"*Instant Confidence*," repeated Mark, "has it been working for ya?" He asked.

"Well… no, I'm nearly finished it and I'm still too self-conscious to have people catching me read it." Mark burst out laughing and I began to chuckle along, the absurdity overwhelming my insecurities. When we had settled down Mark continued:

"Anyway, did you decide what subject you're dropping for second year?"

"Well," I said, "it was a hard choice, if I had my own way I would have dropped classics and continued studying economics and anthropology, but they have conflicting timetables so I can't. It's mad, they prevent anyone from studying the most social of business courses along with the most social of anything, and when I complained to them they just said 'oh, it happens sometimes, it's not intentional which subjects will conflict, but we see your point…' And I was good at economics too, it was the only subject I got a 1st in."

"So you're sticking with anthropology then?" Mark asked.

"Yeah. For ages I couldn't decide, then my mam got my nana to do a card reading over which one I should study, she went on and on about how economics was the right decision—she saw me working successfully and getting rich and all that shite, and of course that pushed me to do the opposite."

Mark laughed. "Tarrot cards is it?"

"No my nana just uses a normal deck, but yeah, I don't put any stock in it. She's known for 2 things; being manipulative and for doing card readings, and no one else can put two and two together. I wouldn't be surprised if my mam told her to give me that kind of a reading, but then, my mam's a true believer. She once went to a palm reader after booking 10 months in advance, that's 10 months for them to snoop around your social media and say at the very least 'I see you've got 3 kids,' my mam was eating out of her hand after that, even though she's on Facebook and has no idea what she's doing on it."

"Ah sure," said Mark, "So you're studying anthropology because you think your parents don't want you to study it?"

"Well, no, at least I hope not" I sighed, "it's more the fact that economics seems easy to study, I mean it's an easy subject and most colleges cover it, but I feel like this is my only chance to study anthropology since Maynooth's the only college in Ireland that does it, and it's still interesting."

"Can you explain what it is yet?"

Bracing myself I made a start—"it's the study of humanity through the lens of culture using ethnography as its main research tool. Basically an anthropologist hangs with a group of people for a long time, 1-2 years, and compares their culture to his or her own and others he or she's studied, and then uses all that to try and understand our social behaviour. One of our lecturers puts it that it's studying people at the micro level and then making macro claims regarding human behaviour if that makes sense. I like it because it often takes a theory from psychology, say, and sees if it's applicable to a completely different type of society to the one the psychologist was starting from. It's good in that sense, it knocks the ethnocentrism out of you."

"The what?"

"The belief that we're the centre of the universe."

"Sure mushrooms do that," Mark laughed, "and books" and laughed and laughed a great snowballing laugh "and what will you have on your CV? I've studied anthropology, so I know that I'm not the centre of the universe, please hire me! ...And anyway, doesn't any old journalist or travel writer do all that?"

"Yeah, yeah," I shrugged. "But it's interesting, and I imagine it's more focused on the research and theory than those. Plus this term we're doing a mini-ethnography assignment, we have to choose a group of people to hang out with and write up an ethnographic report."

"Oh yeah," Mark wiped away a tear, "and who will you be hanging with?"

"I was thinking of asking my sister Kate if she could help, I've been wanting to stay a couple of nights with her in Galway and she's always had mad friends. It would be a good way to kill two birds with one stone."

"A couple of nights in Galway would be class, and it seems very anthropological," Mark laughed, "turning research into a holiday."

"Yeah," I said, "as if journalism is much different."

"What about the rest of your summer anyway?" Mark asked, "are you still with Kinky, what's the craic with her?"

I shook my head as my face turned red. I carefully looked around the train and, dropping my voice, returned—"Kinky, what a mess man. After we were a month together she invited me to her neck of the woods, a pub near her house, and I thought I was in for the win, you know, have a pint or two and go back to hers, instead we had a pint and she broke up with me."

"Ahahahahah—Jaysus man—hhahahahahahaha—What—ahahahahaha—Why?—hahaha..." When Mark had settled down I continued:

"Get this," I dropped my voice to a near whisper: "she had this stupid idea in her head that we weren't to sleep together for a month because, I don't know, she thought I'd want to take it slow cause, you know, I'd never slept with anyone, and she wanted to take it slow herself for once, despite calling herself 'Kinky Kitty,' for fuck's sake." I started laughing, "the amount of other stuff we did and she broke up with me for that."

"What happened, what did she say?" Mark asked.

"She broke up with me because of it! She said she couldn't bear to be my first because she knows how important it is, and she's afraid of how close it would make us, and how it's too much pressure on her, then she said some vague things about her first time and how she wished it were different and I need to be sure I love someone beforehand and…" I sighed, "fucking shitshow."

"Jesus," Mark laughed.

"And get this," I continued, "she told me all that and I said 'fair enough' or something like it, like, what else could I do, and we hugged and went our separate ways, but then, as I was on the bus heading home, she messages me—'Hey, soz about all that, I do like you though, I think we should stay friends… maybe even with benefits!' She wanted us to be friends with benefits after she broke up with me cause of you know what."

"Fuck," said Mark, "that doesn't make a lot of sense, and how did you respond to that?"

"I messaged her that I'm not interested. We can be friends ok but after that I'm not interested. Wasted enough time." Silence again until I continued, my voice calmer but tinged with regret:

"…I know I didn't love her, maybe I didn't even like her all that much, but we got on ok, she was nice enough, and what does love have to do with sex, only…" I sighed, "only anyone I ever really fancied I've been too shy to make a move on, and most of that comes from being embarrassed about not having done it."

"Well, you're right," said Mark, "sex is great and all, but the first time's overrated, only virgins, writers and film directors give a shit about the first time."

"Well, obviously her first time left a bad impression. I've sort of been ignoring her since, I feel bad, but she knew from day one where I was at, so why did she drag me along for a month? And the whole time there's this stunning woman in my classics class I could have made a move on but I didn't, I know that's not Kinky's fault, but," I shook my head. I didn't know what to say.

"Ah… you'll get there someday," Mark said, trying to comfort me.

"Well… I did," I mumbled.

"What! With who?"

"It doesn't matter. Let's just say what's good enough for James Joyce is good enough for me."

"You didn't…"

"I did. But it wasn't a dodgy job, I paid well enough, I organised with her directly online, so I'm not planning on feeling bad about it. Only, you're right, only virgins give a fuck about their first fucking, fuck. I didn't even enjoy myself much, especially since she kept asking me if I was over 18, I even tried to take out my I.D. before she fobbed it off and got on with things, for fuck's sake," I shook my head as the image of her came back to me.

"Christ," laughed Mark, "this is the funniest train I've ever been on," it looked like his ribs were hurting.

"But," I continued, "the point is it's done. And I'm glad it's done, at least now I'm over myself, at least I'll be less shy to go for what I want."

"Asked for I.D. by a prostitute! Hahaha," Mark cracked.

"Escort" I elbowed, "but yeah, and she told me she was studying Law in Trinity. Well, maybe she is, living and studying here can't be cheap, but after she kept asking me how old I was, and the way she was asking man, as if I was some 12 year old kid looking to buy a bottle of vodka. I couldn't warm to her after that. No, fuck me, I didn't get much from it at all, but at least the box is ticked. The worst thing is, it was so anti-climactic, so unmemorable, such a non-event, yet a woman who calls herself 'Kinky' of all things broke up with me because of it. Imagine if someone I liked did the same thing? 'No' I thought, fuck that."

"Mad," said Mark, "I wonder what must have happened to Kinky on her first time."

"I don't know man. My dad says that most men are doomed to live their lives as the main fool in a comedy, while most women live theirs as the main character in a drama."

"Maybe," Mark said, "they've a harder time of it than we have, you should hear some of the mad stories I get from my sisters. We've never had to worry about our drinks being spiked. That shit isn't funny."

"Yeah, well" I continued, "I'm not going to hold a grudge against Kinky or anything, maybe I should've been more patient or acted better with her, and maybe she's holding a grudge against me, but after all that, I can't see us being good friends or anything. The amount of messages she was sending me. Every hour of every day while we were together, message message message, even messages while I ate, and she had no patience. She asked me once why I wasn't messaging back and I blamed it on having no credit, so she bought me €20's worth, and I still didn't message her back. That alone was wrecking my head. Plus... she knew from the start what my story was. I'll never make sense of it all."

"She'll probably never make sense out of you too," Mark laughed.

"Yeah, I don't know" I sighed. "I guess all I cared about was losing my you-know-what, and all she cared about was respecting it, so yeah, I probably deserved to get dumped. But what a weird month that was. How was your Summer anyway?"

Anthropology's a Drag

'My brother's coming! My brother's coming!' thinks Kate excitedly
While I sit in the warehouse that is Hueston station waiting for my train to Galway. The bookmark fell out of *Ulysses* so I had to dig through Joyce to find my place in Joyce, and for the first time in a long time I read joyiously of Joyce, pure joy Joyce joyous Joyce where's my page Joyce what does it matter Joyce sure you weren't following the plot anyway you auld codger-reader of Joyce. And just when I lost him I thought that I had finally found him Joyce. Yes. That's right. A man too obscure to be read left to right, top to bottom, start to end. His plot so thin he asks to be read upside down and back to front, he asks you to look for him, and his plotless plodding words shining joyously reading Joyce until you get to page 346 and it feels as if you're a naughty pupil and Joyce is giving you unending lashings of his disciplinary cane as you turn from page to page of the slowest caning you ever did see, only I've never been caned and we're not used to our teachers caning us anymore. But it feels like Joyce is caning me, and with a gleeful smiling mien he raps my knuckles with his disciplinary cane for daring to follow Joyce through mud and the profane. It's the problem with Joyce; he's the smoking teenager wanking down dodgy lane and he's the sadist headmaster with his disciplinary cane.

Giving up, but not before finding my original place again, I put my book away and allowed my eyes to lazily follow the pigeons as they shuffled along coo cooing comfortably for crumbs, or perhaps they're just coo cooing a song. I like pigeons, they're not as shy as the rats, but then, we've probably killed a lot less of them than we have rats. I wonder if rats ever get out of the labs? What would they have to say to the rats they met on the street? I like rats too. Funny, we've cleared this island of its plants, trees and predators, not to mention filling our cities with overlooked and unkempt habitations, so they must feel as though we've invited them in to stay with us, and yet, for all that, they must also be aware that we often try to rid ourselves of them. What strange greedy animals we are—to want to rid our streets of other animals which, as far as *their* concerned, have invited them in. Small, meek, opportunistic and frisky, lovers of warmth, company and a free meal, we are so like them, but I suppose there's nothing like a human for hating a human. Funny that. Self-love, self-hate, and the extension of that to love for others and hate for others, how much do the other animals feel these things? And what are humans anyway only rats without tails and pigeons without wings. Well, anyway, come, if you'll join me, it's time to board the train.

I enter the train as my self-narration fizzles in and out. This seems to happen every time I read a book written in 1st person for too long thought Martin as I sat down. Self-narration. The 'I' in Martin, describing Martin to Martin for Martin the Martian. Yes. Come to think of it, I think I'm having a crisis. Can't you tell? And now my mind's too jumbled to read, and I can barely carry myself right now, never mind anyone else. No Mark today. But why not? I can speak with him if I wish. Yes, I prefer imagining a conversation than talking to just myself, but no, not Mark, I can talk to him readily enough. Who then? Kate? Hmm. Why bother with a fake-Kate when I'm heading straight to the real Kate anyway. So who shall I give this seat to? Who shall it be? Who shall I talk to?

Mart*i*n looked around the train and saw a woman reading *Romeo and Juliette*. 'You cannot escape Shakespeare!' came an echo in our head. 'Who said that' thought Mart*i*n—'Watchem?'

"You cannot escape Shakespeare lads, one way or another you must read Shakespeare for your exams."

"yes sir, I remember, but my school days are finished now. Now I can read whatever I want."

"And what are you reading now Martin?"

"*ulysses* sir, or trying to."

"Haha," Watchem said in Martin's head, "you can't escape Shakespeare in *Ulysses*, he's there too Martin, he's everywhere. Come, you've only read *Macbeth,* and you wrote beautifully about it, although I think you put too much of the blame upon Lady Macbeth myself. Try another."

"did you say that sir? ididn't write that in into the backstory."

"Story structure was always another struggle of yours," he ribbed. "What are you doing these days anyway Martin, how have you been?"

"well, i'm studying anthropology at the moment sir. as well as classical studies. It's interesting enough."

"And what's anthropology Martin?"

"it's the study of mankind, of us, through the careful study of a small group of people who are different to us, to see what we all have in common I guess, and what differences between us have been socially and culturally constructed, if that makes sense." Watchem nodded, but said nothing. Finally he changed the subject.

"And what about writing Martin? I quite liked your old essays." Martin nodded, but said nothing. He made Watchem change the subject:

"And what's bringing you to Galway anyway Martin?"

"I'm going to see my sister sir. I'm staying with her for a couple of nights. She's agreed to help me out with an ethnography assignment, you know, let me hang out with her and a group of her friends and take some notes and that. How they talk, how they dress, I guess stuff like that. She's an artist you see, a painter."

"Really? And what kind of stuff does she paint?"

"Oh, landscapes, portraits, some religious motifs, some abstract work. Some of it is really good, similar to Van Gogh here and there, she seems to play with realism and his kind of abstraction, although her subjects always seem a little safe."

"Safe? And what would you paint?"

"oh, everything" Martin smiled. "The toilet just before getting sick perhaps, seen through a drunken lens. Lads knacker-drinking in the park. My dad running naked on New Years, a train station from a pigeon's perspective… I don't know."

"The ordinary," said Watchem.

"To highlight the extraordinary," said Martin, shrugging and tapping his fingers against Joyce.

"It's funny" Martin continued as Martin, "my sister moved to Galway when she was 18 to attend college, but dropped out after 2 years. Then she lived for a while in Paris, then London, a bit in Liverpool, finally she settled down back in Galway. She's incredible like that. Very brave I mean, to move out and start her own independent life so young. So I guess I'm always stuck feeling that her art should reflect that. I admire her so much... Instead, her painting's kept close to what our mam has taught her."

"Your mother's a painter too?"

"Yeah, but more as a hobby, although she sells the odd painting. She tried to teach all of us, and my brother is pretty good, but I can't even draw a cat" Martin sighed, "I don't know what I can do, except college seems easy enough:

Read what we read
Write like we write
And all year long you'll be told 'there's a good boy, you're doing alright'."

"So what's the problem?"

"Well" thought Martin, "have you ever read *Great Expectations*?"

"Of course," said Watchem smiling, "Dickens, *nearly* as a good as Shakespeare haha. What about it?"

"I'm scared sometimes that I'm living it," said Martin. "Like, college is training me to be a kind of gentleman, it's knocked many old ideas out of my head. But am I learning anything of value? Or rather, am I learning anything which will make *me valuable*? Or will I end up like Pip, a fish-out-of-water-gentleman who doesn't know how to earn his own keep, pining after something he should never have been allowed to reach. I don't even have the benefit of the unknown benefactor we call a grant. I'm working flat out for my degree, and sometimes I feel like 'yeah, I'm getting there,' and other times I feel like—where is 'there?' What if I'm going nowhere?' Like, last week I was helping my dad out on a job in a priests' retirement home, talk about fancy by the way, they each had a bedroom, flatscreen, bookshelf, radio,... and their communal area was every socialite's brown-nosed dream, and filled to the brim with whiskey. I have to give the priests one thing, for believers in an imaginary friend, they've somehow secured for themselves a lot of real-world perks, maybe I should be an atheist priest... anyway, where was I? Oh yes, at one stage my dad told one of the priests that I was studying ancient Greek and Roman history, and so the priest first started speaking to me in Latin, and when I couldn't answer him he started speaking to me in ancient Greek, and I just stood there feeling like an idiot. And when dad tells people instead that I'm studying to be an anthropologist I feel just as stupid. It's great for him I guess—to brag about his son, I hope to do it too someday, but I don't feel worth bragging about," Martin sighed, "because then I have to explain what anthropology means, and then I have to hide that I don't think it means much and I don't know what I'm doing. Not only do those old priests seem educated far beyond me, but if I do become an anthropology or classical studies lecturer then I'm afraid I'll just become a different type of priest, you know? A believer in impotent ideas, useful only within my discipline or college, an intellectual shut-in."

"You could become a teacher" offered Watchem.

"In this country? No. You need Irish for primary schools, and what secondary school wants to hire an anthropology or classical studies teacher?"

"Well, you're only in your second year Martin. Relax a bit. Just focus on graduating. Any degree is sure to stand for you, and since Ireland's in a recession college is probably the best place to be to wait and see wait and see."

"I know," said Martin, "finish college and worry later. I know. Thanks sir, although you're starting to sound like my mother now. Still, I'll buy you a pint someday I'm sure." Shaking his head clear of the company Martin took out his book in the hope that Joyce's swirling thoughts would be enough to engulf his own, but after 6 difficult pages without a word sinking in he put the book down, bookmarked it where he had started, sighed, and thought out something along the following:

Always Always Always Pip,
Great Expectations today
But tomorrow I feel like shit.
Because there's no one writing my story
No Dickens guiding my ship
So my life will have the original ending
Deserving of a real-life Pip

The Train Arrives

'My brother's coming! My brother's coming!' thought Kate excitedly as she waited patiently in her car near the station at Galway. She hadn't seen Martin in months, and she had never had the pleasure of having him come over without their parents, let alone stay for 2 nights. It was an opportunity she was keen to take full advantage of. As a teenager she often had to babysit Martin and Shay, and the 3 of them always enjoyed themselves as Kate would make up a game for them to play. 'Restaurant' was one of their favourites. She would sit the two of them down at the breakfast table, put on an over-the-top French accent, and give them a menu with exaggerated options and strange food combinations—'High-Juice' being a particular favourite for the boys as they would watch their sister get upon a chair and poor them each a glass of orange juice as she held the carton as far from the glass as possible, that way the juice always poured in with a lovely frothy head. Nobody can serve up orange juice like Kate. But since moving out their relationship had lost a lot of their previous intimacy, and while Shay seemed to be developing along and had made the effort to stay with Kate twice already, Martin seemed to Kate to be a little more shy, slow, placid even. Out of the 3 of them Martin was the only sibling to flat out refuse to go to any of the Gaeltach's as he felt from an early age that his Irish was beyond saving, but in missing these chances to immerse himself properly in Irish he had also robbed himself the chance of experiencing those periods of freedom which Kate and Shay had, that they needed, to grow and stretch themselves. There were talks at one point of Martin going to Zambia, a trip organised by his school for 4th year students, but Martin, despite his keen application, wasn't chosen to go. 'So' thought Kate, 'I don't think Martin's ever had a holiday by himself, and if he's really become that reluctant to stretch himself, then I'm going to stretch him myself. Now, where is that boy....'

Seeing Martin walking towards her car in her rear-view mirror Kate got out and gave him a big hug as Martin's arms awkwardly returned same with lukewarm strength. She took a step back and said "Wow, you look as young as ever!"

"Thanks" Martin said as he rubbed his face and smiled, "I need to grow a beard or something."

"Nonsense. Here, give me your bag," said Kate as she took Martin's bag to throw into the boot.

"Get in," she said as she made her way around the car to sit behind the wheel.

"How was the train?"

"Grand yeah, no hassle."

"Did you have something to read for it?"

"Yeah... I'm trying to read *Ulysses* at the moment, but I find I can't read it in large chunks without going on autopilot."

"*Ulysses* huh? Must be hard going while you got plenty of college stuff to read."

"Yeah, well, it's the only one of the readable 3 I haven't read, and since I finished reading the *Odyssey* for college, and *Ulysses* was inspired by it, I thought 'now's the time,' but it's a struggle."

"Well then," said Kate, "When I was struggling through *Ulysses* a friend of mine said that of all the books he's read he thinks the only way to read *Ulysses* is by reading other books at the same time. He told me that many people size up *Ulysses* and make the mistake of trying to plough through it too quickly when it needs to be given a lot of patience, and it's true," she nodded. "I've always such a pile up of books that when I was reading *Ulysses* I was trying to speed my way through it, and I nearly gave up on it, but once I started reading other books and just read couple of pages here and there—only then did I start to really enjoy it."

"I didn't know you read *Ulysses*" Martin said.

"I felt like I had to when I was living in Paris" Kate laughed, "so many French people were trying to talk to me about Joyce that I started feeling embarrassed. But it's true, if you start reading other books and give *Ulysses* the patience it needs, it becomes much easier to process. And there's 2 chapters towards the end which are definitely worth reading." Kate's mind wandered back to a painting inspired by the last chapter in particular. It had Joyce kissing Molly's neck, his little round glasses half-steamed and nearly falling off him, while he uses his fingers to squeeze some milk from her breast into his cup of tea while she bears it all with an eye-rolling and slightly disapproving patience. She smiled as the painting came back to her, she saved a picture of it at home, 'but,' she thought, 'I won't show it to him yet, better he reads on without any spoilers.' Still, her smile remained, she made a lot of money from that painting.

"Yeah, maybe you're right" Martin said after some time, "well, if you have anything lying around I'll take it for the train back."

Kate tried to hide the gleaming smile she felt inside. "Well, I do have something… have you come across Marcus Aurelius in your classical studies?"

"No, not yet, we're covering the Augustan period at the moment, and we've been moving fairly chronologically."

"Right," said Kate as she tried to modulate herself, she had little faith in college. "Well, sure, Marcus Aurelius was one of the later emperors I think, probably long after Augustus. Anyway, it doesn't matter, what matters is that he wrote a book called *Meditations*, it's not academic, but it's a great read, I think you'll like it, and you'll enjoy it all the more since your studying the Romans anyway, and it references a lot of the Greek philosophers, the Stoics and that."

"Sure, I haven't heard of any emperors that wrote their own books, well, except Caesar and his campaigns, yeah, I'll give it a go."

"Great," said Kate, and 'great' thought Kate, smiling to herself as things fell into place. 'Let the stretching begin' she thought.

"What are you reading anyway?" asked Martin.

Kate sighed and replied: "I'm reading *Lisa: the story of an Irish drug addict*, written in the 1980s."

"Are you not enjoying it?" Martin asked.

"No, that's the thing, I love it. It's one of the best books I've read in a LONG time, but it turns out it's out of print and hard to find, I just happened to be lucky, I found it in a charity shop and took a chance. I'd love to give it to you when I'm finished but I've promised it to half a dozen people at this stage. I need to buy more copies of it, because someone needs to make an adaptation of it, big time."

"Like a series?"

"Yeah, it could be a series, but it strikes me more as a play" Kate said. "I've already earmarked a couple of pages to paint from, but that's as far as my talents go… it's just mad that a book like it has slipped through the net."

"You paint scenes you come across in books? I didn't know you did that" Martin said with a side-long glance.

"Hahaha. Of course I do and of course *you* don't know. You've only seen my parent-friendly paintings, the type of paintings mam used to teach me. Wait till I show you what *I* choose to paint," she beamed.

Martin stared at his sister as she navigated the roads, "fair enough" is all he could think to say while Kate tried to organise her thoughts and the best way to proceed. Finally she continued—

"Listen Martin, you asked if you could do your ethnography project hanging out with me and some of my artsy friends, right?"

"Yeah," said Martin, "and I wanted to see you. I feel bad I haven't made the effort sooner."

"Forget it," smiled Kate, "but listen, this weekend, I'm going to show you a little of the world I live in, and it's nothing like the world you're used to if you're only used to living with mam and dad. Not that there's anything wrong with how they live, you know I think they're great, but my world's a little different, okay?"

"Sure," said Martin adjusting himself, "I guess I wanted something different."

"Okay, so you'll keep an open mind?"

"Yeah," said Martin, but he was beginning to feel more and more self-conscious. "Why?"

"Well," continued Kate, "the party I was thinking of for your ethnography assignment is tomorrow. But tonight me and my roommate are having a couple of people down, they'll be going to the party tomorrow as well so you'll get a chance to get to know them first."

"Yeah," said Martin, "sounds good."

"And," continued Kate "I've made a batch of brownies for us tonight. Like, Amsterdam brownies" Kate began to laugh, "Well, you're in college, maybe I'm not giving you enough credit, surely you've had a bit of weed or hash at this stage?"

"No," said Martin, "I haven't tried anything except drink. But… I'm happy to. Really, to be honest, what with working flat out in the shop and not living on campus, I sort of feel like I've been missing out on the proper college experience."

"Good," said Kate as she relaxed a little, "you're right. Look Martin, I'm not going to make you do or take anything that you don't want to, but my brownies happen to be *amazing* and safer than safe. And sure, if it turns out you don't like them, it'll be better to find out tonight where you'll have your own bedroom and that than in a pub or some stranger's house."

"Yeah," said Martin, "I've read a few books here and there where characters smoke or whatever, like *The Colour Purple*, that definitely put me in mind to try it."

"What a book," said Kate. "Didn't I tell you?"

"Yeah, you have me sussed when it comes to books and tunes," smiled Martin, "anyway, I've figure weed can't be that bad since I've heard from enough people who have gone to Amsterdam and had a great time. I'm happy to try one." They nodded and Kate felt delighted, but Martin continued, half audibly and staring out the window: "You know … I know I'm quiet and that, and … yeah, I haven't done too many mad things, but I'm not as shy as I used to be… I'm up for trying new things." He looked at Kate before turning back to the window. 'I need to try new things' he thought.

"That's great," said Kate. "Martin, if you keep up that attitude, you'll have a weekend you'll never forget."

Brownies and Butt-Plugs

They arrived at Kate's house and Martin was shown inside and greeted by Kate's housemate, a 40-something year old man he had met once before. He was of average height, had a round ruddy clean-shaven face and eyes hidden behind rose-tinged glasses which, despite his floral shirt and denim jeans, gave him what Martin took to be a rather guarded air.

"Howya, how was your trip," he asked while extending his hand. Martin shook it and replied: "Fine, yeah, no hassle."

"Martin, I think you met Jamie before," said Kate, confirming for each each other's name.

"Yeah," said Martin, "during the holidays I think. How's things?"

"Grand yeah," said Jamie flashing a smile.

"Come," said Kate, "I'll show you up to your room and you can throw your bag in." She led him up to a box bedroom containing a queen-sized bed with a painting over it, a wardrobe, side-desk, an overhead light and a reading lamp. Martin smiled. When the family had stayed over before he and his brother were always left to share the bed-suite, now, without his parents, he had a bedroom to himself. He smiled too at the painting. It was the first one he passed in the house that his racing mind was able to rest on. It was of a group of four elephants emerging from a forest into a water-logged clearing; serene, peaceful, a little understated. The three adult elephants are walking and facing forward with clear purpose. Only the little tuskless one is half-turned and uncertain, but at least the little one shows an acknowledgement of being watched.

"It's beautiful. One of yours," he gestured with confidence.

"No, that one's by Vincent Booth. To be honest, I only hang my paintings around the house when I want to get a feel for how they'll look on a wall, and even that's difficult. I don't know how mam does it, I can't look at one of my own for more than two minutes without wanting to fix it" Kate shivered.

"Fair enough," said Martin, hiding a little surprise.

"Anyway," continued Kate, "I'll leave you to it, you know where the bathroom is and all that, and there's a couple of towels in the wardrobe if you want a shower." She checked her watch. "It's nearly half 5, Irina and Shane should be down in half an hour and we'll get the party started then."

"Thanks," said Martin, "I'll leave the shower for the morning, but yeah, I could do with the bathroom... thanks."

"Sure" Kate smiled, "it's so nice having you Martin," she said as she went in for a hug, "I want you to have a great time."

"I'm sure I will," he mumbled into her shoulder. Kate left him to it and headed downstairs.

"All good?" asked Jamie.

"Yeah, he seems happy."

"Did you tell him we're having brownies?" He asked.

"Yeah, he's keen," smiled Kate. "Can you believe he's never had one?"

"You know, we could offer him half a tab if you want to really blow his mind open."

"No no," said Kate, "baby steps, plus he'd never sleep on a tab, and tomorrow's going to be the real test. Mad," she said shaking her head, "he's been through a year and a half of college and he's never had so much as a toke," she said softly. "He's getting college from the safety of his nest. He probably can't even boil a pot of pasta yet," she frowned.

"Yeah," said Jamie, "it doesn't make for a great education. But sure, he seems to be making an effort," he smiled. "By the way, you know I'll probably be changing later tonight...?"

"Yeah," said Kate, "Don't worry about it, he'll be fine, worst case scenario he'll say something stupid and ignorant, but there's not a bad bone in his body. Anyway, help me lay out some snacks and get the place ready."

As Kate and Jamie laid out bowls of crisps and Maltesers, Martin did his business and splashed some water on his face. He dried himself with a hand-towel and stared at himself in the mirror. Forcing a smile he thought 'well, so far so good,' but deep down he felt a little exposed, for while he was delighted with the idea of finally trying a brownie, he felt self-consciously young in the company of his sister, her 40-something housemate, and god-knows-how-old guests who were on the way. Still, forcing himself a returning smile he repeated out loud—"so far so good" and made his way downstairs.

"So" offered Jamie as Martin descended down to them "how's college going?"

"Yeah it's alright, classical studies has been interesting. It's opened me up to a lot of ideas and reading. It's been an eye-opener seeing how ideas so old can feel so new."

"Oo!" interrupted Kate "before I forget." She went to her bookcase and quickly pulled out a copy of *Meditations*, "here."

"That's a great book" added Jamie, "it really distils a lot of the stoic stuff." Martin nodded as he was handed the book. "Great," he said as he quickly thumbed through it, "like new."

"Keep it," said Kate, "sure you might need it for college anyway."

"Sure, thanks," said Martin. "I feel bad now I didn't bring you a book."

"You should always bring a book," smiled Kate, "I should make it a house rule—BYOB—Bring Your Own Book!"

"Next time," said Martin as he ran back upstairs to leave it on his bed. As he came back down the doorbell rang—'Here! Here!'

"They're here!" Kate repeated as she went to the door. Jamie, meanwhile, seemed to be busying himself in the kitchen as Martin stood shifting from foot to foot while looking around the room and taking none of it in.

Irina and Shane came into the room from the hall, each flashing Martin a smile and a greeting, and Kate followed shortly behind.

"Irina, Shane, this is my oldest younger brother, Martin." A medley of greetings sprang up and Martin, feeling self-aware and longing for the distraction of a drink, extended his hand to the pair and awkwardly shook with each. Irina asked Martin about his trip down and Martin gave as polite and short an answer as he could to avoid repeating himself. Taking a step back he found himself leaning slightly off a table.

"Martin's reading *Ulysses*," said Kate as she walked towards a set of speakers.

"How far are you?" asked Shane.

"Not far," said Martin, "Stephen Dedalus has just finished teaching a class and hearing some anti-Semitic stuff from one of the other teachers."

"Oh yeah," nodded Shane, "not too far."

"It's anti-Semitic?" asked Irina.

"No, no," said Shane, "sure the main character is from a Jewish background. But Joyce never shied away from representing the times he lived in."

"Yeah" Martin nodded, "actually, when I was reading your man's rant about Jewish people ruining everything it did strike familiar, except now xenophobes seem more concerned over Muslims than anything else."

"Exactly," nodded Shane, "and mark in the book that the teacher making the rant is an English man living in Ireland, and in those days too. I think you'll find that still true today, people who are likely to experience discrimination need to be extra careful that they don't end up discriminating against others, I think Joyce was subtly trying to make that point by which of his characters he writes as being anti-Semitic."

"How's that" asked Irena, "people who are discriminated against should be more understanding, not less."

"It can be that way," said Shane, "but more often than not when people are attacked they become defensive and prone to lashing out. Audre Lorde put it exceptionally well: she argued that since those in charge direct their hate downwards to the plebs, and the plebs have no way of directing that hate back up in any real or meaningful way, they instead have to hate people equal or even worse off than them. Wealth trickles up and hate trickles down. You see the same thing play out in Malcom X's autobiography. And if an English man in Ireland is being picked on he's likely to turn to a scapegoat, another kind of outsider, to pick on in turn." Martin nodded, Shane seemed to be making sense to him, and an old unanswered question for him was starting to form in Martin's mind. Suddenly the sound of a piano started playing through the speakers, followed by the rest of the digitalised band.

"Lovely," said Irina, turning towards Kate and the speakers.

"I thought something was missing. Sounds a little like Chet" Martin ventured.

"It's Wayne Shorter" Kate answered. "He played with Art Blakey and Miles Davis, you remember Art Blakey I'm sure."

"*Moanin'*," said Martin with a grin, "I'll never forget it."

"You like your jazz then," said Irina approvingly.

"Thanks to Kate" Martin smiled. "When I finally set up my own email account she sent me the links to a few songs, *Moanin'* by Art Blakey was one of them, the swagger that came out of those horns blew me away... blew me away" Martin smiled to himself, shook his head and came off the table.

"Yeah," said Kate, "me and Martin developed a great system out of it. We take it in turns now to email each other the links to 3 songs with a little feedback on the last 3 we received."

"I've definitely benefited from it," said Martin, "in fact, it's how me and Kate mostly stay in touch, and even when we don't say much, sharing the music is always fun."

"That's a great idea," said Irena.

"Yeah," said Kate, "it's dead simple. You can take as long as you want getting back, and you keep it up till you die! Having someone constantly sending you the best of what they're listening to really helps to expand what you think is out there, and knowing that you have to send 3 songs in return is the perfect incentive to keep track of what you've been enjoying. Martin's gotten me into Rory Gallagher, *Kila*, early *Thin Lizzy*, which is much trippier and laid-back than the stuff they're famous for, and I've been getting Martin into jazz, punk and whatever else I've been listening to."

"Yeah," said Martin, "if it wasn't for Kate and jazz, my mate Dan and Rory, and our dad for *The Beatles* and classic rock, god knows what I'd be listening to, because, really, with the exception of *Lyric FM* and the odd bit of excellent trad, Irish radio is severely lacking." There followed a round of agreement, and as Kate and Martin continued going back and forth Jamie emerged from the kitchen with a bowl of brownies in one hand, a pot of fresh coffee in the other, and a polite "hey guys" and nod to Irena and Shane down the middle. He laid the bowl and coffee on the coffee table and went about shaking hands with the newcomers as Martin looked on and smiled.

"Does anyone want tea?" asked Kate on her way to the kitchen.

"Yeah, sure I'll give you a hand" Martin said as he followed her in.

In the kitchen Martin could see his sister buzzing around collecting cups, filling a couple of saucers with milk and oat milk, getting the sugar, spoons, napkins and a jar of biscuits. Martin helped to pile them onto the coffee table as the kettle started boiling. Finally Kate gave the coffee table a final glare, asking with her eyes if anything was missing from it before asking aloud if anything was wanting. Martin smiled, the whole thing reminded him of their granny, their very own queen of Irish hospitality.

"Looks great Kate," said Irena and they all began to sit on the couch and armchairs around the coffee table and fill their mugs. Martin, going back to the kitchen to finish making his tea, was the last to sit down.

"This is Martin's first time trying a brownie," said Kate with a smile as she reached out to grab the first, "dig in," she said.

"Just make sure to only eat one," said Shane while taking his and looking towards Martin, "it'll take a while for you to feel anything, half an hour or an hour at least, so don't even think of eating a second one until you can at least feel the first."

"Sure," said Martin as he reached for one. "But, we're not having brownies for dinner are we?" He asked. Laughter broke out around the table and Kate explained "We're going to order Chinese once we've had these, think of them as starters."

"The best starters," said Jamie, "the kind that give you an appetite."

"Mmm" put in Irena, "they're delicious, thanks Kate," she said followed by a second volley of compliments. When everyone had had at least one Jamie got up and shuffled out to the open. "Well," he said "I'm going to change into something more comfortable. Order me my usual Kate darling."

"Sure."

He smiled and winked at her before charging upstairs. Martin's eyes followed his disappearance, and as he couldn't possibility imagine how someone could dress down from a t-shirt and jeans he asked the table: "Is he coming down in a dressing-gown or what?" This caused an uproar of laughter as a piece of brownie flew from Kate's mouth into her coffee. As the 3 of them settled down Martin could only sit and hang onto his smile for fear of looking distressed without it. In fact, everyone had been so good-hearted that he felt more confused than uncomfortable.

"No," said Kate finally with a smile, and, taking in a deep breathe, continued, "Jamie's a transvestite, you know, a cross-dresser. He'll likely be down in a dress, heels, wig and make-up in an hour or so."

"Oh," said Martin, "fair enough." He looked around. Everyone seemed to be smiling away, but no one was meeting his eye, and Martin felt an air of expectancy about them. Taking a breath and clearing his throat with an "em," he started: "not that I'm having any problems so far, but am I missing any more surprises or what?"

"Well," said Kate as she shot a look at Irena and Shane, and finally looking at Martin. "Why don't you take your tea and follow me—let me show you some of the paintings I'm working on."

"Sure" Martin said with a shrug, he didn't know what to expect anymore.

Kate led Martin into her studio, switched on the light and closed the door behind them. Martin looked around in wonder; he had been in the room a handful of times before, but he had never seen it like this—in the past the small room consisted of nothing but a stool, a canvas and a small table covered with some tools of her trade, now, the first thing that hit Martin was a strong smell of incense, after that he was shocked to find the place in a clutter. There was the same stool, canvas and table, but the table now held an ashtray, an incense burner and a pack of incense sticks, as well as the usual tools he was somewhat familiar with. There was also a cushion on the floor with a canvas lying face up beside it, and many other canvases stacked around the room, as well as a Bluetooth radio lying near a socket with an Ipod settled in it. The wall was covered by finished and half-finished paintings, as well as many photos and torn pages from books. The last time Martin entered this room it had seemed to him a near carbon-copy of their mother's studio, now, although it was physically the same, it was dressed much differently. His eyes danced around his head as he tried to get it altogether, but there was one detail his eyes were drawn to, and after he felt like he had a grasp on everything else, they rested upon one of the paintings put up along the cream-coloured wall. Putting his cup of tea on the table he walked closer to get a better look. Inside the large canvas sat a woman wearing long red leather boots, a black and red corset, and red-rimmed glasses. In one hand she held a riding-crop vertically so that it near touched the ground. Her other hand, which rested serenely on her crossed legs, held the leash of a dog-collared man who was kneeling naked and frozen below with his lips pressed to her boots in a devoted kiss, the look on his face was one of devoted rapture as his soft pink lips met those bold red leather boots. There was a lot of exquisite detail in the painting, but the only other detail Martin could fixate on was the fox's tail coming out from the man's behind, and their faces! Martin couldn't believe their faces, he stared and stared as Kate drew up beside him, finally he had to let it out: "It's Shane and Irene!" He said, and he felt his face begin to blush.

"Irena" corrected Kate. She stood now beside Martin, watching his face carefully with an encouraging smile upon her familiar face. "Well, what do you think?" She finally asked.

"It's wonderful!" Martin said, "I mean... I don't know what to say, but... it's a wonderful painting." He looked at Kate as if he was coming up for air, and then his eyes plunged once more into the painting. He noted the proud possessive look on Irena's painted face, the bold gleam in her eyes. His eyes slowly took in the lovely golden red velvet chair she sat upon, he noticed how close the borders of the painting were to the couple, and the feeling that it gave, as if they were the only two people in existence. "It's wonderful" was all he could bring himself to say. He looked again at Kate and back to the painting as the image of one began to paint the other.

"I'm glad you like it" Kate said warmly, "I'm really proud of this one, and I just need to finish a little of the background, but,... well, you can see why I tend to hide these types of paintings when the folks visit." Martin laughed, shook his head and took a long and slow breath. "It certainly beats the old barren landscapes," he said, and, indeed, for the first time Martin saw a painting which revealed something of his sister beyond her original teacher and her skill with a brush, and even as he continued to look at it the painting seemed to stare back at him and whisper its own secret influence. Martin felt a new curiosity to look through his sister's art more thoroughly. Jamie's words echoed back to him now; 'the best kind of starter' he thought, 'the kind that whets your appetite,' glancing around the room he saw a few other canvases with a similar theme; of people bound and tied, of couples dominated and dominating, there was one other of Irena and Shane, but the others were of different people. Martin was speechless. In his sister's work he had become used to seeing the idyllic bodies of the ancients and the Renaissance, but now he was surrounded by normal figures, average and even odd body types, and how real and intimate they all seemed! There were other paintings which were fairly unadorned and honestly done portraits, some of which he recognised, some he didn't, but each and every object within the room now seemed electrified—as if each one told a little more of the depth he hadn't known his sister or her work to possess. Finally he looked at Kate, smiled and said, "I could spend a while in here." Kate, returning his smile, replied: "Tomorrow, take all the time in the world, but, well, we still have to order the food! But, listen Martin, the main thing I want to talk to you about is this; the thing is you've got two options for your ethnography project tomorrow.

I can take you to an art gallery where a friend and colleague of mine is opening up her own exhibition, which will be ok but a little boring to be honest, I mean, I'm her friend, kind-of, and even I don't want to go. Her work is good, but hardly anything new. Or…" and here she tipped the scales towards 'or…' with a winning smile, "instead, we can join Irena, Shane, Jamie and a few other friends and go to an event called *Misneach*, which would be a lot more fun and a lot more interesting, both for us and your project since, well, it's a sort of pan-fetish event held here in Galway once a month." Martin, still smiling and lost in a sea of thoughts, took another glance at the portrait of Irena and Shane, and, with a soft laugh, nodded and said "yeah, fuck it, why not." Kate continued: "Seriously, I know I'm springing a lot on you, but we'll only go if you're comfortable, I'm easy myself. But me and Jamie were discussing this last week and, when I told him about your project, he was kind enough to offer to introduce you to some of his other friends who happen to be transvestites, it would give you something to focus your project on, what do you think?"

"Well," said Martin, "it'll make for something different alright, but, why couldn't you have told me all this by email or something?"

"I'm sorry," said Kate, now also glancing at her painting, "but this stuff is hard to share by email, I wouldn't even know where to begin. The thing is, if you were to go to *Misneach*, you would also have to dress in fetish, it's a club rule that anyone going has to be, well, into it. If you were to arrive in a shirt and jeans they wouldn't let you in—I guess the idea is if everyone's compromised then everyone's safe. I was thinking you could go in drag, I mean, we're the same build, so I could give you some of my clothes, a wig, do your make-up and all that, plus you said yourself that your project should be immersive, didn't you?"

"Right," said Martin, "yeah… I could go dressed as a woman. And how would you be going?" He asked, feeling ready for just about anything except seeing his sister walking around with a whip in her hand.

"It's a little easier for women," smiled Kate, "I have a few Halloween costumes to choose from. Skimpy devil or skimpy cat-woman normally go down well. I'm not as into the fetishes as the rest of them, not that we have to go into detail!" she winked, "but once you're open-minded, respectful and discrete, it's a very welcoming community, and, aesthetically, it's opened up a whole new world to me."

"Yeah" Martin nodded, "I can see that…."

"What I love about it," continued Kate "is that BDSM-themed art allows me to express, in a way I've never been able to express before, not just the sexual act that you see on the canvas, but of a whole sexual history. Does that make sense?" Martin nodded pensively, so Kate continued:

"Like this, for example, what I want people to see when they look at this painting is that I'm not just trying to speak for one sexual act, but for hundreds and thousands, like, how many times can a person have sex, especially with the same partner, before one decides to up their game to this?" Kate indicated to the painting, her eyes shining. "Can you see it Martin? It's like cops and robbers for adults, and most kinksters have a toy chest to rival any spoilt child's. That's what's at stake here, I don't just want to capture the moment, I want people to feel the history involved," she bit her lower lip as Martin reflected on what she said, he had to give it to Kate, she could certainly put the 'mm?' into BDS.

"Is this painting going to be given to them then?" He eventually asked.

"Irena and Jamie? No," said Kate, "to be honest, although it's definitely not the main reason for my interest, it's a very profitable theme. This painting already has a buyer—one of my old contacts from London, anyway, we better go back in and order the food, but, by all means talk to them about the painting, or about anything really, as I've said, once you're respectful and discrete they're very open people."

Kate and Martin walked back to the sitting room, Kate with her empty cup and Martin stuck with a near full cup of cold tea. Irena was on her phone as Shane sat staring into space with his hand on her leg. Jamie was still busy getting changed as the faint sound of Sinead O' Connor's *I Want Your (Hands On Me)* could be heard from upstairs over the now more mellow jazz which was playing from Kate's main speakers.

"Well, what does everyone want?" asked Kate taking out her phone.

"I'll have a satay chicken with fried rice, please" Martin said, "and I'm going to make a fresh cup of tea if that's alright."

"Of course, make yourself at home. Here, take my cup with you and leave it near the sink" Kate said with a smile. Martin made his way to the kitchen while Irena and Shane gave their orders. As Martin waited by the kettle he couldn't help but smile, 'God, what did I agree to' he was thinking as the kettle clicked, and he chuckled softly at the idea that tomorrow he would be dressed as a woman and attending a pan-fetish event. With everything that had happened he was surprised to find his limbs feeling a little sluggish as he poured his tea and milk, 'the brownie!' he thought as he finished putting his tea together and made for the couch. Shane saw Martin fall into the couch and could see that Martin, despite hanging onto a nervous smile, appeared a little flustered.

"How's the brownie treating you?" He asked as Martin put his cup on the table.

"Yeah, think I'm starting to feel it, in my limbs a bit," he said sitting back. He looked at Shane and Irena and tried to let go of the image of them he had seen, but even still, he couldn't help looking at Irena's jeans and imagining instead the red boots and black tights. He shook his head with a smile and found himself meeting Shane's eyes and holding onto them like a couple of buoys.

"It'll probably take another bit yet then," Irena said without looking up.

"So… I guess we're all going to *Misneach* tomorrow then." Martin said as cool as he could, even feeling overly aware of his age again as Kate began rattling off the order over the phone.

"Yeah, so you're going then" beamed Shane. "You'll have a great time."

"Hope so," said Martin, "sure, it'll be something different, for me anyway… I love your portrait by the way," he said, looking from one to the other. "If you don't mind me asking, did Kate just use your faces and her imagination, or … em … did you pose for it?"

"Oh, we posed," laughed Irena putting her phone away, "this one wouldn't have had it otherwise," she said as her hand fell on his which was still resting on her leg. Martin smiled, the way that they looked at each other—he could feel the love between them, it seemed to him not just a love of lust, but of boring domesticity and trust. He saw something of the same love in the painting, along with all the playfulness they seemed to have, that, and the fact that he was starting to feel high, took all the nerves from his own smile. Suddenly he broke in: "and what about the tail, if you don't mind me asking, did Kate add that in?"

"No," laughed Shane, "that was a butt plug with a fox's tail attached—a bit of a novelty I guess. Also, of course, it's not a *real* tail."

"Oh," said Martin, lost now for words. Shane continued: "Listen Martin, a butt plug, or anything anal, isn't just for gay people you know," he glanced at Kate, who seemed to be struggling on the phone, and he lowered his voice for Martin's discretion. He continued: "No, they're not even just for us kinksters and occasional subs like me. The thing is, we *all* have nerve endings up there, all men at least, and it's pleasurable, *undeniably* and *physically* pleasurable, understand?"

"It's pleasurable for women too," said Irena without looking up.

"And," continued Shane "well... I'm not saying it's for everyone, but it would certainly be for most if they gave it a try. Remember," he said, falling back into his own chair and raising his voice again, "for years and years Irish people have been afraid to masturbate, maybe you're too young to remember, but it was drilled into us that masturbating is a sin, hell, it was beaten into most of us. And it's absurd and most of us now know it's absurd, and yet, when it comes to sex and masculinity, we have been extremely boxed in, more than we even realise, stunted even..." he took a breath and some space to reflect before continuing; "it's unhealthy. Frankly, it's a tragedy. This country has spent centuries being bullied into boxes by the Catholic Church and their ignorant and hypocritical, sexist, women-hating homophobic priests, and even now, as more and more truth is coming out about the Church and their hypocrisy and their horrible actions, we are still mentally stunted. It's like... it's as if we've been shaped by hands long dead, for their ghostly echoes still fill our heads."

"Now there's a line" said Irena looking up, "you should write that one down," and with that she reached for her bag and pulled out a small diary which she handed to Shane. "What's that" Martin asked slowly, "you keep a diary?" Shane nodded but continued his writing as Kate put her phone away and turned the music back up, she now started clearing the table and getting it ready for the delivery as Martin began sinking deeper into the sofa. Shane, closing his diary and leaving it on the table, got up and started helping Kate. Martin, looking at them both, wanted to help, but he couldn't bring himself to get up.

Martin was shocked as if woken from a dream when Irena spoke up and asked him "are you alright?"

"Yeah, I'm grand, just feeling heavy, but my heart seems to be racing."

"You're high so," she laughed. "Just relax, remember to breath and your heart will slow back down in a bit" Irena said encouragingly, "and you'll be able to move right enough when the food comes," she laughed, and kept laughing until Martin had to ask what was funny.

"Oh, Shane's just reminded me," she said, "in order to tell my left from my right I used to have to bless myself, and I still have to, although I've been pagan now for years," she laughed, "and it was so bad that when I took my driving test

I had to bless myself at every junction, my driving-tester must have thought I was crazy!" and with that Irena's laughter seemed to flow right into Martin and soon he was laughing, and Irena laughed some more which only made Martin laugh, and suddenly Martin couldn't remember why he was laughing, and the idea that he was laughing without knowing why was so funny that it made him laugh, and Irena laughed and began to cry from laughing until the tears streamed down Martin's face and the next thing they were both laughing and slapping their chairs like a couple of desperately pinned-down wrestlers calling for release. When he finally had some control of himself he found that everyone seemed to be giggling away.

"I haven't had a laughing fit like that in ages" Irena said as she wiped her eyes. Suddenly Jamie appeared back downstairs in a long black wig, a long black dress, red lipstick with a matching gold and red necklace, tights and a pair of black high heels. Martin, his face ruddy red and his blood-shot eyes wet from laughing, took a glance and said "you look amazing" before convulsing into another fit of laughter. "Isn't he precious?" Jamie said as she made her way to the speakers. "Can we have a break from the jazz Kate darling?" She asked while thumbing through Kate's Ipod.

"Do I have a choice?" laughed Kate, "at least stick on some Reggae or something easy. I can't stand techno before midnight."

"You read my mind" Jamie replied, and soon the room burst into a new light as a Reggae tune bounced it's way along with a familiar voice.

"That can't be Sinead O' Connor?" asked Martin astonished.

"The one and only," said Jamie as she made her way to the couch. "With the best Reggae album Ireland ever produced."

"Didn't *Sly and the Family Band* do the music for it?" Irena asked.

"Sly and Robbie" Jamie replied. "I only wish Sinead would make another one, but sure, if Sinead could be told what to do she wouldn't be my Sinead."

"I never would have thought of her doing a Reggae album" Martin said.

"These are dangerous days, to say what you mean is to dig your own grave. Now here, get up and dance with me Martin, you look like you're about to fall asleep." Before Martin could say anything Jamie was pulling him off the couch, when he found his balance he tried a couple of shuffling steps before standing stock still and feeling embarrassed. Everyone but Irena now seemed to be dancing and Martin made a move to sit down and join her when Jamie pulled him close and whispered 63xplaing with your eyes closed honey. Dance as slow and awkward as you want, no one's going to care, nobody's going to stare, but you need to give it 2 minutes with your eyes closed before I let you sit down again." Letting go of him Jamie closed her own eyes and started pulling moves straight out of *Pulp Fiction*. Martin laughed and took a nervous breath, shook his head, closed his eyes, and danced. And for the first time since he was a child, Martin danced and enjoyed himself.

A parting gift received

In what felt like no time at all the food arrived and the dishes were handed out. As they sat to their meal Martin found himself asking Jamie:

"So, when did you start dressing up as a woman?"

Jamie shrugged and answered, "oh, over 10 years now. And tell me, when did you start dressing *that*?"

"Like what" blinked Martin in surprise, he had to look himself over to remind himself just what it was that he was wearing (black schoolboy shoes, black socks with multiple holes, jeans ripped at the knees from use, boxers with several holes, a light-blue short-sleeved shirt and a brown zip-up jumper), "like this?" (safe, plain, dull).

"Yes, like that," smiled Jamie.

"I guess I've always dressed like this," said Martin.

"You mean" pushed Jamie, with a raised eyebrow, "that you went from being dressed by your parents to dressing yourself while wearing the same kind of clothes all your life?"

"Eh…" flustered Martin.

"Please," laughed Kate, "Martin might dress himself physically, but he still wears whatever we buy him for Christmas and his birthday, my brother's the only kid I've ever known to constantly be asking for clothes for his birthday! … Once it's not something that rocks the boat" Kate joked. Martin shrugged and replied: "yeah… I guess that's true. I just hate shopping for clothes, so I guess I do ask for clothes for my birthday and Christmas… and yeah, Kate bought me an *Iron Maiden* hoodie before and I wouldn't wear it, I just didn't want to be identified as a metal-head when I listen to all types of music."

"That's fine hun," said Jamie, "I'm not here to judge, the point is, I always find it bizarre that non-trans people take such an interest in what *we* wear and why *we* wear it, whereas when it comes to so-called 'normal' people I find, when they're being honest, that they only dress as they do because it's how everyone else dresses. I mean, no one in Ireland dresses as they do in Japan say, and vice versa. So… before you judge how someone else decides to dress, take a second to reflect on the clothes you wear, because this is what's so frustrating about so-called 'normal' people, they judge us constantly, and yet, by definition of being 'normal' they are rarely, if ever, judged. And they have no idea the damage their judging does."

"Fair enough," said Martin, a little in shock.

"I don't mean to get defensive hun," continued Jamie, "but I've lost contact with an awful lot of people for dressing how I dress… the kind of people who are meant to stick by you no matter what, understand?"

Martin nodded.

"And…" Jamie struggled, "and… it goes so deep hun, gay people, trans people, women, black people, disabled people… the judgement that's experienced, the discrimination, it goes so deep that we internalise it, like… have you ever met a woman who's sexist against women?" Martin nodded and thought of his own mam's sexist comments towards Katie Tylor, such as 'she's disgusting, women shouldn't be allowed to box.' Martin sighed, met Kate's knowing nod with his own and replied:

"yeah, I have."

"Well," continued Jamie, "a famous transvestite by the name of Panti Bliss once made an argument that everyone, even gay people, are homophobic in Ireland, and of her and people of our generation I can tell you that that's true. And it's true because we internalise all the judging, the abuse, the questions, the discrimination. And so I know you're a good kid, and you're only asking what, to you, is an innocent question, but I promise you, if you had to justify, every single day, why it is that you dress as you do, could you imagine that making you more self-conscious, especially when we're dressing as we do to better reflect how we feel inside?"

Martin nodded, he was painfully self-conscious at the best of times anyway.

"Anyway," continued Jamie as he looked around the room "I don't mean to get so serious, but this is good. Let me say this now before tomorrow; when you go to *Misneach*, when you meet some of my other friends who happen to be trans, don't meet them as a sociologist—"

"Anthropologist," mumbled Martin.

"Right, anthropologist, meet them as Martin, meet them as one human meeting another, and if what they're wearing causes you any feelings of discomfort or confusion, then please respect the fact that, as far as *we're* concerned, that's *your* problem, not ours. I don't judge you for how you dress, so don't presume the right to judge me."

"Okay…" said Martin, then, looking directly at Jamie, he added: "Thank you."

"In any case" Shane came in, "in my humble opinion, we should all be nudists anyway."

"Oh, our father's a bit of a nudist," said Kate.

"Yeah" Martin nodded gratefully, "any time I've locked myself out of the house at 2 or 3am and he's had to open the door, he's always been naked."

"Probably to discourage you from forgetting your key," laughed Irena.

"Oh he's just a dirtbird," laughed Kate. "I remember back when I was living with them, so I must have been under 18, dad was trying to get me to taste something that had cucumber in it, I told him I always gag when I eat cucumber, 'in that case' says dad, 'why don't you try cutting them up first'." The table came together in an eruption of laughter, which seemed to erode any lingering tension or guilt Martin was feeling, he smiled.

The next day Martin woke up from a sweet but lost dream, and slowly his mind started pulling together pieces of the night before. He found himself smiling, blushing, laughing and shaking his head as bits of yesterday starting drifting back. Eventually he got up, threw on his holey boxers and a shirt, grabbed a towel and made his way to the bathroom. He stared at himself in the mirror with a goofy grin, half surprised and half disappointed that it showed him what he took to be his old self, but, smiling and returning his own reflected smile he shrugged and did his business, brushed his teeth while doing his twenty five squats and took a shower. The rest of the house slept on as Martin got dressed and made his way quietly downstairs. Looking around he tidied as much as could while staying quiet, then he made himself a cup of tea and walked softly back upstairs to grab *Ulysses* from his bag. He sat down and started trying to read, but for all the world he felt too peaceful to let Joyce tease and rap him on the knuckles, so he took out a copybook and started writing bits and pieces from the night before. When he had finished his tea, he put his cup back in the kitchen and made his way gingerly to his sister's studio. Again he smelt the lingering smell of incense and now, without his shoes, he felt the soft carpet underneath his feet. Slowly he scanned the walls which were covered in paintings, pictures and ripped pages, but slowly too his eyes came to rest on the portrait of Irena and Shane, for while it wasn't the only picture of a BDSM theme, the fact that he had spent a night with the two of them gave the painting an added depth. He remembered then that he would be seeing them again tonight. He smiled and cringed as bits of their conversations came back to him. At one stage, after they had discussed the dress that Martin was to wear, he asked in turn how Irena and Shane were going—

"Oh, I prefer to let her decide," said Shane with a grin, and Martin blushed at the thought that here was a man infinitely more comfortable in his own skin, and there he was, strung up on the wall, with a butt plug in his ass and a collar around his neck, and somehow exhibiting more self-confidence than Martin felt he could ever possess. Martin cringed to think that while he had finally stopped believing in a Catholic god he too lived a life that was shaped by hands long dead. The boys-only Christian Brothers school, the fact that he had to be baptised to attend, the fact that his teachers practically led him by the hand and pushed him into a confessional box to tell his private 'sins' to a strange old man, Martin shook his head. The fact that even the idea of a man enjoying anything anal was reason for ridicule, Martin shook his head. The fact that half his time spent studying anthropology was focused on the oddities of others rather than the oddities of us, Martin shook his head. Irena too, while sometimes seeming a bit too attached to her phone... both of them, all of them, seemed to be so comfortable, so natural, as if they were all at home. 'Sexual deviants.' 'Stoners.' 'Hippies.' 'Trannies.' 'Perverts.' Martin shook his head as words he didn't invite seemed to flash and vanish, and he started looking at some of the other more explicit paintings, and everywhere he saw the same openness, honesty, comfort and bravery. 'Even if these people were only naked' he thought, 'they would still be more substantial than me.' The paintings, while ranging here and there in style, in levels of picture-like precision to abandoned abstraction, were all shockingly normal: here were bodies of the middle-aged, the underweight and overweight, the too short and too tall, the imperfectly perfect. His gaze even met a grey-haired wrinkled woman handcuffed to a chair and blindfolded with nipple clamps attached to her long sagging breasts, her old feet tied to the comparably youthful looking legs of the chair, and her head back and lips grinning—every detail seemed to say, without a shred of pride or malice, 'this is me, this scene is mine, and your gaze is for *my* pleasure, not yours.' Martin, who spent a lot of time worrying about his little pudgy belly, about the occasional spot on his face, and about how he's perceived by others in general, felt desperately silly gazing at them all. He shook his head and his mind took him back to a *Metallica* concert he went to years ago, and the delirious surge of unselfconscious joy he felt while listening to the song *So Fucking What*, and how his mind often took him back to that song and that sense of abandon, and here were people who lived it, at least as they had been painted. Martin shook his head.

When Kate came down she found Martin sitting pensively with a cup of hot tea beside him on the table, an A4 *Easons* copybook on his lap and a pen in hand.

"Morning!" she said brightly, "how'd you sleep?"

"Great yeah, thanks," said Martin as he pulled himself out of last night and back to the present.

"And how do you feel?" asked Kate, "all good?"

"Yeah," repeated Martin, "I feel great, no bad effects to the brownie or anything, just my mouth felt a bit thirsty when I woke up."

Kate smiled and followed: "Well, that's cause weed isn't poisonous you know, not that I want to be too critical on alcohol, I mean I still drink occasionally, but just goes to show huh? I haven't been drunk in years now, a little tipsy is about all I allow myself to get."

"Yeah," nodded Martin, "although I never really get hangovers, but yeah, it was good thanks, no complaints. Won't be my last I'm sure, it didn't make me grumpy like drink sometimes does."

"No," laughed Kate, "I've known a few people to fall asleep after a smoke, but I've never seen it make anyone feel down. By the way, while you *can* have a drink while smoking, maybe one or two at most, it's best not to get drunk and high at the same time. Choose one or the other on a night out unless you want to get sick or black-out."

"Sure," said Martin, "thanks."

"What are you doing now anyway? Are you writing for your assignment?"

"No" Martin said with a soft laugh, "I'm just scribbling away about last night I guess, I don't know."

"Scribbling away?" asked Kate, her eyes flashing, "scribbling away in a *copybook*? Have you no diary?"

"No," said Martin, "I normally just scribble in whatever copybook I happen to have, I mean, I haven't tried keeping a diary since I was a kid, and that was short-lived I guess, I don't think I write enough to merit one." Kate shook her head and walked over to the bookcase, saying as she went "a copybook won't do at all Martin, I never knew you were so ridiculous. Like, how many copybooks have you lost?" Martin said nothing but watched in wonder as his sister pulled out a soft blue diary and thumbed through it. "This one's fresh," she said, and walking over to Martin she handed it to him. "Maybe you haven't been in college long enough, but believe me, copybooks are apt to get lost, forgotten or thrown out. And copybooks are for *copying* for christ sake! Copying the words of your lecturers, copying notes from the books they have you read, a copybook is no place for your own writing, even if it is only scribbles."

Martin stared at her and the soft blue diary being thrust upon him, finally he took it.

"Em, thanks," he said.

"If you really want to thank me then use it," said Kate, not without a smile, but not without force either. "Listen," she continued, "to each their own, but if you'll take my advice you'll write all future scribbles and personal thoughts here, *here*, understand, and, once a month, maybe, you should rewrite what you've written onto a computer and save it onto an external hard drive or somewhere safe. Don't trust Facebook or any of the rest of them to keep the story of your life, god only knows what Facebook does with the information we give it, and I think it's only a matter of time before that website gets pulled down, hacked to bits or whatever else, and you could wake up to find that everything you've put on it is gone and buried. And don't be using copybooks that are or will be mostly filled with second-hand words which you'll leave forgotten or thrown in the bin. I'm serious Martin, if you have any respect for yourself and what goes on in that head of yours, then you have to learn how to respect your own thoughts, so either write in a diary now or regret later."

"Sure" stammered Martin, "but..."

"No buts!" said Kate. "If it takes you one year or ten years you fill this diary. Got it?"

"Okay, I got it."

"Grand so, I'll get started on breakfast," and with that Kate was gone towards the kitchen, but, looking back, she topped and watched as Martin sat still and dumb. He opened up the diary, thumbed through it slowly, and opened the first page and stared at it, and held his breath. For the pages looked to him like a new snowy field which froze him in place, and he was reluctant to start leaving his own clumsy searching mark upon them. Suddenly he looked up to see Kate approaching him, and before he could say anything, she grabbed the diary, grabbed the pen from Martin's hand, and, opening up the first page, she quickly drew a smiling emoji-like face with arched eyebrows and a line for a joint stuck in its lips with a whisp of smoke to show it was lit. "There," she said handing it back to him, "a stupid smiley face to ruin your perfectly white page, now you draw one" and Martin did, his own face no better or worse than his sister's, although somehow his had rather large, rounded eyes which gave it a sad look. Kate leaned into the page and nodded approvingly.

"Now date it she said" and he did. "Listen," she continued: "if you want to be any kind of artist, or even if you just want to live, then you have to understand that we can never make more perfect an unmarked page or an empty canvas. Perfection is leaving things alone, perfection is death. 'Nothing's as dead as a diamond.' Do you know who said that?"

"N-no" Martin answered.

"Never mind" Kate continued, "I can't remember either… Salvador Dali had a similar one though; 'have no fear of perfection' he said, because 'you'll never reach it,' the point is, many things should be left alone, but as for diaries and their snow-white pages, fuck 'em! There'll always be another perfectly white page, unspoilt by you or me, or another canvas that my brush hasn't ruined, but the purpose of a diary, or art for that matter, is not perfection, understand?"

"Then what's the purpose?" Martin asked.

Kate held his questioning gaze for a long time, and it seemed to him that she was about to answer, but, taking a breath, she smiled and said: "How am I to tell you the purpose of art or keeping a diary Martin? Hell, who's to say there needs to be a purpose? All I know is—if you're occasionally going to scribble a thought somewhere, *please* don't let it be in a copybook. Before you're finished college you'll have filled more copybooks then you'll know what to do with. And like, 5 or 10 years after you've finished college you'll stumble on them, flick through them once maybe, and throw them in the bin. That's what happens to copybooks. College is all about taking a huge range of different people and requiring them all to read and write the same things while charging you an arm and a leg, and you'll only lose your own thoughts in all that mess. But a diary that contains your own thoughts, your own voice, and perhaps the voices you respect the most.

Something like that doesn't just end up in a bin, and it can be more useful than you'd ever imagine... trust me, have I ever let you down?"

Mart*i*n, frozen, looked at Kate, and then, suddenly reanimated, Mart*l*n took the diary and wrote beside the two smiling faces: *"Yes, I trust you, thanks Kate."*

"Yes. Thanks Kate." Yes.

"By the way," I said, "I love your friends."

"Thanks," smiled Kate.

"Are they how you've become so open-minded?"

"Well, part of the reason I'm sure, why?"

"It's just... I feel like college is helping me to let go of some of the ideas that have wormed themselves in, but, I mean, where do you go then for new ideas to replace the old ones?"

"Well," smiled Kate, "I've already given you one book, Marcus Aurelias, he's a good place to start, after him I'd recommend Alan Watts and Walt Whitman, and finally, my own personal hero and guru, Virginia Woolf. Someone once said something like—'if you find your guru, kill them,' but the beauty of those 4 is that they're already dead, there's no agenda to their work, just a wish that the rest of us would think as freely as they did."

"Mm," I said, "well, I'll see how I get on with Marcos then."

Intermission

(Brown sauce optional)

Half-Pipe

I sat and stared on what I feared

Pathetic

It would have been better if I approached it once and walked away
But instead I sat on it, dwelt on it, was consumed by it—pathetic.

For my 11th Christmas I received them:
a clunky pair of rollerblades,
The best kind of gift—one to grow into;
Unlocking new worlds of thrills and skateparks
A new space to grow, an adult-free world to explore with my friends.

On dry weekdays I would wait until I was sure Dan had finished his homework
to his father's satisfaction.
Then I would go to him, my best friend, and the two of us would try for hours to
successfully grind on his well-waxed corner,
Or we would prop up a ramp and skate up it as fast as we could,
Grabbing our blades in the air,
Turning 180s and 360s,
Jumping and falling,
Jumping and falling
Jumping and falling
Until we landed successfully.

Our repertoire of moves was limited and simple, but we enjoyed ourselves.
We were out of the house, away from our families and left to our own devices,
what more can a child want?

We created a space for ourselves where we could grow without direction, without parental oversight.
I didn't realise it at the time, but skating was another step into adulthood, another beginning of the endless process of self-development.

Skating is different to other sports.
For one thing, very few Irish fathers have had a failed career in skating
My father watched me skate with perfect indifference, perfect silence. A facilitator, not a spectator. Perfect.

Skating isn't football.
There's no coaching, no winning or losing, no outside input,
The only competition was what you made of it –
The need to improve, the joy of showing off

And Dan was something else—my trailblazer
At least once a week the 2 of us went to one of two skateparks
Our parents taking it in turns to bring us
Once a week I had a space in which to grow

The highlight of our week was our weekend outing,
Ramp City near the airport was our favourite.
It was noisy, chaotic, fast and dangerous.
Snoop Dogg, spinning wheels and endless crashing was the soundtrack,
The smell was wood, oil, sweat, skin-burns and occasionally blood.
The feeling was freedom, adrenaline and growth –
The slow progression of being able to go down a ramp to mastering it,
Eventually going down in such a way as to increase your speed for the next one and gain in momentum and air.
The ground gave us our platform for speed,
but it was off the ground that we wanted to be.

Between the two of us, me and Dan, we fell into a pattern –
Dan would break some limit, do something we had never done before,
And I would follow him
Slow and steady.

I didn't mind being 2nd best to Dan,
It came naturally.
In school there was no comparison;
he was 'king of the focloir,' one of the star pupils,
and I was one of the class rejects,
Hopeless at Irish under a teacher who cared for nothing else.
'You need to be great at something to be good at anything.'
Was it Oliver Sacks who said that? Well, anyway, if it's true, then the reverse is true too, and so my complete inaptitude in Irish crippled me completely, academically, for many years.
For a long fucking time
'Fuck the focloir' was my crime, and my self-esteem was sentenced, locked away and very much left behind.

So I couldn't follow Dan academically,
in school my friend was on another level.
He was unapproachable, but outside of school,
slow and steady,
I could follow him on my rollerblades.

Dan would do something new,
and slow and steady I would follow,
By that I mean I would try and fall,
and fall,
and fall,
until I landed whatever move it was that Dan had done with seemingly half the effort it took me.
I thought he was just a natural back then,
I think I know better now.

In the end I settled into my role as the fall guy.
But I was still one of the gang,
I had a place and position to grow into.
And the positions of and set by adolescence are far more flexible and rewarding than those found in adulthood.

Yes. There is something about being a fall guy, about being a failure, that, if you can keep a positive attitude, makes you very endearing.
At least it made me endearing when I wasn't so before.

My failures in school were only pitiful,
I didn't have the wit or the imagination to turn failure into spectacle,
I was no class-cl*own*, just a class-ass—or so I felt.
But on my blades I could fail with a smile, with a laugh,
and pick myself up and keep skating.
I made enough jumps, cleared just enough 360s, to maintain some sense of progress.

And skating has this going for it –
To some extent every skater is a fall-guy or gal.

Skateboarders particularly.
Skateboarders spend more time sprawled on the ground,
ass on the curve,
than any other athlete, (I'm sure of it).
Falling is bread and butter to a skater.
So being the guy who happens to fall the most, in skating,
isn't such a negative role to play,
and in any case I was happy.

But Ramp City got renovated,
New ramps were improved and installed.
And one of these ramps became my wall.

It consisted of small ramp that led to a camel's hump
followed by another camel's hump,
slightly higher,
which connected and led down to a half pipe.
The trick was that you had to go down the first ramp and take to the first bump with as much speed as possible to allow you to skate up the final bump and down into the half pipe.
In other words:

you had to commit yourself from the start for the final part,
otherwise you wouldn't hit the final bump with enough speed to go over it,
never mind having enough momentum to stop yourself from falling face-first
upon reaching the half-pipe.
You had to commit to finish from the start.

Dan mastered it in a day.
After a few failures he cracked it,
and the increase in speed it gave him literally allowed him to reach new heights.
We congratulated him;
high-fives, pats on the back, the lot—people we never talked to before came up
to congratulate him.
He winked at me and said, "you're next."
"Alright, no worries, I can do it, I'll try it next week though, no point doing it the
same day and stealing your thunder."

Yeah, right.

And over the next few weeks I sat and stared on what I feared.
Pathetic.
Imagine a now 13 year old me in a sometimes busy, sometimes quiet skate park,
sitting on a ramp, and staring at it, eyes open, nothing moving.

I never even tried.

I could just about clear the first hump,
but I always stopped myself from going down the second.
I couldn't commit to it.
This was unlike anything else in the skatepark.
I couldn't stand over it and simply let myself drop and fall to get over myself,
because there was no way you could make the second hump without some proper
speed and commitment.
I couldn't do it.

I once spent the entire time we were there,
probably a good hour and a half,

sitting and staring on my fear.
My friends took turns sitting with me for a spell,
and I would joke and make merry and promise that I was just building myself up to it,
lying to them,
lying to myself.
Trying to conjure up courage from a spell of empty words,
But I was never equal to that ramp.

Meanwhile Dan was going from strength to strength,
and I couldn't follow him anymore.
After another few months he amazed us all by doing a backflip,
it was incredible.
We got a photo of him upside down in the air and a video followed,
It circulated in our school and made him a living legend.
'Good-man-Dan.' 'Dan the backflip man.' 'Daaaaa(m)n!'
Absolute legend.
Inspiring us all round as all my skating friends were progressing,
and I wasn't.
All I could do was sit on my fear and stare at it.

Sometimes I wouldn't even look at the ramp,
I tried to forget it was there
And without it I became more imaginative and daring,
I even learnt a trick before Dan,
but within the hour of seeing me doing it he could do it too.
He could do it better.
No amount of imagination could bring me back to his level,
I knew exactly what I needed to do,

And I couldn't do it.

After spending years skating and loving it, falling and getting back up,
I found my wall,
the one ramp where I never fell because I never tried.
Dan was showing me what lied ahead,

I knew exactly what I had to do to progress and follow my friend,

But I couldn't do it,
I just couldn't bring myself to do it.

No matter how hard I tried.

I physically brought myself to where I needed to be,
I sat there and said, 'I won't skate another goddamn ramp until I've attempted this one.'
But I couldn't bring myself to do it,
Mentally, I wasn't able.
Pathetic
Dan was my hero,
And I became my own villain.
And like all villains; I saw myself as hateful, pitiful, unnecessary.
Life is hard enough as it is.

I haven't skated now in over 10 years,
and I see Dan once in a blue moon.
He still skates occasionally,
and tells me he still loves the thrill of doing a backflip.
He has a couple of kids now and a good job,
and he'll continue to be a trailblazer for those brave enough to follow.
Dublin has sprouted a number of outdoor skateparks which weren't there when we started,
and Dan even got to open one of them and get his face in the local paper,
I smiled bitterly when I saw that newspaper photograph.
I should have been there

(In the background of course)
Near my friend.

For the longest time I continued to feel like my 13 year old self –
self-hating, cowardly, and wishing to god for someone to pull a gun on me and say, 'now you try this ramp right now son, or I'll blast your fucking head off.'

But I remained paralysed with fear.
When I heard Johnny Cash singing *The Wall* for the first time I cried,
I couldn't even attempt something that, at worst, would have given me a bloody nose or broken arm.
To this day I've never broken a bone in my body. A coward's boast.

There's no positive spin I can put on my 13-year-old self,
when I didn't even try enough to fail.
There's nothing funny or noble in someone who sits and stares on what they fear.
Do it or don't do it,
surpass or move on,
anything but sit on it.
Perhaps I could lie to myself and say –
'well, I'm sure I could do it now,'
but I know it's a lie.
I once spent a month preparing to do a skate-free backflip to redeem myself.
I watched hours and hours of good technique on YouTube,
but when I went to the backgarden to make the attempt,
I became 13 again,
I couldn't commit,
from the start,
on what I needed to do.
For a long time it seems I stayed 13.
For a pathetically long time.

I went through a crisis,
I became so down about it that I started staring at myself in the mirror and forcing myself to cry, because I felt that someone who feels so low should cry,
Should look as bad as they feel.

I slapped myself and hit myself and argued with myself for days,
But eventually I gave it up and moved on, or time moved me on at least.

Life continued, and new walls presented themselves.
I started debating, and found a new environment in which to grow.
Debating led to stand-up comedy

And to this day I'm baffled by the amount of people who tell me how brave I am
How they could never do what I do.
Sure, my first few times doing stand-up were scary,
but it was nothing like that ramp.

In a way, I'm just continuing my trajectory of being the fall-guy who tries to put a positive spin on it.
'Falling with style' as Buzz Lightyear once said.
But it's true,
What is good stand-up comedy but 'falling with style?'
Well, apparently, some people can't bring themselves to do stand-up,
Others, like my mam, can't bring themselves to swim,
And I can't bring myself to skate that ramp
Or do a backflip.

So what's the morale?
Are we all cowards?
Or am I just trying to make myself feel better?
The thing is—skating gave me an environment to grow and develop,
and it was wonderful until I hit that limit.
And when I didn't have skating anymore
I became depressed, I withered.
I knew something was missing.
I needed some new space to develop without supervision.
I tried basketball because my family weren't into it,
I tried music,
I tried martial arts,
but it wasn't until I started debating that I found that space again.
That space where we get to create who we want to be,
That room to grow.
Now in stand-up comedy I am constantly blocking myself,
Getting in my own way,
But it never feels insurmountable, in fact, I love it.

Now, my 13-year-old self, sitting alone and pathetic, is left there to rot in Ramp City.

Sometimes I want to pick him up, give him a hug, tell him it's okay and bring him home
by finally doing a backflip,
but I don't.
I've left him in that skatepark, a lost child,
mine but not me,
A scared ghost of myself,
A pathetic reminder that, physically, *I am a coward.*
A reminder that I have to find other ways to put myself out there and to grow.
I had to learn new ways to be brave
But it's not heroic,
It's survival.
I'm no longer as pathetic
Just more practical.

There must be a version of me that's tried it
Another me who's in that way brave
But now I feel myself somebody different
And I'm no longer ashamed.

Oh Leap of Faith! Take the plunge or walk away
But do not stay, do not stay,
I've learnt it's better by far to be a coward
Than one who cannot walk away.

Blessington Basin

Blessington Basin
Blessed Basin
What characters you hold!
Sitting, reading, smoking, writing
Running, laughing, meditating
Setting of unending stories rarely told
Home of bards and birds
Of rats and rogues
Coming to cleanse sober our spirits and our souls
Staring down into the murky waters that you hold

A place of barking humans
and honest dogs
Historic Basin
Awash with sun and inspiration
As adults push enfants round
As they stare up at the flawless clouds
Nodding approvingly at every sound

Now two old women pass hand in hand
As joggers keep time by their rounds
And my mind, within you, soars unbound
In this place where I'm always lost
And never wanting to be found

It's hard to write bad poetry in such a basin,
Sitting among blue sculptures hugging their stony walls
In the centre lies a giant turtle that's always sleeping

And in the shrubbery are fairy-homes, discrete and small
Come and sit my friends, press pause
Close your eyes, let go, let everything fall
And trust our little stolid soldier to guard it all

For "you'll never know how sweet it seems
Or just how much it really means…"

I would only add two things to you, oh basin:
First, a monster of a blackboard,
lovingly maintained (by your lovely 'good morning' caretakers) with a good selection of coloured chalks
So that I may read the thoughts of the happy and the lost
Second, Dublin's first (and Ireland's second) statue of one of our best *female* writers—Iris Murdoch.
As colourful as Oscar Wilde's but not so frivolous,
I imagine her statue with its back to us, leaning over those black rails,
Staring out into the waters, swans and ducks
Contemplating a home that for so long has turned its back on her,
(We can do better than that little mangy plaque telling us where she was born!
Make amends here and now—and bring knowledge of her home).

I throw my lucky old Irish penny to your human-made waters,
Blessington Basin,
And wish my will be done.

Scrubbing Rocks

Brush your teeth! Scrub your rocks!
Before removing jocks and socks
Scrub, scrub, scrub away

To your station
Every race and every nation
Scrub, scrub, scrub away

Clean, Clean, Clean!
Before the pillows, before the dreams
Scrub, scrub, scrub away

Remove the sand, remove the grease
Lay out 2 clean sheets
Scrub, scrub, scrub away

Brush it out and brush it in
Like sunburn peeling off the skin
Scrub, scrub, scrub away

The metallic taste of blood still warm
Clean the rocks and clean the gums
Scrub, scrub, scrub away

All that remains of your day
Gargle, spit, rinse, relay
To scrub, scrub, scrub away

Prologue to Jamie's Lucid Dream Diary

I woke up from a dream last night which didn't want to let me go, so I hit the snooze button and lingered in its afterlife for another 10 minutes before getting up for work, but my mind is still floating around that dream, and I'm distracted, so that it feels like I'm still dreaming. Bits of my dream float in and out of my headspace, like the wreckage of a ship that had once carried me.

The dream was in some ways sensual and seductive, it was in other parts a sort of conveyer belt of happy memories. I was standing at the bottom of Grafton Street, where Molly Malone used to be, and a mix of family and friends came and went, some I talked to and some I didn't, while waiting for a bus which I suppose was never to come, just talking and letting my mind wander. But what I can't shake from my dream is that in it I felt like a better 'me,' like I was my best self. Not that I looked any different, or had acquired any special skills or knowledge, but it felt something like I was handling myself expertly, as if I was beyond second-guessing, doubts and self-criticism. Since waking up I feel more strongly than ever that I don't normally handle myself so well, either I am too self-conscious, too self-critical, or just too aware of myself. In so many day-to-day interactions I am so painfully aware of myself. But in that dream I was as I want to be. And so I'm picking up and examining the now useless pieces of driftwood to see if I can find what it was that made me feel as though my dream counterpart was a more complete me than the me that woke up, than the me that writes in this diary. It's as if I went to sleep as a shadow and awoke a shadow, knowing full well that my true substance was left behind in that dream.

To make it all the worse I didn't wake up alone, but he was there, my other half. Only so lost in my wrecked dream was I that his very presence—any presence—was irritating. It didn't take much to hide my irritation though, as he had been caught in the grip of a death-dream. His had been some nightmare involving swarms of attacking insects, and he spent a fair amount of time unburdening his troubles on me, or the space between us at least. Distracted as

I was in my own dream-wreck I was able to give enough easy responses to help him forget his. I only wish I knew what was better about my wonderland self. What could she do that I can't? What does she know that I don't? And will I ever feel so perfectly complete and solid again, or am I to come to terms with the idea that I may always feel myself as just a shadow of what I could be?

Jamie, checking the time, put her diary away with a sigh and got back to work, as distracted and air-headed as ever, the dream lingering in her mind like a persistent and vindictive fly. When she got home she determined to try to talk it out with her partner, Alan, feeling that by now her dream might take centre stage, as fragmentary as it now was. But it wasn't until they were through with their routine evening banalities that she could find the space to bring it up, after their dinner, after their barely changing afterwork conversations, after Netflix and a bit of reading, it was while they were in bed, just as Alan began feeling safe for a good night's sleep, that Jamie threw out her line.

"You know, my mind's still caught in the dream I had last night, I mean, it wasn't such a nightmare as yours, but… it felt like I was a better 'me' in my dream than I really am, I mean, when I'm awake. Does that make sense?"

"Better how?" asked Alan, hiding his trepidation, for he was over-aware that Jamie's timing in opening up these novel and unexpected conversations usually robbed him of much sleep.

"I don't know. That's the problem. I felt …," she sighed, feeling already that words were to fail her, "I felt self-assured, or, like, I wasn't judging myself, I had this sense that everything I was doing was as I wanted to do it, and everyone was perceiving me as I would want to be perceived," she shook her head, "it's hard to explain."

"Who's everyone" asked Alan, "who was in your dream?"

"Oh, loads of people. I can't remember all of them. I remember flirting with some of them, which was weird, you know I'm terrible at flirting. There were some old college lecturers, old friends, family, workmates, Patti Smith made an appearance, and all the time I felt… free of myself, as if everyone I talked to understood me perfectly, and I could understand them too, like, not just what they were saying, but I could feel how they felt about me, and it all felt so… positive."

"*Free of myself*" Alan repeated.

"Yeah. Like, there was no need to judge myself, because I knew that I was handling myself so well. I can't explain it better than that," she sighed. After a long pause, in which Jamie began to give up hope of further conversation, Alan came in.

"I wonder," he said, "you know, I often wonder how the company of others affects us, like, how I talk differently to my friends than to my family, how I can be less self-conscious around you compared to my colleagues. Did you notice that in your dream? Like, were you acting differently with different people, or were you just... you?" Jamie thought about this for a while, it seemed plausible.

"Maybe," she said at last, "I mean, yeah, I don't think I was concerned about how I was perceived, or it wasn't something I had to worry about, and I could enjoy all the random interactions all the more for it. I don't know," at this stage it was almost impossible for Jamie to remember specific details from the dream, she shook her head and asked, "have you had anything like that, a dream where you felt like a better you?" After another long pause Alan answered.

"No, not quite like that. But I do sometimes, rarely, but enough to look out for them, have a sort of recurring dream that leaves me feeling free. ... sometimes in a dream I find myself with an ability to walk on air, where I can walk vertically up towards the sky. But sometimes it's scary, because I have this sense that if I lose focus I could fall out of the air and hit the ground. But usually, if I have a target to aim for, or if I concentrate on watching my feet, I can walk to the top of a building as the crow flies, I like those dreams, I don't feel like it's a better 'me' in them, but it's exhilarating to walk on air" Alan laughed, "I'm sure most people dream they can fly, but I guess walking on air is enough for me."

As he finished he looked over at Jamie, and was shocked to hear a small gasp, never in his life did he perceive such a thing from her before. Jamie's mind, it turned out, had been triggered, as a memory, long forgotten, began to resurface. This was not just a piece of very ancient driftwood, but whole bodies representing a long lost memory, intact, fascinating, and so strange to her now. It was as if a pod of blue whales, in all their immensity, and singing a long forgotten melody, had just resurfaced after many years from an infinitely larger and more mysterious ocean. If we could only have had a brain-scan of Jamie at this moment! How interesting it would be to see her mind aflame as synapsis long out of touch fired to life these memories once more.

"You've just reminded me," said Jamie excitedly "of a recurring dream I used to have, years ago, a nightmare. I remember it now, I used to dream that I would be walking and I would turn right, and all of a sudden I'd become stuck turning right, I mean, it was as if I were caught inside an invisible revolving door, and I would make myself dizzy and crazy and claustrophobic in my turnings. I would feel a horrible knot growing in my stomach from the effort to stop turning, so I would stop moving altogether and try to calm myself down, then, I would look down and stare at my feet, desperately begging them to behave and stop turning right, when suddenly I would move again only to find I was now stuck turning left, and that's how my dream was, spending a torturously long time stuck turning left or right, spinning and stopping, crying and changing direction, completely unable to walk straight. I even remember, in some of those dreams where I was able to walk straight again, that I refused to turn either left or right… I was so terrified of becoming stuck again… It's amazing. It's so clear now, and I forgot all about it until you mentioned staring at your feet within a dream." Jamie stopped talking but her mind was still racing, memories were now flooding back. She remembered in quick succession waking up disturbed from these dreams, fretting during the day in case they would reoccur again, being awake and panicking herself about what she would do if she found herself locked into perpetual turning as it so often happened at night, fearing as it happened each time that this was the one that wouldn't end with 'it was only a dream….' "Why," she said aloud, "I think that must have been when my mother bought me a dreamcatcher for my room I was so freaked out."

"I guess the dreamcatcher worked" Alan said.

"I guess so … it's just so crazy, I can't believe I forgot all that."

"It sounds like a bad nightmare alright."

"It was, but, it's easy to talk about it, I mean, I'm so removed from it now, it's so strange."

"It sounds almost psychological" Alan offered, "like, I know you hate making decisions, do you think it could have been tied to something like that?"

"I don't know" Jamie smiled, feeling that Alan was working his way to a joke, and said in a humorous tone "why, do you think the dreams stopped when I met you?" Alan cracked up laughing and turned over. "Well," he said, "you do tend to leave it to me to make all the decisions."

"*Most* of the decisions, not *all*. I don't know," she sighed, "maybe it was tied to me being indecisive, I do think I was worse when I was younger, but I definitely stopped having those dreams before meeting you."

"Fair enough" was all Alan could think to say.

"I don't know when I stopped having them" Jamie said.

"You'll probably never remember," said Alan, "after a while I think it's impossible to remember when we had a dream, sure it's difficult enough to remember them, never mind when we had a specific one, and unlike a normal memory, it's not like anyone can help you to date it."

"Yeah," said Jamie, "I normally don't remember mine past breakfast, but the one I had last night, and these ones you've reminded me of, it's so strange, I feel like I'll never forget them, but, I *did* forget, until now. How can we forget dreams so easily, even when we feel them so strongly."

"I have a theory on that one," said Alan, "although I might have told you before," he yawned.

"Go on," she said, "you probably have and I've probably forgotten, I'm sorry you're tired, but you can't bring something up like that and drop it." Alan laughed softly and obliged with a sigh.

"Well, I guess I have two theories, the first is that dreams lack a logical narrative, and so you can't rely on the normal things you do when you want to remember something. Like, if someone asks you in the evening what you had for breakfast, for me, I can only remember what I had for breakfast if I start by remembering how I got up in the morning, like, I have to play it all out. What clothes did I wear, did I have a shower, did I put on the radio, what channel, and then I get to breakfast and I remember, or I usually remember. But you can't do that in a dream. Logical order of events like that no longer exist, the 2nd theory, although I guess they're complimentary, is that there's a kind of sensory overload in dreams, we simply experience too much to remember it all, especially if you believe that time is sort of condensed within a dream, so that time in a dream lasts longer than it does while we're awake."

"Interesting," said Jamie, "and what about in college, did you discuss much about dreams there?"

"Well ... no, I did psychology in Maynooth, and the psychologists in Maynooth hate Freud with a passion, and they're afraid to mention Carl Jung, so no, dream interpretation was linked to Freud, and anything linked to Freud was used either to make a bad joke or to show how far psychology has come, although," he sighed "I know most of that now was a load of shit. You should see how much Trinity students love Freud, it's madness ... It's probably all switched around now after the last exodus... Actually, the only other theory I heard about remembering dreams is that, supposedly, on some level, our brain realises a dream for a dream, and since dreams aren't real, there's no incentive to remember them, since they can hardly be useful to us when we're awake, but I don't know… I could never wrap my head around that one," he yawned again, exaggerating it, ever so slightly, "my friends in anthropology came across scores of different peoples who take dreams extremely seriously, and practise some form of lucid dreaming."

"Lucid dreaming" Jamie repeated. "You know, I think I'm going to give it a go. I'm sorry dear, but you know you love me…" Jamie said in her cutest tone.

"What?" said Alan, faking an irritated tone, or rather, faking that his real irritation was only a let-on one. But Jamie's mind was still too fired-up to notice or care.

"Well, I need to write some of this into my diary, it's just, those recurring dreams, as horrible as they were when I had them, they're fascinating now, and I don't want to forget them again."

"Ok, write in your diary, but can we kiss first and that, I'm going to try to sleep."

"Sure, I'm sorry hun, I know my mind's fired-up, but I won't be able to relax if I'm worried about forgetting all this."

"Sure, no problem." They kissed each other and recited their usual final spell for a good night's sleep, and only when they finished did Jamie switch on her lamp and take out her diary as Alan buried his face into the silent sheets. She wrote a brief account of her long-forgotten dreams, followed by a command to herself to begin researching into and practising lucid dreaming. She then closed her eyes and slipped off again into waters unknown, but with a feeling that one day she would master even these waters, and, perhaps, chase what it was that her dream-self had that her waking-self didn't. 'Yes' she thought, 'I'll track my dream-shadow, and mark my progress, tomorrow I'm starting a dream-diary.'

What's That?

I was walking along the canal one day,
Absentmindedly scanning along the water for joyful signs of life;
Looking for ducklings, fish, dragon-flies, butterflies, when…
– what was that?!
It was a little flying gift of a frog,
Attached to a line by a fatal catch,
And it went around my wandering head with a twist
Circling twice past my bulging question-mark eyes
Landing with a little splash in the water, like this – ?!

What in frog's name just happened? I thought.
And then I saw the fisherwoman with her rod,
Throwing a grin at me as big as a net,
As her little flying frog caught my full attention
And I stood, stopped dead, my mouth as open as the fish I hoped she'd catch.

I closed my mouth, smiled 'good luck' and continued my walk,
… But reflecting along with the water I wondered,
Surely the frog wasn't smiling when it was murdered,
And the fish?
No, … certainly not for much longer.

And I felt empty then, to be innocently looking for signs of joyous life,
As they come under such attacks from my brothers and sisters.
Using Kermit-corpses
As Trojan Horses

Flies and Windows

Charlie walks up to his bedroom
he's followed by a pest
Ignoring a fly he opens up his laptop
and sits down to work at his desk

Clicking away the usual demands
his waking computer always makes
He swipes at the fly with his hands
And playfully slaps his own thick face

'I've a power of work to do' he thinks
rousing himself to the task
'But first I must set the mood'
and so he opens up his first tab –

To YouTube, where he's greeted like a wealthy alcoholic in his local bar
As the website beams
an endless stream
of videos, just for him and free of charge

He puts on his headphones
thinking—'now I can ignore that distracting shit'
As the algorithms direct him without sense
to a personalised bottomless pit

And for each new video that he opens
He makes sure that the most popular comments are well read

as they come together to form the opinions
He comes to feel are in his head

Finally, he manages to open up a new tab
Where he's greeted by Internet Explorer's 'My Feed'
He doesn't recognise the Venus fly-trap
of 36 shallow articles, click-bait and funny memes to see

As 'His Feed' eats up more of his time
The fly continues its hopeless flight
Of its buzzing and pleading rhyme
Feeling the shortness of its life

And nearly 2 hours of mindless buzzing later
Attempts of freedom that always fail
Charlie slaps his face in anger
Only to open up Gmail

Seeing nothing in his main inbox
he quickly checks his social
Where he's directed straight to Facebook
And starts another drawn-out cycle

There he's met by a web of messages,
Notifications and friend requests
Put together by more algorithms
And people that he's never met

And so it's rare for the fly to see
the spider whose trap he's in
Zuckerberg likewise has no sympathy
For those of us trapped within

And with only a day in which to live
The fly's trapped by an invisible wall

Where it's doomed and doomed and doomed to hit
As Charlie hears his mother's call

He puts his headphones away
And closes his laptop reluctantly
Promising he will do his work another day
As he heads down for his food and tea

And so digital spiders have swarmed the web
And perhaps if we too had but a day to live
We would struggle against those which mean to stop us dead
And no more of our time we'd give

Instead we make our beds
And lie until the day is dead
And with polluting pollen fill our heads
And leave no space for regrets

And so we buzz from tabs to windows
Until our days are gone and done
Until our own time reaches zero
And those pesky flies return

Tommy's Rambles

Part 1: Random Rambles from Tommy's Diary, Dates Unknown

The better at listening I get, the more she talks! Maybe I should give up listening...

Friday night, during my break at work I headed down to the Liffey boardwalk to enjoy the sun, escape the job and have a read. A part of me was also hoping to overhear more boardwalk-madness for the poem I started, but no matter. The only madness today was a scruffy looking character throwing bits of his lunch to a mob of squalling seagulls. But as I was reading, the sun was so powerful and lovely for the time of year that I completely unbuttoned my floral shirt and allowed my milk-white belly to get some sun. And of course I felt like a bit of a knacker sitting there with my shirt unbuttoned and my belly sticking out for the world to see. It felt strange, but actually, if I had it all my own way, I would have taken off my shirt altogether. Why are we so afraid, so imprisoned, by the indifferent and fleeting opinions of others—and what even is 'the opinion of others?' for surely 'the opinion of others' can only really affect me by in some way altering the opinion I have of myself. So I am scared of my own opinion of myself? (as it is made up and directed by what I consciously feel to be the opinions of others?). Am I afraid of myself! How odd.

I can sit down now, hours later, shirt on as normal and in my own company, and write—'I will soon be dead, you and everyone else will soon be dead, and all our opinions, which are meaningless to begin with, will soon leak out of our to-be-forgotten heads'—but, in that moment, sitting on a public bench, it's difficult, and shameful to me how much someone's opinion affects my opinion of myself. And so I allow the strange opinions of stranger strangers to stifle me and make me feel a little awkward for unbuttoning my own shirt, and so, unbuttoning my own shirt became more than just a practical way for me to maximise my absorption of vitamin D (important this time of year!) and enjoy the life-affirming heat of the sun, but it also became a liberating exercise, it loosened me up, or rather, loosened me out of ... of what? Social constraints, social pressure, your effect on me? And yes, it did help me to feel more free. Free from you; free from me. How mad.

Anyway—when I tried to relate the thing to Sarah she had a knee-jerk reaction. Now, I was expecting an initial negative reaction anyway because, even despite myself, I also feel that people who hang out in public without shirts or bare-chested are to be thought of as knackers (oh how we're raised!), but what threw me about Sarah's response is that she said she hates it that men can get away with showing their skin and women can't, and she said she'll forever be against the idea as long as there's this inequality. I was left baffled as if she had pulled the rug out from under me, I argued that I've seen women walking or jogging while showing their bellies via sportswear, which I thought meant that women are better capable of showing more skin than men, but even if she's right, and she stuck to her guns (arguing that in school and work women are much more pushed to cover-up which, thinking calmly about it now, is certainly true globally—absolutely when one takes hijabs and Christian 'modesty' into account), but I'm *not stopping anyone from taking off their clothes!* If I had my way, I would make an annual nudist day to be celebrated on the hottest day of the year or some comfortable day of Summer, because, while we go on and on about this idea of people undressing each other with our eyes, what we don't understand is that we're actually doing the opposite. Yes, we dress people with our eyes, not undress them.

Not only that, but thinking about it now, the only naked or half-naked bodies I've ever seen much of have been from films, TV shows (and series), advertising and porn, so no bloody wonder we all have body-image issues! We need a national nudist day, or at the very least nudists should be studied to see how much of a problem they have with their body image. And how much easier would it have been to take off my shirt in public if I didn't have this fixed idea in my head that only knackers take their shirts off in public? And now I must take my hat off to the so-called knackers because clearly they, as a group, care far less for what others think of them than what I care (on reflection, they've probably developed a stronger callus against the opinions of others)!

We silently insist on dressing people, and it's a madness. The only cure for it seems to be to take my shirt off more often, follow my dad's wonderful *example—a man ahead of his time, or rather, not so constrained by his time as I feel myself to be. We should have a national nudist day—the crazier an idea sounds, the more shocking, the more necessary it is to wake us up from our socially induced comas. I need to tease this idea out, maybe add it to the poem I was trying to write earlier about the boardwalk. It could be a 'lesson' given to me by the junkies for which I want to repay them some service or lesson in kind.*

Also, it seems to me an impossible task to count my teeth with my tongue, you would imagine the tongue to be the perfect tool for the job, but alas, I try and feel something like 31 teeth. So if I cannot count my teeth accurately with my tongue how do I expect to know myself with my own brain? How strange.

I sat on my arse drinking and masturbating, thinking about writing but rightly deciding that I wouldn't have written anything good, when my muse comes in saying that I have snake-skin hands and that our bedroom reading lamp looks like an interrogation light. She was slagging me for eating what were apparently her bag of Doritos. As far as she was concerned she bought them and they were hers, I think it's because she's an only child. I weathered the slagging better than usual, in other words, I didn't get upset but propped myself like one of those clowns that keeps taking the hits but keeps getting back up, it seems to be the way to go, I've got a sarcastic partner and a sensitive soul. Still, 'snake-skin hands' and 'a reading lamp like an interrogation light'—amazing!

'Can you zip me up' is one of the most dreaded questions a woman can ask me. 30 minutes ago I was standing behind Sarah, eyeing up the flimsy little zipper and the long Grand Canyon I have to bridge. With one hand I hold the Christmas-cracker zipper, and with my other hand I try to negotiate a truce between the two sides of her dress; pulling, pinching, squeezing and pleading as my other hand tries and tries to tug the flimsy little zipper up and up, but the zipper refuses to budge. A dull panic sets in, I've been here many times before, tugging hopelessly as she makes such comments as 'great, I've gotten fatter,' 'great, another dress that doesn't fit me anymore,' 'great, I'm turning into my mother etc...' Out of all the little jobs women have me do this is by far the worst, the one with the lowest success rate. I'd rather untangle a hundred necklaces or fish out a dozen missing contact lenses from my mother's poor watery eyes than try to zip up another one of their dresses.

I watched Sarah eating this morning with her mouth flapping open. Now, I grew up with people who eat with their mouths open, I'm part of a proud family of mouth flappers, but since Sarah has called me out for eating with my mouth open I'm now in a bind. It takes a great deal of effort not to throw it back in her flapping face if just to show her that we're all fallibly flapping from time to time, or meal to meal. I wanted to say something badly, but I refrained, for what would I have gained? It would only serve to make her more vigilant to catch me out in turn, and turn me into a hypocrite, so I watch her and keep my silence as she makes an orchestra out of a packet of Doritos. Why do we have such self-destructive urges? I suppose our brains are programmed to respond to instances of unfair play, we're ridiculous—our good is the common good, but we're only built to serve ourselves as individuals. I need a drink.

Living in Dublin we learn to walk,
Past homelessness without a second thought.

Part 2: Tommy on the bus

Tommy cut an unremarkable figure at the early afternoon bus stop. He was a young man, of average height and build, clean-shaven, and with clear blue eyes which were shining magnified-blue behind a smart new pair of glasses. His clothes, dull and unassuming, were at least clean and unoffensive. There he stood, like a silent background character even within his own story.

When the bus came he pressed his leapcard politely for his fare and headed instinctively for the top deck. Finding an empty seat for himself he sat down and took out his book and began to read. Comfortable and occupied, his surroundings faded away as his attention became absorbed in his book, and a happy tranquillity took over—the only thing Tommy noticed was the quietness on the upper deck. 'Perfect reading conditions' he thought with a smile. But Tommy made a rare mistake that day; finding that the last 20 pages of his book contained nothing but an index and footnotes he had no interest in. He affectively finished his book, and only 4 minutes into his journey. He felt cheated and stupid for having no other book on standby, and for the first time in a long time, Tommy was bookless on the bus—'fuck' he thought. What was worse, he had left his diary at home, 'probably beside the toilet again.' 'Fuck Fuck Fuck!' he shook.

Closing his book with a rueful sigh he put it back in his bag and started to take in his surroundings. The top deck held about 15 people spread thin throughout, but it slowly filled as it made its way into town. Tommy started looking out the window, down at the people on the street, and saw many wandering around silently behind the glass. He imagined that they were people like himself, travelling from A to B to meet with somebody else. He felt a little thrill gazing down at them all, feeling confident that even if he were to be caught staring, that the metal, plastic and glass separated them more or less completely. He began to feel like he was at the zoo, despite the fact that he was the one boxed in, and he imagined those below to be of the lower primates, making simple journeys for simple motives. He tried to guess the ones who were walking to eat, who were walking for lust, who were walking to quench their thirst, 'monkeys all' Tommy mused.

Suddenly a ping from a phone woke him up once more to the fact that he was on a bus with other people. 'Yes' he thought, 'there are others here,' and a second ping from a phone reminded him of his own phone resting in his pocket. He took it out and stared at the front screen for a while. 'Now why did I take out my phone' he thought to himself. For there was no one that he wished to contact. He opened up Wikipedia and saw that their front page remained the same from the last time he checked it, and so he sat with his mind hovering over the search bar, spending over a minute wishing his brain to come up with something interesting to look up. 'Hmm' he thought, he had already Wikied all the fruits and vegetables that he could think of, every film that he had seen recently, every book—'wait, that's it,' he entered the title of the book he had just finished and spent a few minutes devouring the scanty page written about it. 'Too short' he thought disdainfully, putting his phone back in his pocket.

He looked around again, this time fishing with his eyes to see what his fellow commuters were doing to occupy themselves, and, he thought, 'everyone else is on their phones. Texting, reading, scrolling, listening, liking, commenting, playing... but nobody's making a sound.' As much as he could he tried to see what it was that people were looking at, and found that the majority seemed to be watching something, perhaps on Netflix or YouTube. It struck him that these people might as well be in their own living rooms, and he thought how much he would like to strike up a conversation with someone, but he felt that everyone else already had their excuses lined up. 'People no longer share the experience of a bus ride' he thought, 'but everyone carries with them a technological bubble of contacts, videos, music and photos. It's as if they were all astronauts, carrying with them their own personal supply of oxygen.' He sighed and said to himself:

'I have no one to talk to,
but no one to blame,
for just a few minutes earlier I was exactly the same.'

Looking bitterly down at his bag he again thought of the book he had brought with him and the mistake he had made. 'Well, if other people are absorbed, I better leave them to it' he thought, and he resigned himself to once again looking out the window, thinking that if one of his fellow commuters could only turn away from their phone then he would strike up a friendly and interesting conversation with them, 'for you only live once', and this silence in a crowd started to weigh heavily on him. 'Yes, monkeys outside with their ears covered,' deaf to Tommy on his top-deck pedestal, 'and monkeys inside, with their eyes covered, both by their phones,' and Tommy felt isolated and alone.

But now the bus driver, as if following Tommy's thoughts, stopped to pick up a new passenger, a woman his age, who walked to the top deck and sat down right beside him. Tommy became dumbstruck to observe her sitting down and, 'and, that's it!' No book, no phone, no earphones. He felt his heart start to beat and his ears flush with heat, not at any thoughts of lust, mind you, for Tommy has his Sarah and considers her more than enough trouble. 'But,' he thought, 'here's a person I can actually talk to.' –

"Excuse me," said Tommy, followed by –

"thanks," as he shuffled awkwardly past the woman and made his way off the bus, a good 20 minutes after she had sat next to him, and feeling like the worst monkey of them all, the one who had kept his mouth shut.

Even though he was now physically off the bus, Tommy's mind was very much still on it. 'Why couldn't I have talked to her' he was wondering. At first, the thought that she was just sitting there with nothing to occupy her was just too amazing to believe, and he felt sure that at any minute she would take out her phone, stick in some earphones and immerse herself in a world of her own, but she didn't. Then he became conscious of the amount of time he had let pass, thinking at what point would starting a conversation seem natural and at what point would it seem weird? But he had to admit that his greatest difficulty was the idea of striking up a conversation—it terrified him. How easy it was to assume that he could do it when everyone around him looked for all the world like a phombie. And how impotent he felt when she sat down and he found he could say nothing. The silence which had earlier made him feel sadly amused suffocated him with her sitting there. How unnecessary that silence became, how stupid he felt that he couldn't break the spell of it. Tommy couldn't understand, he believed that he had discarded God, reincarnation, heaven and hell, he believed that he had embraced the meaningless of life, the idea that nothing really matters and so it's best to at least enjoy ourselves and live in the moment and without fear, and yet, even armed with these ideas, he time and time again found himself as mute and scared as a lost child in the dark, only worse, for a scared child isn't half as afraid to ask for help as adults are. 'Well, there's always next time' he sighed as he made his way to the pub where he was to meet his friends, and as he walked closer to them he was able to walk out of the oppressive funk he had found himself in. 'But,' he said to himself, 'next time I will try and have a chat, otherwise I might as well be dead.'

Tommy was the last to arrive at *Whelans*, and he had a bit of catching up to do before he felt lubricated enough to start squeezing in his own jokes and stories to the mix. When the rest of the table finally warmed up to his presence one of them demanded to hear about the now famous story of Tommy's efforts to talk to the so-called *lovely driver*. 2 of the table had heard the story and 2 hadn't, and, despite Tommy's protests, it was declared that either he would have to tell it or one of the other 2 would, so, despite the embarrassment it caused him, a version of the following story was told:

Part 3: Tommy's story

Well, as I'm sure you're all aware, there's a cute pink car that glides around my spot of Dublin, and, amazingly, the car and driver have become something of a legend—the legend of the lovely driver. I remember once being stuck waiting behind two rude and ignorant people on a long flat escalator in Tesco. Despite saying "excuse me" and have them ignore me, fuming away that I couldn't get past them, I overheard the following from another couple being descended towards me: "... she was driving down the Navan Road, windows rolled, and the sweetest trance music was coming from her car."

"Was it a pink Beetle?"

"Yeah, with flowers on it, it must have been her, I nodded as she drove past me and she gave me such a big smile and a wave ...."

Yes, it could only have been her. Even just hearing her being talked about was enough to calm me down and allow me to reach the top of the escalator without wishing unmerciful torture on those standing in front of me as they waved their hands madly about.

I completed my shop in my own headphone haze as I reflected on the lovely driver. For whether you happen to be a cyclist, pedestrian, driver or horse-rider for the day the lovely driver has your back, that's for sure. She'll let you cross the road, she'll give you a wide berth, and she signals her intentions to you perfectly, every time. She has a horn which she only beeps to spread pleasure and delight, for the horn of her vintage Beetle gives of a thrilling old honk which always finds a chorus in the girls and boys she's passing. Not only does she have her whimsical horn, but she also plays the sweetest music from her cheery car. I've heard what I imagine to be wonderful Indian music and the loveliest jazz as she's driven past. Chet Baker seems to be a favourite of hers, or at least it's the only music that I've been able to recognise. You won't believe this, but from her car a beautiful fragrance follows, as if it runs on perfume instead of petrol. Why, she could put the 'car' into any postcard, for her bright old pink Beetle has lovingly painted flowers adorning it, and with her beautiful warm face behind the wheel she would make a wonderful addition to any photo.

There's a rumour that she once stopped to light someone's smoke without ever leaving her car, smiling happily as she did so and waving a pink lighter. Another legend has it that she once handed a bag with a brand new coat in it to a homeless man that she frequently passed, and my very own friend here swears, hand to heart, that he saw her pick up a couple of hitchhikers along the Strand leading to Howth. She seems to be a magnet for warm and light-hearted stories such as these, our very own Bill Murray or Keanu Reeves, and if even half are true that was good enough for me. Why, she's become a character in these parts as good as any Bang Bang, Mad Varnish, Elvis or poor old Chemical Legs. A legend in our own time, and I was determined to talk to her. It wasn't enough that she had driven her car and parked it right in my mind, and I didn't just want to have my own story to tell of her. No, it's just... of all the imprints and marks we leave on each other, the imprint of the lovely driver is always expressed as one of joy and sweetness. She impressed me for this, there's no ambiguity about her, in every story, in every encounter, and no matter who is telling it, she is described as lovely, and considering just how grey and subjective our minds are, I was determined to find out something of her secret—I simply *had* to talk to her.

So I was walking into town one day with my headphones on when I passed her, the lovely driver, on her feet and in the flesh. Judging from her face and her style of colourful clothes it could only have been her. When she passed me my heart raced and I took off my headphones. I stood there in a panic as I watched her slowly walk away from me and wondering how I might approach her when she stopped at a set of traffic lights to cross the road—it was now or never! I retraced my steps and stood alongside her. Afraid that the lights could change at any moment I cleared my throat and asked her—"excuse me, but do you drive the pink Volkswagen Beetle with the flowers painted on it?" She didn't answer me, but continued to stand there without a care in the world. I continued, my heart beginning to sink, "I… I just wanted to say … I love your car, if it's yours… is it yours?" The lights changed and she crossed the road with a quick glance left and right, seemingly looking right through me! How could such a lovely person ignore me like that? I stopped at the corner and put my headphones back on, putting on some *Dead Meadow* until the world was nothing but mournful music.

I continued my way into town, wishing to god that I never attempted to talk to her, and for the next few days I tried to put her out of my mind. But it was impossible. Every now and then I would see her car gliding by, and see her as happy and cheerful as ever. She continued playing lovely music, her car continued to leave a lovely smell, she continued to wave, smile and nod at everyone she passed, and she continued to honk her lovely horn. Why then was she so rude to me I wondered, and how would I ever be able to talk to her, to have my own story worth telling and to learn something of her secret.

Another week passed and my mind was as fixated on her as ever, more so even, for our brief encounter drilled an imprint that I couldn't forget. I wished that I had never tried to talk with her, that I never saw or heard of her. I started to dream about her now, I would dream that I would get into her car and be about to start a conversation when she would begin driving and her car would move off and leave me behind, as if I were a ghost and the car was passing through my phantom body. Or I would dream that I was walking and the lovely driver was everywhere, was every person that I passed, and she all continued to ignore me, and I was left surrounded by a silent and judging crowd of *her*. I was lost, could it be possible that I was the one person that she refused to be nice to? Or was it the case that she was only nice while driving? There was only one thing I could do to find out. I rang my friend here and got him to go through his story of her picking up the hitchhikers in as much detail as possible, and satisfying myself on that I determined to try and hitchhike my way into the lovely driver's car. Of course my friend tried to dissuade me, calling me mad, but I was determined. As the incident was said to have happened on a Sunday, I spent 3 Sundays walking to the road that leads to Howth and waited on her. It's a nerve-wracking thing waiting for someone who knows nothing about it, my hand was constantly twitching out a thumb every time a pink car hummed by, but it wasn't until that 3rd Sunday that I had my wish.

Part 4: The lovely driver meets Tommy

Anusha woke up to a lovely sunny Sunday. She put on some loose fitting and colourful clothes and a pair of sandals and headed downstairs. She sat down to her breakfast of black coffee and a couple of almond croissants with her book, *Conversations with Friends*. She didn't quite know what to make of it, but she felt a pang of displeasure for every fictional cigarette butt thrown willy-nilly by the book's characters, not to mention the amount of takeaway coffees they consumed without ever a mention of a bin or keep-cup. She sipped her coffee and turned the page. She was half-way through breakfast when her nephew, Ijaz, finally came down with his dreamy smile and woolly head.

"Good morning, any new music for me today?" She asked him.

"Good morning auntie, yes, I think this one will go down well, it has a real lazy Summer vibe to it. Where are you going today?"

"I was thinking of driving up to Burrow Beach for a swim and then maybe stop around Howth for a walk and to meditate, why, are you feeling brave today?" She asked with a goading smile.

"I don't know how you can swim in the Irish sea auntie, but yeah, I think I'll join you if that's ok."

"Of course," she said, "and I'll throw in a towel for you just in case," she winked. "I'm going to give the car a quick wash and have a shower after, so you have an hour or so to get ready and finish waking up," she pointed to a pot half-filled with fresh coffee and smiled.

"Thanks auntie" Ijaz yawned. Anusha finished her breakfast and her chapter as Ijaz pottered around the kitchen. Then she filled up a basin of hot soapy water and opened up their little garage to let the water drain. When she finished washing her car she gave it a little pat of satisfaction and headed up for her shower. She had dreamt of owning a little pink Volkswagen Beetle ever since she was a child and she was robbed and hospitalised. During her unpleasant stay at hospital her mother bought her a little pink model of a Volkswagen Beetle, and, sitting there in that quietly busy hospital, it made all the sense in the world that she would have to have one, a real one, and now the car meant the world to her.

An hour later and they were in the car about to start their journey. Anusha started the engine and put on the new music provided by her nephew. She held her hand up to the speaker and closed her eyes, enjoying, for a few seconds, the vibrations as they passed through her hand.

"Louis Armstrong," said her nephew, "something different, but it's nice." Anusha nodded and said "Louis Armstrong, boy, where are finding all this old music anyway?" Ijaz replied "YouTube suggestions mostly, I let YouTube autoplay while I'm working, sometimes you land on a gem." Anusha thanked her nephew for the music. She then adjusted the volume until her nephew gave her a nod and then she lowered the windows, finally, she took out a bottle of soft but persistent floral perfume and gave a few sprays about her and the car. Ijaz, meanwhile, settled into his seat and closed his eyes, he wouldn't last long before nodding off. Anusha looked at him with a shake of her head and a smile and started to drive—now she was in her element.

There are few drivers as confident and as observant as her. She never turns without checking for cyclists, never forgets to indicate, and always errs on the side of caution. Unlike most drivers, she has infinite patience behind the wheel, because it's behind the wheel, more than any destination, that she longs to be. Even when she finds herself being driven by someone else her eyes always search out those brief flashes of eye-contact with other drivers and passengers. Brief and distant. She feels there's something special about catching the eye of another while in a moving car. The eye contact between two people in two fast travelling vehicles going about their own business. It's eye contact without any self-consciousness, without any concern for how you might look, and without any follow-up. An undemanding pleasure. Brief unobtrusive glances. Like lightning, gone and forgotten, the recognition of another, another, another, and so the eyes of others come and go like glimpses of foxes in the liminal early hours. A simple, intimate and secret pleasure that always makes her smile. Even while driving she sometimes finds herself searching for those unobtrusive glances. But, since buying her own car and taking the wheel, her ability now to communicate with those around her has surpassed those passive flashes, now she can nod, she can wave, she can smile and beep, and it's only the rarest curmudgeons that don't find themselves returning her smile, for she drives without hurry, without stress, and always taking the greatest pleasure from her driving.

As they reached the Strand the traffic slowed down and a thumb came into view, attached to a feverishly shaking young man. Anusha gave Ijaz a soft elbow to wake him up and pointed out the thumbing young man. Ijaz yawned and stretched, shrugged his shoulders and smiled. Anusha checked all mirrors and indicated to stop in front of Tommy. She beamed and waved and shouted out "Howth?" Tommy nodded and got in. Ijaz turned as best he could and shook hands. "Good morning, I'm Ijaz, and this is my auntie, Anusha."

"Morning! My name's Tommy, thanks for stopping, nice to meet you both."

"So you're heading to Howth then" Ijaz asked pleasantly, he watched Tommy, who was smiling away and looked to be taking everything in. Ijaz, while maintaining a polite demeanor, thought it strange that they had picked up what sounded to be a Dubliner. They seldom ran into hitchhikers, but when they did, they were *always* foreign, or at least from outside of Dublin. 'What Dubliner hitchhikes his way to Howth' thought Ijaz as he began eyeing Tommy up more carefully.

"Yeah," said Tommy, "Howth." He looked at the side of Ijaz's face and the back of Anusha's head while the ghost of Louis Armstrong sang the *Basin Street Blues*.

"So," said Tommy, "where are you guys from?"

"Pakistan originally" Ijaz replied, "my auntie has been living here for nearly 10 years though, and I moved here about 5 years ago now... and I'm guessing you're from Dublin?"

"Yeah," said Tommy.

"If you don't mind me asking then" Ijaz started in his usual polite tone "how come you didn't take the bus to Howth?"

"Oh," said Tommy, "I ... I couldn't find my leapcard... I guess I could have bought a new one, but... I'm hoping my old one will turn up, I had quite a bit of money on it" Tommy mumbled. Ijaz nodded, it seemed like a weak excuse, but then, Tommy seemed harmless enough, even if he did look a little flushed and excited. Tommy continued:

"To be honest, I was thinking of walking my way, but I thought I recognised this car coming up behind me, I've seen it pick up hitchhikers before and thought I'd try my luck… actually, this car has quite the reputation." Ijaz laughed. "I'll be sure to tell auntie next time we're stopped," he said.

"Why," said Tommy, a little confused, "can she not speak English?" Ijaz really cracked up laughing then as Tommy's face started to go red.

"My auntie has had quite the education. She's a writer and she's been living here nearly 10 years! No, English certainly isn't a problem" Ijaz settled himself down and continued, "no no, she's deaf, that's all, and it's dangerous to lip-read or talk sign while driving."

"SHE'S DEAF?" Tommy nearly shouted, and Ijaz's face began to lose some of its humour. "I'm sorry" Tommy continued, calming himself, "it's just… I didn't know deaf people were even allowed to drive." Ijaz smirked:

"Well, I'm glad auntie didn't hear that one."

"Sorry," said Tommy, he felt he was digging himself a hole. "I… I just didn't know, I've never heard of a deaf person driving."

"I'm guessing you don't know many deaf people?" Ijaz replied.

"No, I guess I don't know any" Tommy admitted.

"Actually, not only are deaf people legally allowed to drive here and in most countries, but they generally make for far safer drivers. My auntie knows better than anyone that she has to be vigilant, that she can't take her eyes off the road, that she has to check her surroundings constantly. Actually, she has to be *more* careful than everyone else, auntie knows of 2 deaf friends who got into accidents through no fault of theirs, and in both cases the driver at fault tried to blame the whole thing on the deaf driver, they're like the elderly behind the wheel, people see them as easy scapegoats, but auntie here hasn't had a single accident in her whole life, here or anywhere."

"Yeah," said Tommy, "that makes sense." He looked at the car in a new light now, and he finally began to realise that it wasn't just a car, a means of getting from A to B, but it was a means of communicating. He looked at the radio. "The music?" He asked.

"Oh, auntie always asks me to provide her with playlists and CDs, she can feel the vibrations and they help keep her focused, and she also likes the smiles the music brings, with the vibrations too she says that sometimes her brain fills in some music for her. You should see her dance when she's given a good beat, you'd swear wasn't deaf."

"The same with the horn?"

"Yes," said Ijaz with a short laugh, his humour beginning to return, "the children love the horn... I guess auntie likes not feeling deaf while she's driving," he sighed patiently. "You'd be amazed at how ... invisible people can make you feel when you're deaf, it's something my auntie talks about quite a bit. How people who can't speak sign don't give her half a chance and get awkward around her. She wasn't born deaf either, and she's all too aware of how people can be rude to her without meaning to, but she doesn't have to worry about that in here... not normally."

"I'm sorry" Tommy said, "I didn't mean to be rude, I just... your auntie is a legend, her and her car, I just had no idea she was deaf."

"Well, maybe keep it to yourself" Ijaz shrugged, "she doesn't need to be reminded that she's deaf while she's driving, she likes the bit of attention she gets."

"Of course," said Tommy. When they got caught in some traffic Ijaz started silently talking to Anusha and the two of them started laughing, Tommy could do nothing but sit and try not to stare, he wanted more than anything to just slip out and disappear.

Part 5: Return journey

Tommy finished telling his story and the table was cracking up with laughter. The insanity of hitchhiking to talk to someone because they're a 'legend,' the idea of Tommy stuck in the backseat of a deaf woman he had longed to talk to, the mistake he had made in thinking that she was being rude to him before—it was all too much. Tears were shed and the table was slapped in abandoned laughter and poor Tommy sat through it all and chuckled reluctantly along. Then, after what felt like 20 years, our Tommy left the pub. Now his blue watery eyes behind his thick-set glasses looked as if they were two overflowing pools of water, restless and sad. His clothes had grown beer-stained and shabby. His face was now ruddy and coarse with a drunk flush and a shade of stubble, and his stomach, which was previously held flat, had now succumbed to the beer swilling inside of him. He got on to a now packed bus and managed to press his leapcard for his fare, and he found himself a spot near the bus driver, facing the rest of the passengers as they stood and sat in front of him. 'A captive audience' he thought, as he held himself steady against the rail. His mind, mummified in alcohol, started a rambling drunken train of thought:

'It's night and I'm on a bus, I'm drunk as a fool, fuck
Green cross at the bus stop, Moowing café and breaking the lights.
Eyes are pox. Shouldn't have taken those last few shots.
Head's in a bliss, a drunken maze, dead-ends and twists,
but at least the bus goes straight, even if it doesn't feel like it.

Liquid lunch and dinner—pissed
had a hunch I'd get to this,
Old Cabra Road, Merry Christmas from Guinness,
Guinness is in my stomach,
Guinness is in my sights,
Guinness is my past, present and future
Advertising at its finest.
My lousy packet of cigarettes has the most disgusting picture of a brain tumour yet all I see is Guinness, Guinness, Guinness.

Is this the same dirty bus where I finished my book? Fuck, what's the difference, how long ago was that?
Back with the monkeys! But at least this time I'm drunk,
Surely this time I can have some fun…
37 ahead.
If I puke now I'm dead
Pouring rain,
Water dripping on my coat within a bus,
condensation's fucked up.

Aren't they getting rid of the 37?
Soon it'll be in bus route heaven,
along with the 121.
I'm on a crowded bus, so why should I feel so alone.'

Tommy's mind slowed down enough for him to take in his surroundings. 'Yes' he thought, 'this time's different, the bus is packed like a tin of sardines, and I'm drunk as a skunk.' He noticed a group of young women standing together who were at least chatting on and off, luckily for Tommy, he could make nothing out of what they said, although only a drunkard could stand immune to glances such as theirs. Tommy noticed too some elderly folk sitting here and there, and most of them were off their phones at least, 'not too many phombies' he thought. Suddenly, without warning, Tommy began to sing:

"Sardines, Sardines, how are all my lovely sardines? Saardiiiines," he stopped and blinked wildly, like a dog farting itself awake, and he asked in the general direction of the women: "Do you feel like a sardine today my miss?" Tommy looked at the group, too drunk to single any one of them out, who in their turn grow silent and evasive. All eyes now darted on and off Tommy the drunk. For his part, Tommy felt simultaneously out of his mind and fully awake. He continued singing about sardines and throwing obscure comments out to his fellow commuters, who were feeling less like passengers and more like prisoners. 'What's wrong with these people' thought Tommy. 'I might as well be tossing pennies in a wish-pond.'

"Bloody sardines!" he said aloud with a belch which made one passenger laugh, and for a second Tommy felt that he might have found someone who would actually talk with him, but this young man, while amused and enjoying Tommy's rambles greatly, made every effort not to engage with Tommy, less he should be associated with a mindless drunk by the rest of the good passengers who sat still as judges.

Tommy was getting agitated, he felt that all his efforts were being met with silence, and while he tried to bounce amicably off the little feedback his rambles generated, it was like clutching at loose vines, and he felt only that he was falling.

"God damnit, you sardines are worse than drunk," he said mournfully, "you're *dead* sober," turning away now to face no one in particular he started singing again: "sardines, sardines, a bus of sober hIck! Sardiiiiiiines" until one of the passengers finally shouted:

"You're the only fuckin' fish here mate, now open your mouth again, just *one* more time, and I'll smash your face in and throw you off this bus!" Tommy turned and stared open-mouthed at the passengers, but he couldn't identify who said it. He closed his mouth, slowly and silently, and opened it again, and again, no sound came out. He was stunned, and so his mouth continued to open and close, indeed, like a fish. Eventually Tommy got off the bus, hearing just before the door closed a cheer and a "good riddance" and "drunkin' knacker." Tommy stared at the bus as it drove on, still flapping his mouth open and shut, and bobbed back to his home, drunk and alone, singing in his head, sardines, sardines, sardines.

When he got in he slowly registered that the front door was unlocked, the downstairs lights were on and his dad seemed to be asleep on the couch with a glass of whiskey in his hand. Tommy sank down on the couch next to his dad and asked:

"Well, how was your night?" After staring at his father's ashen face for several minutes he put his hand to his father's skin. When Tommy drunkenly realised his father was gone the shock tipped him over. Clasping his father's stiff leg for support Tommy preceded to get sick all over the floor. Tommy's mother came down to see her son dead-drunk and getting sick beside her husband's corpse as it held tight to the very last glass of whiskey he ever got to pour.

Part 6: Loosening up

Tommy had no sooner finished his Beamish when another was placed in front of him.

"Thanks John," he said, faking some surprise, "you guys are too good."

"No worries man," returned John, "it's the least we can do for ya… to your da Tom, an absolute legend." The table; Stephen, John, Nile and Michael, raised their glasses for the 2nd time and clinked again to Tommy's freshly laid father. He closed his eyes and took a long satisfying sip. It had been a strange day for him up to that point, and it was only now, in his glass and in his company of friends, that he finally started to feel himself again. Up to this point he had felt numb throughout the day, as if his movements had been pre-programmed and weren't his own as the social strings of the funeral pulled him along. Now, he was finally getting a break from the heavy-handed predictiveness of it all. For the first time that day he felt free from the undercurrent of the spoken and unspoken directions of his mother, his older brother, the priest, and the army of his father's old acquaintances. He was no longer being told to wake up, wear this, go there, read that, rise, stand, kneel, rise, stand, kneel, rise, stand, kneel and feel, feel, feel … 'feel what?' Now he was past the worst of the shoulder pats, handshakes, conspiratorial winks and melancholy smiles, all of which seemed to say, 'keep up the act son, keep your mask on, keep up the brave front.'

'The more boxes they make you tick—the more they box you in' was Tommy's favourite saying in college, 'and it applies all the more today' he thought. Only reluctantly he had played his part. He got up when he was told, he had a large breakfast in preparation for the famishing church service, he showered, put on his new suit—hoping that he wouldn't have to wear it again for a long, long time—and after a scolding word from his mother he finally put on a tie, feeling it like a noose around his neck. He suffered the insults his mother threw at him when it looked like he would leave the house without polishing his shoes to a blameless black hue. He laughed quietly when she told him "if you ever attempt to carry *my* coffin with unclean shoes like that then I promise—I will make you trip and fall and drop my mortified corpse! And you'll have deserved it." She said this with several magical touches onto the nearest piece of wood. He smiled again at the thought thinking now—'what a spell of words! Now my shoes for her funeral must either be funeral-black, or I'm daring her ghost to keep a promise made by her once living host.'

He smiled, but his mind turned again to his sufferings as he remembered his marginalised role in the church as he was forced into reading a psalm he didn't care for in an environment he loathed while his older brother got to talk at length and with free-rein on their father. He let the current of the day pull him along alright, but it pained him, especially as he couldn't figure out whose benefit it was all for. But now that he was seated away from his family and among his friends he felt that now he could finally move without strings and speak without script, and, more importantly, now he might begin to celebrate and remember his father properly, and he swallowed this all with his funeral-black Beamish as he finally began to wake and loosen up. With half the pint gone he stretched himself, shook his head mildly, smiled and said:

"Well lads, I'm glad that's over with. I tell you, when I die, just dump my body out of sight and skip right to the pub, or have a proper Irish wake," he paused and lowered his voice, "none of that church crap," he finished by reaching for his Beamish for another long sip. Michael laughed and said, "right so" and John came in before the silence became uncomfortable:

"I don't know man, some parts of the service were nice, you're brother's speech was a good send-off."

"You can have all that without the church," said Tommy, "and my brother's speech … it was good, but, there was no humour in it, I think if my dad could have had it his own way there would have been at least one good belly-laugh in there. I mean, even in death, he never spilt a drop of whiskey, and I had to drink it!"

"You drank your dad's death whiskey…" muttered Michael.

"Well I could hardly have poured it down the sink. Bad enough having my mam threatening to hunt me with that".

"Well, how would you have given the eulogy then, besides letting everyone know that you're mad".

"I could have done it" Tommy replied, he had been thinking about this for a while, he was dead confident.

"For one thing," he continued, "my brother should have mentioned our father's obsession with trying to jump into his jocks. He'd always tell us 'a man who can jump into his jocks can do anything' and he spent many a morning desperately trying and falling all over the place." Tommy started to laugh as images of his father jumping and falling naked around his parents' bedroom came back to him. His friends caught the laughter too and joined him, until Tommy wiped away a tear and continued; "of course, I've never seen him do it, and I've tried it myself plenty of times, it's surprisingly difficult."

"I've never heard of anyone trying to jump into their jocks, your dad was a character" Nile said good-humouredly.

"Yeah" Tommy nodded. "Not once did I ever see him do it, and yet, seeing my dad naked and failing ridiculously like that," he sighed, "there was something privileging about it. He was approachable, my dad, even now I can remember him and laugh and smile, even now he feels approachable…." Tommy, dwelling on the distance between the living and the dead, watching the dark abyss below the thinning white head, drank his Beamish and said: "I would also have talked about our dad giving us advice all the time, you know, build up a laugh nice and slow with some good pieces of advice he gave us, then hit the crowd with the time my dad convinced me, absolutely convinced me, that if you ever notice a change in a woman's hair to compliment them, you know, and all the times I'd seen him pull off the trick and him getting free cakes in the bakery and free chips at the chipper, and then telling everyone how my dad told me—'now it's your turn, give it a go son' pointing at a local woman we recognised working behind a checkout. There she was working and with no hair, just a funky looking bandana to cover her head, and dad told me to go up to her and say she was pulling it off better than Sinead ever did and how it really suited her, so my dad watches me walk up to this woman with our bags of messages, and a few minutes later she's screaming at me that I'm a prick and I'm sick and my dad's breaking his shit laughing because, as he later explained, it's important to remember that you should never compliment a woman's *lack* of hair, especially not if they're going through chemo. That and, as my dad explained later, never take someone's advice without thinking twice."

"Well" Michael said with a laugh, "That's well and good over a few pints with your mates, but your brother's was the crowd pleaser."

"Well," said Tommy, staring at his pint, "that's how I'll remember him, my dad, a funny bastard" and Tommy laughed and thought to himself 'so there is no great distance between the living and the dead, hey dad? When we can still share a laugh, wherever you are.'

"Cheers," said Tommy.

When Tommy got home that night he went to his room and began to write:

Life is for living,
and so surely we dishonour the dead
by wasting ourselves with this shallow grieving
letting their imagined worms fill our own heads.

Like when Sean Connery passed away, at the age of 90 and all!
And they all said it was a tragedy!? Like those who told me
'I'm sorry for your loss.'
But everyone shall have an equal share of death, so I want to scream and yell –
For those of us who have life left to live, we can only honour the dead by living
ours well.

When he finished, Tommy undressed naked in his room and began trying to jump into his jocks, thinking he'd continue forever until he did it, 'one for you dad' he initially thought. But after several failed attempts he gave up and smiled, deciding that the lesson needed an audience, and vowing he'd try again when he had kids of his own. Kids who would also enjoy the privileging sight of seeing their father fail, and laugh, and learn not to take it all so seriously. Plus, 'let's face it' he thought, 'how can you succeed in anything until you learn to laugh at your own failures.' But Tommy's smile was short lived, for the thought of kids made him reflect that if he had them they would never know their grandfather, at least not in person, 'and anyway,' Tommy sighed, 'that's my life now, a life without my dad.' And so, putting on his dressing gown and running downstairs like a ghost, Tommy poured himself a whiskey from his dad's collection and bolted back up to his room where, away from the well-wishers and funeral extras, he sipped his dad's whiskey and cried his eyes out.

Satellite

An unknowing Star has become the centre of my world.
Her attraction and my infatuation—now my tether and my pull.
I feel like an unmanned satellite; a dreary hull with no control,
Falling forever, forever afraid of calling and forever doomed to fold.

Our mornings are spent on wooden ships in naked lecture halls.
One look from her and I'm set adrift as my heart begins to fall,
Or if She happens to be sitting near I sink deep inside my phone,
Submerged there below the waves, below that lovely choking foam.

By day she's my Helen of Troy, and my unwell mind her wall,
Where I longingly gaze up upon her, feeling two feet tall.
By night she's my silent Homeric Siren, and crushingly I dream –
Her dangling toes becoming strawberries, and I the kissing the cream.

But my dreams fall like silver rain
While She's in bed and drifting off,
i may hit the glass, but leave no crack nor stain
Breathing desperately, or not at all.

Major Tom to ground control –
This is satellite:
I've caught myself in Venus's hollowing hold
And i'm drowning in Her Light.

Unnourishing Star!
Constellation Prize i can't embrace!
Why has my mind inflated you so?
That I've become both the game and the chase…

A Letter to A Godchild

On Monday Charlie found himself with an evening and not much to do. He had planned to walk the dog after their dinner, but by the time they finished the heavens had opened. The rain was pouring and a sense of loss had settled in. As the wind and rain shook their head against Charlie's plans he instead picked up a digital thread and settled in with a sigh to follow where it led, but a few minutes in he shook his head. He looked to his partner who was lying on his bed watching *Supernatural* with his headphones. So Charlie got up with a sigh to see if there was any craic to be had with his family downstairs. Earlier his mam had cooked a gorgeous pot of food, but, thought Charlie, they had had dinner while his parents were watching reality TV. The show had been about reuniting adult-children with their long lost parents who had given them up for adoption. The stories were compelling but, as usual, Charlie sat with his back to the TV as a quiet form of protest. Charlie didn't even share 2 words with his brother whom he hadn't seen in over a month. The highlight of the dinner was when their dad had asked for some tabasco to throw into his food and their mam gave out stink that nothing she made was ever good enough. Dad took the tabasco anyway and showered his food with it while trying to compliment his wife's cooking as best he could. Charlie stuck up a bit for dad and his brother stuck up a bit for mam, and that was the conversational everything of the dinner. Afterwards his dad and brother got up and disappeared into the sitting room to watch a match, and so the three of them sat in what was, for Charlie, an intolerable silence. Soon Charlie and his boyfriend said their thanks, cleaned up a bit and disappeared up to the attic, Charlie's bedroom. It's here that Charlie, disappointed, put down his iPad and looked up to the rain-pelted window with a sigh, looked to his partner with a sigh, and decided to go back downstairs with a sigh. Now his mam was watching *Coronation Street* while his dad and brother continued watching the match, and Charlie felt depressingly lonely. In the end, despite the rain, Charlie brought the dog for a quick walk, thinking as he left whether there was life on Mars. 'Probably,' he thought, 'since Mars doesn't have tv and Wi-Fi yet.'

When Charlie returned he had a quick shower and, down now in his dressing-gown, he tried once more to spark a little craic from his family. His mam was now watching animal surgery, which always turns his stomach, so he headed into the sitting room where the match was coming to an end.

"Diving, all they do is fucking diving," said his dad.

"And shirt-pulling," said his brother as they watched repeated replays from a corner kick showing plenty of both.

"I swear," continued his dad, "the more money they put into football the worse it gets. You never saw George Best, Roy Keane or Maradona diving. They'd take your head off if you even accused them of it."

"It's bad alright," said his brother, "I feel like switching it to the GAA."

"What about seeing if there's any women's football on?" offered Charlie. His dad and brother turned and stared.

"Women's football? You're mad," said his dad.

"I'd sooner watch snooker," said his brother.

"Why not?" asked Charlie.

"They're amateurs," said his dad, "they don't play to the same level."

"But so what?" said Charlie, "You've often said George Best would seem like an amateur if he played today. And I've watched a couple women matches, the women are vicious! No diving, no shirt pulling, just passion, skill and the roughest tackles I've ever seen."

"Skill!?" guffawed his brother.

"Let women watch women's football," said his dad.

"You pair of moanbags," said Charlie, "all I ever hear when you watch a match is how much cheating and diving goes on, how delicate all the players are, how they all care more about their haircuts and boots then they do playing for their club. Well, women footballers get paid fuck-all, hell, they play football *despite* the lack of support they get. So if you want to watch what football was like before the players started to get paid mad-money then you have to watch women's football. You said it yourself dad—the more they're paid the worse they play, so is the opposite not true?"

"I'm not watching the women's football," said his dad, "sure I can barely keep up with the normal football these days."

"I've no doubt they kill each other on the pitch," said his brother, "but that doesn't mean they can play good football."

"Good football? Sure you still support Bohs!"

"GET OUT" shouted his dad and brother. Charlie shook his head and left the room as another 'normal' player went down in convulsions, seemingly trying to hold both his face and crotch together after a tip on the shoulder.

Giving up on his family Charlie checked the calendar in the kitchen and saw that his niece's birthday was coming up next week. 'Oh shit' thought Charlie. He has 2 nieces from his eldest sister, and he happened to be his eldest niece's godfather. Charlie fondly remembers being asked to serve the role, and the pride he felt at the time, but in the nearly 13 years since, he feels that he's been pretty lousy at it. For one thing, Charlie's never babysat his nieces. He still lives with his parents in inner city Dublin while his sister lives in Lucan, and Charlie has no car, even still, he feels that this is a rather flimsy excuse, so his main defence is; 'I've never been asked to babysit, aren't you supposed to be asked to do these kinds of things?' To be sure, in the early years he made a great uncle, playing with the girls out the back garden whenever they visited their nana, spinning them endlessly in circles and wrestling with them out the back, playing chasing, hide-and-seek, dodgeball… Charlie was always good for that, he loves kids. When he played with them in those days it was like he was given special approval to play at their level and to revert himself to a child once more, but as his eldest niece has grown older Charlie has been struggling to maintain a strong bond with her. For one thing, he considers his nieces, as much as he loves them, to be cheeky little shits. He sees them bomb into his parents' house and wrestle over the remote control, changing it from whatever he was watching to something else. This irritates him to no end, because he normally watches the kind of cartoons that he thinks his nieces should enjoy, such as *Stephen Universe, Teen Titans Go* or *The Regular Show*, but all they want to watch are girly live-action shows which seem to focus more on their characters messaging each other on their phones than actually interacting face-to-face. 'The future's fucked' thinks Charlie. He thinks back to when he was a child, and he knows that if he and his brother ever went to visit a grandparent and went straight for the remote that they would receive a good slap each and thrown outside. 'No respect' thinks Charlie.

Charlie often wonders what the kids will be like when they grow up, kids who have never experienced a time before smartphones. He remembers being absolutely shocked when his sister told the family over a dinner that if she could get her 2 daughters microchipped to know exactly where they are all the time she would.

"You can't do that," said Charlie, feeling, somehow, that he must speak up against microchipping for children everywhere.

"Why not?"

"Because then you'll always be worried about them, you'll always be checking where they are, always freaking out. And when would you remove the chips? Would you have liked it if mam chipped us when we were kids?" Charlie shivered at the thought.

"I had better things to be thinking about" chipped in their mother. 'What a joke' thought Charlie, 'what a joke. How short their memories are.' Charlie still remembers all the sneaking around he had to do as a teenager, all the waiting up his mam did, all the lies so that he could spend some time with his friends, with his boyfriends.

"Well, if I could, I would" his sister said, "it would stop me worrying so much about them when they're out. You have no idea Charlie what it's like, and those two think nothing of running off without their phones for hours and hours."

"Listen, sis" Charlie poured out warmly, calming himself to do his argument justice, "people always think that technology can ease anxiety, and it can't, in fact, microchipping will only make you more anxious, because you'll never be able to let go of them, and they'll never get to feel free. Remember when we were kids, do you think we would have wanted to be microchipped."

"Well, it's how I feel Charlie, and unless you have kids you're never going to understand," she said dismissively. 'Typical,' thought Charlie sulkily, 'she never argues, only withdraws, the future's fucked, hasn't anyone seen *Black Mirror*? For fuck's sake.' For the rest of that night Charlie and his sister were cool towards each other, both withdrawing into themselves. Charlie wanted desperately to know how his rebel of a sister could want her own children microchipped, eventually he concluded to himself: 'if a child goes camping with her friend, or cycles out of town, or does something a little out there, to be free, yes, it's dangerous, but if the child gets hurt or even dies then 'so be it' says the child, they are the most fearless things on the planet, and when you're dead you're dead. But now, society has deemed it so unspeakable for a parent to lose a child, especially through anything looking like neglect, and parents can afford to have so few children anyway, that parents have become cowards, the media too has made them into cowards, the media loves a child-in-danger story for grabbing attention, and technology loves a weakness for making psychological inroads and profits. The world is fucked.'

These bits of memories kept Charlie musing along as he made his lunch the next day. His godchild will be 13 next week. She has already hit puberty, an experience he can hardly relate to. He was surprised to hear that her younger sister, now 10, is deeply jealous of her older sister's growing breasts. It's part of the problem, he feels—he really knows nothing of the world of girls. Charlie's own sister is 10 years older than him, so his early memories relate to her troubled teenage years of screaming matches between her and their parents, and her abrupt move out of the house to live elsewhere when he was 8 and she 18, 'how people can change' he thought, 'and what the hell can I get for my niece?'

To top off his ignorance, Charlie was educated in all-boys primary and secondary schools in the Catholic tradition. An education that was designed to keep children from the 'sin' of discovering anything worth knowing of the other sex before marriage, a system which still continues today out of sheer political laziness to change it, or perhaps it has something to do with the fact that, unlike the public, most politicians just so happen to have gone to private schools instead, inside jokes that they are. How can Ireland rid itself of sexism when boys in an all-boys school are sent in 4th year to a girl's school to learn 'home economics' (= cooking) for a few weeks while the girls in turn go to the boys school for a short stint of metal and woodwork? Charlie's school was so strict on this front that they had a policy in which the boys from that school, and the girls from the nearest all-girls school, were always released at different times of the day to minimise the 'risk' of them mingling. Such an outdated system, 'how in God's name does it continue' thinks Charlie. He has seen the abysmal effects of this 'education' on his friends, many of whom, despite, like him, being now in their early twenties, are still either virgins or hopelessly lost around women. One friend in particular has attached himself so much to the first woman who didn't shy away from him that he's now hitched to a psychopath and refuses to acknowledge it for fear of being stuck for another long period of embarrassing advances and devastating rejections. He knows another friend who gave up awkwardly trying to pick up women in the pubs and clubs and just hired an escort to teach him what his school refused to. Charlie, for his part, never had the same problem with women, for he knew early on that he's gay, and thanks to the catholic tradition, he had no problems picking up boys and the kinds of experiences that his heterosexual friends were starved of. 'But I'm also clueless' thinks Charlie, 'I don't know anything about girls, and I have no idea what to get my niece.'

At night Charlie taps away into his diary. He has kept it since he was a teenager, ever since he read Bram Stoker's *Dracula*, and it helps him to think, and the thought hits him—'Why don't I get her her very own diary.' He sits and thinks about it. He knows girls are generally encouraged to keep diaries, 'maybe she already has one?' but he's never seen Lisa with one before. And with a diary he could include a letter. 'Yes, there's a thought.' A letter, he could write to her at length, one that would perhaps help him to reconnect with his godchild. 'Maybe that's what's been missing' he thinks, 'she's no longer a child, she's a moody little teenager, and I don't know how to deal with teenagers, but every teenager wants to be treated like an adult, and I can do that for her at least. Yes, I can write to her, buy her a diary, and sure, I'll put a €20 into the card just in case.' So that night Charlie began writing, and over the next few nights, when not overly distracted by digital threads, he wrote the following for his godchild:

Happy birthday Lisa,

For your birthday I'm giving you a little money, a diary, a book and some advice, so at least one of those things will be useful! But first, I just want to say how happy I am to be your uncle. You are already such a wonderful person and you do our family proud.

So let me start by saying that life is crazy and no one knows what it's all about. People say that life is a gift and there's some truth in that, but it's a funny kind of gift, because nobody asks for it, we can't exchange it and there's no receipt. But here we are! Or here it is, and I suppose we would be stupid not to try and make the most of it.

Another strange thing about life is that by the time you're old enough to start questioning what it is and what you want, you have already been immersed into a specific kind of life. It's important to remember this. I guess we call this our culture or background. For example, my parents (your crazy grandparents) believe in god, especially your nana (both your nanas actually). So I believed in god. I considered myself a Catholic and I prayed to god almost every night, but then the idea of god watching me all the time became, well, weird and uncomfortable, and being gay, I realised that the god I was believing in must be very different to the god that many others believe in. And in college I met someone, a sweet boy from a Muslim family, and as our relationship developed it hit me one day; why, if my parents were Muslims, surely I would also be a Muslim! In fact, if my parents were Jewish, I would also be Jewish. So when I finally decided to think for myself, I became, well, I guess I'm still trying to figure that out, but the point is it took me a very long time and a very good friend to escape an idea I was born into, an idea that was already making certain aspects of my life very uncomfortable! I'm not saying you should become an atheist or anything like it, that's your business, I guess what I'm saying is, to paraphrase Miles Davis (a jazz legend); sometimes it takes a long time for you to be able to think for yourself.

If you remember this it should help you to understand other people. Even the assholes in this world didn't choose to be assholes (why would anyone choose to be an asshole?), they are a product of their environment, their parents and family, and they don't have the education, support or resources to escape the world they find themselves in, a world that others have, knowingly and unknowingly, built them.

And here's the really crazy thing Lisa, everyone wants the best for you, your parents, your teachers, your friends and family, we all want the best for you, but you need to know sooner rather than later that none of us know what that really means. For me, this is the craziness of life. People will say that they want you to be happy, but really, (believe me,) they also want you to be 'successful' and they will put this pressure on you, but 'success' means different things to different people, and their ideas will pull you every which way, and the only thing you can do to not be torn to shreds is to realise your own idea of happiness and 'success.'

For example, when I finished school my parents really really wanted me to go to college, but I wanted to travel the world instead. I listened to my parents and I went to college, and I wish I didn't, because college didn't get me a good job even though I worked hard and got good grades. It was nice, but I think travelling would have been better for me. I listened to my parents when I should have listened to myself, but I wasn't confident enough to do that then. But I also have to remember that my parents love me, and they only wanted the best for me, the problem is that parents don't always know what's best. They know how to look after children, sure, but as you become an adult, they will know less and less what's best for you, and so you need to find that out for yourself.

This is the best and worst thing about life: That despite the fact that other people have had a hand in shaping it, in the end, it's your life, and you have to figure it out for yourself, and while other people can and will help you, nobody knows what life really is or what we should do with it. So, with that in mind, here is my top advice about life, or rather, what I've learnt so far:

People like to say—'nobody's perfect,' or 'everyone makes mistakes.' But let me be honest with you, in reality, everyone is, to some degree, sick, broken, or arrogant, some more than others, and everyone has their 'medicine.' What I mean is, we all have bad feelings sometimes, and we all do things that we shouldn't do, and sometimes for absolutely no reason, so when we're feeling bored, sad or angry at ourselves, sometimes we need something to help us feel happy again. This is 'medicine.' For some people their medicine is TV, or alcohol, or religion, or even work or sports. My medicine used to be video games, Lisa, I used to play video games maybe 6-8 hours every day—I love video games, I can't put into words how much I love video games. The immersion, the shutting out of the world, the isolation, the peace, the private competitiveness, but, for me, it was bad medicine, because it made me lose friends, do badly in school, and video games, especially for me, are extremely addictive (6-8 hours every day!!!). Now, I take my medicine in the form of music, books, friends and meditation. I try to fill my time with these things, and I am happier now than I've ever been. You need to find medicine that makes you happy and that doesn't make you sad. It's not easy, but think of it like this; video games made me very happy, <u>but only while I was playing them</u>, whenever I stopped playing them I became bored, sad and often angry at myself. Anything that makes you more sad when it stops is bad medicine, and anything that feels like it's pulling you in and making you do things you don't want to do is bad medicine. When I tried to give up video games I had what addicts call a relapse, I had many many relapses— times when I started playing a game again, but promising myself that this time I would only play for 1 hour a day. It never worked, always I would go back to the same routine, video games make a liar and a fool out of me. If you find yourself with a medicine like that, walk away, because what you're really taking is poison.

And remember, everyone's different, most people laugh at me when I tell them I was addicted to video games, they think I'm joking, but you'd be amazed the things people have become addicted to, and that experience was no joke for me. Don't let it happen to you, or if it does, you can always talk to me or seek professional help. One word also about professional help—Most of our family wears glasses, (and you'll probably have to too!). Glasses are help for faulty eyes, and nobody bats an eyelid about them these days. In other words, no one feels guilty about needing glasses. But some people feel very guilty and embarrassed about seeking some forms of help, and this is absolutely crazy—if people can be born with faulty eyes, and can correct their vision with absolutely no fuss being made about it, well then, if you ever feel that there is some part of you that's faulty and needs help or a bit of extra support, then, make sure you ask for that help, even demand it if you have to, because you have every right to it, and feel no more guilt about it then if you were asking for an eye test.

Next, Life is for learning. I don't understand what life is, or what to do with it, but in my opinion, life is for learning, for exploring, for trying new things. This comes from external sources (books, school, family, friends, travel, etc) and internal judgment. It's important to learn a lot, but it's equally important to reflect on what you've learnt. What I'm saying is, you have to figure yourself out. Who you are, what you like, what you've learnt and what you want. And listen, you might never know the answer to these questions, maybe it's impossible to know 'who is Lisa?' That's ok. The important thing is the experience—that's what this diary is for. I write in my diary maybe once a week, and it's a chance for me to keep track of what I've experienced and learnt, and to ask myself these questions. I hope you use your diary too, because the better you know yourself the easier life becomes. One thing I recommend about keeping a diary is this— keep a physical one (like the one I bought you!) and write in it whenever you feel like it, but also keep a digital one on a laptop or a hardrive, and update this once a week or month. The advantage of typing out your handwritten diary is that it gets you into the habit of re-reading and re-writing what you've already written, and this gives you space to reflect. Also, on a computer, you have the advantage of 'Ctrl F,' by hitting these 2 magical keys you're able to search a computer document for a specific word, date or phrase. As you get older, the ability to 'search' through a digital diary will seem like an absolute superpower, there's simply no better way I know to search through your own mind so accurately. You may not see the value of it for a few years, but trust me, when I talk to other people who keep diaries we always have the same complaint—we wish we started sooner!

Also, TV is bad, at least in my opinion. I absolutely loved TV when I was growing up, and I still love some shows and cartoons, but the older I get the more I hate it. TV makes us lazy. Being lazy is nice, but only work (mental and/or physical effort) seems to gives us satisfaction. When you achieve something you feel proud, happy, satisfied, amazing, but I don't know of anyone who felt proud from having watched TV. You don't have to stop watching TV (I haven't, not yet anyway), but don't let TV become a big part of your life, and yes, Netflix not only counts, but Netflix is a form of TV that is even built better to addict you to it.

So far, I've found the most important things in life to be people, reading and music. Everyone is struggling to understand what's going in life, and everyone is making little discoveries on how to live a good life and how to be happy. Spending time with people allows you to learn what they are doing and what you might be able to do, and connecting with people is something we're built for, at our most basic level, and it feels great.

Also, reading and music are forms of magic that we now take for granted. Stephen King helped me to think of it this way—reading is telepathy, a superpower, if you are reading these words then, in a way, I am in your head and you are in mine, and that's a very intimate connection. It means that, no matter where in the world I may be, right at this very moment, we're close. If that isn't telepathy and magic I don't know what is. It's a strange relationship—reader and writer—but few relationships are more personal or intimate. Don't take reading for granted. On the other side we have music. If reading is telepathy than music must be empathy. Music allows the feelings of one person to enter another. A lot of music now is made purely for making money, and for me this music is often empty, but really good music wants you to feel something, wants to move you, wants to tell you something. Here's some music I recommend you to try, if you want:

Yoko Ono—'I Love All Of Me.' Yoko Ono is a remarkable woman, she loved someone very much, and for that, most of the world decided to hate her. She was bullied, attacked and made into a living joke, and yet, here she is singing about acceptance and self-love, even in a world that criticises us for who we are.

Bikini Kill—'Rebel Girl.' Kathleen (the lead singer) sings about being a teenager, about finding your way and finding a kindred spirit; someone you want to be friends with. If you think that all sounds soppy and sentimental then you haven't heard the song yet, because when Kathleen steps up to sing no one, and I really mean NO ONE, rocks harder than her.

Lisa Hannigan—'Barton.' (She's my 2nd favourite Lisa!) In this song Lisa sings about depression. People don't like to talk about depression, but it's a part of life, and we can't escape it, instead you have to make peace with it, and sometimes, when you're feeling depressed, it's nice to find something to match how you feel. This music helps me when I feel sad, because it reminds me that I'm not alone.

Nina Simone—'I'm Feeling Good.' Because depression doesn't last, and as Nina knew, it's the simple things that wake us up from it and allow us to feel good again.

Anyway Lisa, that's my advice, maybe it's not much good, but it's honest. The last thing I'll say is this—there's a free to watch documentary on YouTube called 'Human' in 3 volumes, please watch it, it will teach you more than school ever will (the same goes for the book I've included). And I just want to say that I am always here for you if you need me, and whatever crazy things happen in your life I will always be happy to listen, and I will always be honest with you. You have my number and you know where I live!

And I promise, for your next birthday I'll stick with a normal present ☺ *.*

Finishing it the night before Lisa's birthday, Charlie read over it and shrugged. Some parts he was happy with, others he wasn't, but deciding at the very least that it would do no harm he printed it out and stuck it into a lovely blue diary he had bought. He wrapped the diary and book together (*Sophie's World*) and put them into a gift bag along with a card from Easons. In the card he stuck €20 and wrote 'Happy Birthday Lisa, I hope you have a wonderful birthday! There's a longer message inside one of your other presents for you to read in private and when you have the time. With all my love, Charlie XXX.'

On the day of Lisa's birthday Charlie's mother hosted a big party with a lot of guests. Charlie fidgeted for most of the day before finding Lisa relatively alone and giving her her present. Lisa opened the card, making sure to read the message before pocketing the money. 'What's he talking about, another message?' She opened up the presents, revealing a book and a diary with a few A-4 pages folded up and stuck in the middle.

"Oh," she said, "ok, I'll read it at home," she promised, thanking Charlie with a quick hug and wandering off, turning her back just in time to hide her confused face. 'What is it this time' she thought, 'Charlie always gets me the weirdest presents.' Last year Charlie had given her Louis Stevenson's *Treasure Island*, a book she had tried to read out of a sense of duty, but of which she only managed 5 pages before giving it up for the 2 *Diary of a Wimpy Kid* books that she had also received from someone else (and had actually asked for!).

The diary and now moneyless card were put into one of several bags which contained Lisa's other gifts. Sarah, Lisa's younger sister, walked sheepishly around Charlie, expecting to receive €5 or €10 in compensation for the fact that it wasn't *her* birthday. Charlie, oblivious, gave her nothing, but walked into the kitchen to take a beer, feeling that for better or worse a weight was now off his shoulders. He remembered back to all those times as a kid when his uncles would slip him some money, sometimes doing it in such a way that he would be home for several hours from his grandmother's house before realising that his pockets contained a £20 note or such. He thought how wise his uncles were back then, and decided that he would have to learn the slip-technique for future birthdays. Sarah, realising she was getting nothing from him, disappeared out to the back garden, giving Charlie an unnoticed scowl and a shake of her fist.

5 years later and Lisa is tasked with clearing out her room as her family get ready to move to a larger house in Co. Meath. She notices some paper in the middle of one of the several diaries she has kept unused under her bed. She opens it up and reads through it before throwing it in the bin with a shake of the head, for what time does an 18 year old have for the words of a crazy uncle addressed to a godchild he barely sees and knows, 'silly Charlie, he's never even added me on Facebook.'

Spending Too Much Time on My Phone (Again)

'A soft bed makes a soft body,'
And a hard life makes a hard woman or man,
So why we see ourselves as autonomous individuals
Is what I'm struggling to understand.

For I find myself being submerged ever deeper
Into this 'social' digital land,
Where we wrestle our individuality
Among trillions of things made by different hands,

I wonder if it will be too late
For our individuality not to be damned?
Or will it be lost and engulfed forever
Into these little screens of digital quicksand.

Passing by Your House

3 months ago my partner and I managed to buy a house,
and since settling in I now pass by the house where my grandmother used to live.
This fact was pleasant in the first few weeks,
but now it's becoming a nightmare.

From the outside the house is the same: a two-story terraced house with a large front garden, black gate, and a cemented path leading to where you are faced by a large red door. After the house was sold to new owners I rarely saw it, and never dwelt on it. It had ceased to exist, and I only visited it in rare dreams and fond memories.

But with my new commute to work I rarely pass it by without notice, and even when I do, this fact always seems to catch up with me. It's as if the house, realising that it was unacknowledged in the morning, say, comes to find me at work, especially in the afternoon, and goes through my orifices like vapour, and wipes its feet on my mind and makes itself at home. I feel it like one of those 'walking on your grave' shivers that, logically speaking, must originate within us and radiate out, and yet they feel for all the world like an outer force, a warning which, if anything, serves to make a mockery of that barrier we call skin, or rather, 'me' and 'not me.' In this way the house is haunting me, very much like a ghost, for what are ghosts if not involuntary thoughts? I have even considered changing my route to work, but what would be the use? Since all efforts to avoid something only brings our mind ever more upon it, and it seems so daft to let a door have the road.

I'm in work now, and I know I will notice it on my way home—I always do. One reason is that there's a large green hedge that blocks my view of it on the way into work, but catches my attention on the way back, like a goal on a pitch which my eyes can't resist, striking home every time. Also, on my way home, I'm always walking on the same side of the street as the house (I get very anxious if I'm not on the correct side of the road as soon as possible). Or perhaps this bloodhound image of the door has been sent to find me, if just to remind me, not to forget it on the way home. What a needy house it has become. I've spent a great deal of time thinking of all the silent and patient forces slowly acting towards destroying it (continental drift, soil creep, war and meteorites to name a few), but, I sense, these same forces plus a million more are aiming to destroyed me first, and that house will have the last laugh, and as my consciousness slips away from this world my mind won't be clinging to her, my favourite person, but clinging feverishly to that bloody red door, and I will be plunged into darkness, clinging onto a piece of bloody driftwood, that is my nightmare.

Well now. I know my grandmother has died, that she existed, and that she will endure in my mind as long as it's well. And perhaps this is why her old house, a place I loved so much, now haunts me, for it feels as if her essence has seeped into it, and, as I walk past it twice a day, I find myself thinking more of the house than of her. It is as if that bloody red door has soaked up all the vapours my grandmother had to offer, and my mind is stuck revolving around an object that, with each passing, still demands more, and more, and more.

John Banville showed us the trap: I exist, therefore I think. I exist, and at times I *must* think. What fools that we cannot go without thinking while think we're intelligent? Who can choose what and when they think? Not me, no, my mind came with no manual, and no control settings have been found. Yet we have the nerve to consider rocks dumb because they cannot think? Well, if you can only do one or the other, and never learn to do both, there is no difference, because I sometimes feel as dumb as a rock when I cannot stop myself from thinking, and thinking, when that red door finds me and knocks. I see it in the book I'm reading, in my daily walking, in my very living. I feel it knocking upon my skull, like a piece of dead skin upon my lips, my fingers just itching to peel and pick.

Three times so far I have seen someone come out from that door, exiting the house where my grandmother used to live, and so have *you* entered the undirected theatre of my mind. Once, when I passed while you were leaving, I peered deep into the old long hall, and glimpsed the beautiful modern paintings you have strung upon the walls. I was shocked. Once my grandfather's watercolours hung along that wall; moody meditative scenes of trees and water, how misplaced those modern paintings were, and yet, how I wanted to enter then, and touch those paintings, to soak in every pigment, and let them paint over the hall within my head, how I wanted to breathe in the life you've brought, and forget all about those sad watercolours and that old red door—guardian now of so many memories, shut and dead. And how I have watched you in embarrassment, and wondered if you recognise me, if you have ever felt any of this special attention which is drawn towards the house you now live in. Tell me, have you ever got a whiff of Superking Black in the kitchen? Did you ever clear out those empty Jameson bottles from the shed? Sometimes I imagine myself talking to you. Oh, we used to have great conversations at first, I imagined myself telling you that my favourite person used to live here. How your house was once my grandmother's house. I go on to tell you how happy and free I had been in those days, and how much I would love to enter through this door one more time. Would you let me in, just one more time? Would you really?

Well, here at least, what choice do you have. I enter your house with you behind me, in respectful silence, while I soak it all in one more time (in an attempt to shake it off). And you politely start asking me all kinds of questions while I try and make us a cup of tea,
Laughing nervously,
As I reach for the place where the teabags used to be.

After I have had my fill of the place, after I have explored each and every room, we sit over our cups and I tell you how I once enjoyed a period in this house freer than anything I had ever felt. It was during the transitional period, between my grandmother's death and the house being sold to you. My family had already mined the house for objects to hang their memories onto, and left it silent, empty, and completely compliant, so that the house became *my* house, and I would often say to my friends on a night when the pubs were trying to kick us out—'hey lads, let's all go back to my dead granny's gaf!' And we did, and we bloody enjoyed ourselves. We spent many nights one winter drinking there, smoking, playing cards and revelling until the morning; when my friends would leave and I would lovingly clean up the house and think of her that used to live here. Or sometimes I would go there alone, just to roll a spliff, have a cup of tea and sit there, quietly reading or doing nothing at all, feeling my grandmother to be with me, feeling sadly sublime and at ease, really free, completely free.

Perhaps you think I'm crass for having had sessions in my dead grandmother's house, taking advantage of its emptiness. But it wasn't like that. My grandmother, when she was still able to manage stairs, had lived in a grand

4 or 5 story Georgian house on Berkeley Street. This is the house of my half-remembered, half imagined early childhood. The house where, in the year 2000, my dad stripped naked with one of his brothers and ran screaming down the streets (a pair of jokers in my incomplete cerebral deck). But even so, that house has no hold on me, and I've walked past it hundreds of times without a conscious thought. It doesn't follow me to work, and, in fact, I have to carefully look for it in my mind and out of it. You see, my relationship with my grandmother only blossomed during those turbulent teenage years, when we begin to flirt with freedom as the world starts to pile its expectations upon us, and those where the red door days. It started somehow during a family visit, over HB ice-cream and strawberry jelly; that I would come down to her some Saturday to do her shopping as it was becoming too much for her. She puffed a cloud of Superking and said only if it were no trouble. But once I started going there on my own that was it, I had found my heaven on earth, a place where I always belonged. I was there nearly every Saturday and many a weekday since that day and the day she died. In no time at all my grandmother's presence had lost the stuffiness of babysitting duties and childishness, and took on beautifully all the trappings of a true friendship. And though I went down on my own most times, down there you never knew who you'd meet. Her house was our family's town market square, our local, our church. Cousins, siblings, parents and their offspring all mingled there, wonderfully, and I miss it.

For 10 years I visited that house, doing odd jobs for my grandmother, or just sitting down to a cup of tea. When she wasn't there I would let myself in, having long been given a key so that she wouldn't have to walk to the door, and I would sweep the kitchen for her or wash the dishes. When she returned, normally with one of my uncles, we would all sit and chat. Our family was never so well connected than in those days, and when my grandmother passed away the only thing that brought her back to me was that house, and knowing that whenever I was happy—she was happy. Her ghost, in every memory she invoked, told me so. Yes, I know my grandmother would have approved of everything I did there. The drinking and singing, the wild parties and jubilee of a free house in inner-city Dublin. My grandmother's 'essence,' whatever that may be, was substantial beyond those biscuit-tin totems and jaded jinnee lamps. She showed me a way of living that surpasses all of that, and I went to that house to pay tribute to what she taught me. When you want to honour a musician you do so by playing their music, and so I lived those unsolicited hours in her house by hers. Because that's how it was, when her body was too feeble to live fully, she lived fully through us, and I shared everything with her, as I share it all again with you, over another cup of tea, and tell you of the person my grandmother used to be.

Now at family gatherings her memory kindles our conversations, her twilight years being what seems to me the golden age of our family, and I've spoken to many a stranger whose only connection we share was knowing her, but so tender is that connection that they never remain strangers after. Think of the thing you're fondest of, and the joy you feel when you find a kindred spirit, that's only close to the feeling I get when I meet someone else who knew her. Knowing my grandmother is the quickest entrance there is to my heart, and I was thrilled to share her with those I already loved. Indeed, that she got to meet and get to know my partner before she passed, and approved of him and 'us' fully, was the best external sign our relationship could ever have received, and among the best gifts this mad world ever bestowed on me. No, indeed, please understand, I, like all in my family, invited my friends to her house far more when she was alive than when she was dead.

Yes, my grandmother, with her contagious laugh and shinning eyes, she was substantial, she was wholesome. She had a child's innocent curiosity tempered by weathered patience and polished love, and she had a mind that was kept happily and lovingly alive by us. She wasn't some greedy gossiping bookkeeper, no, not once did she betray my confidence or use someone else's information in any mean-spirited or self-gaining way, and she treated what I told her, which was everything, better than anyone, certainly better than myself. For she saw the very best in everyone, and treated everyone accordingly, without even a hint of an ideal that she expected us to reach, it was all she asked that she saw us alive and living, smiling and growing. In that way, she gave us the best possible light in which to see ourselves, in which to grow. Perhaps this is what I miss most, her unconditional love. For what parent can give their child unconditional love these days? When children are no longer mere accidents but actual decisions—investments even. What a farce. We have been raised by generations upon generations of surprises, by the sometimes wanted, but often unwanted, by-products of sex and desire. The psychologists and their lot have yet to catch up with this fact of our shared human history—but I put it to them like this:

> Another accident? Another surprise!
> So we'll love him unconditionally
> Throughout his unplanned for life.
>
> But this one was planned, you see?
> And so a blessing he may be
> But we've invested an awful a lot
> So he is conditionally free
> And of course we will love him, (but conditionally).

Anyway, I tell you one thing, if my grandmother had been our priest during our first confessions, not one of us would have left the church. Yes, this house, for me at least, has become a church without priest, and that bloody red door stands like a crucifix without any faith nailed to it, revealing the sad ugly art that it is. There's a lesson for the church for you, at least when my grandmother was on her way out, despite doubts and fears that shook her occasionally to her core, in the end she died graciously and with a smile, surrounded by her family. And as I pass that house and my eyes are drawn to that bloody red door I try, like a failing Catholic, to attach some meaning to it all once more, but you're here, and she's gone, and even now I see you closing your door on me.

At this point I imagine your patience has waned, and I hear you thinking 'what have I done, inviting this utter lunatic into my house, just to hear him babble about his grandmother and how terrible *my* house has become for *him,* let it go son, and get out!' Here my mind exhausts itself, and our conversation comes to an end, and I find myself back to the waking world again, the solid world of changing houses closed to us by unchanging doors. But, despite it all, I promise I will never knock upon your door, for in reading this you have let me in enough already, and perhaps, just perhaps, you're reading this behind the very door that now haunts me, and the thought makes me smile. I too have moved into a new house only recently, and god only knows the ghosts I sleep among and the survivors who ruefully walk past my own front door. Hell, if I came a knocking, I doubt I would let myself in. I suppose it's our burden to bear to make peace with a new commute through life, to free ourselves from these silently screaming objects and all that we attach to them, and to dwell on those left behind and carry them with us, and only them, and leave rocks and doors as there are, mocking us

with their unthinking, now, and forevermore, until we too shall share in the intelligence they keep,
the intelligence of the dead and the dumb,
their quiet,
their peace.

A Poem for Walt Whitman's Atoms

'Tell me,' asked a foolish man to his teacher:

'How is it that when I cast my mind back
it's only me that I catch?
And when I try to imagine someone's face
It's only mine that comes back?

'And how is it that when a poor begging brother I pass
it's to my own needs that I latch?
Grasping money I know I don't need
walking on without looking back?

'And how is it that when I try to listen to her
It's only my own thoughts I can track?
And when she wants me to love her
It's my own itch I want scratched?'

The teacher sat down with his student, and taking out pen and paper he began to explain:

'You are, my son, beginning to see the light,
Now sit with me and we'll set this right.
First, examine this:
I love (God, God loves) me,
Now, remove the brackets and we see,
We are left with only 'I love me.'

'Do this exercise a hundred times a day,
changing the verb and noun as you please,
Because *Everything* comes back to you,
And you will see,
That while you are alive, my son,
There's simply no other way it can be.
So, if you want to be unselfish,
This is key:
Each time you look *at, for* or *to* someone,
You must say to yourself—'*Why, that's me*!'

'And so you remember yourself by remembering others
And you give to yourself when you give to the beggars
And you love yourself more when you love her better
Realise this, my son, and you may one day let go of Me, me, em? Me!
And once again sing your body electric
Living unselfishly and free.'

'Once again?' Asked the fool, 'you mean we've been through all of this before?'
'Yes, indeed!' laughed the teacher: 'it seems I am struggling through it all once more.'
'And I'll continue to struggle though it all again
and again
and again:
This is the one thing of which I'm sure.' For the only way the world can be both eternal and always new is if "every atom belonging to me as good belongs to you."'

The Vegan Haikus

(To be read horizontally/across)

I sat on haikus
'Prisons for words' I once thought
But people can change

For example—meat
Something I no longer eat
Why? I'm glad you've asked:

I love animals
Now, my actions match my words
Vegans love them more

"Organic," "Free Range"
I was hypnotised by words
– Shadows of a farm

Chickens cannot care
Which label mocks their corpses
Labels are for us

Sheep will follow sheep
Most people eat animals
Only sheep eat sheep

No anaesthetics
For pulling teeth, clipping tails
We make their life hell

Who's on the menu?
Finger Lickin' Good? Eat Fresh?
You're Lovin' 'it?' 'It' is 'death.'

Eggs are foetuses
Milk is kidnapping and rape
Who died for your plate?

Our countryside's sick:
Woods grassed clear, our streams toxic
'Fresh air?' smells like shit!

Bugs tried to tell us
It's never rabbit season
Who likes Elmer Fudd?

Make Batman vegan
Athlete? Detective? Hero?
Need for flesh? Zero.

'Make mine Marvel!' Why?
Their heroes protect the weak?

With the crowd is how
Insanity goes down best

Not while they eat meat

Or Nazis once thought
That they were superior
While killing millions

Each farm is Auschwitz
For the animals concerned
Forget not—but learn

Slaughterhouse workers
Are paid to kill and suffer
To satisfy taste

Or it will be us
One day farmed by aliens
Wouldn't that be just?

Militant vegans!
But who has the body count?
Whose taste has victims?

If you need help, use –
Earthling Ed's YouTube channel
You've nothing to lose

Would you eat your pet?

How are we different?
In slaughtering innocents?
Worse, we breed them first

When we pay for meat,
We pay to keep; a system
Of torture and grief

If cosmic justice
Exists, we'll all come back as
cows, chickens and pigs

Slaves and Sexism –
Tradition was no excuse
Why stop at abuse?

To become vegan
There's just one thing you must quit
Ignorance That's it

I used to laugh at
Vegans, but I was naive
Truth sets us *all* free

Talking Shit and Backflips

On a long bright Summer evening I agreed to meet a couple of friends at the Monument in the Phoenix park. I cycled out that way and waited for them there with a book in hand, but one man in a pair of wine-coloured shorts and matching top caught my eye, for near the Monument he stood and stretched, and streetched, , and streeeeetched. His stretching exercises were so conspicuous that I took him for mad, and so I sat on my ass to enjoy this free spectacle, amused and glad. And I started to wonder whether he was seeking attention or if he were immune to it instead, but I wasn't long watching him before my mind grew sad. My wandering mind, not content to stay on the grass, stretched me back to a Rory Gallagher tribute gig I once went to with my dad, where, despite the band failing miserably to resurrect Rory's live energy, I willed myself to dance despite myself, when, in the corner of my eye, I saw my dad videoing me on his phone. Now, to appreciate what that did to me, I must mention something—but how can I put it? Have you ever heard a phrase or a quote that seemed to strike you physically? A moment when you grasped at a string of words and held desperately onto them—hoping, I guess, to make a charm out of them to wear with you for the rest of your life? A favourite quote perhaps, or prayer? For instance, I once watched online a *Sly and the Family Stone* concert where Sly said such a string of words that I wrote them down, stored them, saved them, and often wore them around me like such a charm. What he said was something like this:

> "We want you joining in with us on this one, to clap, and sing, and feel the music with us. Don't wait for approval from your neighbour, for your neighbour is more than likely waiting for approval from *you*."

I wrote those words down like a spell, a spell which rattled around my mind and came out any time I found myself wanting to let loose, go wild and join in at a concert. 'Don't wait for approval' said Sly, 'hell, them boring people standing around looking real awkward—didn't you know it? They're waiting on YOUR approval!' said Stone, and many times when I was feeling good I did just that—I danced like a lunatic until I was past the point of caring, only to find I was no longer dancing on my own. That's what those words did for me—and they meant more to me than any 'holy Mary mother of god' ever did. And yet, at that lacklustre concert, when I invoked those sly words and began my raindance for a more lively gig, I saw my father recording me on his phone, and those spell of words were dissipated and I was left feeling like a stuttering child pushed out into the spotlight, and so stutter off the dancefloor is what I did. For what spell of words or positive thinking can beat a parent with a smartphone? Goddamn, how musicians can tolerate phones at their concerts is beyond me. Anyway, in trying to video me dancing, my father instead recorded the moment when those words were tested and found wanting. And yet, here was this man, in the middle of the park, stretching out in the open for all the world to see, and so I stared and began instead to watch his watchers and write in my diary, trying to make my mind up about him and his magic while he stretched on happy and oblivious.

Streeeeetch. Stretch. Stretch. Stretch. Stretch. Stretch. Stretch. Stretch.

Some stretches later and the first of my friends arrived, there on his bike he came with a big bag of cans and ice.

"Story buddy! What's the craic?" He greeted me with his thick Brazilian accent. I smiled, for it always makes me smile to think how Dublin-speak seems to get under the tongue so fast, and I put away my neglected book and diary as Renato rested his bike beside mine and sat down to lay his cans on a plastic-covered bed of icy slush. I greeted him in turn and we bumped fists, and, after we settled a bit of business, we got to talking:

"I'm grand, any craic yourself?" I asked.

"The same old man," he sighed, "still doing deliveries, still saving money, still fighting with my housemates. You remember Felipe?"

"Sure" I lied.

"He's bought some new camera gear, he says he wants to start producing porn, but his girlfriend's against it."

I laughed, yes, I remembered Felipe now.

"Doesn't Felipe have a porn addiction?"

"Yeah," Renato laughed, "but who isn't addicted to porn? His girlfriend wants him to get help, find a therapist, but Felipe wants to start producing his own videos instead, crazy guy."

"Well," I shrugged, "who knows, it could be his calling."

"Are you joking?" Renato mocked, "what money is in porn? I watch porn every day and I've never paid for it."

"True," I nodded. "I suppose you'd need a niche to make any money."

"A what?"

"A niche, I mean, he'd need to make something very specific, you know, like… specialised."

"Yeah… but what hasn't been done in porn?" Renato asked….

"What about balcony porn," I threw out, "your house has a balcony."

"Fuck off man," laughed Renato, "if balcony porn doesn't already exist, Ireland isn't the place to start."

"True… a new porn niche… that is a hard one alright."

"My friend is crazy," said Renato, "he needs help… nearly everyone's addicted to porn these days but he watches a lot man, *a lot*."

"I'm lucky," I said, "when our house finally got a computer and the internet, my mam told us that she had it set up so that if we ever went on a porn site the Gardai would be informed and arrive at our house."

"Really!" Renato laughed.

"Yeah well, call me naive but I believed her for years, I was terrified of looking at porn on the house computer, there used to be the odd bit of porn on TV, things like *Eurotrash*."

"I remember," smiled Renato, "we had *Eurotrash* in Brazil, I used to watch it when I was like 10."

"Exactly, but, I don't think I watched porn online until I was 20."

"*20!* Fuck's sake man, really?"

"Yeah," I laughed, "but it was good, and even at 20 I rarely used it, then, when I started getting more into it, I don't know… I found it harder to get by without it, you know? Like my imagination used to be all I needed, I used to imagine mad things, and always good enough to get the job done, but after a year or two of watching porn it felt like my imagination wasn't working anymore, like my brain got too lazy, so after that I started limiting myself, and I still limit myself, to watching it about once or twice a month."

"Yeah," Renato shook his head, "I don't think I could masturbate without porn."

"Yeah, it's mad, I escaped a porn addiction because I was stupid enough to believe my mam, but I'm grateful for it now."

"Yeah," nodded Renato, "and it will get worse, every kid has access to porn now, and even for my friend to see a therapist, in Brazil, that would never happen 5 or 10 years ago, now it's normal."

"Yeah... but I'm glad therapy's become more common."

"Yes," nodded Renato. "But kids today are fucked, once they get their first smartphone or iPad they might as well start saving money for therapy down the line."

We took a few sips in silence, and I looked towards Mr Stretch who was still stretching away when Renato asked:

"Did you see the Pope when he visited?"

"No," I replied, "it wouldn't be my cup of tea... Did you?"

"No, I told my mother I did, haha, I had to send her a photo I found on Google. I wanted to go but I was busy man. It was a good day for deliveries."

"I didn't think you were religious," I said as coolly as I could, for despite knowing Renato for little over 2 years I felt very close to him, for I enjoyed his company without finding my own behaviour much altered by it, and I believe he felt similar, for we often referred to each other as my Irish or Brazilian brother.

"I'm not Catholic," he said. "And I don't follow the Pope, but I believe in something man, not the Church I guess, but most of us are raised Christian in Brazil. I don't know, but I think I believe there's some God, afterlife and purpose. And you, let me guess, ATHIEST?"

"I guess so," I shook my head.

"Pssssdt," he hissed. I continued:

"I used to be religious, then atheist, then spiritual, and now I guess I'm a sort of spiritual atheist, but I don't believe in a god, in no way, shape or form, I don't." I opened another can and took a cool sip, and looked towards Mr Stretch in the hopes of changing the subject when Renato asked:

"So how do explain all this then?"

"I don't. I mean, I can't. I can't explain any of it, I can't explain anything, and even when I think I can it never seems to do any good..." I sighed, "I often feel like Cassandra when it comes to these things."

"Who?" Renato asked.

"Nevermind," I said, "it's from an old Greek myth, sure even the ancient Greeks tried to explain all this without pointing to god, there's an ancient Roman book called *The Nature of Things* by Lucretius, in many ways it reads like the original *Origin of Species* in that it's a solid attempt to explain everything without grasping at gods. It's funny, but I guess the nature of things is that things don't change, because we're still grasping at straws."

"So you think life and everything in it is just one big coincidence?" Renato laughed, and my brain alighted as his comment set up a runway for a favourite argument of mine to take off, and his laughter fired-up my worst self like rocket fuel. So I answered him, with increasing energy; "Yes man, and I can prove it to you." Taking a long gulp of courage I shuffled up on my knees, reached down and grabbed a euro from my right pocket. I showed it to Renato and explained:

"In English we call a coin toss 'heads' or 'tails.'"

"I got it," he said.

"Good, well, it's like this, before I toss the coin, can you tell me, with 100% accuracy, whether it'll land heads or tails, this side or that?"

"No," said Renato.

"No, and why not?"

Renato drank his beer and shook his head—"because I cannot tell the future," he said.

"Exactly," I said. "Now, here's the point," and here I tossed the coin, caught it, and covered the result with my left hand:

"The coin's been flipped right?" He nodded, "so, did it land 'heads' or 'tails'?"

"I don't know man, I can't know for sure until I see it."

"Exactly" I continued, "so we don't know the result of the flip until I move my hand, and so we're both ignorant, right?" He nodded, and I showed us the result.

"So it's landed 'heads,'" I said, "now, here's the difference between an atheist and someone who believes in god… a catholic looks at the world around them and, based and what they see, they decide that the way things are now must have been an inevitability from the start, that it was simply inevitable that the Earth would be Earth and humans would be humans and life would exist as we know it, understand? So a catholic takes the result of the present coin toss and projects backwards that this result was inevitable, which is literally backwards-logic, whereas I see the world around me and I believe that there was nothing inevitable about any of it. The fact that we now know the results to be 'heads' does not mean that 'heads' was fated to be the result, and that it could just have easily been 'tails'.

"In other words, if all of time were to begin again, then we probably wouldn't be here, perhaps the dinosaurs would still be reigning supreme, You see? Perhaps the coin would have landed differently…. But what I'm trying to say is this—you cannot use the world around you as evidence for god because the world around you wasn't an inevitability, it *was* just chance, and if you don't believe me then just try to predict the next coin toss." So, still on my knees, looking at him intently and with the coin ready, I dared him to predict the next toss, instead, he said: "Ahhh come on man, it's different," with a shake of his head.

"How?"

"A coin toss is meaningless, but we're here man, living, alive, thinking, feeling, living. We're *here*, you can't tell me we're not here or that it means nothing."

"But we are here and it does mean nothing," I said. "I know it's hard, but think of it this way, we know we're here *only because* we're here. But that doesn't mean he *had* to be here, and it says nothing as to why we're here, we're simply here, the coin landed in such a way that we've been made conscious of the result, but if we weren't here, and there's countless planets where we're not by the way—not to mention 4 billion years of the past and the billions of years to come—then we wouldn't have been conscious of the result, and that's life as far as I can make it."

"So there's no purpose, no meaning," Renato said, and I started to feel some sad weight in his words.

"No," I said, "that's the crisis point we reach, we realise there's no meaning, no purpose, and the thought terrifies us for a moment, but you have to learn to see the other side too, there's no meaning to life, there's no purpose in living, and so life is, whether you choose to see it this way or not; one never-ending-Sunday. It's a day off my friend. We have no worldly obligations, no divine purpose, no inherent meaning or grand destiny to follow. We're simply here until we're not, and so we should learn to enjoy ourselves. If there's any meaning to life it's to enjoy it, and to clean up after us so that others, now and future, can also enjoy it, because what else could you ask for? What else *would* you ask for?" Renato shrugged.

"But," I continued, "the difficult thing is that, for most of us, I think enjoying life comes naturally, but, for those of us who have been misguided, by religion to say the least" I nudged, "we have to re-learn how to enjoy life. It becomes something like a required taste, or maybe even a skill or muscle to be developed, but religion only gets you so far, because either you'll always suffer from doubts, or instead, you will have to give yourself up to your own ignorance and carry on with a blind faith, but, and I really believe this, the majority of all religions, especially those in the 'West,' cripple our ability to enjoy and understand life. For one, they all claim that we're above other animals, which is absolute nonsense. 2nd, historically, if not so much recently, they all put women and homosexuals down and try to keep them down, and last and most stupidly of all—they divide us! They divide us internally with their ideas about 'right' and 'wrong,' 'good' and 'evil,' and teaching us from the time were kids to feel guilty and ashamed of whatever 'sinful' thoughts enter our heads from heaven knowns where, then they divide us externally by saying that WE know best and everyone who isn't US is going to hell.

"Christianity, Judaism and all the Muslim sects are nothing but nonsense, even worse than believing the earth is flat—because the earth couldn't care less what you make of it, the earth doesn't change its rules, shape or trajectory based on our thoughts, but the way you think about other people shapes other people, because we're malleable, understand? I am who I am partly because of how my parents raised me and how others have treated me, and so 'god' distorts how we see ourselves and how we act around others, and that shapes the world we live in—completely."

"Ahh fuck off man, you've smoked too much!" Renato said, in a lighter tone at least, and we both vented out a little with frustrated laughter, but, with some lingering weight Renato continued:

"So, you don't believe in heaven then, no afterlife, nada."

"No," I said, "nada, but, and here's the really crazy part, the reason why there cannot be a heaven is because, as individuals, we don't really exist. So there cannot be a heaven for individual souls when individuality is a myth."

Renato shook his perplexed head dismissively:

"How can you say individuals don't exist, what are we then?"

"Look man, we are never, *never* only an individual. Nobody lives independently from the world they live in. It's impossible, because we're a part of this world, we're completely ingrained in it, and we maintain an invisible umbilical cord with the world from which we are forever taking in water, oxygen and food, and if you separate yourself from the world you die. So, physically, we're not individuals, at least in the sense that we cannot be disconnected from this world. Next, think of babies. If our mothers were out on a walk, gave birth to us, left us by the road and kept on walking we'd be dead, unless we were picked up by someone else. So a baby has to be part of some kind of a family to make it into adulthood, and that family will, at least to some degree, make the adult that that baby becomes.

"Now, psychologically, we feel ourselves to be individuals, but how many of our actions can we truly claim are individual? I mean, I had no choice over my gender, my nationality, my metabolism, my height, my first language, my school, my family, my sexual preferences, and, if you were to remove or change all of that, who would I be? Even this distinction we make between who we are on the inside and what's going on on the outside is only a difference of perception. We perceive the world from within our bodies, but we really are a part of our environment, and not a separate self-determining part, but a living connected part. So much of the sciences, physical *and* social, are spent researching and showing us how we are shaped by our environment, and so much of art and architecture shows us that our environment can also be shaped by us. But we're never brought up to feel this connection. So if you identify yourself by, say, your brain within in your body, then of course you will fear death, for death will be the end of your brain as a living organ, but if you come to identify yourself as a part of the world, in which you are so connected, then death becomes a small thing.

"And the philosophers will forever be looking within, and the cosmologists will forever be looking out, but as long as they are asking 'who am I' they will never be able to find an answer—because 'I' doesn't exist, or rather, it's like—"

"Hahaa! What's up!" crashed Ciaran our not-long-enough-awaited 3rd party, coming in on his bike and probably saving Renato from me and saving me from myself.

"What's the craic?" He asked.

"Nothing man," Renato replied, "just this guy talking crazy."

"DAMO the INSANO," Ciaran shouted.

"Yeah man," I smiled, "what's the craic?"

We got into another round of fist-bump introductions as Ciaran settled himself. I took a sip and shook off what remained of my last rant and felt instead the new air that Ciaran's presence brought. Here was a different kind of friend: I enjoyed Ciaran's company precisely because it *did* have an effect on me. Ciaran was born of Irish parents in a rough part of Algiers and spent most of his life there before taking advantage of his right to an Irish passport. His father, he once told me, had knocked up his mother, and together they fled as far as possible before his father's original wife found out as hers was an IRA-proud, country-catholic family, and god knows what they would have done if they ever caught up with his father.

Both Renato and Ciaran grew up in far rougher settings than mine, and in knowing them I often felt I was learning something of my parents, aunts and uncles. Their tales of being robbed, beaten, attacked and shot at, of driving drunk and bribing the police, of random fights with gangs on the streets, filled me with a voyeuristic light-headedness, and Carian's slightly more racist and sexist humour gave me a degree of flexibility and abandon that I enjoyed in his company while hypocritically condemning behind his back. Hanging out with Ciaran was, for me, like taking too many shots of tequila, except I not only ended up physically hungover, but morally hungover too. A small price to pay though, for he 'alienated me from myself' as Carl Jung once put it.

"Say, what's that weirdo doing," said Ciaran pointing towards Mr Stretch and snapping me out of my head.

"He's been stretching and exercising like that since I got here," I said.

"What a looney," Ciaran laughed. "HEY LOONEY! WHAT ARE YOU DOING?" Ciaran shouted towards him, but Mr Stretch, either too far to hear or thinking better of responding, kept up his energetic movements. Startled by Ciaran drawing attention to us I got up.

"I'm going for a piss," I said.

Streeeeetch. Stretch. Stretch. Stretch. Stretch. Stretch. Stretch. Stretch.

I hopped on my bike and flew down past the Monument and into the undergrowth where, while pissing, I heard a strange noise. I looked to my left, expecting to see a squirrel, but was startled instead to see a rat run down a tree and disappear into the grass. I smiled and thanked the rat as it gave me something amusing to report back. Getting on my bike I again flew past Mr Stretch.

"Man, I just saw this big fucking rat running down the tree next to me while I was taking a piss," I cycled in—knocking Renato and Ciaran's conversation off the grass.

"Fuck man, how big was the rat?" Renato asked.

"I don't know, like this big," I said, indicating about a foot.

"That's tiny," laughed Ciaran.

"Yeah" cracked Renato. "Rats in São Paulo grow like dogs."

"In Algiers they grow to this" said Ciaran, indicating about a metre. I dropped my bike, sat, and took up my beer as my friends continued invoking imaginary rats capable of eating mine in one gulp. Having enough I grabbed my bag and determined to roll up a bit of hash.

"Where'd you get that?" Ciaran asked. I nodded towards Renato.

"My friend," said Renato, "takes it through the airport from Spain, up his ass," he laughed as the hash stuck stubbornly to my fingers and the paper I was trying to roll.

"ASS-HASH," slapped Ciaran, "classic, does it smell like ass, Damo?" He asked me.

"It smells ok to me," I said, wiping my sweaty fingers on my shorts.

"Fair enough," said Ciaran, "sure probably half the drugs in Dublin came here through somebody's ass."

"Wouldn't be the worst job in the world," I said.

Streeeeeetch. Stretch. Stretch. Stretch. Stretch. Stretch. Stretch.

"Ass-hash, that reminds me," said Ciaran, "did I ever tell you the one about my mate and the two shits?"

"No" we laughed, "go on."

"Oh, wait to you hear this one," said Ciaran, already starting to chuckle as the story came back to him.

"So my mate," he began, "was out dancing in some club when this bird knocks into him and spills her sickly-sweet cocktail all over his brand new shirt, fucking *ruins* his shirt, right, and now he stinks like a drunk candy-shop, but she apologises again and again and buys him a drink and so they begin hitting it off. After a bit of dancing and that she invites him back to hers, so he goes back to her place, gets lucky, bang, and in the morning he wakes up, only now she's gone and there's no sign of her. So he's in her house and he's sobering up, and he's trying to find his clothes but they're missing. He sees his keys, phone and shoes left by the bed, but all his clothes are gone."

"Fuck," said Renato.

"Yeah man, so he's naked, in this one's house, and even his socks and jocks are gone, and he has to get back home, so he figures that this bird must have run out of the house with all his clothes to leave him having to go home naked."

"Why would anyone do that?" I interrupted.

"Aw man, this was in college, and in student accommodation it was a weekly occurrence for us – the naked walk of shame," answered Ciaran. "Anyway, so he thinks—'well, fuck her, I'm going to get my revenge.' So he takes a shower, and then he goes and takes a shit in her bathroom sink."

"No," I said, a smile spreading across my face as the mental image formed in my head.

"Yes," continued Ciaran, "then he goes and takes another shit in her kitchen sink!"

"Fuuuuck." Me and Renato erupted in laughter.

"The two-shits man!" Ciaran said when we had settled down, tears in our eyes.

"But wait, it gets worse. So he wipes himself off, grabs one of her towels, wraps it around his waist, and makes for the exit, only he opens the door to leave… and she's standing outside about to go into the house."

"Fuck."

"And… in her hands…" struggled Ciaran, "were my mates clothes in a bag, she felt so bad about ruining his new shirt that she went and got his clothes dry-cleaned for him." And with that he had us knocked and rolling on the grass in stiches. When Renato could breathe he asked:

"Then what happened?"

"Man…" Ciaran wiped his face, his body still convulsing, "he grabbed the bag, said 'thank you very much,' and then he ran for it, naked anyway, and still carrying her towel around his waist." We laid on our backs in abandoned laughter as the scene played out in our minds.

Streeeeeeetch. Stretch. Stretch. Stretch. Stretch. Stretch. Stretch. Stretch.

As we came back around from our 10-count knockout, feeling the pain from our laughed-out ribs, I decided to throw out my own funny shitty story when Ciaran shouted:

"FRONTFLIP!" It seemed Mr Stretch was finished stretching. What followed was a series of frontflips, cartwheels and handstands.

"He's gotta do a backflip," Renato said, and my heart began to pound.

"DO A BACKFLIP!" Ciaran shouted. But, thank god, Mr Stretch took no notice. Still, in less than two minutes he did do a backflip, several of them.

"What a weirdo," said Ciaran, turning back to face us. "Hey, I got another shit story for you Damo."

"Look," Renato interrupted. The three of us looked back towards Mr Stretch as a small crowd of even smaller kids flocked over to him. From the distance we could tell they were talking to Mr Stretch, who began showing the kids a couple of his stretches and to demonstrate a cartwheel for them, he then moved away from the kids and continued doing different gymnastic routines as the kids began doing his stretches and trying to mimic his cartwheels.

"Haha," slapped Ciaran, "he hasn't picked up any chicks, just a gang of kids, what a loser." I sipped my beer and said nothing, feeling ashamed of myself, wondering why I had joined in in mocking Mr Stretch. Here we were, sharing this public space, us on our ass, sipping beer and smoking joints and talking shit, and here, too, oblivious to our stares, jokes and shouting, was Mr Stretch, inspiring a group of children to try his gymnastics out for themselves, and I felt depressed. I felt we were put in our place by a group of kids, and I was struck by how much better children are than us. They don't judge, they don't joke, but they see someone having fun and doing something different and they not only *want* to join in, they *do* join in.

Why do we grow 'up' at all
when when it's just to become stunted and small?

I went home that day with my tail between my legs, searching, I guess, and not for the first time, for a new way to be brave, for I understood then how much I wished I was Mr Stretch, or how much I wished I could rewind my brain to that of a child's. I felt so bummed out about it that when I got home I started to roll myself another spliff to cheer myself up; my intention being to lie on my bed and listen to an Ann Briggs or John Martyn album, only, as I was rolling my spliff and thinking of those kids it hit me—*aren't all recreational drugs an attempt to return to childhood?* The idea was so obvious that I couldn't finish my spliff, but instead I poked and prodded this thought out on my diary, and the more I did so the more sense it all made.

Alcohol – the more you drink the more your body functions like a baby's. You also lose your inhibitions and become less self-conscious, much like a child.

Social lubricant. Helping adults to drop our masks of insecurities and our hang-ups and just get on with getting to know the people next to us.

Weed – everything feels fresh, vibrant and new again. Everyday objects become fascinating. The world loses it's dead dust of experience and everything shines like new.

Acid and mushrooms – a cerebral rebirth, bringing us back to our earliest childhood, when the world was so new it was positively strange. Boundaries between things disappear so that all we know is that, on a certain level, everything is connected, and everything is spectacular.

Cocaine – cocaine is to an adult what a sugar-rush, caffeine or a victory is to a child. An inflation of ego, of confidence, a bubbling over of raw energy.

Heroin – from what I've read heroin is a return to the cradle, to the arms of your most beloved parent figure, a 'warm gun.' A return to the sense of security childhood brings as we return to a time when we were completely helpless, (and so when we received the most help).

I was so dumbstruck by this idea that I sat for an hour just thinking—is this all I am: An adult wishing to return to childhood? The idea in itself was not so bad, I've lost track of the amount of philosophers, writers and artists who have made a similar claim, but then, is there no better path to take than drugs? Is that really such a stretch?

Part 2

Tightrope Thursday

Martin sat in a pub with a pint in hand. He checked his watch—12:30. He assumed his workmates would join him for a drink as it was lunchtime on Halloween and very little work was being done, but now he was starting to fear that he would be spending his lunch alone. He sighed and took out his diary to help him kill the time:

[lunchtime—pub, poem?—'liquid lunch'?]
Halloween liquid lunch in The Black Sheep
Waiting on workmates with 4 empty seats
And I'm reminded that it's me…
I've become the 'man with the plan,'
the organiser of pints and nights that spiral out of hand,
and I'm left to wonder if I'm happy with who I am?

My workmates aren't here, perhaps they're getting work done,
a sneaky one on your own is less fun,
but 'nobody' tells no tales,
and my costume hides red eyes and lets me take sail,
And anyway, it stops my own company from growing stale.

Throwing beer into an empty stomach, I feel stupid and left out
But in an hour I'll be back to teaching,
—Good! For I reflect well off of others, but badly off myself

Don't we all?
I drink my pint and feel 2 feet tall.

Martin reread his poem, took a sip of his craft beer that somehow tasted like a condom, sighed, and looked back to the entry before it:

> *I've taken to doing twirls as I'm walking to and from work. Just a single twirl as I'm walking. At first I found I could only do it when I thought nobody's around, but I'm getting better at doing them as the thought occurs, because I still find it very difficult to look stupid and odd, but I imagine it gets easier the more you do it, and we have no idea the level of autonomy we really have until we put it to the test. I guess autonomy's like a muscle. Going vegan has been a good workout for my autonomy. I don't think my parents have forgiven me yet. Ah well...*

Suddenly Martin was saved by three of his workmates coming into the bar: Ian, Des and Frankie, as they brought Martin's good mood back to him. His face now beaming, Martin closed his diary and put it back in his bag, and in a short time they were all sitting together with a drink and in high spirits, and Martin was able to let go of his own gloomy mirror. Being Halloween, they were dressed up as follows: Martin was in a Spiderman hoodie that could be zipped up to cover the face completely, creating the bulk of a costume when zipped-up fully, but beneath the waist no effort was made as he wore a pair of badly ripped black denim jeans and clunky black school-boy shoes.

Frankie was dressed as the builder from The Village People's YMCA, with a white t-shirt, sunglasses, blue jeans and builder's hat; a costume that complimented his new bushy moustache, and, all-in-all, he looked the part. Ian was 'dressed' as a generic law enforcer. His costume consisted of a leather jacket, a fake gun and a pin-on badge he got from a pound shop the day before, and Des was partly mummified in toilet paper. None of them, bar maybe Frankie, would have won 3rd prize in a costume party of five.

"Cheers anyway," said Martin as he raised his glass.

"Cheers," they drank.

"Thanks for waiting for me, jackasses," said Tom as he walked in and towards them.

"Feck off Tom," said Ian, throwing his hands in the air as if he were tossing Tom's words back at him, "I saw you chatting to a group of students long after the bell."

"Excuse me for being so professional," said Tom. Martin laughed; "The only reason your classes run over is because you start them so late."

"Plus," added Frankie, "a professional would have dressed up for Halloween."

"Yeah bru, you should be out buying a costume," said Des.

"I don't need a costume ye bastards, I'm scarier than all of yas without one." Tom, who looked something like a thawed-out Viking at the best of times, made no effort, wasting his 6 feet 3 inches of height, long hair and scraggly beard. Martin, who had worked in the school for nearly as long as Tom, had already known that his friend would suit himself, that he wouldn't dress up, and that there was little point in waiting for a man who ran on his own time at the expense of everyone else's. "Come on Tom, get a pint and stop moaning."

"I'll have a pint if you're going up," said Des.

"I'm not getting into rounds! I've only time for one anyway," said Tom on his way to the bar.

"I'll get you back after work bru, don't be such a tight cunt."

"How's the mummy room going?" Martin asked Des, "I see you got your costume out of it."

"Yeah, but it's brutal, it takes less than 2 minutes to wrap up a couple of students and take a photo, so I'm killing the rest of it just watching *Simpsons* Halloween episodes, and the last group of students were proper shits, they just sat there looking at me, and one student actually said: 'Teacher, what's this? I'm not dressing up in toilet paper, I'm here to learn English,' so I told them 'we are learning English! Today we're learning prepositions! Now the toilet paper goes *over* your head, *under* your legs, *around* your arms, *on* your body and, when you need the toilet, *up* your ass! Like that I had them all wrapped up in 5 minutes." Ian cracked up:

"Aw man, I'm stuck doing Halloween charades, I probably had the same group before you, coming in looking at me as if they were already pissed off, and one of them asking 'what English are we learning?' I just said we're learning action verbs and wrote some on the board as they did the charades. Another group came in like 'Ooo Ooo we're not doing charades, this is kids' stuff.' I told them 'if you don't like the activity you can leave,' fuck that shit."

Martin let the conversation breeze through him as he started to roll a hash joint. He felt good that his workmates had come in the end, and the steam they were letting off was warming him up better than any alcohol could. He knew that each of them, in their classrooms, were excellent teachers. But he also knew that the therapy-like complaining that often happened at lunch was needed to keep them sane back in their classes. Instead, his mind was on the 10 grams of hash he had bought from one of his students. 'How can these Brazilians buy and sell weed cheaper than us?' He was that way lost in his thoughts when Frankie noticed what he was doing.

"Martin, for fuck's sake," said Frankie.

"It's grand man, hash doesn't smell until you burn it, and I'll have my face zipped up for the rest of the afternoon, and sure, it's not like we're doing any real teaching today." Frankie laughed and shook his head, "You're brazen," he said as Martin finished packing in the top of the joint and made a move to go out the back. He was followed by Tom and Ian like the cat that's got the vegan cream.

"He's a mad cunt" Frankie said to Des.

"Yeah bru, let's get another pint in, that fucker didn't get me one, what a cunt."

Martin, Ian and Tom stood out the back passing the joint, Ian and Tom taking weak puffs to minimise the risk of red eyes.

"Seems alright," said Martin, looking at the joint as if reading a descriptive label.

"So, do you have everything ready for tomorrow" Tom asked him.

"Yeah, I have the ring, I've booked us in for a nice dinner in a fancy restaurant, I've got some craft beers hidden away to celebrate. It's not as epic a plan as I wanted, but it should be good, he wouldn't want a spectacle made of it anyway," Martin replied.

"Well good luck man," said Ian, "Let us know how you get on."

"Definitely." The lads finished their wee smoke, with Martin putting it out and throwing the butt into a bin a few feet down.

"Most of the groups have been alright," Frankie was saying to Des, "They get excited enough just being here for Halloween."

"Well it's an Irish holiday," said Tom, his words landing ahead of him as he approached the table, "they should be excited."

"It's a load of shite," said Martin sitting down, "What's Halloween? After you're too old for trick or treating or acting the bollax around bonfires it's just a bunch of messy parties and kids throwing fireworks into shops. I used to work in a dodgy little shop and Halloween was a nightmare, plus my grandfather died on Halloween, and I even had a phone robbed on me on Halloween, Halloween's shit craic."

"Yeah," said Ian, "I hate Halloween, I hate drunks in masks, it makes them feel brave, like 'Ooo I'm wearing a mask, you don't know who I am, so I'm going to be a PRICK," he said, dropping the 'prick' as if it were a brick—aimed towards heads he wished to split.

"So you're not going out tonight then?" Frankie laughed.

"No mate, I'm tempted, of course I am, but NoNo! I've never had a good night on Halloween, NEVER, just like Martie here. I've always ended up getting kicked out of places because some drunk prick with a mask starts on me."

"Fair enough," said Martin. "Sure I'm only going out for a few hours myself, I don't want to wreck myself before tomorrow," he said, trying to convince himself more than his friends. This night he had to balance going out and making sure that he would be misery-free and in good spirits for tomorrow.

"Good man Martie," said Frankie, "so you're all set then?"

"Yeah man, think so," he said sipping his beer.

"How did you decide who has to propose and that?" Des asked.

"Well, I can't speak for every same-sex couple, but in our case it's an easy one, he believes in marriage and I don't."

"Jesus," Frankie laughed.

"So why get married if you don't believe in it, TELL ME THAT, MARTIN?" Ian asked.

Martin shrugged, "Well, we're 8 years together tomorrow, I love him, and I don't see myself loving anyone else. It will make him happy and that's good enough for me."

"8 years" whistled Des, "and how'd you meet?"

"Well…," Martin thought how to answer, "it was at a kind of party with my sister… And in the smoking area I got to sharing a joint with this guy called John Paul, and, I don't know how to describe it accept at some point I felt, like, I realised, 'hey, I could kiss this guy!' And talking to John I couldn't get the idea out of my head that I *could* kiss him and he would let me, and he knew it too, because I completely zoned out to what he was saying until suddenly he was waving at me. When I came back to reality he smiled and asked if I wanted to kiss him. Well" Martin shrugged, "I was so nervous that I burst out laughing, and John laughed, and when we settled down that was it. He bought me a drink, we ended up sharing the rest of the night together, and we woke up wanting to share our lives together. It felt right. And to top it off that was the first night I ever spent a man."

"Serious!" Des asked.

"Yeah," continued Martin, smiling into his drink, "I knew I was bi, but I guess I was happy enough not acting on it, you know, thinking I'd go in for a less complicated life, but, to borrow from a Christy Moore song, 'thoughts which I didn't invite' hit me hard that night, and my life with John has been the least complicated it's ever been."

"Fuck," said Frankie, "I didn't know you were the romantic type, but is it not weird to be getting married if you don't believe in it?" He laughed.

"Yeah, well," Martin shrugged, "to be clear, I hate pretty much everything tied to the Catholic church, humanist weddings included. I just don't see why something as personal as love needs to be made so public. My cousin had a humanist wedding where they mixed two big jars of sand together and stupid things like that, now they're stuck with a big jar of sand in their house that they can't get rid of, I mean, who wants that lying around their house? But sure, if it will make him happy, what better reason is there? Even if I don't get it, there's plenty about me that John doesn't get but he goes along with anyway. Plus, I think if we're married we can get some tax breaks, so that would be sweet."

"Who's changing their name?" Des asked.

"No one," Martin replied.

"Did you vote in the same-sex vote?" Tom asked.

"Yeah man, of course, I'm all for choice. Actually, one of our worst fights came during the same-sex vote when I said how much I wish we could vote to legalise weed first, John flipped a bit, so I think he's given up on the idea that I would ever want to marry, so tomorrow should be a good." Martin finished and reached for his beer.

"Well, good luck bru," said Des raising his glass and clinking his, which set them all clinking. "Will you be dropping the knee?" Frankie asked.

"No harm I guess, he's a bit more traditional than I am, and worst case scenario it'll probably give him a laugh." Martin got up and stood with a stupid grin on his face, feeling the effects of a single pint like only he could, and thinking fondly of the party only a few hours away he said: "Drop the knee, give the ring, then go down and make him sing" and with that he started making his way to the toilet and leaving his friends laughing. After his piss he studied his eyes in the mirror to check their condition, 'not too bad' he thought. He slapped his face three times playfully and headed back to the group as they were finishing off their pints. Martin finished his and they headed back to school, light as toilet paper.

Pre-Drinks Before Free Drinks

After 2 and a half hours of more half-arsed Halloween activities Mary, their manager, called it quits and gave permission for the remaining handful of students to go home. Most of the teachers were packing up and heading off while Tom headed to the top-floor toilet to roll a joint. In the staff room Martin, Frankie and Des were hanging around waiting on Tom and trying to decide on their first pub. They had to get to The Liffey Bar by around half 6 where they would meet Mary along with some of the admin staff and other teachers for a free round or two.

"I say we go to Cassidy's," said Frankie, "they have a pizza and pint deal there, we need soakage."

"Cool, let's go Bru," said Des, "I hate hanging here after work—I'm out!"

"Good luck guys, enjoy yeah," said Ian coming in from the toilet, and they all said goodbye solemnly as they lost a drinking buddy before the first round.

"See you man," said Martin, "Alright, I'm going to wait for Tom, you guys head off and we'll meet you there."

"Alright bru, let's go," said Des. The 2 of them left as Martin sat down and took out his diary to kill some time:

> *Tightrope Thursday, staff room:*
>
> *Going to Cassidy's with the lads*
> *With an engagement ring and a bag of hash*
>
> *Just don't burn, just don't crash.*
>
> *But first I wait for Tom*
> *How does he always take so long*
> *Hope he's rolling something strong...*

He sat over the 6 lines for a minute when Tom burst in.

"Where's the lads?" He asked.

"On the way to Cassidy's Butch, figured we'd smoke one and follow them down."

"Is Ian gone with them?"

"No man, he's gone home."

"Fair enough," said Tom. Martin smiled, "Let's go Tom, I've been waiting on you for ages."

"Yeah yeah ya jackass, just give me a few more minutes." Tom organised his bag and locker while Martin turned to the computer and stuck on an old song, *My Gal's Pussy,* and leaned back on his chair with his hands behind his head.

"What are you listening to?" Tom asked.

"It's catchy," said Martin, "and just wait for the lyrics, a little reminder that we're as filthy now as we were back in the 1930s."

By the time Tom was ready and the two of them were leaving they were in stitches, and in 5 minutes they started walking down their usual lane to share Tom's smoke.

"So Sean didn't cop you had one earlier?" Tom asked.

"No sure, I had the hoodie zipped up for a while, although it was stuffy," they passed the joint back and forth for a while before Martin threw out his daily icebreaker:

"My warmer for the class today was—if you could have access to any fictional technology, what would it be?"

"What does that have to do with Halloween?" Tom asked.

"Ah I get so sick of this Halloween business, just answer the question."

"Well," said Tom, "easy answer—a teleportation machine."

"That would be terrible," said Martin.

"Why? If I had a teleportation machine I could sleep in for longer, get more stuff done, never be late for work."

"You'd still find a way to be late for work. And think about it, when North America started coming out with freeways and motorways and all that, didn't a load of small towns lose all their business from commuters? Well, imagine if you could teleport wherever you wanted to go, then eventually all the small coffee shops, pubs, cool little hangouts, they'd all be gone. We'd only be left with the likes of McDonalds, Wetherspoons and Starbucks. We'd all be teleporting and losing the world around us, the places and spaces between destinations, the world of serendipity."

"Yeah, maybe," said Tom, "But come on, even if it was just set up from my house to the school I'd be happy. Who wouldn't want that?"

"Suppose… but you'd probably get fat."

"Well, what would you want?"

"I'm still trying to figure it out."

"Well, come on, let's finish this smoke and join the lads," Tom said, taking a third drag. "How long are you staying out till anyway?" Tom asked.

"I'll say I'll probably head around 8, maybe half 8 at a push."

"Fair enough, you sure I can't twist your arm to stay to stay till 10?"

"Normally man, but you know I got to be fresh for tomorrow, plus I'm a lightweight."

"That's true, you really cannot drink."

"I'm a cheap date," Martin smiled, taking the last drag.

They headed to Cassidy's where Martin bought himself and Tom a round as they sat down with Frankie and Des on a bench just outside the front. Des and Frankie were grinning from ear to ear, and there was the unmistakable feeling of a dirty joke or a freshly cut secret hanging in the air.

"What are you clowns smiling at?" Tom asked.

"This," said Frankie as he handed Tom a small plastic bag half-filled with white powder. Tom eyed it carefully under the table. "Coke?" He asked.

"Yeah think so," said Frankie. "You remember Marcus who came from your class?"

"Yeah, wait, which Marcus, skinny Marcus?"

"No man, sound Marcus, the one who works as a bouncer in Dicey's."

"Oh, *that* Marcus, he gave you *this*?"

"I said it to him once that if he ever patted someone down and found something good to pass it onto me, well, I said it in a 'I'm joking but I'm serious' kind of way" Frankie said with a building laugh, "and today, before we finished, he handed me this little baggie yee**oOO**W**!**"

"You're joking," said Tom.

"No joke mate, we've taken a bit 10 minutes ago and it's good, haha, feeling it."

"I'll be back so," said Tom, getting up for the bathroom, "you joining Martin?"

"No man, I'll stick to spliffs and pints," he replied, feeling his tightrope beginning to wobble.

"Good man," said Tom while heading off.

"Bru, what a legend," said Des, "the best a student's ever given me was a pair of socks."

"In my first month in the school one of my students gave me a weed brigadeiro," said Martin.

"Fuck bru, did you eat it in the class?"

"Yeah, towards the last half-hour anyway, but really, he must have overcooked the THC, it did nothing."

"So do all your students know you smoke?" Des asked.

"Not anymore, I had a really sound class at the time, I keep it to myself now… so, do you think there'll be many students in The Liffey Bar tonight?"

"I fucking hope so," said Frankie, "I'm not planning on going home."

"Are you chasing tail too man?" Martin asked Des.

"Always bru, always, just not anyone from my class again." Martin smiled, remembering the story. "Didn't you say she apologised for ratting you out?" He asked.

"Bru, so what. What's the point of her apologising? I've already received a formal warning and I could be fired. If I see her tonight I'm going to trip her up on the dance floor and dance on her head."

"Who are you going to trip?" Tom asked sitting down and passing the bag back under the table.

"That fucking student who ratted me out to Sean in work. What happened was we bumped into each other on a night out, had a good night, slept together, bam, I hear nothing from her after that, everything's sweet in the class as if nothing happened, then 2 weeks later I go on a date with another one from the class, this one then goes and tells everyone that she's got a date with me behind my back, then the first chick I slept with rats me out to Sean; telling him I'm sleeping around with every good-looking student that steps into the place, cunts bru," said Des, riling himself up. Everyone laughed and Tom slapped Des on the back, calling him the Tinder-Teacher. The whole table started sharing their student war stories when Frankie cut in:

"Let's order some pizza,"

They eyed up the chalk board and took turns ordering at the bar.

"So" asked Des, "will you be having or adopting any sprogs after your married?"

"It's tempting," said Martin. "Adopt a couple of kids and become a stay at home dad, that would be living the dream in my book."

"I could picture you as a housewife," laughed Tom.

"Well," mumbled Martin. "I wouldn't mind staying at home and cooking, cleaning and minding the kids, and writing man. My own mam wasn't a 'stay at home mother' because she was lazy or unskilled, she was a 'stay at home mother' because she was smart enough to work from home, and if my writing ever takes off that's where you'll find me—only, I hate to disappoint you, but I won't be dressed as a housewife, thanks very much, househusband suits me fine, I had my night in drag, and I can tell you sincerely that it's not for me… Dressing like a woman did nothing for me but give me sore eyes, sore feet, and what felt like half a wig's worth of hair down my mouth. And eye-liner man, that stuff gunks to you all the next day and left me in work having to tell every customer that 'yes, I happen to have 2 very precisely given black eyes,' … no thanks."

"What had you dressing in drag … just for the craic?" Frankie asked.

"It was for an anthropology assignment. Hang with a group of people, join in whatever they're doing, read a bunch of bullshit and then write about it. It was an eye-opener, because I spent a night with a group of transvestites, and my sister, probably trying to help me, told them out of nowhere that I was her little brother and a transvestite finally coming out, and so this group of guys in drag decide to take me under their wing and they all start talking to me and sharing their horror stories with me—about how one lost his wife and the respect of his two adult daughters when they found out, about how one hasn't talked to his parents in 18 years, about how one was bullied at work for daring to dress in drag at a Halloween party, how another lost his best friend and mentor over suicide—and I had all these stories under false-pretences and I felt like an utter scumbag. To make it worse, when I started doing my academic reading to get those mandatory references all I could find, across all my anthropological, sociological and especially psychological reading were variations of the same question; 'Why do transvestites exist? What compels a man to dress as a woman? What's the reason for this *disturbance*,' and that's the last thing I cared about after spending a night with them, all I wanted to know was why do the rest of *us* care so much, why do *we* give them such a hard time? After all, until I dressed in drag, no one ever questioned me over what I've worn, but when my mam found out I had a night in drag she was trying to get me to see a shrink. I honestly thought she was going to hold an intervention. And for what? Those guys were some of the nicest people I've ever met, and they're given hell for daring to dress how they want."

"That's pretty shit," said Franky. Martin took a drink and continued: "So, I had my night in drag and found I wasn't a drag queen, I had an assignment which I threw in the bin because I couldn't bring myself to write about all those personal stories got under false pretences, I made up a new assignment out of my ass, and I got a 2:1 for it. That was anthropology for me, 5 years … well, spent."

"I spent my college years in the pub," laughed Des, prompting Martin to look at Des with envy.

"But anthropology must have had some uses," said Tom.

"Maybe," said Martin, "but I read a book, all too late, which pointed out that the truly practical subjects start with their subject's present knowledge and teach from there, whereas the more a subject relies on teaching its own history the more impractical it's likely to be, and that's what I came away with, I'm an expert on the history of anthropology, and it's not even a good history. And of the best anthropological books I've ever read, things like—*Black Like Me, Really the Blues, A Room of One's Own, Germs, Guns and Steel*, none, bar maybe the last, were written by an anthropologist, and none, including the last, was even so much as 'suggested reading' by any of my lecturers, instead, they had us read books like *The Modernity of Japan*, where a guy who lived in a tiny part of Japan writes a book as if he's just discovered the Japanese, and he can say everything there is to say about them in one book, as if the Japanese can't speak for themselves, as if Anime and Studio Ghibli didn't exist."

Martin sighed, "I'm no anthropologist. I'm an English language teacher and even worse—an unpublished wannabe writer. If anthropology has any merit, find someone who practises it to explain it. All I did was waste my time and gave myself a big head before realising what my job prospects were."

Martin had no time for self-pity as the pizzas landed and he was once again put on the spot.

"What! Is! That?" Frankie asked, pointing to a mess of red with some veg thrown on top.

"It's just veggies man, bread and sauce, I'm giving veganism a go… they didn't have any vegan options so I had to ask for a vegetarian without the cheese, story of my life these days."

"You're a fucking idiot," said Tom, throwing the words like a live grenade.

"Bru, you've watched that Netflix documentary, didn't you?" Des asked.

"Well, yeah," said Martin, "but I wanted to give it a go before I watched it, it just helped to give us a push."

"You mean John's gone vegan," said Frankie, "and he's making you go vegan."

"Yeah and no" Martin sighed. "We're both giving it a go, and honestly, we're both really into the idea."

"You're both fucking idiots then," said Tom.

"Why man?" Frankie asked, "is it for health or the animals or the environment or what."

"It's for all of that," said Martin, "but mostly it's that we love animals. In just about every way you can measure it, pigs come out as smarter or at least as smart as dogs, and I felt really uncomfortable knowing that while still saying to myself that 'I love animals' while eating them. Then there's the environment side of things. My favourite quote of all time is "be the change you want to see in the world," so after doing my homework and realising how much it impacts the planet and how well we can get on without meat and milk and all that… I had to give it a go. Meat doesn't do us any favours."

"Of course it does," said Tom, "it's tasty, it's nutritious, and if pigs were so smart they wouldn't have made themselves so delicious."

"Don't be thick," said Martin, "it's all arbitrary what we eat and don't eat. Albert Camus once wrote: 'We get into the habit of living before acquiring the habit of thinking,' and it's true, especially when it comes to what we eat. Just look at our students: I've never had a Turkish student who ate pig, even the ones who drink and smoke have it ingrained in them not to eat pig, have you had any who eat pig?" They shook their heads and Martin continued: "Brazilians think we're crazy for putting milk in tea, and I've seen streets in Vietnam were all they do for a living is raise and sell cats and dogs for meat, and all the Vietnamese friends I made over there said the same thing as Tom when asked why they eat them; 'because they're tasty,' plus, they say, they 'only eat the ugly dog' which is a breed that looks something like a boxer. We don't eat dogs cause we see them as pets, but I'm telling you, a pig is just as smart as a dog, so where's the logic in eating pigs and not dogs?

"We're top of the food chain," said Tom, "so we can eat what we like."

"First" Martin began, "as a group, we are at the top of the food chain, but so what? Just as our collective intelligence allows us to eat whatever animal we want, that same intelligence is also what allows me to eat healthily without having to eat animals. And second, the idea that we are justified in doing something merely because we can do it is the justification made for every horrible action ever committed throughout history."

"What about chickens," said Des, "they're thick as fuck bru, healthy to eat, good protein, why not just stop eating pigs then?"

"Well, once I decided that pigs were too smart to eat it no longer made sense to only eat the 'stupid' animals. There's no justification for it, plus, after doing a little research, I'm pretty sure eating chickens isn't as healthy as you think. They're pumped full of antibiotics, and besides protein, which you can get from lots of fruits, veg and nuts, what's so healthy about chickens?" In the silence Martin started working on his sloppy pizza before Tom came in with:

"You'll end up sick. You're already too skinny, and you're the youngest looking 28 year old I've ever met, you can't even grow a beard! You'll be even weaker and sicker as a vegan."

Martin sighed and replied: "A vegan diet's healthier man, vegans have way less chance of getting any sort of heart disease, we have less risk of developing cancer, and you can still be healthy on a plant based diet, healthier even."

Tom shook his head. "You'll need to take supplements every day and you'll have no energy," he said.

"Man, the no energy thing is a complete myth. Do you remember our last Christmas party when the two of us got steaks and spent the rest of the night in meat comas? We couldn't even make it onto the dancefloor—and that's from meat. Since going vegan I have as much energy as ever. And supplements? The only supplement vegans need to take is B12, and many people are deficient in B12 regardless of their diet. And the only reason why meat-eaters *might* get away with not taking B12 supplements is because they inject or feed it to the animals on the farms. So we both take the same supplement, only I'm now taking it directly instead of through the meat-vine."

"You know what your problem is" threw in Frankie, "you're too much of a Dubliner, if you ever stepped outside of the Big Smoke you might have noticed that we don't treat our cows and chickens like they do in the States, not only are our cows out grazing all day, but most of Ireland *is* grassland, good luck trying to grow soy and almonds here mate."

"We've got cows in Dublin" Martin laughed, "and I've been outside the county, but you're probably right, maybe farming isn't as bad for the planet as we do it in Ireland, and maybe it isn't as cruel to the animals, and maybe our meat is of a higher quality" Martin shrugged, "but it's still cruel. It doesn't matter if you give an animal a hard or an easy life—killing without necessity is cruel. But to say Ireland is natural grassland is false. Humans have been destroying Ireland's natural forests since we've arrived. If we farmed less we could rewild more, it's that simple. And so many people in Ireland die because of high cholesterol and heart disease, and that's from their diets. And why am I the only one tired of the old joke that when you get out to the country air and roll down your window the first thing you smell is shit. Inner-city Dublin smells better than the countryside Frankie. Since going vegan it's hit me, for the first time in my life, that the countryside isn't supposed to smell like shit all the time—and it's not the cows' fault, it's ours. You slag me for being a Dub, but as soon as I leave the Big Smoke I'm entering the smell of big shit. And if I can learn to get on as a vegan, then why not? And look," he said before Tom could get a word in, "before you lay into me for being a hypocrite this or a hypocrite that, as far as I'm concerned, the most environmentally sound thing a person can do is to commit suicide. That's a fact. I know I'm not going to save the planet by going vegan, I know I'm still going to be using plastic and relying on fossil fuels one way or another, I know I'm still going to step on the odd ant or snail or whatever, but I'm giving it a go, I like the idea of not intentionally paying for animal abuse, I like trying new things, and it's been on my mind a while, so what's the harm?"

"Animal abuse!" Tom exploded, "We're the apex fucking predator dude, we're designed to eat meat!" Martin sighed, out of all the anti-vegan arguments he'd been suffering from over the last while this one really bit into his patience. He replied:

"We're not an apex predator, we're just not. Just think, if you see a squirrel, or a baby duck, or a three-legged dog, do you feel hungry? Do you want to kill that vulnerable animal with your predator instincts, like a lion or a wolf would? Or do you go 'awww' and take a photo? This idea that we're designed to eat meat is bullshit, and even if it was true, so what? Evolutionarily speaking, where did our hands come from?"

"To grab things bru," said Des.

"To grab what, specifically?" Martin pushed.

"Trees," mumbled Tom.

"Trees, that's right, we've evolved these hands and arms like our primate and monkey cousins to climb trees, now when's the last time anyone here felt obligated to honour our biological heritage and climb a tree? Or take dairy—for nearly all of human history we have been without cow's milk, so why is something so recently introduced declared 'natural' for us to consume? And as I said, if our collective intelligence allows us to eat whatever animal we like then it also allows us not to eat them. We have oat milk now, vegan cheeses, meat substitutes, is it not drawing a line in the sand to say our intelligence allows us to eat what we want, but doesn't allow us to extend that idea in order to eat more ethically and sustainably? Eating meat is bad for the environment, bad for our conscience, bad for our health and it's literal torture and death for the animals."

"Got off your fucking high horse," said Tom, "we're designed to eat meat, meat's good for us, and more natural than that fucking mess you call a pizza."

"DON'T BLAME THIS PIZZA ON ME!" Martin shouted, "I've had nice vegan pizzas, it's not my fucking fault this place doesn't make them. And what's so healthy about eating meat?"

"Protein," said Des.

"Protein!" spat Martin, "look up how many vegans have died from a protein deficiency, then compare that to how many people die from high cholesterol and heart disease. Or just look at the biggest and strongest mammals on earth—gorillas, elephants, rhinos, hippos, giraffes, bulls, cows, guess where they get their protein from?"

"From grass," said Tom, "we tried eating grass during the famine and look where that got us."

"I don't eat grass, I only smoke it."

"I give it a week," said Tom.

Martin sighed heavily. He was getting too riled up. While he could argue sober all day long, after a beer or two he had to be careful. 'I've been vegan now for over 3 weeks already you fucking prick' he thought, but he kept quiet and swallowed his thought along with another mouthful of his shitty let-the-side-down flop of a pizza.

"Yeah boiii! More chicken for me," said Des digging in.

"And more cholesterol," mumbled Martin.

"So," said Tom, "I take it we'll be staying out all night?"

"I'll probably leave before nine," mumbled Martin.

"Yeah" elbowed Frankie, "those of us with our freedom and protein will be out all night, or until we find someone. Every man for himself and all that… but… don't suppose you have a free couch if any of us lucks-out? I'm not paying for a taxi out to Ongar at 3am again."

"We'll see how the night goes," Tom shrugged.

"Fucking rent bru," Des said, "I've been trying to find somewhere closer to the city centre for months."

"They should get rid of some of the churches," said Frankie, followed sharply by a "Here here" of agreement from Martin.

"What?" Tom asked.

"The churches," said Frankie, "there's too many of them in Dublin, at least half of them should be turned into apartments."

"Fucking right," said Martin, beginning to cheer up.

"You can't," said Tom, "most of the churches here are historical buildings, hundreds of years old."

"You fucking can," said Frankie, "a city is for living in mate. Its buildings should be for the living."

"YES!" thumped Martin.

"Most people still going to church have a foot in the grave anyway," said Des.

"And they could still pray" added Frankie, "give them the basement or a room on the first floor for praying and build the apartments above."

"You can't" pleaded Tom, "those churches are some of the oldest buildings in Dublin."

"Fuck em," said Martin. "Frankie's right, there's too many, Joyce said it would be a puzzle to walk through Dublin without walking past a pub, but it would be an impossibility to do so without walking past an empty, miserable, sad-looking church."

"Did you know," said Frankie, "the Catholic Church owns more land than any other religion, business, person or entity?"

"Criminals," said Martin. "You here that? They own more land than anyone else and they preach what? Charity? Double-speaking criminals. Yet we'll have to wait another two hundred years before any politician even suggests converting them into something useful, and there'll be Tom, still alive, talking about the 'historical significance!' The whole planet's going to go kapoof one day, and the churches will collapse one way or another, so why not get some actual use out of all that land? 'Houses of god?' empty, surrounded by homeless people, it's a sick joke. If god exists, and I highly doubt it, then Sinead O' Connor's right, he's become a ghost in his own home."

"Sinead O' Connor's nuts," said Tom.

Martin, glaring at his friend, continued, "look, before I gave up on god completely that description described god perfectly, for what else could god be but a miserable, unlistened to ghost, if the love of god can only be expressed through people then people are making a mockery of god by leaving his so-called houses standing empty."

Tom shook his head, "Look," he said, "some churches in England and that are starting to be converted into museums, nightclubs, art galleries, stuff like that, which keeps the building intact, I'm all for that. Plus, I, for one, while accepting that the Earth will one day go 'kapoof,' still think humans, or some evolved version of us, might still be living on in space, so we should preserve history when we can."

"We need houses Bru," laughed Des, "not museums and nightclubs."

"Listen" Martin forced his way in, "I'm going to tell you a secret, humans won't make a success out of space travel cause space travel's a myth, it's not real."

"JESUS," said Frankie, "you're a moon-landing denier Martie?"

"The lack of protein's getting to him," said Tom. The lads laughed and slapped the table for a good minute before Martin finally managed another word—"No, the moon landing was real, but listen, LISTEN! … it was also a myth." Martin, losing the reins again, had to wait and fume another minute before he could continue—"Listen, listen… what's a spaceship, huh? What's a spaceship?" The others quietened down for half a second before Frankie answered: "It's a ship—for space."

Martin, regretting life and trying to get his argument out right, continued when the fresh volley of laughs died down: "listen. A spaceship is a container, right, it's not a 'ship' like the kind we use to travel the oceans, a spaceship, unlike a 'ship' is an airtight container. It has to be airtight or it wouldn't work, right?"

"Right," said Tom, "So?"

"So," continued Martin, "So it's an airtight container made from earth, right, and what does it contain? More earth. Water from earth, oxygen from earth, food from earth, along with some earth-grown people, right, and then it gets blasted up to space using earth's fossil fuels. So a spaceship is an airtight container made of earth, fuelled by earth and containing earth, and designed with the sole intention of keeping the so-called 'space' out until the spaceship arrives safely back to earth."

"Yeah, because it's necessary," said Frankie, "it doesn't negate actual space travel, Neil, Buzz and Michael still got to walk on the moon."

"Except they didn't," said Martin, "for what's a spacesuit except just a smaller airtight container made of earth and containing earth?"

"Jesus," laughed Des banging the table, "what you want bru, it doesn't count unless they take off the suit?" Martin, dismayed by the continuing derision rather than the awe he thought his argument deserved, continued, "I'm just saying that 'spaceship' is the wrong word, if I took a ship to France, say, but stayed inside my car, even on the ship, and then drove off the ship in my car, and spent a week driving around France without even so much as opening my window, would you say that 'I've been to France?'"

"It's a first step," said Tom, "we can't expect people to be running around spacesuit-free on the moon until we've done the legwork."

"Terraforming," Martin shook his head, "Earth will likely be long gone before we have the technology for it. And even if we had the technology, it wouldn't be possible to terraform the moon until we have something resembling world peace. Can you imagine what the Russian and Chinese governments would do if the U.S. started terraforming the moon? Or vice versa? Look, I'm all for satellites, for sending robots out into space, but space travel, and especially space-tourism, are myths, they're disgusting myths made to exploit rich pricks. Not only because you'll never be able to actually 'enter' space without dying, but space travel assumes that we're not already traveling through space, what do you think the earth does all day long?"

"Martin the Martian," laughed Des.

"You're nuts," said Tom.

"Let's go," said Frankie, "it's time for the free beer."

"Fuck your space travel, fuck the church and fuck your blood-soaked protein," mumbled Martin as he wobbled off his chair and followed his mates through the tilting streets.

One for the Road

The 4 lads arrived in *The Liffey Bar*, an awkward blot of a spot that leaned more towards being a nightclub than a bar proper. Lighting was lacking and the music deafening, which made a mockery of conversation and turned all to muzzled shouting. An attempt, perhaps, to isolate its occupants to their own thoughts or lack thereof, and so to increase the speed at which the bottle or glass was clutched, supped and polished off. If Martin felt tipsy before, this place was designed to finish him off.

When they arrived they found Mary, Sean and 3 other teachers at a table against a wall and near the dance-floor.
"Well, there's the lads," shouted Sean, "how are ye now?"
"We're grand Sean, sorry we're late," honeyed Tom sweetly, "have you been here long?"
"No we're just here, we got some food in the Sugerbowl first," said Sean.
"How's the student turnout?"
"I think there's a few from another school on that table," said Mary, their main boss, pointing, "but most of them won't be here till 8 or 9, well, I'll go up to the bar and sort out the drinks." Mary left them as the lads got settled on the next table. In a moment a bucket of bottled Corrs and an opener landed down among them.
"That's it," said Mary, "a bucket per table, and when they're gone they're gone."
"Cheers Mary, class," shouted Frankie reaching for a bottle as Mary went back to sit with Sean and the older gang.
"It's more than I expected Bru," said Des as he took one.
"15 bottles," said Tom, "someone's going to have to do without a fourth one."

"First come first serve," said Des necking half of his bottle. The rest of them followed in their race to the bottom. "Fucking piss-water," said Tom. Martin looked at his watch, 7:23pm. He thought he told John that he'd be home before 10, so he he'd have to leave by 9. 'Fuck it' he thought, 'I'll get my 3 free beers in anyway and leave them with the fourth.' Martin drank and the beer poured straight to his head as the world went from tilt to spin. He looked to the lads for a bit of conversation to chew on but found them sitting still like islands as a sea of music stormed around them.

Martin frowned, either he would have to shout or move his body intimately towards the ear of his would-be listener, and he hadn't anything in his brain witty enough to merit the effort. Instead he put down his empty beer bottle and went to the toilet, shuffling past the dance floor on his way. After his piss he checked himself in the mirror, 'how did I get so drunk' he thought 'don't fuck up tomorrow!' he ordered his mirrored-self. He zipped up his hoodie and determined to make it back to the table as Spiderman, hoping that by hiding his face he could escape the increasing feeling of self-consciousness that was coming over him, but on his way back through the dance floor a student dressed as a witch grabbed him and dragged him to the centre, he recognised a group of the school's students through his mask and forced himself to dance, feeling like the puppet and the puppet-master rolled into one.

He continued that way for some minutes, but as much he tried to let go and have fun the difference between how he was feeling and what he was doing grew too much for him, and he walked away from the students and drunkingly searched for his table through the muffled vision of his mask. His colleagues laughed and pointed as Martin finally sat back down, unzipped his hoodie and began sipping a new beer.

An hour blurred past and Martin found himself sitting at the table alone when, at half 8, Mary, Sean and the older crowd started gathering their things to leave, saying goodbye to Martin and leaving him in charge of 3 extra bottles of Corrs which they didn't drink. Martin shrugged and grabbed his fourth bottle, meaning to cool himself down. He checked his watch, 9:10, and felt it time to finally get off the tightrope. He did a round of messy goodbyes and went to leave when Tom caught up with him.

"Are you alright man?" he asked.

"Yeah, just it's getting late, I need to go and I've probably had too much to drink."

"Are ya gonna be sick?"

"Ah, I'll be grand, I just need to get some air."

"I have one rolled," said Tom, "sure come on, we'll have a chat and you can take a few drags for the road."

"Sure, a drag or two will sober me up," said Martin, and they left the bar together and found town to be a sprawling mess of costumed drunks, far-off fireworks and surrounding sirens.

"I forgot it was Halloween," mumbled Martin as they headed to the relative quietness of the Liffey boardwalk to smoke in peace.

"How drunk are you?" Tom asked in good humour.

"Yes," said Martin, making Tom laugh. "Ah, I'll be fine," he continued, feeling overly self-conscious again and taking the spliff lightly as it was passed to him, "I'll walk home, it should sober me up, and once I get to bed early enough I'll be fine for tomorrow, for work, for proposing, for the future!" He stood staring out to the water. "madness," he whispered, "I'll be engaged tomorrow," then he turned to Tom and continued, "what about you? How's Frankie's mystery bag treating you?"

"Yeah it's definitely coke, not too strong, but should keep the party going. I'll be dying in work tomorrow."

"Yeah, be careful, back in college we used to call coke the reset-button, but the night always catches up with you in the morning."

"The reset button, I like it," laughed Tom. "sure you don't want a sniff to see you home?"

"No, thanks" Martin shook, "when I was a teenager I got so hooked on video games that I nearly dropped out of school, and I had so many relapses I got depressed, from what I hear of coke I've been afraid to get into it, I'll stick to my hippie drugs."

"Fair enough," said Tom, "I say most of the teachers and students will be in bits tomorrow... I'm seeing more and more of our students in there, think tomorrow will be a Netflix day...."

"Netflix!" Martin scoffed, "I don't know why you can't play games with your students instead. *Scrabble, 30 Seconds, Scategory.* It gets them practising their English more than Netflix."

"Well not all of us can drink without getting hangovers," returned Tom. "I'll have fuck-all energy for games tomorrow."

"Well, hangover or no, I'm glad tomorrow's Friday. Seems the best way to end tightrope Thursday."

"What?" Tom asked.

"Nothing."

"No what?" Tom persisted, "what's a tightrope Thursday… are you that nervous about tomorrow?" Martin sighed and looked at Tom, who somehow appeared relatively sober.

"No man, a tightrope night is one where there's a chance of fucking up, a night when you got to call it quits early, or make sure you're fine for the next day. It's a night with a very hard landing if you're not careful, and in being careful it's a night when you can't fully relax."

"Well you're nearly home free," said Tom.

As the 2 of them walked and smoked a couple of Gardai started approaching from behind. Gerard, the older of the 2 guards, said "Bingo" and tapped his nose. He pointed out the pair in front of them to his younger colleague, Leo:

"Looks like a couple of stoners, maybe a dealer, let's see if we can get one of em back to the station, being out here on Halloween is no craic." He had no sooner said it when he felt a cold drop land splat on his head. "And fuck this weather," he said.

"Sketch," said Tom, "2 guards behind us." Martin half-turned and saw them, his heart leaping to his throat. He squeezed the joint out in his hand and shoved it in his pocket, hoping that would be the end of it, but the Gardai marched in front of them and cut them off.

"What was that you were smoking?" asked Gerard squaring right into Martin's face as the younger Gardai stood looking up at towering Tom.

"It's just a cigarette," said Martin.

"A cigarette! That's a funny smelling cigarette."

"Well! It was a cigarette."

"You sure it wasn't something else? Now, you give me whatever drugs you have right now or you'll be in serious trouble."

"It was a spliff," said Tom, "we're sorry Guard."

"I'm not talking to you," said Gerard without looking up, instead he stared hard at Martin thinking—'this cheeky pup here needs to learn some respect.' He also noticed that, between the 2 of them, Martin was the one with a coat and a bag, 'if either of them is a dealer, it has to be the little one.'

"It was a cigarette," said Martin, his brain failing him and clutching at the lie no one was believing, 'it was a cigarette! It was a cigarette! It was a cigarette!' screamed his brain, 'and how can they prove otherwise now that it's out?' was all his bubbling mind would spout.

"Right," said Gerard, "Leo, handcuff him."

Leo promptly got in front of Martin and Martin held out his hands before him to be cuffed.

'Can they do this?' he thought. "Ok, it was a spliff," he said. Gerard beamed a smile and winked at Leo, "there you go now, it's not often you get a confession on the spot," he then pressed a button on his walkie-talkie—"we need a pick up now, the Quays, near *The River Bar*." Martin's head went dark, and that image of the beaming Gardai, smiling and winking away because he had finally told the truth, left a murky smudge on his brain that he couldn't shake off, 'this guy's a bully' he thought.

"Look guard," said Tom, "he's on his way home, he's proposing to his partner tomorrow, he's just being drunk and stupid, I'll get him in a taxi and see him home…" Martin couldn't hear anymore, he stared at his handcuffed hands, 'why am I in handcuffs? Am I really going to the station? I can't be. Surely I'm only getting a scare. For fuck's sake, Tom's off his head on coke, where's his handcuffs, why, it wasn't even my smoke!' With a flash a Gardai car pulled up and ran over what was left of Martin's optimism. Gerard led Martin in, getting in on one side, putting Martin in the middle, (his bag crushing against his back), and Leo on the other side. Martin saw a look of hurt on Tom's face before the door shut. 'Well, fuck it, at least that fucking asshole is off the hook' he thought as the car pulled off.

"Shop Street Gardai station," said Gerard to the driver, thinking to himself 'Well now, this will do nicely.' Gerard also wasn't a fan of Halloween, especially when he had to work it, and this night he was suffering from a particularly bad headache which was compounded by the screaming, fireworks and sirens that Halloween night brings. 'Now,' he felt, 'I can take things easy enough with this clown.'

Stripping for Strangers

Martin sat there in silence. It felt strange to be squeezed in so intimately between two Gardai, and he felt uncomfortable with his bag pressing against his back. It was too silent. He desperately wanted them to stick on the radio, but instead his thoughts went from wondering why Tom wasn't taken to his image of a tightrope Thursday and how he was now truly, completely and utterly fucked.

"Can I ring my partner," he eventually asked, "I said I'd be ho—"

"Shut up," Gerard interrupted as he tried to get a handle on his headache. "Not a word until we get to the station."

Martin went quiet again. His younger brother had joined the Gardai less than a year ago, and he now started debating whether or not to name-drop him when they reached the station, 'but he's been a guard for less than a year' he thought, 'and what if this gets him in trouble.' He decided then that as unfair as he felt his situation to be, he wouldn't drag anyone else along. 'I just have to ring my John' he thought, 'he'll be worrying soon.' Somewhere in the back of his mind was also the thought that if he could only somehow convey to the Gardai how nice of a person he was he might still just get a slap on the wrist and be let off...

Tom entered the bar and found Frankie and Des on the dancefloor.

"Martin's been arrested," He shouted.

"What, fuck off?" Des said.

"I'm serious, we we're smoking a joint and 2 Gardai came from behind, Martin got thick and started lying about what we were smoking, his name and address, just... being a thick, and they've thrown him into a squad car."

"Fuck off," said Frankie.

"I'm fucking serious." Tom shouted. "I'm going to the station," he said.

"Wait," said Des, "Isn't his brother a guard? He'll probably just get a warning bru."

"I don't know… I don't know what to do. I'm going, I have to check on him," he said, "I'm going."

"Well, fuck, let us know how you get on," said Frankie.

"You're staying here?" Tom asked in shock.

"Yeah, well, I'm not going to the Gardai station out of my head and with a big bag of coke on me," said Frankie.

"Yeah bru, and anyway, what the fuck can we do for him?" Des said.

"Fine," said Tom shaking his head, 'it wasn't even his spliff' he thought. "Well, I'm going, hopefully they give him a warning and let him out, I need to see if he's alright." He got his bag and coat and headed to the station, cursing out loud the whole way down.

"Fucking hell," said Des watching Tom head off.

"Martin, what a fucking mad cunt," said Frankie.

"Martin the martian. Fuck it bru, let's get another round in, I need to shake that off if I'm getting laid tonight."

Martin was led out of the car and into the station in a haze of drunkenness and depression. There he gave his details to a bored looking Gardai slumped behind a counter and was brought into a small holding room with a long bench against the wall, one high-up barred window and one overhead light. The room was dim, cold and hard, and left Martin feeling miserable as his eyes searched for something to distract him. Instead the room impressed upon him the dim, cold and hard reality of what was happening. The Gardai took off his handcuffs and made him sit down.

"Are there any drugs in this bag?" Gerard asked as he took it.

"Yeah, 10 grams of hash."

"10 grams. Are you a dealer?" Gerard asked.

"No, personal use," said Martin in a low tone. "Thought I'd save some money buying in bulk, joke's on me… I work full time in a language school, I'm not a dealer."

"We'll see," said Gerard. 'Why bother asking' thought Martin.

"Open up his bag," Gerard told Leo.

They each took out a pair of blue gloves and put them on before Leo opened up the main part of the bag, first pulling out a book—*Leaves of Grass* by Walt Whitman, Martin didn't know whether to laugh or cry.

"What's this?" Leo asked. "A stoner book is it?"

"It's a book of poems, it's good," said Martin. He continued, in the hope of making some connection with them—"Walt Whitman wrote it. You know, they used this book as a plot device in *Breaking Bad*."

"So you think your Walter White do you?" Gerard laughed. 'Fuck me' thought Martin.

Leo didn't look impressed, and Martin felt further and further away from coming to a feeling a friendship among them, 'clearly they're not fans of poetry' he thought. Next Leo pulled out Martin's diary.

"And this?"

"It's my diary," said Martin.

"Diary of what?" Gerard asked suspiciously. Martin slowly shook his head in disbelief.

"It's just a diary, thoughts, ideas, I don't know, whatever I want to write. Have you never kept a diary?"

"Do we look like we're ten?" Gerard asked as Leo started flicking through it. When Leo slowed down and started to read some passages Martin's heart sank. It was a relatively new diary, but still, he felt deeply violated and humiliated as each page felt like a naked snapshot in someone else's hands, and no one else had read a page of it since he found his brother flicking through it when they were teenagers, and Martin gave his brother such a dig for it, and ever since kept it from him (unsuccessfully) by any means necessary. Now he was watching some stranger, who had handcuffed him earlier, flicking through it at his leisure. He was mad, even as he felt so numb, and he wanted nothing more than to crawl away into a hole like some guilty looking insect. 'And for what?' he thought. Leo continued flicking through the pages and stopping at parts were the handwriting was somewhat legible:

[08/10/2019]

In the park smoking a joint. I had a dream last night where my dog had sex with another dog and then gave birth to a squirming wiggly shoebaby. The owner of the other dog was very upset, he looked like the Gentleman Trainer from Pokémon Blue, and he shouted at me and then punished his dog by somehow merging it with a nearby wall, so that only half his dog, a poor black Yorkshire terrier, was sticking out... The shoebaby was a great curiosity, and people kept gathering around me to look at it. It had no features of a baby to speak of, but it was small, alive and squirming, and I remember cradling it carefully. I was glad to be rid of it when I awoke. I wonder, it would be lonely to grow up as a single shoe. ('what the fuck' thought Leo)

[10/10/2019—Street]
Guy driving by and beeping, why? I see you!

[15/10/2019]
In the Phoenix Park watching the singlets, they look like moody teenagers now with their grey coats and sunken necks. Just smoked a kief joint and had a great little cycle, have 2 hours to kill. I saw a crane or a stork earlier, it looked like a drug dealer.

A bee sees better than me,
A world of ultra-violets I'll never get to see.

There's people rolling down the hill,
abandoning all to the thrill,
but self-consciousness keeps me still
and stops me from having my fill.

[21/10/2019]
Getting people to engage with you is the hard part. To get them off their phones, away from their books, to pull them from their own headspace. Once you can engage with them everything gets easier. Next comes the nervousness to find common ground. The blues bar last night was really good—but it was missing it, the talk between strangers. Common ground was already laid out for us. All we had to do was break the ice and engage with each other. And I failed, but am I the only one who feels this failure so miserably?

[29/10/2019—House, afternoon]
Saw Sinead O' Connor last night with good old Mark, Sinead looked high as fuck. Great gig, only wish she played something of her Reggae album. Anyway, concerts are for closing your eyes and losing yourself

to the music. Anyone who takes out a phone during a concert should be shot.

[30/10/2019]
TV has destroyed our ability to entertain each other and social media is killing our ability to communicate with each other. Me and John have now agreed to have 3 tv-free nights a week. On Mondays we're going to choose some activity to do together starting with a jigsaw puzzle. It's a wonderful idea, why didn't we think of it sooner? I guess it's because our brains are geared towards laziness and easiness. Madness is what it is.

[Later]
Tomorrow will be an interesting Halloween, I have students and fellow-teachers all at me to go out and have a mad one, but—.

"I wish you wouldn't read it," Martin finally said, as politely as he could manage, "it's very personal." He wanted to cry, it was in his mind like a fact that he should be crying, but he was surprised to find that really he felt very little.

'Madness,' thought Leo as he closed the diary with a shake of his head for Gerard, he looked at Martin's sorry figure and shook his head again, for in the space of a few pages he lost sense of where he was or what was happening. He shook his head and felt he had to say something:

"He mentions getting high quite a bit in this," he said, putting it away. "But there's no details about buying or selling."

"Should I take a look" asked Gerard, "any numbers?"

"No," said Leo, "it's just gibberish."

"I'm not a dealer," said Martin. "I'm sorry it's illegal, but I'm not trying to break any laws, you know it's legal now in Canada, several states in the U.S., decriminalised in many European countries, it will be legal here too in a couple of—"

"Shut it" Gerard interrupted and slapped Martin lightly across the nose. "It's not legal now, you hear? And look of the state of you. Who knows what we'll find in this bag. But I tell you now. You're biggest mistake was lying to us, if you had of been straight from the start I would have thrown whatever you had into the Liffey and let you walk off, but you didn't, you lied to us, and you need to learn not to lie to the Gardai."

"I'm sorry," said Martin, "I was scared, I'm drunk, it's hard to think straight."

"You're out of your head is what you are," said Gerard as Leo continued through the bag, pulling out the bag of hash and passing it to Gerard who put it on the window sill, followed by his papers, tobacco, and another plastic bag with green leaves inside it, Leo passed them all to Gerard.

"What's this?" asked Gerard waving the bag of leaves, "You're lying to us again?"

"It's green tea leaves," said Martin. Gerard looked at him as if he had 2 heads. He opened the bag And smelled it. Well! It certainly smelt like green tea.

"We'll see what the lab has to say about that," said Gerard, putting it on the window sill with the rest. Now Leo pulled out a couple of empty plastic tubes used to store pre-rolled spliffs.

"I see you've been to Amsterdam," said Gerard with a grin, putting the tubes on the window sill with the rest of his property-turned-informers. Martin bit his tongue despite wanting to return that weed is technically illegal in Amsterdam.

Finally, Leo pulled out a small black box, he opened it up and saw an engagement ring inside. "Now what's this?" said Gerard, "did you steal it?"

"Off course not man," said Martin, "It's an engagement ring, I'm proposing to my partner tomorrow, I tried to tell you… I just want to go home, I was literally on my way home."

"Then you shouldn't have broken the law," said Gerard, his headache increasing.

"How much did you pay for it?" Leo asked.

"The hash?"

"No, the ring."

"It wasn't much," said Martin, rather embarrassed. "A couple of hundred, he's practical, he never wears expensive jewellery out of the house, he's afraid it'll get stolen or lost on him."

"You're gay?" Gerard asked before he could stop himself. 'Fuck' he thought, 'I shouldn't have asked that… but he doesn't seem gay, and he's getting married? How old is this kid?'

Martin shrugged, "I'm bi," he said. "Bisexual."

"Does he know you're proposing?" Leo asked.

Martin took his time again, struggling to think straight as his mind fired neurons through a scrambled maze of alcohol, weed and stress. "Yes and no. We're together 8 years, but I don't think he knows I'm proposing, if I still am. Please, I would love to ring him and let him know I'm alright. I was meant to be home by now."

"Worry about yourself," said Gerard, "you've enough trouble to be worrying about." The ring was left on the bench along with the diary, book and other odds and ends.

"Now stand up, empty everything out from your coat pockets and put it all on your right, then put the coat on your left." Martin dumbly did as he was told. Gerard grabbed his phone as it was set aside and started going through his contacts and photos, Martin again felt violated, but said nothing this time, he only said a silent prayer that there was nothing that would land him or anyone else in trouble. After a minute Gerard put the phone on the window sill. Next they made him stand up in the centre of the room.

"Are you wearing underwear?" Gerard asked.

"What?" Martin asked, unsure of what was happening.

"UNDERWEAR, ARE YOU WEARIN' ANY?" Gerard repeated.

"Boxers, yeah," said Martin, his mind waking up to this odd question.

"Right, take off all your clothes bar your boxers and then sit back on the bench," said Gerard. Martin let his brain carry this out as robotically as he could, afraid of what he'd do if he let himself think. He stripped down to his boxers as the Gardai also began to wish that there was something to distract them in that unflinchingly cold room. When Martin was finished he sat back on the bench, pale, thin and near-naked as the two Gardai went through his clothes and emptied out his pockets, which contained a large wet cloud of tissues owing to his seasonal head-colds. He watched with a sense of disbelief as the younger Gardai made a point of stepping on them. They then took out his lighter and, finally, pulled out the half-smoked and now sorry-looking spliff he had shoved down there an hour earlier. It was the only thing in the room that Martin could empathise with.

"Well well, there's the smoke that started all the trouble," said Gerard, sounding satisfied and putting it on the window sill with the rest.

"Imagine how much happier you'd have been now if you were honest with us," he said.

"Yeah," said Martin, half audibly, 'thanks Tom!' he thought sarcastically, and his mind flashed back to the smile and wink that the older Gardai gave when he finally told the truth, that smile, to Martin, said 'we got him now,' and dissipated any sense of humanity or mercy he felt he could expect from this man, who even now seemed only to be teasing him, now helpless, with the thought that he could have helped himself a great deal if he had been honest sooner. 'all such fucking nonsense' thought Martin, 'they might as well give me a beating for being gay they're enforcing laws that outdated' he thought. 'And fuck Leo Varadkar. Why the fuck do we have a Taoiseach who's admitted to doing the very thing that's landed me in prison? If he had been in this situation he would have had it legalised by now.'

When they were through with their search they told Martin to put his clothes back on. After he was dressed Gerard gave him back his phone, tobacco, tubes and lighter, "you can keep these," he said. Martin half-smiled and said thanks. He then made a move to pick up the stamped-on tissues from the ground.

"DON'T TOUCH THEM," barked Gerard, "leave them there."

"Sorry," said Martin, "I don't like leaving a mess."

"Don't worry about that," said Leo, "someone will look after them." 'I hate people cleaning up my own mess' thought Martin, looking sadly at the trampled cloud of tissues. He got his coat and bag and followed the Gardai out of the room to another which resembled more of an office, but with the 3 of them still standing. "What's your number," Gerard demanded, taking out his own phone.

"08-7-7-4," Martin stumbled, trying to remember his number through the haze. Gerard glared at him; "are you serious?" Martin closed his eyes and his number came to him, he rattled it off. "Again," said Gerard. Again Martin rattled off his number.

Gerard asked for Martin's phone and held it in one hand and his in another, he rang the number Martin gave and gave it back to him after it rang. "Now" Gerard said, "I'm going to ring you on Monday or Tuesday, it'll come up like this, 'Private Number,' and you make sure you pick it up. If you cooperate we'll get this sorted in a couple of weeks and let you get on with your life, alright, if you don't, we know where you work and where you live, and we'll pick you up and make your life hell, understand. Cooperate with the Gardai, that's your lesson tonight, understand?"

"Yes," said Martin, "You'll ring me Monday or Tuesday, I'll pick up, but… can you ring me between 12:00 and 1:30, I'm sorry, but I really can't pick up a phone while I'm working."

"Fine," said Gerard, "make a note," he told Leo who wrote the times in his notebook.

"Go on then, go home," said Gerard.

"What, really?" Martin asked, somehow feeling more numb and intoxicated.

"Yeah, exit's behind you, don't forget to answer your phone, and we'll talk to you next week and clear this up when you're sober," he said with a wink and a smile. Martin couldn't tell if he was being mocked or reassured, he could only nod his understanding.

"Thank you guard," he said, "goodnight," he nodded at Leo, who also said goodnight, and walked out of the station. He walked for 5 minutes without stopping before heading down to a quiet lane to throw up. When he was finished getting sick he cleaned himself as best he could, cursing the guards for taking all his tissues. He checked his watch—10:45. He sent his brother a message:

Hey bro, how's things? So, haha, I'm after being picked up by the Gardai for smoking a spliff. Even though there was 2 of us smoking I got singled out and brought to the station. The stripped me and that and found 9 grams of hash on me. They said they'll ring me on Monday or Tuesday. I didn't mention you at all in case it got you in trouble. If there's anything you can do for me let me know, would appreciate it. Its been a long night.

He then messaged John: "*Very sorry, I'm alive, be home in 40min x.*" He started walking home, his hand in his pocket and squeezing his phone as a life support. His first message was from John, "ok" it said. Martin noticed the lack of an 'x' and knew he was in trouble on that end, and kept walking. Eventually his brother got back:

Shit man, you shouldn't be carrying large quantities like that! Did you have a scales on you? If it were me I would look you up on the system, see you have no record, and throw your hash in the bin and forget about it. Worse case scenario they will send your hash to a laboratory and then process it, which means you will have to go to court. It is VERY unlikely you will receive a conviction, but you might need to pay €2,000 for a sols to represent you just to be safe. I'm in work on Sunday. I'll check the systems then and let you know what's happening. You should be fine, the guards know there's no point bringing someone to court for weed unless they already have a conviction, but if they found a scales on you could be fucked.

Martin read the message and got back: '*Thanks, no scales, thank fuck, I'll probably call you at some stage over the weekend, thanks.*' With that Martin headed home as fast as his legs would take him.

When Martin got into his house it was 11:40. He knew by the lights through the sitting-room blinds that John was waiting downstairs. He took a breath and let himself in, having already decided to say nothing of the arrest until he heard from his brother, or at least sobered up, otherwise he would ruin his plans and their anniversary for something that could all have been forgotten about—(oh how he hoped it would be forgotten about).

"I'm sorry," said Martin, coming into the sitting room. John stared at him. "You look wrecked," he said, shaking his head, "you should have told me you were going to be out so late."

"I wasn't planning to be out this late," said Martin.

"Don't give me that shit," said John. "You always go on as if you're held hostage, every time you go out! If you want to stay out, then you can stay out, you're an adult for fuck's sake, but you need to tell me, that's the deal."

"I know," said Martin, "I'm sorry. There was a lot of free beer, I drank too fast, I didn't notice the time... I'm sorry John, I didn't mean to worry you." John shook his head. Martin looked to be in bits, so John sighed and said more calmly: "Well, I'm going up. Are you following me or do you need to eat something? There's some leftover curry and rice."

"Thanks, I'm fine, I'll follow you up, I just need to brush my teeth and that."

"Bring some water up with you... and the basin," said John, he looked Martin over before deciding to bring the basin himself. He passed Martin with a sigh and headed to bed. Martin sat down for 5 minutes and tried to slow down his racing mind. He took out his diary and wrote:

[30/10/2019], at home

Trust me to get picked up the day before I'm to propose. I left the Halloween staff party in The Liffey Bar around 9 with Tom joining with a smoke he rolled. We were both caught together, but Tom got the young and sounder guard while I got the grumpy prick. After initially playing dumb I came clean and said it was a spliff, but it was too late as far as he was concerned. They put me in a car and let Tom walk off. What kind of half-arsed justice is that? I think they picked on me because I'm smaller and Tom probably wouldn't have fit in the car. I'll have to be more careful in future now. Hopefully they'll forget about me, but it probably isn't over. I'll probably be summoned to court. It's crazy. I was handcuffed on the streets, put into a Gardai car, they were making snide remarks about the state I was in [...]. Halloween is not my day. All around me illegal fireworks were blowing up, but I got handcuffed cause some fucker caught a whiff of a spliff. They didn't even ask me where I got the hash from! They couldn't have cared less! Fucking pricks. Weed's been the best thing in the world for me until suddenly it wasn't. 'You must have been in Amsterdam' said the prick with a smile, what a fucking joke.

Fuck fuck fuck fuck fuck fuck!

I was so close to getting home, so fucking close. Why did I have that smoke?

Then he went to the bathroom, shaking his head at himself in the mirror. "Well, you fucked up," he told himself. He shrugged apologetically and brushed his teeth and got ready for bed. While they were lying down John said a curt goodnight and rolled over, Martin answered goodnight and lied on his back, floating up and down the waves of his restless mind until he blacked out and slept.

The Morning After

Martin woke up to the sound of John's alarm. John got up and started getting dressed as Martin slowly came round. Memories from the night before barged in and cleared the last-orders wasted drifters that constituted what was left of his dreams. His dreams would go unrecorded for some time as Martin felt that it wasn't worth tracking himself when he was currently hating himself. It hit him that while he slept his heart tapped away contently without once stomping on the floor or banging on the roof, his hair grow by a flea's foot, his body flushed out the remains of last night's drink and fear, and all this and so much more his body took care of without a care in the world, unconsciously, without stress, without any Gardai—

"How's the head?" John asked.

"It's grand, I'm alive," mumbled Martin. 'How does John get up so fast' he thought.

"Mmm," said John, "well, happy anniversary, I'll let you make it up to me tonight."

"Happy anniversary John, I'm sorry about last night, and I love you," said Martin.

"Mmmm," John replied, "happy anniversary, love you too, now get up before you fall asleep again."

Martin moaned, turned his head away and said: "You know, when I want to sleep, it's the most difficult thing in the world, and when I want to wake up it's even more difficult. Sleep acts like a stereotypical teenager, it only does the opposite of what I'm asking for." John rolled his eyes, pinched Martin by the toe, and told him again to get up.

By the time Martin was dressed John was already out the door. Martin ate half a bowl of salted porridge and moved some expensive beers he had been hiding into the fridge, as well as placing a photo album he had prepared in a convenient spot that he could pull out during the proposal. He quickly glanced through some of the photos, showing their life in Vietnam, several nights in Misneach, even more nights spent at his sisters, and his most precious photograph; the one of John and his grandmother smiling together. "For eight years we went out and had a life," Martin mumbled to himself, "then I went and got arrested."

He closed the photo album and grabbed his coat and bag to leave for work, having decided to stick to his proposal plan despite feeling in turmoil over the night before. The guards could take his hash and his clean record, they could strip him on a whim and force him to live under the passive voice, but they weren't going to come between him, John, and their life together. Or so Martin quietly determined. . But during the walk to work and for most of the day Martin had second thoughts, troubling thoughts, and with no bouncer coming to the rescue.

Martin arrived at work early, without once looking up from his two feet, glad as he was that he was still walking straight. With reluctance he made his way into the building. He was in no mood to teach or talk with anyone, and he winced when he saw Ian in the staff room.

"Alright man, how was last night, was it good? Details, Martin, DETAILS!"
"Man, it was a good up to a point, then… well…"
"WHAT? WHY?"
"I don't want to talk about it, not here," he said, for fear of another teacher coming in.
"Okay man, no problem, what about after work? If you want to talk, if you don't mate, no problem." Martin looked at Ian and thought about it, he would have nearly 2 hours to kill before John could get to the restaurant. 'Talking about it would be nice,' he thought.
"Yeah man, I'd be free for a coffee or something after work."
"Yeah, great," said Ian. "ok, we'll talk about it then, but listen mate, whatever it is, if you can't do anything about it now, forget it, I know it's easier said than done, but forget it."
"Thanks," said Martin. "Don't worry, I'll cheer up, it's easy in the class to forget everything," said Martin, hoping what he said was true.
"Yeah mate, no worries," nodded Ian, showing a humane discretion which often laid hidden behind his centre-stage mannerisms.

Martin got the materials he needed from his locker and put them in his bag, he then went into the kitchen to make a cup of tea. Although it was still too early to teach, he didn't want to stick around in the staff-room if he could help it, but he waited on his tea like a loyal friend. As Martin stood watching his friend getting ready Tom came in, and he approached Martin and the warming kettle.

"Ya alright?" Tom asked.

"As can be," said Martin.

"What happened to ya?"

Martin checked around the staff room before replying: "Well, I got brought to the station, strip-searched, found with 9 grams and let go, and they're going to ring me next week, probably, after that, I don't know," he looked at the kettle as he finished, wishing the old thing to reach the boil faster.

"Fuuuck, did you tell em your brother's a guard?" Tom asked.

"No, I talked to my brother when I got out, he's going to check the system on Sunday to see if I'm being processed or not, if so, I guess I'll be brought to court and pray I don't get a conviction."

"You won't get convicted," said Tom, "just for a bit of weed, sure, I hate to say it, but they probably would have let you go by the Liffey if you didn't start giving them a fake name and that."

"Don't start that with me! I lied about what we were smoking. Alright? But I never gave a fake name." A thousand thoughts and insults fought among Martin's mind, each screaming and promising to spit acid on Tom's remarks, instead he stood staring at the now quietening kettle. As soon as it clicked he grabbed it to poor his cup—but too soon—as the waiter boiled and sputtered everywhere while he tried to pour.

"Fucksake" sputtered Martin as scalding water splashed around his hand.

"Sorry," said Tom, "...you know, I went down to the Gardai station, I told them at the desk that my friend was brought in, but they wouldn't give me any information." Martin shrugged:

"Thanks," he muttered as he put the kettle back. "I didn't know you did that."

"Well, it didn't do any good, did they keep you there long?"

"An hour or two I think, I don't know, I don't want to talk about it here. I feel like shit over it" Martin said as wiped away the spill-over.

"It'll be grand," said Tom, landing a friendly pat on Martin's wooden shoulder. Martin shrugged again, "yeah, well, we'll find out on Sunday."

"It'll be grand man," said Tom, "trust me, I've friends who've done way worse. Sure I have a friend, taller than me, who picked up a 4-foot-something guard, called him a leprechaun, and spun him around till the guard got sick, and he got off scot free."

"Thanks," Martin said, wondering if it was people like Tom's friend that made the Gardai so happy to be dealing with the likes of himself. He took his tea and his bag and headed to his classroom, getting there 20 minutes before the class was to start. He turned on the computer, closed the door, and, ignoring the well-chosen display of recommendations that would normally win in directing his first order. He typed for some live Rory Gallagher, turning the volume up as high as he could get away with, and he sat there with his eyes closed, letting the wailing guitar solos sweep over him and take him away so that he could hear nothing else, inside or outside his own head. And yet… Tom's comment about him lying to the police buzzed around his brain until he took out his diary and wrote:

Fuck Tom.

Friends…
They'll push you to your limits
But never take the blame

In isolation I am desperate
But in a group I go insane

Filling In

When the first student arrived Martin reluctantly lowered the volume and put away his diary, but instead of making easy conversation like he normally would, Martin, for the first time since he began teaching, decided to *look* busy. It was only when the bell rang and his class was half-filled that he shook himself from his stupor and made a start. He gave the class their usual Friday test, cursing himself that he didn't make it 8 pages long, and tried again to write. But his hand felt like lead, and all he could write was the quote for the day: "Life is a cruel master, she gives the test first and the lesson after" Daymond John. After the test some of his students asked why they didn't see him at the Halloween party—"I left early," he said. T then, breaking his first smile of the day, weak as it was, he told them that he was finally proposing to his partner and so he needed to be hangover free.

"Don't be so nervous teacher," said one of his students who had noticed Martin's sullen mood, "you'll be fine."

"Yeah," Martin smiled, "sure anyway, I'm too nervous to teach, let's watch some Netflix."

During the break Martin stayed in his classroom, silencing his mind again with the raw energy of of an increasingly louder Rory. He sat there in guitar-assisted sedation for a few minutes when Frankie came in and Martin had to lower it down.

"Well, what the fuck happened to you last night?" Frankie asked with his friendly laugh.

"I don't know man," said Martin, "I was smoking with Tom when 2 guards came from behind, I was singled out, got handcuffed, brought back to the station, and … fuck."

"Tom says you were giving them a fake name and address," said Frankie.

"Tom's a prick," mumbled Martin. "I tried to fob of the spliff as a cigarette, but I NEVER gave them a fake name or address. Tom can go fuck himself." Martin calmed himself and fleshed out his side of the story, he then asked, "and how was your night anyway?" As Frankie took some air in through his teeth and shook his head.

"Haha fucking shit, not as shit as yours, but me and Des were left on our own with no one to mind our gear, so some prick stole our bags, our coats, the lot. Des's keys were stolen and I couldn't get a bus home that late, so the two of us spent three hours walking around town in the early hours, fucking freezing, me dressed as a pneumoniatic builder and Des covered in beer-stained toilet paper."

"Fuck," said Martin, a smile beginning to spread as he pictured the pair.

"Yeah," continued Des, "by the time we found somewhere that would let us in we had to pay €60 each for 2 hours sleep and a shower. Then we had to go into Penny's on the way into work to buy a new set of clothes to work in, fucking shit craic, I'm bollaxed mate."

"Jesus," said Martin, "you *do* look tired. Fuck Halloween, Ian was right."

"Yeah Martie man, anyway, let's get some lunch and a pint, I'm dying, and you need to get away from that computer before you start cutting yourself."

"Nobody cuts themselves while listening to Rory Gallagher," mumbled Martin as he surprised himself by turning off the computer and finding himself back again, a lost little lamb among lambs in *The Black Sheep.* But it didn't take long, sitting in the usual seats, for Martin to cheer slightly up now that he found himself with a friendly cohort of bouncers who could bar his blues away. And over cauliflower wings, a pint, and a laugh Martin was reminded by Ian and Des that the world was something that existed beyond his own suffocating thoughts.

In the afternoon class Martin got into an argument with one of his students which left him deep in thought and frustrated, but he shrugged it off and stuck it in his back pocket as he went down to the staff room to wait for Ian, his mind once again perpetually swinging from wishful optimism to crushing depression. He tried again to get a handle on his thoughts by writing them down, but all he could write was: *will we survive this?* And the thought depressed him so much that he couldn't face it, so he tried to bury the sentence in frantic ink, which only created a desperately conspicuous mark on his page. All he could do was wait for news from his brother… When Ian came down his presence resurfaced Martin, and the 2 of them went to a Costa where Martin bought them a couple of coffees as Ian found a place to sit. Martin gave Ian the story, who listened well; and for the first time, perhaps because Ian had no part in it himself, Martin felt the weight of last night a little lighter to manage.

"I had a mate," said Ian, "who was caught with 50 ecstasy pills in college, 50! Like that he was arrested and brought to court, and the judge asked the guard if he had any previous convictions, the guard said 'no,' and judge struck it out, no penalty, nothing. You have a clean record mate, a decent job, a house, no way a judge is going to ruin your life over 8 grams of hash, no way."

"I know man, it's just shit," said Martin, "all thoughts lead back to it."

"I know mate, I'm not going to say forget about it, cause you can't. Of course you're depressed, but listen, you know it's going to be alright. You just have to wait for these pricks to ring you, yeah? That's shit, but probably they won't bother, I don't think they'll bother man. And if they do, no one's going to convict you. The amount of shit that goes on during Halloween, and the guards want to convict YOU? No fucking way. I'd throw that case out man, OUT! NEXT!"

"Yeah man," smiled Martin, "it's just the timing of it, you know, I'm proposing today, I think, and I haven't told John anything, and I hate keeping this from him, but his parents are very old school about these things, every drug that's illegal might as well be heroin as far as they're concerned, and even John's prickly about me smoking sometimes. I don't know what to do."

"I thought you told me John smokes too, no?"

"He smokes, yeah, but once in a blue moon, he's too much of a health-freak to smoke like a habit, and he prefers his craft beers. But it's more the fact that I was smoking out in the open like that, in the middle of town, when we're finally getting our adult lives in order. He's going to think I'm an idiot."

"Mate, on the way over here I smelled weed at least twice, did you?"

"Yeah," sighed Martin, "I smelt it."

"On the street! Every fucking day there's people smoking on the street, and the amount of times I have to tell my Brazilians that weed's ILLegal in Ireland, half the time they don't believe me! There's people smoking everywhere! I've even had students rolling joints in my class for fuck's sake. Yeah, you should have been more careful, but shit happens. You were just unlucky man, fucking unlucky. And you got done on Halloween for fuck's sake, the amount of shit that goes on Halloween—and they want to convict you for a fucking joint?"

"I know man, it's hypocrisy, it's stupid, you can drink yourself to death legally but we're the 'dopes who smoke.' But since I've bought a house and our job's Gardai-vetted I'm fucked if I get a conviction. Like, life-as-I-know-it-would-be-finished fucked, not to mention John's life, and I still don't know whether to tell him tonight or not."

"Listen mate, do what you have to, but personally, if you're asking me, I think you're right waiting until Sunday. Imagine you tell John and it causes some big fight, and then you find out from your brother that they're not chasing it up, fuck that, of course tell him after if you have to go to court and deal with it then, but at least you'll be dealing with a fact, not a fucking what-if scenario. But listen mate, that's my thinking, you got to do what you think best—yeah?"

"I know," said Martin, "but when you find yourself in such a fucking mess, suddenly it becomes very hard to trust the same thinking that got you there in the first place."

And Leaving Out

They finished their coffees and went their separate ways, with Ian wishing Martin all the luck. Martin headed to the restaurant, still getting there early, and waited out the front. He watched the people flowing past him as he tried to clear his mind while his eyes became two searchlights searching for his John. When John came into view they smiled from a distance and then kissed and headed inside.

"I don't know why you always wait outside in the cold," said John in good humour.

"It's less distracting," said Martin.

"What?"

"I hate waiting inside. Either way I'm waiting, but inside I also have to pretend that I'm not looking too hard, then I have to worry about waiters approaching me, then I start feeling a ripple of a nudge from those around me, excited to see who my date is. Out there I can look out for you with none of that, people normally leave you alone when you're outside...." Martin somehow got all this out in front of the "Please Wait" waiter as John was too busy chuckling to stop him. Even in 8 years their irregularities still surprised each other. Martin smiled, so far they seemed off to a good start. The waiter led them to their seats.

"Did you have a smoke while you were waiting?" John asked.

"No" Martin answered, a bit surprised. "I don't smoke every day you know."

"I know," laughed John, "only asking... Plus, you know, I'd rather you high than drunk, Mr two beers and I'm cranky."

"Well, I'm not high and I'm not planning on being drunk or cranky."

"Fair enough. Well, happy anniversary," said John, planting another kiss before they got seated.

"Happy anniversary," said Martin with a smile. 'I can do this' he thought, 'I can give him a good night, and a decent proposal, nothing else matters tonight.'

"Well, how was your night out anyway?" John asked.

"Yeah, it was good," Martin sighed, "I just didn't mean for it to get so …out of hand."

"Well, you weren't out mad late I suppose, although you did seem pretty out of it, I didn't even mean to be that mad at you, but you should have messaged."

"Yeah, I'm sorry, I wanted to message earlier… I just drank too much too fast, all that free beer, but it was good. Most of the lads were chasing after students once our bosses left, that's always fun to watch."

"They're mad," said John, "I get student-teacher relationships happen, but the way you go on in your job it's about all that happens … I'm not sure it's all that funny," he said, "it doesn't seem professional."

"Yeah, well, it's not as predatory in language schools as it would be in a normal school or college. Most of our students are around our own age or older, and a lot of them are more qualified than we are. At the moment I have a Chilean doctor, a Turkish politician, I've another student who owns a construction company with 20 odd staff—or so she says. I've taught psychologists, instagrammers, Frankie even has a professional male-model in his class."

"Well… that one could be tempting," John laughed.

"Yeah, Frankie hates him because he attracts all the attention. Then you have students who come here on holiday mode, they show up to class hungover or high and just want to complete their visa requirements. I get sleeping with students is complicated, and management have to keep a lid on it, but I'm not so sure it should be condemned. One of the teachers I worked with is engaged to a Brazilian student she started dating 2 or 3 years ago, they seem happy out."

"Have you ever been tempted," John asked teasingly.

"There was one student, a woman from Brazil… if I was single I might have tried something."

"A stunner?" John asked.

"No, not a stunner, but she had a great sense of humour, a lovely smile that lit up the room, plus, she was the only student I've had who really liked the background music I put on, by the time she was leaving the 2 of us were having great chats over which live version of a Rory song was the best. She said that I introduced her to the first guitarist that was as good, to her, as Johnny Winter. I could have kissed her just for that." John shook his head and cracked up laughing and Martin smiled.

They ordered a bottle of wine and starters when Martin asked: "So, how was your Halloween anyway?"

"Grand," beamed John, "I went on a run after work, got back, watched some horror films, dished out some sweets for the trick-or-treaters, can't complain."

"Sounds good," said Martin, "I'll make a point of joining you next year."

"Did you really have a bad night?" John asked.

"No... I'm just tired, and, I guess I feel... bad, I upset one of my students today."

"How so?"

"Well, I have this real loveable bear of a student, always joking and flirting, but he does my head in because for all that he's very lazy when it comes to putting in the work. He has an Irish husband and yet he's still in my pre-intermediate class, and he's working in a shop in town and he hates it, I know how that feels, and so I'm already struggling to keep my patience with him because, well, if he would only put in a bit of work he'd ace the IELTS exam."

"Mmm," said John.

"And, anyway, besides being lazy, I feel like he's spiritually stunted, and we got into a discussion and I got a bit heated."

"As you do," said John.

"As I do. The thing is, he told me, after giving out to me for somehow missing me at the party, that really I'm a good person, that I'm 'good on the inside' he said."

"That's sweet."

"Yeah, it was a lovely compliment, but, I don't know what mood I was in, because instead of just thanking him for it I said; 'you know, to say I'm a good person on the inside is another way of saying the world's been good to me.'"

"Oh no," laughed John, "you didn't go Alan Watts on them again did you?"

"I did. This student hadn't a clue what I was on about, so I explained to him that to say I'm a good person is akin to saying that I have a good family, good friends, a good job and a good partner."

"A *good* partner!" John said.

"The *best* partner," smiled Martin. "Anyway, I went on about how there's no 'inside' separate from an 'outside' and all the rest but I'd lost him. Then he tells me, a few minutes later... to a random question I put to them, that his dream is to win the EuroMillions so that he'd be rich enough for himself, his husband and his family, and still have enough money left to help all the children in Africa. He's mad about the children in Africa."

"Fair enough," John reasoned.

"Yeah, but, I start arguing with him again, asking him if he's ever given money to the homeless in Dublin—'no'—he says, 'because they harass me at work and they're all drug addicts.'"

"Oh no," laughed John.

"It gets worse," said Martin. "So, as you imagine, I go back to the 'outside/inside' thing 'and anyway' I says to him 'I do drugs and you just told me that I'm a good person.'"

"You didn't!"

"I did, I didn't go into details, I said drink is a drug and I did other things when I was younger, and sure we all like to drink, but only the homeless seem to be judged for it. And they actually have a good reason to take drugs, what's our excuse? …Anyway, my student eventually gets back to me with this idea that I have a good soul and that most homeless people either have a bad soul or a lost soul."

"Oh god," John laughed.

"So I ask him 'what's a soul?' and of course he can't answer, so I ask him 'do you think dogs have souls?' and he says 'no, because they don't have personalities,' finally some of the other students wake up and start arguing with him that of course dogs have personalities and one by one they start to describe their favourite dogs."

"Of course," nodded John.

"So I let them argue amongst themselves as I tried to get a handle on myself, and the class finished ok I guess, sure being Friday helps, but, I just, I just really hate when people try to tell me that humans have souls and other animals don't, I really struggle to respect people like that, especially when they won't even bother to explain what a soul is. It's such a human thing to do. We make something up, and then we go around kicking and belittling other animals for not having it. If it were a game it would have been abandoned years ago, and I know this student isn't trying to be malicious, but I wish he could see that he's setting humans up to be this, this fucking tumour, severed and unconnected, and so stupid."

"Calm," said John, "breath… it's ok, sure, if *we* have souls of course dogs have souls, in fact, dogs have twice the number of souls that we have."

"How's that?" Martin asked.

"Why, because they've got twice the number of feet." When the penny dropped Martin beamed his biggest smile of the day and had to excuse himself to the bathroom for fear of crying. 'What did I do to deserve him' he thought. He did his business and splashed some water on his face, gave a weak smile to his mirrored-self and took a breath.

"So," said John as Martin sat down, "I take it you didn't convince him anyway."

"No" Martin replied. "He's another enigma, an openly gay man who believes in a slightly-more-tolerant Catholic god who created humans to stand apart from other animals. I don't know. I can't even teach this guy English, and I'm actually good at teaching English, so I don't know why I thought I could teach him a bit of philosophy."

"Well," said John, "speaking of philosophy, I've been thinking of an argument against Creationism, I call it the coin-toss argument, you want to hear it?"

"Of course," said Martin.

"So, what do all creationists use as proof that god created the universe?"

"Easy, they use this," said Martin, gesturing the world around him with his hands. "they use the evidence of the existing universe and cast their 'logic' backwards."

"Exactly. So, you take a coin, right, and ask the person if they can predict a coin toss with 100% accuracy, and of course they can't, but you push them first, get them to admit that they can't predict the coin toss because they can't predict the future."

"Right."

"So, you flip the coin and hide the result with your hand, then you ask them if they can tell you, with 100% certainty, if it landed heads or tails, right?"

"Right, so they're no longer being asked to predict the future."

"Exactly, but they still can't give you an answer because they can't see the result, they can't see the evidence."

"Right," nodded Martin.

"So, you show them the result, let's say it's 'heads,' and then you gesture around you and say that this 'heads' represents the world as we know it."

"Right," said Martin, "I get it… so then you ask them to predict the next coin toss."

"Exactly," said John, leaning back in his chair with the rare satisfaction of delivering a well-understood point. "and they can't," he continued, "then you drill the point home, the point being that the world as the world is now is *not* evidence that this world was fated to be as it is."

"That if we could flip the coin again, chances are everything would be different."

"Exactly, chances are we wouldn't be here."

"Maybe the dinosaurs would have continued."

"Only there'd be no 'us' to mark the result."

"Mmm," said Martin, "I like it! It might go well with the electric-current theory."

"What's that one?"

"Another by Alan Watts: that consciousness is felt like the closing of an electric current. Electricity, you see, regardless of the distance, will only travel if you close the circuit. The length of the wire, or the time it takes for the electricity to travel through it, that doesn't matter. And so we cannot measure, feel or even hold to account the time before or after life, as the tools to measure 'life' and 'time' are part of the very same system being switched on… And it's funny, but every intelligent thing, be it machines or animals, always turn on in a state of standby, awaiting instructions. Computers take seconds to follow instructions. We take years. True, we also have instincts, pre-programming, but even the pre-programming is built upon the world that was, if not still is. Yes, it seems the smarter something is, the more external input is going to shape it."

"Alan Watts said all that?" John smiled.

"Well, his thoughts should be allowed to grow, even if he's dead. Sure, what did he do anyway but grow and share the thoughts of others?"

"True," said John. "And there you go," he smiled, "try the coin toss argument on them, that'll make you happy, and just think, if you got me a little interested in philosophy then there's hope for you yet with your students." Martin smiled.

"Well, I don't have a philosophy that isn't a watered down version of Alan Watts, and I owe that to Kate."

"Mmm," said John, "but you package it better," he winked, "and you can have the coin-toss argument as your own, consider it an anniversary present," he smiled, "besides the card I'll give you later."

"Thanks," said Martin, "I got you something small too,"

"I hope it's small," said John more seriously, "you know we don't normally get each other anniversary gifts."

"It's very small," shrugged Martin, wishing to himself for another coin toss on yesterday.

But then a thought occurred to him, he continued: "Yesterday I showed my students a short film on YouTube about animal testing, I was disappointed it didn't mention veganism, sure animals don't care whether we torture them to eat them or to experiment on them. But anyway, it didn't take long for it to come up in the following discussion, where one of my students argued that since Jesus multiplied the fish and bread eating fish can't be a sin, the irony. I've seen so-called Buddhists, Christians, Muslims, Jewish people, and possibly more use their religion to defend their 'right' to eat animals. Disgusting."

John nodded, Martin continued: "I really can't put it into words how sad it makes me. Not that atheists are much better on this front, but using religion to justify eating animals is madness. The problem, and it was my problem too, is that the oppressors make the rules, we don't pay any attention to the oppressed, which is the mentality that has allowed, and continues to allow, the very worst actions of human history. How can I get my students to understand this without them asking for a new teacher?"

"You can't," sighed John, "you can give them a nudge maybe, but at some stage they have to decide for themselves. But it is crazy, most religions preach world peace, and most even preach that peace starts at home, but unfortunately they leave out the victims in the fridge and those being gnawed to the bone. You'd think they'd add to their message to leave animals alone."

"Exactly," smiled Martin, "and am I getting you into poetry or what was that about?"

"Shut up," laughed John, "coincidence! I draw the line at poetry."

They ordered their mains and topped up their wine as Martin continued to enjoy himself like a convict on probation. When they felt the waiter's presence gone John continued:

"You know, you hair's getting long again."

"I know" Martin groaned, "I need to find a new place, they have a new barber at Tony's and I somehow always get stuck with her and she treats me head like a pin-cushion."

"I know," John laughed, "you complain about her every time you go there."

"Well it's true, and I don't know what to do about it, I feel like asking her for a safe word or something."

"You could try finding a new barber," John laughed.

"Yeah, I know, but everyone else at Tony's is fine, even if Tony still thinks I'm just out of secondary school, last time I had him he actually asked me what I was planning to study."

"I just don't understand you," laughed John, "you've been going there since you were a kid yet you've never seemed to like it much, and now you're afraid of one of the staff, meanwhile I got at least 3 places I recommend for you."

"I'm not afraid of her… I just know she's going to hurt me," they laughed. "But, you're right," Martin sighed, "I've been going there for 20 odd years and it's never been much craic, but Tony's is right next to my parents, if I get my haircut someplace else he's going to notice."

"Let him!" John said. "Have you ever shared two words with him outside of his barbershop?"

"We nod at each other," Martin answered, but his answer was rolled over by John's eyes:

"Fuck em, the new place I'm going to actually give you a bottle a beer while you're waiting, you can't ask for better than that."

"But," said Martin, "you're happy to pay 20-30 quid for your hair, I don't think I've ever paid more than 15."

"You're hopeless," laughed John.

"I miss Vietnam," returned Martin, "getting your haircut outside is living the dream."

"Mmm, once you don't think too hard about everyone's shavings blowing in the wind."

"Still," argued Martin, "I have colds and hay-fever here, I never had no hair-fever in Vietnam."

"Well, *you* can go back," mumbled John.

"I'm kidding, 'hair-fever,' get it? I was just setting up a joke."

"An old joke."

"Ok, ok, sorry." Martin decided to clear the air by telling John about the pizza in Cassidy's that let him down, and the story of his pitiful pizza led them to wonder back at how naive they once were.

"It's crazy," said John, "I was once told by a doctor to avoid Guinness because of my hemochromatosis, out of curiosity I compared the iron content in Guinness to red meat."

"And," nodded Martin.

"And red meat has nearly ten times the amount of iron than Guinness gram per gram, chicken over 4 times. Guess what the doctor never mentioned avoiding?"

"Madness," agreed Martin. Thinking back to his class talking about their favourite dogs he wondered who was truly mad, the one student he considered to be spiritually stunted, or the others who defended the personalities of their dogs—for the individual student believed in a divinely ordained, if not to be understood or questioned, line of separation between humans and the other animals, the other students didn't, but ate them anyway. One sounded like dogmatism, the other cannibalism. Loving dogs and eating pigs. How naive they used to be.

For dessert they finished their wine with some dreams. John began:
"I didn't tell you about the mad dream I had last night."
"Oh?"
"We were staying in a hotel, you, me, Irena and Shane, somewhere in the countryside. On our way to the hotel you got it into your head to adopt a dog, so you dragged us all to a puppy farm."
"As if I'd buy a dog from a puppy farm," snorted Martin.
"Well," continued John, "you dragged us there, and then you spotted a Cavalier King Charles Spaniel puppy and begged and begged me for us to adopt it. You and that puppy were begging so much that eventually I said yes, then you took out a briefcase, put the dog inside, paid for it and we were on our way again to the hotel. When we got into our room Irena and Shane knocked on our door and told us that they were sneaking off to the woods for some midnight shenanigans if we wanted to join. You paid lip-service to the idea of you staying in and minding the dog while I went out and enjoyed myself, but then you started pouting and sulking as I got ready until I had enough and said that I'd watch the dog and you could go out. You beamed your smile, leapt out of bed, handed me the dog, kissed me and ran out of the room."

Martin laughed, John had acted and mimed Martin's parts so well he couldn't help but laugh.

"That was it," continued John, "I watched tv alone in the room with the dog while you were probably having a threesome out in the woods."

"I could have been looking for mushrooms," smiled Martin, "but sorry, besides the puppy farm it does sound like something I'd do."

"Mmm," smiled John, "well, if we ever do adopt a kid you better get used to the idea of *both* of us taking our turns at going out and having fun."

"Of course," said Martin, his mind trying to make the jump from puppy to kid, from dreamt to dream. In the silence John asked:

"Well, have you had any mad dreams lately?"

"No," sighed Martin. "Well, I have a piece of a dream from a few nights back. All I can remember was that I was back in my old bedroom and my clothes were having really kinky, even violent sex." John nearly spat out his wine. "What! What kind of a dream was that?" Martin shrugged.

"I just remember some images, like snapshots. There were jumpers fucking trousers, trousers fucking shirts, my whole wardrobe was flying around having an orgy, and some of it seemed pretty violent and rapey, but I can't remember anything else."

"Jesus," said John, "on that note let's get the cheque," he smiled, his foot rubbing up against Martin's leg.

Back at their house Martin produced the collage book he had made for John, and then started taking out other small gifts, ending with the small black box. With both of them sitting on the couch Martin proposed. John said yes and they hugged and kissed and chattered like 2 nervous virgins sharing their first bed. Then John said he had to tell his family, which ended Martin's dirty thoughts, so that he went to the kitchen to get one of the giant craft beers he had put in the fridge. He took his time in the kitchen, smiling as John spoke proudly to his parents. When John finished the call Martin came in with the beer and glasses.

"Very nice," said John, taking the bottle and inspecting it with care. "Celebration Stout, must have been expensive, by the way, my folks pass on their best and congratulations."

"Thanks," Martin smiled, "There's another giant beer in the fridge, and sure tomorrow's Saturday." Martin, who wasn't fussed about craft beer and who normally hated getting drunk smiled at the thought, and a lyric from U2's *Until the End of the World* played out in his mind. The first time Martin heard the song he misheard 'dream' for 'drink,' and felt the misheard version to be infinitely better. 'Well, perhaps it will do to get drunk tonight' he thought, 'I only have to stay on top of my sorrows until Sunday.'

"Aren't you going to ring your family?" John asked.

"I don't know, I think I'll ring them tomorrow," said Martin, "I just want to enjoy the moment."

"Sure," said John, looking sidewise at Martin. 'It's odd that he doesn't want to tell his parents' he thought, but when Martin sat beside him and put his hand on John's leg John smiled. On the surface, he always felt Martin's actions odd, but still, he felt a deep love for him that made his surface oddities trivial. They poured their beers and raised a toast, drinking to a long and happy life together.

Saturday

With the proposal finished Martin drifted through Saturday morning and afternoon as cheerfully as he could, at least while in company, but when he was alone he felt sick. He pretended to John that he had a great idea for a poem so that he could spend a good chunk of the day staring at his laptop, but he found that he could write absolutely nothing, he couldn't even bring himself to try. Instead, he tried as best he could to shut off his brain. But more than anything else, he simply didn't feel 'present,' his need to get to tomorrow, to get some idea of where he stood, gave him the sensation that time wasn't moving, like a watched kettle, and it drained him. He felt like the kind of lifeless husk he so often associated with John Banville novels.

He couldn't read or touch his guitar, he couldn't write or work on any stand-up material, he couldn't seek out friends or family, all these things now felt like amputated limbs to him, he only felt the phantom pain of their existence, as if these things were gone and gone forever. He felt he could do nothing except wait. Wait in the space between his past actions and their unknown consequences. Wait in a prison of uncertainty. Wait. He never contacted his parents or anyone else about the engagement. The thought of interacting with people repulsed him, especially people he would have to hide the truth from. The only person he wanted to hear from was his brother, and only in relation to his own situation. In this way the gravity of his arrest made Martin selfish, for as much as he would have loved to escape his own thoughts and problems, his seemed unable to rotate around anything other than his arrest. In fact, Martin, as a person, was reduced, as everything else going on in the world now felt criminally trivial in comparison. He was reduced in the way that all traumatic events reduce their victims; reduced to the passive voice, reduced to a single event. Pre-arrest and post-arrest Martin. Reduced to waiting. Waiting. Wait.

He had been arrested and let go an hour or two later, but all the good that was in him was still in that dingy little room in Shop Street Gardai station, stripped near-naked and desperate, waiting to be told to put his clothes back on. It took all of his effort to pick himself up enough to get through dinner without arousing too much suspicion from John. John cooked for the two of them and even the food, despite John's flare in the kitchen, took on the blandness of prison food and the stickiness of guilt in Martin's mouth, and while Martin did his best to guard himself and put up a happy front, he couldn't help but close himself off from the one he loved. Martin felt particularly wretched when, despite his sullenness, John started getting frisky, and Martin had to let him down as gently as he could, complaining of tiredness and a headache.

"What's wrong," John pushed, "you're not stressing about the wedding already, are you?"

"No... no" Martin sighed, "I'll never regret proposing to you, I just don't feel great. Getting drunk on Thursday and Friday is catching up on me," he lied.

"Aw, is this your first hangover?" John teased.

"Maybe" Martin smiled weakly, "I'm sorry."

"You're fine," sighed John, "I just want you as happy and excited as I am," he said with a hug and a kiss. "Well," he continued, "I'll go up and have a read if you're not in the mood for anything. Don't stay up too long, a good night's sleep will do you good."

"Thanks."

When John was gone up Martin forced himself to write in his diary in an attempt to regain some sense of balance against the emotions that were toppling him from the inside out.

[02/11/2019, night, at home]
I'm still waiting on word from my bro on whether those 2 guards are going to follow up on me or not. It's Saturday night and he says he'll let me know tomorrow. John has gone to bed, before he left he was clearly in the mood to do stuff, and maybe we could have, but I just can't see myself getting in the mood. I'm feeling pretty fucking depressed about these 2 clowns hanging over me. I can't even make love to John on the weekend of our engagement. I feel shame, fear, guilt, desperation. I feel depressed. It comes in waves, 'a black eyed dog...' On Monday Mark and the old gang are going to see a Miles Davis documentary in The Sugar Club and I'm trying to keep myself together. If Shay gives me bad news tomorrow then I will have to come clean to John. He'll be pissed

that I didn't tell him earlier, and 8 years of softening up his stance on my illegal habit will be thrown out the window. I guess I'll be on CBD for now on until it's legalised, which is fine for anxiety, but doesn't do much for parties where it's drink drink drink. Ah sure, I'm sure I can spin all this for the best in the long term, but I have a shit few days ahead of me yet if all this goes south. Well, at least tomorrow I'll either be off the hook or no longer having to hide anything from John. 'A change is as good as a rest,' is probably one of the truer sayings. 'Fuck the police,' that's also a good saying, cunt bags. 'Protectors of the peace?' What's more peaceful than a stoner, on his way home, with an engagement ring in his bag, and on Halloween fucking night? The State, the power to inflict violence. To kidnap someone against their will, deny them contact with their friends and family, steal from them, hit them, bully them, all with the backing and support of the State.

I feel depressed.

But I can't blame the Gardai… hard as it is not to. I suppose, in the same way that we've been preached to for years by priests who have secret families, mistresses, to say nothing of young boys, so now we find ourselves policed by those who have smoked and tolked and driven whiskey-soaked. And yet we mustn't hate them for their inherent hypocrisy—for you cannot hate someone without inviting them to hate you back, and we need the police to change with us, not through opposing and reshaping them, but by highlighting that we all fall prey to impulses, and we are all in need at times of a little restraining, not by cold unfeeling metal cuffs but by a hand on your shoulder, a sympathetic ear and a human touch. For the police are entirely human, and it takes a human to help a human. But Fuck, if I was caught passed out from drink I like to think I'd be sent to hospital to get my stomach pumped and then get directed or nudged towards an AA meeting, instead, I get arrested for a smoke…

Fuck
They fucked me in the ass while letting Tom walk off scot free, they did their job half-arsed, and I guess I was the cheekiest cheek on the night,

and I'm getting spanked pretty fucking raw right now. I'm trying not to be bitter, but I'm failing, because, fuck me, everywhere people are smoking weed. Leo Varadkar admitted to smoking weed, and he's our Taoiseach for fuck's sake. He should have legalised it. Snoop Dogg is coming to play in Ireland and he's literally hired a full-time blunt roller to be at his beck and call. I went to see Sinead O' Connor recently and she seemed high as fuck. I went to see Biig Piig and half of her songs are about getting high. I heard Blind-Boy use his grinder during his podcast, and he used it like a joke, so it's hard for me not to be salty. We need to legalise it. If I get convicted, black-listed, life restricted and flushed down the toilet then I will have to become a legalisation radical. Was feeling flush now flushed, grand to fucked, fuck.

Weed
      was
            the
                 best
                      thing   O
                           for ||--''
                               me,   /\
                                    until
                                         it
                                             wasn't. Now?
                                       I feel stupid, afraid...

What kept me from going home as I wanted? Or why did I say it was a cigarette?

Should I blame Tom?

Or some inner working of my mind perhaps?

A chance word said to me at some forgotten time?

But why should I play at being both the judge and the defendant of what I don't even consider to be a crime—except my crime of getting caught?

> *'We forge the chains we wear in life,' said Dickens. No. Too simple. Some chains we forge, some we're born into, some thrust upon us, but anyway, who forges a chain for oneself except out of ignorance?*
>
> *Why must we always walk on a tightrope of near-zero autonomy and absolute responsibility—until we lean or are pushed too much to one side and take a fall, which, if we survive, we'll scrutinise until the next fall, the next time? And who the fuck decided that smoking weed should be a crime? Goddamn North American racist politicians who just wanted to legalise a way to lock up blacks and Mexicans, and even they're starting to legalise it. Fuck.*

Martin finished writing, adding some details to the above doodle, and put his diary away. In bed he snuggled his face into John's large upper-arm and promised to be more in the mood tomorrow, which made John feel a little better.

"I'm just tired" Martin re-lied, his face still lightly pressing into John's arm. "It's been a long few days, I just need a good night's sleep."

"I hope so," said John.

"Yeah, don't worry… I love you" Martin said, kissing John and rolling over, hoping to end their conversation for the night.

"I know," said John, "I love you too." Martin turned off the light by his bed and embraced the indifferent and unquestioning darkness with relief, and sometime later he fell into a desperate sleep.

Sunday

On Sunday John got up military-fashion and went for a jog while Martin complained of a bad night's sleep and rolled over to fake a lie-in. When John was out of the house Martin took out his phone and turned it on. After an hour or so and while he could hear John in the shower Martin received the message he was waiting for and the answer he was dreading:

> *Hey, they sent your hash to the labs so it will have to be followed up. Sorry. They'll probably ring you in the next week or two, or call to your house with a court summons. I really, really don't think you'll get a conviction, but get a sols on standby to represent you to play it safe. You can call me if you want.*

The message seemed to sweep away all that remained of Martin so that for half an hour he felt like a non-entity, he just lied on his bed with a book lying closed beside him. Slowly he recovered, being pulled back to reality by his bladder. He went to the toilet, took a shower, got dressed, said a few words to John and then went back upstairs and confined himself to his laptop. He looked for as much information as he could regarding the law and being caught in possession. He saw that there was some news about Ireland bringing in a 3-strike system relating to weed; where those caught in possession would have to present themselves to the HSE rather than go through the court system, but that this change would not come into effect until August next year.

He went through Reddit posts of those who went through similar situations and found that things seemed to be as his brother promised, he would go to court, pay some cheeky solicitor around €2,000 to represent him for 2 minutes to an uninterested judge, and be let go without a conviction, perhaps having to make a charitable donation. He sighed, the only thing left to do was tell John. Martin went downstairs and sat beside him. John put away his book and looked at him.

"What's wrong?" He asked.

"I need to tell you something... something that happened on Halloween," said Martin, staring mostly at the floor.

"That night I actually left the pub to go home around 9, and Tom came out with me with a smoke for the road and wanting to have a chat. So we started smoking along the boardwalk and 2 Gardai came up on us from behind, I got rid of the smoke as quick as I could but it was too late. I was singled out and asked what we were smoking, I tried to fob it of as a cigarette, I was ... very drunk, and very stupid. Anyway, the guard got the hump that I was lying to him, so I got handcuffed, put into a squad car, brought back to the station and strip-searched down to my boxers. They found me with 7 grams of hash. They let me go after they got my details, and that's why I was home late. As soon as I was out of the station I talked to my brother, he said that they would probably check my file, see I've never caused any trouble before, and would likely throw my hash in the bin and not follow through with it, and that he'd find out today what the craic is. Well... Shay got back to me there, he says my hash has been sent to the labs and so it will be followed up. I'll probably have to go to court, hire a solicitor to defend myself, avoid a conviction, which Shay says I will, and... I guess that's it. I'm sorry, I'm so sorry. I wanted to tell you straight away, but between not knowing what was going to happen with it, and finally having a plan to propose to you, I just wanted to wait until I knew from Shay rather than having us both worry and waiting for what could have been nothing... I'm sorry" Martin finished, his eyes watering, and he looked to John for a response, to make or break what was left of him. John took a deep breath and said:

"Well, I guess it's not as bad as I thought it was going to be when you said you wanted to talk. But... jesus Martin... I'm sorry you had to go through all that, it sounds horrible."

"What did you think I was going to say?" Martin asked, somehow relieved at the idea that it could have been worse, and more than willing to cling to John's sympathy.

"I don't know, I thought you were having second thoughts about the engagement, or that you made out with someone on the night, I never expected an arrest, not from you, even if you are an idiot for smoking in the middle of town." Martin smiled.

"I would never cheat on you like that, and of course I want to marry you, if you'll still have me."

"Of course," said John, "but you have shit timing, I understand you not wanting to tell me till you knew where you stood, but it kind of knocks the wind out of our engagement... you should have told me."

"I know," said Martin, "trust me to get arrested the night before I propose. They even pulled the engagement ring out of my bag, guess they weren't romantics, the older one definitely seemed to have it in for me. They even pulled out my diary at the station and had a good flick through it, they humiliated me," said Martin.

"Well, what were you doing smoking a joint in the middle of town on Halloween? You must have known the place would be crawling with guards."

"I don't know that I was thinking," said Martin, "you can imagine the mess town was in, and I wasn't any better. I was drunk and I guess I thought the guards would have more to worry about than a couple of lads sharing a joint."

"And why didn't you have the smoke at home?"

"It was Tom's smoke," Martin shrugged, "but yeah, I should have had one at home, I won't be smoking again anyway, not like that."

"No," John agreed. "You can't smoke in town like that again, no way." John looked at Martin, who sat staring at the floor, and gave him a hug. Martin felt loved and cried with relief, not knowing what to do or say now.

"Your job's Gardai-vetted, isn't it?" John asked, after the longest and dearest hug of Martin's life.

"Yeah, but I don't know if that's just my school or all language schools."

"And I wanted you to visit my American cousins..."

"Sorry," mumbled Martin. "I didn't think about this affecting my ability to travel."

"We could lose our house if this affects your job" sank John. "Not to mention killing the buzz of our engagement." He looked at Martin, who was back to staring at the floor with watery eyes. With a sigh John gave him another hug and whispered in his ear: "Oh Martin, if you were anyone else I'd kill you... but we'll get through this, we'll get through this together."

"Thank you, I love you so much."

"I love you too."

Monday

Martin woke up on Monday, still reluctant to work, but at least having made a week-long plan for his two classes. He would spend the week teaching his morning advanced class about Irish history and finish by showing them *Michael Collins* on the Friday. For his pre-intermediate afternoon class it would be Irish folklore followed by a Friday showing of *Song of the Sea*. He had done these topics a few times before and he knew the material like the back of his hand. On the way in he sighed as he passed his grandmother's old house, wishing he had her to lean on, and he stopped off in a Centra along the way to buy a new carton of oat milk. In work he bit his tongue and rolled his eyes when, while waiting for the kettle to boil, Tom came in and joined him.

"Well," started Tom, "ye alright? Any news from your brother?"

"Yeah," mumbled Martin, he looked to make sure the staff room was clear before continuing, "looks like I'll have my day in court, but my brother's pretty confident I won't get a conviction…"

"You won't," said Tom, "of course you won't. It'll be grand."

"Hope so," said Martin. "Anyway, I don't want to talk about it, I just want to forget about the whole for a while." The kettle clicked and Martin poured his and Tom's cup, he shook his carton before opening it and poured some in to complete his tea.

"They shouldn't be allowed to call that stuff milk," said Tom, smiling.

"What would you have it called?"

"It should be called oat juice," said Tom. "It's stupid calling it milk, sure it's probably 90% water anyway."

"What about coconut milk?" Martin said, "do you want to start calling that coconut juice? And what should peanut butter to be called? Or about bourbon creams? Did you know Tesco's chocolate bourbon creams are vegan?"

"…they're different," muttered Tom, "they're not pretending to be milk, butter or cream."

"Man, the biggest difference between oat milk and cow's milk is that *this* was actually made to be consumed by humans. You're drinking something that's biologically designed for baby cows. By the way, cows, like us, have to give birth before they produce milk, so they are continuously impregnated through sexual violence, and guess what happens to their babies?"

"Cows aren't sexually violated!" Tom said.

"What would you call what happens to them?"

"Most cows are artificially inseminated, so 'artificial insemination' is what it's called, or 'AI,' my cousin works on a dairy farm, he'd punch your head off if you said he was sexually violating cows!"

"But calling it 'AI' doesn't make any sense. Humans are artificially inseminated all the time when they're struggling to have kids—imagine if I 'artificially inseminated' a woman without her permission, what would you call *that*?"

"Sick," scoffed Tom, "and what happens to the baby cows then? Sure they're just farmed like the rest of the herd."

"If it's a female cow then yes, but the first thing they do is to separate the baby from its mother so that the likes of us get all their mother's milk, and the baby cow is then given formula. And cows are naturally maternal animals, I've watched enough footage of mothers being separated from their newborn babies to put me off milk for life. And if the baby cow is a male then it's soon shot and shipped off as veal, or turned to dog food, because dairy cows are a different breed to the cows used for meat. They don't grow as big or as fast so they're not profitable, and no offence to your cousin, but farmers are only paid to care for what's profitable. I'm not saying they're saints or devils, but their sole purpose is to extract as much profit as they can from the bodies of sentient animals, and there's simply no way to do that without cruelty involved."

"Whatever," said Tom. "Even if baby cows are chopped up for dog food—dogs also have to eat!"

"One of the oldest-lived dogs on record lived on a vegan diet," said Martin.

"*Really?*" Tom said.

"Really," said Martin, as he made his way to the computer to print what he needed.

"So you want to turn all dogs vegan?" Tom continued.

"Why not? They make far less fuss about it than us."

"That's the thing—vegans put themselves under this extreme diet, and then try to convince everyone else to follow suit, it's militaristic."

"What's extreme is unnecessarily raising, feeding and then killing an animal to satisfy someone's taste for their cooked flesh. What's militaristic is getting upset at vegans for asking you to consider the side of the victims."

"Whatever dude," said Tom, "I still wouldn't call what happens to cows sexual violence, it's pretty insensitive to actual rape victims, we do what we do to cows to feed people."

"Well why should 'rape' be the one word in the English language that can be used to describe what happens to humans, but can't be used to describe the exact same process happening to an animal? If I say: 'I kicked my friend' and then 'I kicked a dog' you wouldn't get upset about my choice of words. The only logical reason why people get upset at the idea of cows being raped is that they're paying for it to happen and they don't like to hear about it."

"I would consider bestiality rape," said Tom, "but what's done to cows is necessary to feed people, if it's not for sexual pleasure, it's not rape."

"That's stupid. You don't have to rape someone for sexual pleasure, you can do it for revenge, to show dominance, because of peer-pressure, none of that justifies or determines the action of rape, and if eating meat and dairy are choices, then what's the difference between taste or an orgasm? They're both forms of physical pleasure, and neither can be used to justify an action that has an unwilling victim."

"Whatever man," said Tom, "our ancestors ate meat, other animals eat meat, it's normal to eat meat."

"Give me strength!" Martin said, "nobody ever, EVER, brings up their ancestors or the animal kingdom in any other argument or context, because it's stupid. When you chose this as your job did you ask: 'would my ancestors have approved?' When you bought that jumper did you think: 'wait, do other animals wear jumpers?' Talking about your ancestors and other animals is not a reason, it's an excuse, and a bad one, nobody has ever defended a rapist by going—'well, your honour, you see, lions have also been known to rape each other, so my client was just doing what's natural,' you sound like an idiot."

"Ok dude," smiled Tom, "I'll have a think and talk to you later" and, with that, Tom went out with his tea for a cigarette, smiling at how easy it was to get Martin's mind off his arrest.

And Monday

Martin got to his class and wrote his quote of the day: "Be friendly to everyone.

"Those who deserve it least need it the most" Bo Bennet.

"Well teacher! How was the engagement?" asked his class.

"Great," he said, "yes," Martin beamed.

"Congratulations!" they shouted.

"Thank you. Now, there's a lot that can happen between now and the actual marriage. So, reviewing and using the 0-3rd conditionals I want you to write a sentence for each on my upcoming marriage." His favourite examples were:

1) You have no in-laws until you get married.

2) Teacher might have a kid after he's married.

3) Teacher would be broke if he had a traditional Irish wedding.

4) Teacher would have been able to pay for a traditional Irish wedding if he had studied something more practical.

He led the class through a discussion on the quote, asked about their weekends, cleared through the grammar (mixed conditionals) in record time and then explained his plan for the week:

"So, on Friday we're going to watch an Irish movie called *Michael Collins*, but to give you some context for the movie I'm going to take you through the history of Ireland this week, from 1845 to 1922." Martin wrote the time period on the board and began a mind-map by pulling the bits of information the students already half-knew. He then gave his class a handout on the famine and finished by getting the students to listen to and examine Sinead O' Connor's song, *Famine* while filling in some missing lyrics. Martin was touched that, for the first time, a student, a Chilean in his 50s, not only recognised Sinead, but told Martin that he had actually seen her play in his country, in 1990! Sinead's lyrics led to Martin discussing the possible link between the famine and Ireland's current problems with drink and drugs.

"But" Martin determined to settle, with one eye on the time, "the sadness which is still being felt today didn't just come from the famine, we'll continue the sad history of sad old Ireland tomorrow," and with the timing of one who's kept the same job for too long, the bell went.

Happy with the class and happy to be feeling like a teacher again, Martin's happiness was cut short when he pulled out his phone and saw a message from his mother. She had seen through the digital grapevine that Martin and John were engaged, and she was furious that she wasn't informed by her son, or so Martin understood as he read—*I see your engaged. Congratulations. Please ring me after work*. Martin messaged her back that he was sorry, that he wanted to tell her in person, and that he would drop down to them after work so that they could catch up properly. His mother *was* livid, and between their messages and Martin's actual arrival she spent the time arming herself with as many stones as she could muster to fling at him. As for Martin, he got through the afternoon class on autopilot, and avoided like the plague any more philosophical discussions. When work finished he got out as quick as he could and, as there was still some lingering daylight left, he made a point of walking home through the Basin to try and calm himself before the storm. Taking 5 minutes to sit on a bench Martin looked at the sorry-looking trees and, following a thought, he took out his diary:

It's the trouble of trees
That they lose their leaves
When we need them most.

For while they give us shade
From Summer's showers and rays
In Winter they become lousy hosts.

How I feel like those trees,
stripped bare to the bone,
Lonely in waiting
For Summer to come

He stared at his own words, surprised that he had been able to write anything half decent. Tapping away on his diary he continued:

And why is it that 'I,' when on its own, is the only letter that is automatically capitalised? Could it be that 'I,' when left alone, feels the need to overcompensate? That it has to stand tall as it were? 'o' can stay small, 'a' of course, 'x' has to or it looks like a number. But 'I'? even to be alone in writing 'I' has to compensate for being alone, that's mad. Anyway, time to face my family, at least grammatically, 'I' sits small and comfortable there.

And Monday

Continuing on Martin let himself into his parents' home and was warmly greeted by George, the family dog, otherwise known as Rocky 3 due to his breed and predecessors. Martin got on his knees to hug and rub the excitable boxer and soak in all the love the dog poured out. 'George' he thought, 'Georgie, Georgie, George.' He remembered the last time he called down to his parents, (what a different time that felt!), and his mother making him laugh by saying that George knows when she's about to go out by the perfume she puts on.

"As soon as he smells it," she said, "he becomes depressed. No cheering him up, no fetch. Needy dog." Martin smiled at the stump-wagging thought. 'Needy dogs. No wonder we love them, they've got plenty of space for our excess love to pour into,' he thought. When George finally settled down to 4 paws on the ground Martin got up and started walking through the hall where his mother began:

"Martin! I *should* say 'congratulations,' but instead all I want to say is that I'm furious, FURIOUS you didn't tell us you got engaged, not even just to ring us afterwards. I have told your brother and sister and they are just as furious. They think you've abandoned us. I can't believe you've treated us like this, to treat us like we're nothing, Richard, what do you have to say?" Maggie finished by glaring at her husband as she caught her breath.

"Your mother's right son, I've never heard of someone proposing and not telling their mother, you've really upset her."

"ME! Don't be stupid Richard, he's upset ALL of us, you were only telling me earlier how upset this made you! And your sister was nearly crying at what you've done when I told her, 'mam' she said, 'I don't think Martin sees us as family anymore.'" Maggie finished by glaring again at her husband, this time because he was 'a feckin eejit. This wasn't about *her*,' she thought, 'this was about making sure that Martin never treated the family this way again.' Martin, for his part, had to struggle not to smile. 'This is all so odd' he thought, 'after what I've been through.' The first rebuttal that came to him was to point out all the times that his parents told him that same-sex marriages were 'an utter sham' and an 'indulgence.' He remembered, even after he told them of his bisexuality (in preparation of introducing them to John), that they said it was 'all well and good, but he had better settle down with a woman,' because, as they had seen it, love and marriage was about 'a man and woman starting a family.'

During the same-sex marriage vote Martin went through all of this and more. He had listened to his parents explain that marriage was for starting a family, and when Martin offered that same-sex couples could adopt, his mother came out with 'such a thing isn't natural, or god wouldn't have made it that a man and a woman were needed for conception.' This brought the argument to 'god,' and the idea that 'he' created a natural order to things which people perverted (for god-could-only know what reason). Martin argued in return that children who are born deaf, blind, autistic, or in any other way 'out-of-the-norm,' were never suspected of perverting god's natural order in the way that gay people are suspected.

"How," he had once argued to his mother, "can you love an autistic child for what she is, and never suspect her of going against what 'god' deems natural, but you think gay people are unnatural? If autism exists from birth, and you think an autistic child is natural and blameless, then you should at least think the same of children born gay."

Martin spent a good part of his life arguing with his parents in this way; arguing against their ingrained and forced-fed ideas of god, of gender and gender roles, of sexual orientation, and of outdated racist beliefs. And over the years he became able to argue most topics calmly and compassionately with his family, because, despite their differences, there was never any doubt that they all loved each other sincerely. It's to the backdrop of this long history of loving disagreement, born from the far older and far more insidiously persuasive influence of the unloving and self-serving Catholic Church, that allowed him to usually argue with his parents while keeping his cool, and it gave him the calmness to reflect on the absurdity that now, for the first time in his life, he was subject to an outpouring of abuse because his parents had actually *wanted* to hear about a proposal towards a same-sex marriage.

But Martin instead sat at the edge of the couch and began rubbing George for support, wishing, at the very least, not to rehash his way out of this current encounter. But he had to say something, he was only in the door and his mother was standing over him and demanding an explanation. 'Well' he thought, 'she can hardly get more upset then she already is, I might as well tell the truth.'

"Look," he began. "I'm sorry I hurt you guys."

"Sorry's not good enough" cut in his mother, Martin shrugged.

"Listen, I've been depressed the last few days."

"WHY?"

"I'm telling you mam. Look, the night before I proposed to John I … I got arrested for smoking a spliff in town, okay?"

"WHAT?"

"Look. It was Halloween, I was sharing a smoke with Tom before heading home, and all of a sudden I was pulled into a Gardai station, strip-searched down to my boxers, found with 5 grams of hash, and sent home. I've talked to Shay about it and he's only told me yesterday that the Gardai are following through with it and, basically, in the coming weeks or months I'll have to appear in court and pay a stupid fee for a solicitor to make sure I don't get a conviction. All this has been hanging over me, turning me to bits, and I only told John about it yesterday when Shay told me that it's being followed through. Up to that point, and even now, the proposal just… it hasn't felt real, or not anything I can bring myself to celebrate, so, I'm sorry I didn't tell you guys. But the idea that I've turned my back on this family is absolutely ridiculous, and you know it is." Martin finished. He was beyond fed-up with the whole thing, and he quite enjoyed the idea of shocking his mother out of her anger.

"DOOBIES!" came Maggie, she wasn't expecting this, "I always told you not to be smoking doobies, that you have a problem with drugs. You're unbelievable. Of course you got arrested, you're a fucking eejit."

"Son," started his dad, "now hold on Mags. Son, how serious is this?"

"It's fine," said Martin, "I made a stupid mistake, I got caught. I'll likely be 2 grand out of pocket according to Shay, but we have a bit of money saved."

"You're not fine," Maggie said. "But this should teach you not to smoke anymore, I can't believe it, my own son arrested!" Martin stayed quiet, he thought about this question on and off, would he cease smoking? He was rather surprised John didn't hint at it, and at first he thought the idea seemed favourable, that he was tempted to, but, now more than ever, he didn't think he would stop. 'They can take the weed away from the stoner' he began to think, 'but they can't take the stoner away from weed.'

"Great," said Maggie with angry sarcasm, reading into Martin's silence, "You're not going to stop, are you, you're a drug addict. I told you as soon as I knew you smoked that you would become an addict, I told you Richard."

"I'm not an addict," said Martin. "And I'm not a criminal, any more than dad was when he used to drive after a couple of beers and a glass of wine, or you are when you bought that TV box to get all the channels, in fact, I'm *less* of a criminal, they might as well have arrested me for being bisexual for all the sense it makes. Smoking is victimless. The drug laws were made by the U.S. government to allow for 'legal' prejudice against blacks and Mexicans. The U.N. copy and pasted their drug laws from the U.S., and now the U.S. are starting to legalise it and the U.N. haven't caught up yet! I refuse to see it as a crime."

His parents were shocked.

"Of course you don't, an addict will believe only what they want to keep their habit," said Maggie, not knowing whether to start screaming or crying.

"Are you telling me, son, that you never thought of all the criminal organisations you're funding by your smoking? Gangs sell the drugs you take, and they're the ones destroying our country, and you don't think your smoking does any harm?" Martin nearly laughed.

"Look dad, I don't know what kind people you think I hang around with, but do you really think I'm buying my weed from hardened gangland criminals? The people I buy weed and hash from are mates. I get weed from people who grow it in their gafs. They buy the seeds legally and grow them illegally. I get hash from lads who sneak it in through the airport from places like Amsterdam or Spain, where weed is also illegal but not enforced.

"Most of the people I buy from are in college and are selling on the side to fund their studies, they're not gangs. And if the government really cared about stoners funding gangs, then they would stop being so pig-ignorant and they would have legalised it. You know, the Gardai didn't ask once, not once, where I got the hash from, they didn't even ask! All that time I was arrested I was steeling myself up to keeping quiet on my contact—and they didn't even ask! They couldn't have cared less dad. They also let my mate Tom walk off even though they saw him smoking with me! I'm telling you, I was just an easy mark to take them off the streets on a Halloween night, and that's it, I was unlucky."

"Unlucky?" said his mam, "You're unbelievable is what you are!"

"You're in denial son," said his dad, "these gangs traffic people into Ireland just to grow it for them, and you don't feel any responsibility for any of that?"

Martin stared at the back of George's head as his hand worked slowly and mechanically on the dog's thick neck. 'Responsibility?' he thought. Martin was getting sick of this. Just as his parents had finally become lovingly accepting of him and John, all it took was one half-smoked spliff falling out of his pocket to make him the black sheep again, to give his parents a new stick from which to poke and prod him, and he was sick of it.

"Listen dad, when you buy clothes or a new phone, you don't think about the child labour, do you? The sweat shops?"

"Enough of that!" Put down his father, tossing the argument out the door. "I'm not condoning sweatshops, but buying drugs is bringing people illegally into this country to grow them, and that's a fact! It's been all over the radio, and it funds gangs."

"Oh, so you want to talk about illegal workers? Then look at the kind of people who are brought to work in our slaughterhouses, slaughterhouses rely on the most desperate of immigrants and have them working 12-hour shifts in hotbeds. That's 12 hours of work killing animals and then 12 hours of sleep in a bed that has just been slept on by another worker. Can you imagine what a 12-hour job of killing animals does to you? Would you like spending 12 hours a day killing meek, scared-shitless farm animals? Studies have shown that those kinds of jobs cause higher rates of suicide, depression, domestic abuse, rape, and, haha, drug addiction and violence."

"So that's it," said his father, "you want to smoke dope, save the animals, hug a fucking tree and give us the middle finger as we watch you end up in jail. You want us to sit by and watch as our son becomes a goddamn stereotype."

"Or you could end up on the streets" rejoined Maggie.

Martin sighed, regretting his loss of focus, regretting pushing his parents' buttons. He continued:

"Caring for animals is also about caring for people, but forget it. Look, I care dad, about people, myself, you, mam, and sometimes I care too much, about not wanting to hurt others, not wanting to get in anyone else's way. And if I thought for a second that my smoking was harming anyone then I wouldn't smoke. Some of the very people I buy weed from have been in this house and have been entertained by you guys! I'm not buying weed from gangs."

"You shouldn't be buying it all," said Richard.

"Here! Here!" nodded Maggie.

Martin shook his head. "You say that, but look, you remember what I was like as a teenager, the ulcers, the therapy, my lack of self-esteem. Now, I've been smoking for 10 years before this arrest, and these have been among the 10 most stable years of my life. Shay will tell you that most Gardai who catch someone smoking look the other way. Why? Because it's an arbitrary, stupid, victimless crime, and it's only a matter of time before it's legalised. They've legalised it in Canada, 2nd largest country in the world, I don't know how many states in the U.S., 10 or 14, it's essentially decriminalised in most European countries, you can grow up to 4 plants for personal use in Spain, and *so* many people smoke, you have no idea, no idea.

"Dad, you who got me into the *Beatles, Thin Lizzy, The Boomtown Rats, Bob Dylan,* you want to lecture me on smoking? Every musician you listen to, every writer you love, even Shakespeare smoked weed for fuck's sake! And you think I smoke because I'm an addict? Okay, I smoke weed because I love it, I'll say it, I love it, I love smoking weed. But so what? It helps my anxiety, and more than anything else, for me, it's so much better than being drunk. Being drunk makes me stupid, aggressive, moody, depressed, and every event, every family gathering, it's drink drink drink drink drink. I hate it. On every level, in every test, scientists show that weed is at the very least safer than alcohol.

"If I wasn't drunk that night, on *free* beer, I wouldn't have been arrested. And you want me to give up weed? If anything I should give up alcohol! Even the Gardai who arrested me pulled out one of my smoke tubes and said, 'you must have been to Amsterdam.' I couldn't make this shit up! The goddamn Gardai who arrested me rubbed it in my fucking nose that he had smoked in Amsterdam! And I'm not an addict. I don't smoke every day, okay, despite what you think, I don't. I smoke, for the most part, socially, because it helps me to be social, it helps me to enjoy gatherings and parties, and to stop worrying about whether I'm fitting in. But sure, you and everyone else get to drink alcohol, every single day if you want, even to death, and yet you get to take the moral high ground because alcohol is legal and weed isn't. Well, fuck our legal system."

With that the front door was opened, George got up with a bark to investigate, Maggie and Richard looked at each other and Shay walked into the room.

"Howya," said Shay as he ducked himself through the hall. "Well, it's the man himself! Congratulations," he said as he saw Martin.

"Thanks," mumbled Martin.

"Welcome to the mad house," said Maggie.

"Martin's been telling us about his arrest," said Richard.

"You told them you got arrested? Well."

"Yeah…" said Martin.

"Fair play to yeah, might as well get the slaggings started. You've been having some mad week huh."

"Yep, thanks."

"Slaggings?" Maggie said, "he needs an intervention and a drug councillor."

"I don't know about that," said Shay. "Even the guards feel it will have to be legalised eventually. Honestly mam, the guards suffer far worse from the alcoholics than we do the stoners."

"Good grief," sighed Maggie. "Do you's want dinner anyway. I'll get you a beer son, sit down."

"If there's a bit of dinner going, oh god yes," smiled Shay.

"I haven't even started *our* dinner yet," said Maggie. "I've been too… frustrated," she said as she went to the fridge and got Shay a Guinness. "Do you want a can?" She asked Martin.

"Oh, why not."

"I'm doing steaks, salad and chips," said Maggie, "you can have salad and chips or order yourself a takeaway."

"I'm not staying for dinner, thanks, we've food in the house," answered Martin, taking a can and a glass from his mam.

"So Shay," said Richard, "Martin would have us believe the Gardai aren't going to follow him up on where he bought his hash, surely they're going to follow it up in their own time?"

"No," said Shay dismissively. "No one cares about that. Sure anyone with a couple of hundred quid can start growing weed from their gafs now, or there's thousands of lads entering the country every day with the stuff on them or in them. The guards don't care, they know themselves when someone like Martin goes before a judge the judge will throw it out, 99% of the time, with maybe a charity donation, so they won't be arsed chasing dealers through Martin. They only bother about that stuff if they find large amounts of coke or something."

"But what about all the cannabis-busts they make every week?" Richard asked, "surely they're looking for the stuff, you hear about a drug-bust every other week on the radio."

"Yeah but that doesn't mean the guards are looking for them" smiled Shay. "Most drug-busts come from some nosy neighbour who makes a complaint about a grow-house, or about dodgy lads coming in and out of a house at all hours, and once the Gardai have a complaint or 2 they pretty much have to act on it. But besides that they don't care, I know a lot of Gardai who turn a blind eye to people smoking or who smoke themselves when not on duty. I turn a blind eye myself if the person's sound because it's not worth the paperwork. I know of the guy who caught Martin, he's an old-school country guard and they say he's been a crank lately, just unlucky," Shay shrugged, "his wife's probably cheating on him or something."

"Unbelievable," muttered Maggie as she put the chips on, "but you wouldn't be an unlucky stoner if you weren't a stoner. You can't argue your way out of that!"

"Then does he really need a solicitor," Richard asked.

"Probably not, no. But judges are wacked. They've no consistency whatsoever. Rather than having Martin represent himself and risk pissing off the judge it'll be better to pay someone all the judges know anyway to bore them with the usual safe bullshit. No offence, but with the way you get into arguments I wouldn't dare put you up to represent yourself. You'd probably ask the judge if he's vegan and get yourself thrown in jail."

"Fair enough," mumbled Martin.

"So that's it then," said Maggie, "you'll have learnt nothing from any of this."

"I've learnt," said Martin, "to be more careful, much more careful, to never smoke out in the open like that again," he shrugged, "obviously I've learnt to communicate better with you guys. I don't know what else there is after that. I just want to put this behind me, it's ruined the buzz of our engagement, and I'm still depressed when I think of what a conviction could do, and while you don't agree, I feel like this is all a waste of everyone's time. I read that Ireland's bringing in a 3-strike policy for smoking where, for up to 3 times of being caught, you'll be referred to the HSE rather than the courts. It's meant to be coming in in the Autumn. I know you don't like me smoking mam, but really, honestly, it's just a matter of time before it's legalised, and what? I'm supposed to wait until our country catches up with common sense? If everyone did that then this country would never have changed anything, never."

"It beats getting arrested," said Maggie as she seasoned the steaks.

"Is that true?" Their father asked Shay, "about the 3 strike thing?"

Shay shrugged, "I haven't heard anything about it. It would make sense except I'm sure the HSE don't want to be dealing with it either, they're already stretched too thin." Richard shook his head.

"Look son, I hear what you're telling me, but despite what you think, you don't know everything. I think those doobies do make you dopey, and lazy. Everything you see about doobies shows how lazy doobie-heads are," Martin sighed and replied.

"Look dad, the idea of stoners being lazy is a stereotype. Sure, some people, *while* they're smoking, maybe, they don't want to do anything, but even that's not true for everyone. I don't think smoking's made me lazy. I have a good job that I love, a house, I'm engaged, and I'm writing a few bits and doing stand-up when I can, I don't know what else you want from me?"

The family went quiet after that. Martin, Shay and Richard sipped their pints while Maggie started frying the steaks. She was disappointed that her main goal, of reducing Martin to humble rubble for failing to tell the family of the engagement, hadn't gone to plan. But on that thought she spoke up: "Well, you're still to ring your sister and apologise to her for not telling her of your engagement. You should ring her now."

"I'll ring her when I get home mam, I promise. I'll be heading once I've finished this," he sipped as his mam got the salads together.

"Well, if you're sure. Can you give him a lift Richard?"

"Yeah, no bother." Martin smiled and looked at the beer in his dad's hands.

"No, I'm grand," he said. "I could do with the walk back. No point risking two family members being arrested in the same week."

And Still Bloody Monday

Martin got home and settled as John asked after his parents.

"They're grand, mam was really upset that I didn't tell her about the engagement, I thought getting arrested would have made for a good excuse but funnily enough that just upset her even more, but they calmed down eventually."

"You told your parents about the arrest?"

"Yeah… I wasn't planning to, but sure, I can't do anything about it now. I just have to face up to it and wait for it all to be over with."

"Well, that's all well and good for you," sighed John, "but I won't be able to tell mine any time soon."

"Well… I guess that's up to you, I can't ask you not to after I've told mine."

"Are you kidding?" John scoffed, "My folks still view all illegal drugs as if they're all different names for heroin. I had a long and desperate enough time letting them in to the real me, I couldn't even get away with coming out as bisexual."

"What?" Martin said, "I came out as bi because I am bi. Are you getting mad at me for that?"

"No, it's just, you got to ease your parents into the idea that you'd be spending your life with a man, I just had to come out as gay. And now you get to tell your parents you've been arrested, if I tell mine I don't know if they'll still want me to marry you!"

"Well… I'm sorry," said Martin. "My brother arrived down to the house and he helped ease things over by giving a typical Gardai perspective, maybe that might help with yours?"

"No, that won't help." Martin sat in the silence, not knowing what to say, when John continued: "I'm sorry, I don't mean to be upset, but my phone's been buzzing with messages and calls about our engagement, and I have to pretend that I'm excited when all I can think about is whether or not you'll get a conviction. I feel like I can't talk to anyone about it and I'm just shocked that you've been able to tell your folks."

"I'm sorry," said Martin. "I'm still in the doghouse with them, my mam tore into me for a good while, she also made me promise I'd ring Kate when I got home."

"Sure, ring Kate, I'm sure she'll love all this."

"I'm sorry John."

"It's fine, ring Kate, I'm going to go for a run."

Martin sat in silence as John got changed and left, only mumbling another apology as John went out. He then picked himself up and called Kate.

"Well, congratulations," said Kate, "I was wondering when you'd call."

"Sorry Kate, and thanks, how's things?"

"Grand yeah, so, how'd you propose?"

"Well… we went for a quiet dinner in town, then back home I had a few personal gifts put together, I told him how much I loved him and all that, and that was it I guess. Fairly quiet and simple."

"It sounds perfect, are you happy?"

"Yeah,… well" Martin sighed, "I'll tell you the full story of it. I was arrested on Halloween."

"*WHAT!*" said Kate in soprano.

"For smoking a spliff."

"**What!**" Kate said in baritone.

"Yeah, I was just leaving a staff party out of my head and got caught spliff-in-hand, green-handed I guess, and, I don't know, I tried to argue with the guard that it was a cigarette—"

"Oh Martin."

"Yeah, learnt not to argue with guards. Anyway, the spliff was out by the time they caught up to us so I figured I was safe."

"Who were you with?"

"Tom, you remember? Looks-like-a-Viking Tom."

"Oh I like Tom, what happened to him?"

"Nothing! They let the bastard walk off…. To be fair, Tom did what he could for me, he even went to the Gardai station to check up on me, but they turned him away at the door. But yeah, we were passing it back and forth and I got nailed."

"Shit," said Kate, "so then what?"

"Well, I got taken in a squad car, brought back to Shop Street, strip-searched, found with 10 grams of hash and let go. The next day I proposed to John without telling him anything and 2 days after that Shay was able to check the systems and it turns out I'm being prosecuted, so now I've told everyone, John and the folks I mean, and... I guess that's it. I'll have to go to court at some stage, look sorry for myself, and hope I just get a slap on the wrist... fun."

"Jesus Martin, how has John taken it?"

"Ah he's been great, very supportive when I told him, although I think he's starting to vent a bit now."

"Serves you right," said Kate, "you shouldn't keep things from him like that."

"I know... I was just hoping the guards would forget about it, I thought I'd wait till I knew before panicking everyone."

"And you didn't think to put off your proposal?"

Martin sighed, "maybe I should have," he said.

"YES, YOU SHOULD HAVE," said Kate. "Well... you said you told the folks about the arrest, how did they take it?"

"Ah, mam went nuts, she was already upset for finding out about the engagement through John's Facebook, I really thought being arrested would be a good excuse but..."

"You're mad," laughed Kate.

"Well," continued Martin, "they calmed down eventually, although mam was making out as if I've deserted the family, actually, she put those words in your mouth."

"Oh," said Kate, "I'm sure I said something bad against you. I wouldn't be going too hard on mam, she might exaggerate like crazy, you know she loves a bit of drama, but she means well."

"Mmm," said Martin. "fair enough."

"So anyway, you got engaged, you got arrested, any other news?"

"I think that's enough news from me for a while, I just have to wait for the guards to get in touch... teaching's grand. Actually I have a funny one for you."

"Go on."

"I was playing Scrabble with the afternoon class after the test and one of the students spelt out zas, z-a-s."

"That can't be a word."

"That's what I said, they're always changing their arm, but I looked it up just in case and it turns out 'zas' *is* a word."

"So what does it mean?"

"That's the worst part, apparently it's short for pizza."

"ZAS! Short for pizza?"

"Well, just 'za,' but it's a countable noun."

"Good fuck," laughed Kate, "imagine trying to order a Hawaiian za over the phone."

"I know right, like 'pizza' is such a fun word to say anyway—peets-za!—it's a brilliant word. And then I thought, well, fuck my life, here I am trying to teach English while the language is going to the dogs."

"What's next," laughed Kate "we'll be using 'ips' for chips."

"Or 'ger' for burger."

"Oh god," laughed Kate, "imagine how angry everyone would sound—I'll have a cheese—gerrr."

"I'll have the vegan ger and ips." The two of them were cracking up and tears started streaming down. "Thanks Kate," said Martin, "I needed a laugh."

"Yeah," Kate said between giggles, "yeah, no worries, are you alright anyway."

"I think so," said Martin, "think seeing mam and dad helped, although they think I'm a drug addict, you'll let me know if they plan an intervention for me, right?"

"Sure," laughed Kate.

"…I miss nana," said Martin. "She would have had a laugh at all this, and help me calm down the folks. Do you remember when mam found out about my night in drag?"

"Remember!" said Kate, "mam kept calling me and screaming at me for what I did to you, she thought I was trying to turn you into a woman or something."

"Yeah," laughed Martin, "and when they told nana all about it nana had to ask them 'what's a crossdresser?' And mam said it's a person who dresses like the opposite sex and goes out and about, and nana, all plain and sweet, says to them 'sure then I must be a crossdresser, all those years I spent cycling in France with Jimmy I was dressed as man, sure there were no clothes for female cyclists back then.' Mam and dad didn't know what to say."

"I know," said Kate, "you know, I think the folks still think that that night had something to do with turning you bi."

"I know," Martin sighed. "When I told the folks that I was always bi they said, 'well how do you know if you've never had a boyfriend?' As if it makes a difference, as if heterosexuals are never taken seriously until they've had sex… with nana I never had to argue about any of that crap, I never had to justify how I felt or why I did what I did."

"I know," said Kate. "She meant the world to me too."

"I know," Martin sighed. "Anyway, I suppose that night in *Misneach* did help me in a way, I mean, not towards being bi, but being more comfortable about it, so… thanks Kate."

"No worries, sure we've had some great times at it, I need to have you and John back, well, when you put your arrest behind you."

"Yeah… how's the old gang anyway?"

"Ah they're grand," sighed Kate, "I still see them once or twice a month, they're always asking about you guys."

"That's good, anyway" Martin continued, "yeah, I'm ok, I get depressed thinking about it, it comes in waves, you know, until it's behind me… it's just the fear of getting a conviction."

"Sure what can you do," she said. "I'd say the chances of you getting a conviction are one in a million, but if you do get one—what's the worst case scenario?"

"I could lose my job, it's Gar—"

"You won't lose your job," interrupted Kate, "if you get a conviction your job won't know anything about it, Gardai vetting is a one-time deal, isn't it? So, put that out of your mind, you might be stopped from getting *another* job as a teacher, but if you keep your head down you should have enough time to figure something else out… anyway, even if you lost your job, it's only a chance to start a new one."

"That's true," brightened Martin.

"What else would you do anyway, besides teaching?"

"Well, assuming I don't magically make it as a professional comedian… I don't know… I reckon I would have made a good sex-worker, but I don't think the folks would approve."

"Or John," Kate laughed, "then again… my brother a sex-worker, are you telling me if our parents were gone that's what you'd be?"

"Who knows," shrugged Martin. "I lived with them a lot longer than you, and sometimes I think—are you ever truly an adult while your parents are still alive? I mean, the amount of things I either had to hide or felt I couldn't do living under their roof."

"Mmm," said Kate, "do you know what I did?"

"Yeah," laughed Martin, "you moved out, I don't know how you did it at 18, I admire you so much for that."

"It wasn't all good, believe me. But, you know, I get where you're coming from, but there's nothing worse than an adult who blames his life on his parents, especially when the parents are as good as ours, I mean, we hit the parent-jackpot."

"Yeah… you're right," sighed Martin.

"And," said Kate, "as much as I love my freedom, do you know, if mam and dad were as free growing up as we've been, I don't think we would be here."

"I know," said Martin, "although I never thought of it quite like that. It's mad."

"Well, my point is," said Kate, "you won't get a conviction, but if you do, the limits and restrictions it would put on your life… who knows, there could be a bright side to it, if you know where to look."

"Thanks," said Martin, "yeah… maybe things would work out work-wise, but, I'd still be fucked when it comes to visiting John's extended family in the States. I hate thinking we may not be able to travel to the U.S. together because of me."

"Mmm," said Kate. "well, I get it, not knowing, limbo-land, it's not where you want to be."

"No," said Martin. "Limbo sucks, it sucks so bad even the Catholic church got rid of it, and that's saying something."

"But it's not forever," said Kate soothingly, "even if it's where you are, the time will pass one way or another. Are you reading anything good at least?"

"I'm finally on Walt Whitman. I'm enjoying it, the guard going through my bag didn't look impressed though."

"Great book," said Kate, "glad you're finally getting around to it… They went through your bag?"

"They even had a glance through my diary."

"Fucking hell," said Kate.

"I don't even want to know what they read" Martin laughed. "What are you reading anyway?" He asked.

"*Blackwood Farm*, I'm picking up Anne Rice again, it's good so far, very good, forgot how much I loved her writing, she has a flare for descriptions."

"Yeah," said Martin, "been a while since I've read any of her work. Think I got stuck on *Memnoch the Devil* when Lestat was taking 50 odd pages to describe a hotel bar."

"Yeah," laughed Kate, "she's definitely a writer I can paint from. And did you read the Alan Watts book I gave you?"

"I did, thanks."

"Well," said Kate, "if you're feeling down pick him up again, or continue with Whitman, they're good sympathisers."

"Thanks," said Martin. "Anything else lined up for me?"

"Of course! *Three Guineas*, another one by Virginia Woolf, it's not as well-written as *A Room of One's Own* but it's very good."

"Sure," said Martin, "looking forward to it, *A Room of One's Own* was one of the best things I've ever read."

"What about me?" Kate asked.

"Yeah actually, *My Father's Wake* by Kevin Toolis, it'll remind you of Albert Camus' *The Myth of Sisyphus*, except it's actually good."

"Oh my god," laughed Kate, "*The Myth of Sisyphus* was horrendous, and it started so well."

"It finished good too," said Martin, "but yeah, the main body of it was poor… but if you want a good book on death and dying *My Father's Wake* is where it's at."

"Okay," said Kate, "anyway, I'll have to let you go, thanks for the call, I sent you your tunes earlier today, congrats again and good luck with the guards, keep me posted, and tell John I was asking for him, I've already messaged him my congrats."

"Sure," said Martin, "thanks Kate."

Martin put his phone away and sat waiting on John to come back.

"Well" John said wearily, eventually coming in with a bag of chips. "I got a bag for myself after the run, ate them already. I got you a bag too in case you didn't get dinner in your mam's."

"Thanks."

"How's Kate?"

"She's grand yeah, she was asking for you, and saying that I'm an idiot for keeping things from you, and… yeah, I filled her in on everything and she cheered me up a bit."

"That's good," said John, "Well, it's getting late, I'm going to get ready for bed" and with that he walked past Martin without a look. They went to bed in a subdued mood that night.

Tuesday

While walking to work Martin winced, held his breath, and his heart thumped as loud and as randomly as a toddler's drum solo as a Gardai car flew down the road with its sirens blasting. Cursing and shaking his head Martin continued, but he was surprised to find his senses twisted and newly tuned to alert him with a wave of anxiety to any nearby Gardai. During the course of one night they had gone from 'Protectors of the Peace' to disturbers of his peace of mind, and he was saddened by his own reactions. In work he started his Tuesday morning class with a discussion on the day's quote: "You inherit your parents' trauma, but you will never fully understand it" from *BoJack*. Then he checked to see what his students could remember about The Famine. He wrote the most important points on the board as the students worked through them:

– *Many people died* ("How many?"), *247xplain. 1.5 million (*"Good, well, not good actually. What else?).

– *Many people emigrated* ('sigh,' "how many?"), *247xplain. 1.5 million.*

– *The people in charge continued exporting food to England and to English armies abroad, one of the reasons the famine is often considered a genocide* ("Good, what else?").

– *English became the dominant language at this time (*Good, gives me a job, what else?*).*

– *The famine happened between 1845-1852…*

After a couple more points Martin focused their attention back to emigration.

"So," he said, "in the film we'll be watching on Friday, which is set between 1916 and 1922, you'll see Eamon de Valera, our then leader (unfortunately), heading to the U.S. to try and get support and money to help with our fight for independence. Now, why do you think he, and many others, went to the U.S. looking for support for what was happening in Ireland?" This led the class to discussing about the huge amounts of Irish Americans; the children, grandchildren and great-grandchildren of those who left due to the famine. When Martin was satisfied he continued:

"Yes, you see, how England treated us during the famine would come back to bite them in the next few decades. But there's one other thing we shouldn't forget about this period (1845-52), and it's that when the Irish emigrated at this time they did so as extremely poor and extremely desperate refugees, heck, there were even Irish immigrants who arrived into these countries without even being able to speak English. And many people, including us Irish, forget that when we arrived in the places that we emigrated to the most, such as…?"

"Boston,"

"… New York"

"Liverpool."

"Good," Martin continued, "the local people hated the Irish emigrants like most people today hate the idea of any poor refugee arriving in the thousands and tens of thousands. Only it was worse, because back then you were actually allowed and encouraged to be openly racist. So most places around England and the U.S. had signs put up saying 'No Blacks, No Dogs, No Irish' or 'Irish need not apply.' In other words, the Irish were discriminated against and often hated at this time, and there were even some English people who claimed that we were an inferior, barbaric race, incapable of higher learning" and, with that, Martin led the class through a slideshow of these and other racist signs and cartoon-drawings aimed against the Irish. Eventually one of his students cleared her throat and asked:

"So what happened then?"

"What 'what' happened?" Martin asked.

"Well, what happened that made the Irish so hated to being so loved in the U.S.?"

Martin smiled, as this question took him back to another class entirely.

"It was a number of things," said Martin, "but the most obvious answer, although it's very sad to say it, is that unlike other immigrants, the Irish looked like, and still, unfortunately, look like the status quo, that is, we looked like those who were already in charge." He gave the class a moment to reflect on this before continuing:

"What you need to understand is that an Irish immigrant arriving in New York, say, had a much easier time mingling with someone of English or Scottish decent, or German, or Dutch, or French, or even Italian, although the Irish and

Italians tended to hate each other in the U.S., I suspect because both groups arrived late to the party, but that's another story… Anyway, if you think back to those signs—'No Blacks, No Dogs, No Irish'—well, it's sad but true, but all an Irish person had to do, in theory, was put on a convincing English or Scottish accent! And that was then, now, a North-American has a choice of declaring him or herself as 'Irish-American,' and when something's a choice it becomes a privilege, but someone of African or Asian descent will always be labelled as such long before they can even open their mouth.

"Unfortunately, these people don't have the luxury of declaring themselves to be African or Asian, they *are* declared to be African or Asian, and it's an important difference. You also have to reflect on the fact that, and back then especially, people are and were afraid of mixing races, so that if a white person got with a black person and they had a child, their child would only be seen as black, or a so-called 'half-caste,' and generally treated as a black citizen. Whereas the Irish looked so much like those already in charge that within one or two generations we were able to leave the racism against us behind, not because of anything that we did, but simply because of how we looked. If you're interested, there's a famous film called *Gangs of New York* which gives a 249xplain249ed version of what it might have been like as an Irish immigrant around this time. *U2* wrote a song for the film called *These are the Hands that Built America.*

"Now, there's some truth to this idea that Irish immigrants built a lot of the infrastructure of North America, especially its railway system, and even the White House was designed by an Irish architect, but black people were also the hands that built America, as well as the hands that fed America, clothed America, entertained America, created wealth for America, and created America's most original and loved music, and yet, they are also the most imprisoned people in North America. The Irish complain that we never received enough gratitude for what we did, but at least we got paid and had some level of choice in the matter, whereas black people were made to work as slaves while living in a world that mistreats, abuses and victimises them for how they look, never mind anything about gratitude."

Martin cleared his throat. He wasn't happy that he was doing most of the talking, his job was to stoke conversation, not smother it, but he felt he had to finish what he started.

"What I want you to realise," he continued, "is that the English used to put us Irish people down the exact same way they used to put down black people, they really believed both 'races' were really inferior species, and to prove their point they made us inferior by treating us as inferior, but when English and Irish people started mixing in places like Liverpool, well, the children they raised looked like typical English children, spoke like typical English children, and, assuming they were treated like typical English children, they developed exactly how typical English children were expected to develop. Of course, under the same circumstances, black children would have developed exactly the same too, but they never got that chance. They were segregated for how they looked then, and, in many ways, they're still being ostracised for it now."

"That's terrible," said the student.

"Terrible and true. The good news is that the Irish, as much as we love to moan about the severe way we were treated, we mixed into North America and England in a way that other immigrants could only dream of, simply because the barriers and walls created by racism didn't apply to us. We simply mixed into 'white' culture and society. If you want proof, there has been a total of 16 U.S. presidents who have claimed Irish decent. That's 16 out of 46. Yet there hasn't been a single U.S. president of Asian, Mexican or native-American decent, but there has been at least 16 presidents who have described themselves as Irish-American.

"Obama was the first president of African-American descent, and even he claimed Irish descent as a bonus! Obama even came to Ireland, had a Guinness, spoke a few words of Gaelic-Irish, and the rest of the U.S. loved it! Why? Because, and again, this is sad but true, the Irish are the only white, 'western,' English-speaking people with zero colonial guilt and with zero war guilt, at least at the national level. Throughout history we have been England's victim, (one of their victims), and even when Irish people did horrible things in other countries, and they certainly did, they did so under the banner of *English* colonialism, under *their* empire. Even when the Irish fought in WW1 and WW2, we did so as part of the *English* army, (but we'll get to that more tomorrow).

"The point is, we have the sad history of a victimised, exploited and colonised country, but we look and speak the same as those in power. That's what makes Ireland so unique; we have the history of the oppressed, and the face the oppressors. This is also the bad news, that too many Irish people have either forgotten all of this or, more likely, we have never been taught to understand it in the first place. And so, despite how historically stupid it is, there are many Irish people today who have little to no sympathy for refugees, and who are also racist and xenophobic, despite the fact that most of these people will have family living in places such as Australia, Dubai or Canada."

"Do you think the Irish are racist teacher?"

"...Well. Yes, unfortunately, there are some Irish people who are racist, and I think how our government treats refugees is really, *really* disgusting, and I often wonder how *we'll* pay for it in the decades to come, but, more than that, there are people in my family who are racist, I've had teachers who were racist... hell, at times, I guess I've been racist... growing up I've said some racist things and laughed at some racist jokes I should never have laughed at. So, yes, Irish people can be racist, but we'll never be otherwise until we admit it and make a conscious effort to improve, and improving," continued Martin, no longer speaking to his class, but to the ghost of a class, "improving means asking not what's lacking in others, but what's been lacking in us."

Martin looked around the class, and feeling it to be more sombre than he intended (even given the topic!), he continued: "But in saying that the Irish can be racist there's one more thing we should understand, it's also possible, and actually common, to be black and racist, or gay and homophobic, or a woman and sexist against women. We have a famous trans woman in Ireland, Panti Bliss, and she gave a speech where she said that despite being an openly gay professional cross-dressing male, that she was also homophobic. According to her, it simply wasn't possible for people of her generation not be homophobic because of how we were raised, and when I think of that I think of my mam, who is sometimes sexist against women, or me, who had been a bit homophobic before accepting myself as bisexual. We're so afraid now to be identified as racist, or sexist, or homophobic that... we're not even trying to improve anymore. But being racist in itself doesn't make you a bad person, what makes you a bad person is being proud of your racism. It's like learning English, what do I always say is the most important thing in learning English?"

"Being willing to make mistakes," said one student.

"Exactly," said Martin, "not just willing to make mistakes, but happy to make them, because when you make a mistake you have the opportunity to grow, to change, to improve, so people need that space to make mistakes. We need to live in a world where it's possible to make a language mistake and to be corrected with patience, kindness, and to be given the reason why it was a mistake.

Similarly, we need to live in world where a person can admit to being a racist once that person is willing to change, otherwise we push discussions on race to the fringes, where people are more likely to be racist and proud rather than racist and honest about their reason for it, which, every time, will always boil back down to ignorance and some level of fear or self-hate." To finish the class Martin showed his students the famous speech by Panti Bliss in the Abbey Theatre; one student cried, several seemed moved, and the class went over the time in the ensuing discussion.

And Tuesday

"Hello," said Martin, picking up his phone and turning down the music.

"Hello, that Martin?"

"Yes"

"This is the Gardai you ran into on Thursday, how's things, you well?"

"Em, yeah, thanks, as well as can be… yourself?"

"Grand thanks. Right, I imagine you want this to be over as quickly as possible, so come down to the station after work and we'll have a chat about your situation. Now, you don't *have to* go down to the station, but it'll be better than if we have to go to you, understand?"

"Yeah," said Martin.

"Good. So Shop Street Gardai station after work, yes? What time will you be here?"

"…half 5."

"Perfect. See you then."

Martin put his phone away and started pacing the room as his head went into a tailspin. 'Thursday' he thought, 'in the space of a few days I'm to meet again the man who has turned me inside out and back to front.' His hands were shaking. He took a seat, took 5 deep breaths, and messaged his brother about the exchange, wondering if Shay had had a hand in the speed of everything, but his brother replied:

No I didn't get a chance to talk to anyone, but it's probably a good thing that they're pushing ahead without waiting for the lab results. You can mention me when you meet them, no harm. Good luck. Martin, struggling to calm down, opened up his computer and again sought to drown his mind in the murkiest versions of *Off the Handle*, *Do You Read Me* and *I Wonder Who*.

By the time work had finished Martin felt only a little calmer as he made his way to Shop Street Station, marvelling at how different the building looked now that he was sober. He walked in, unsure how to present himself, when Leo recognised him.

"Well, it's yourself," said Leo. Martin was relieved to see the younger of the two guards first.

"Yeah, I was meant to come after work," he stammered.

"I know all that, Gerard, the other guard, will be with us soon, follow me." He led Martin to an interview room with a table and a couple of chairs, a very different kind of room from last time he thought. Leo left him there and signalled to Gerard who was dealing with someone else, but he caught Leo's signal and both understood that he would follow shortly. Leo entered the interview room and found Martin standing in the room as he was left. He smiled.

"Have a seat," Leo said as he took one opposite the table. "How did your proposal go?"

"Yeah," said Martin in surprise, "I mean, he said yes."

"That's great," said Leo, "congratulations."

"Thanks," said Martin as Gerard came into the room.

"Well," started Gerard, "how's things?"

"Grand," said Martin. Gerard took a seat beside Leo and looked across at Martin. He felt more bored than anything. On Halloween he remembered a cheeky little shit who was out of his head on god knows what. At the station he expected to find a good mix of drugs in Martin's bag, but contented himself on the 10 grams of hash. When they looked for a record on their system they found only that Martin had reported his phone stolen several years ago, (also on Halloween), but what really struck Gerard was finding out that Martin was 28 despite looking 18. Now, looking at Martin as he was sober, he had even less patience for this business.

"Well," said Gerard after he had his fill, "I called you to the station rather than present you with a summons to your house, I'm guessing you've kept all this to yourself."

"No," said Martin, "I've told everyone, I mean, my partner and my family." Gerard and Leo were amused at this, and Martin also smiled nervously.

"Well," said Gerard between laughs, "that's a new one for us, and did you talk to anyone *useful* about this, like a solicitor?"

"Just my brother," said Martin.

"So you're brother's a solicitor?"

"No, he's a guard."

"WHAT!" Gerard nearly jumped out of his chair. "You're joking?"

"A guard," whispered Leo.

"Yes," said Martin. "My brother's a guard."

"You're brother's a guard? Why the fuck didn't you say that on Thursday then!" Martin, who was only starting to feel in control of his nerves, found himself shaking again at this outburst.

"Who's your brother? What's his name? Where's he based?" Gerard pushed. Martin gave the particulars, including a short but accurate description, when Leo chimed in.

"I know him," he said, "Shay-zee, sound lad, joined the guards just after me."

"Jesus fucking Christ," said Gerard. "This is... this is an embarrassment." He leaned back in his chair, shaking his head and staring at the ceiling, after a few moments he returned his gaze on Martin.

"Why didn't you tell us? Why didn't you get your brother to ring us?"

Martin, exasperated, tried to explain:

"I didn't want to get him into trouble... I mean, he's my *younger* brother... he's not long in the guards... I don't know, I thought it would look bad to have his older brother throwing his name out while being arrested. I rang him when I got out of the station, and he said he'd try to get a word to you, but I didn't know what to do on the night," he wanted to add 'I was drunk, scared and intimidated, and how was I to know my brother was a get out of jail free card,' but he kept quiet.

"For fuck's sake," said Gerard. "Never in my life... What do we do now? Your hash has been sent to the labs, this arrest is in the system, he *have* to follow up on it, a couple of years ago we'd be able to blip it off the computer, but now... fuck, we *have* to process it—and your brother in the fucking guards!"

"What about the tea leaves," offered Leo, "what if we just entered that back from the labs?"

"No good," said Gerard, "they were sent together, and the labs will have to write in the hash. By the way, what fucking dealer are you using that you're getting tea leaves?"

"I bagged the tea leaves up myself," said Martin, "I'm trying to cut down on the tobacco."

"THEN DON'T SMOKE!" Gerard thumped. "Give them up. I've been trying to give up cigarettes these last 2 weeks, and it's hell, but it must be better than smoking tea leaves."

Martin didn't know what to say. He had never in his life smoked anything that didn't have THC in some shape or form, and was he to explain to the Gardai that hash can't be smoked by itself? He was beyond baffled by all this.

"Look," continued Gerard, trying to calm himself, "it's not for me to tell you how to live, if you want to smoke tea leaves to give up smoking, fine, it's a new one for me. But why the fuck didn't you tell us your brother's a guard?"

"I'm sorry," said Martin in disbelief, "I wasn't thinking straight," he offered. "I was on a work night and the job had bought us a lot of free drink."

"Yeah, you were out of your head," said Gerard, recovering himself a bit, but still sounding put out, "that was your first mistake, and lying to me, that was your worst mistake! If you had of told me you were smoking hash straight away, or told me that your brother's a guard…," he shook his head. This was becoming too much for Martin, he decided to risk something.

"No one's more sorry than I am," he said, "you know, I was smoking that joint with a friend, and he—"

"FORGET IT!" Gerard cut in. The last thing he wanted to hear about was the other guy. "What's done is done, there's no good thinking now about what you should have done." 'You started it' Martin wanted to say, but he stayed quiet. He could see, although he could hardly believe it, that Gerard was actually feeling guilty about the whole thing. At the time of his arrest Martin had a vague notion of getting the Gardai on his side, showing them that he wasn't a bad guy, and now, they actually *were* on his side, and by the sounds of it, he was still going to be brought to court.

"Look," said Gerard, "we'll get this sorted by the end of the week. Tomorrow or Friday we'll get you in and out of court, alright? In and out, and let that be the end of it."

"… Sure," said Martin, "But… it would destroy me if I got a conviction, my job's Gardai vetted."

"You won't get a conviction," said Gerard. "What was it you said on Thursday?" Martin had no idea, "can I ring my partner?" He offered.

"No, (for fuck's sake), you said it will be legal in a couple of years, didn't you?" Martin nodded dumbly, he had no idea. Gerard continued: "The courts know it's not a serious crime, 99% percent of possession charges like yours get no conviction."

"Yeah," said Leo, "I have mates now in the guards who have been in exactly your situation now, you won't get a conviction."

"In the court," continued Gerard, "I'll tell the judge that I found you with 3 or 4 grams of weed, that you were completely compliant, and we don't expect to see you back,… who's the judge tomorrow?" He asked Leo.

"O' Leary, he's in court tomorrow and Thursday, and he's been a grumpy prick ever since he found his wife cheating on him."

"Fuck's sake," said Gerard, "who's on on Friday?"

"Rooney," said Leo.

"Grand. Rooney's alright. He's quick, easily bored, and goes light on convictions. Right, can you make it to the criminal court on Friday, when's your lunch?"

"12:00 to 13:30, but I could try and get out early and get a taxi down," said Martin, still in disbelief.

"Grand," said Gerard. "I'll sort it out and give you a ring with the details."

"Do I need a solicitor?" Martin asked.

"Yeah," said Gerard, "to be on the safe side, I'll ring your brother and we'll sort someone out to do it on the cheap, how much to do you make a year?"

"Around 28 gross," answered Martin.

"Too much for legal aid, but look, between us and your brother we'll find someone to do it on the cheap." Gerard shook his head. "I can't believe your brother's a guard and you didn't tell us," he said, "you know something? You're a fucking idiot."

'Fuckers' thought Martin as he began his walk home. He left the Gardai station after going through a few more details. His peripheral vision was non-existent as his feet took him on autopilot towards home. In some ways he felt as if he was walking out of a tragedy and into a comedy, but the comedy had all the warmth and humour of a bad Kafka novel. When he was a good distance from the station he took out his phone and rang his brother.

"Well, how'd you get on with them then?" Shay asked picking up.

"It was weird," Martin replied. "They're sorting it out that I'll be in and out of court on Friday, both of them promising I won't get a conviction. Gerard said he'd be in touch with you to try and sort me out with a solicitor to represent me for cheap."

"Well, that's good."

"Yeah… it's all a bit mad, Gerard gave out to me for not telling them on the night that my brother's a guard, apparently a phonecall from you after the arrest would have had the whole thing forgotten about…"

"Don't start that on me, how was I to know?" said Shay. "You remember back when I was in the Gardai reserves? I got pulled over for speeding and when I told the guard 'sure I'm a guard myself' your man said, 'so bloody what.'"

"I remember," laughed Martin, "you said to him 'you must have been one of them whistleblowers' and your man wanted to arrest you and get you kicked off the force."

"Exactly, I thought that was my career in the bin. You can't blame me if I was slow to stick my neck out for you. You're the one walking around with a load of hash in your bag and a lit joint in your hand."

"Yeah, okay, I'm sorry. I'm just feeling sorry for myself."

"Here, my phone's ringing," said Shay, "it's probably Gerard, I'll talk to you later, stop stressing."

"Alright, thanks." Martin put his phone away, ashamed of himself for relying on his brother, ashamed for wanting more of him. Shay. A year and a half younger and a foot and a half taller. Even as children Martin had given up seeing himself as the elder of the two, it was enough for him that in his mid-twenties he finally began to feel at least equal to his more precocious younger brother. Now his smoking had stunted him back to feeling like a preadolescent teenager, up a tree, aloof and scared, as his brother dominated the football pitch and called the shots.

Martin got home, getting an Indian takeaway along the way. He stuck it in the oven on low heat and wrote:

My brother's more craic than I,
It shames me to admit.
He's the full round in the pub
While I'm an open bag of crisps.

My brother has his guitar you see,
And a catalogue of songs.
While I have to wait for the 3rd chorus
Just to sing along.

Not to mention my brother earns more than me,
And sports his lovely badge.
While I get harassed by his co-workers
For smoking a little grass.

When John arrived from his weekly game they sat and ate and Martin explained the newest developments. Martin was still lost in a sense of disbelief, and it irritated him that the absurdity of it all wasn't felt by John to the same degree.

"I was arrested for a stupid crime that shouldn't be a crime, and the people who arrested me are now doing everything they can to help me escape a conviction. It's madness. They would have, if they had the option, swept the whole thing under the carpet as soon as they found out my brother's in the guards. John, I'm telling you, they're actually embarrassed to be dealing with me!" He said, trying to align John's way of thinking to his own. John just shook his head:

"It's mad alright, but you were still incredibly stupid to be smoking in the middle of town, and on Halloween, and you're lucky Shay's a guard, that isn't something you should count on."

"I'm not trying to count on my brother," mumbled Martin. "I'm just telling you what's been happening. It's supposed to be good news."

"Yeah," sighed John. "I'm happy for you, but it's been hard for me. I don't have anyone else to talk to about all this, and I'm still having to pretend that I'm over the moon about our engagement when really I'm worried sick about you getting a conviction. Everyone from the 5-a-side football were congratulating me and passing on their congrats and well wishes and I just had to sit through it. And of course I'm happy the guards are on your side, but if you're expecting me to indulge your indignation then forgot it, I'm not there yet."

"Well, at least it'll be over this week," said Martin into his food.

"Yeah," said John, scrapping his fork along his plate and wishing they had stuck on the tv. He had found it easy enough to support Martin while he needed supporting, but Martin looking for sympathy for being a victim of absurdity was grating on him, especially now that Martin had also confided in his parents, brother and sister. Who was there for him to talk to? Or who would be worth talking to after revealing that his partner, love of his life and recent fiancé, was a stoner stupid enough to get arrested the day before he proposed. John ate his curry and tried to line-up his thoughts in the hopes of getting them off his chest when Martin's phone rang.

"It's Shay, I'll take it in the kitchen, stick on something if you want." John stuck on *The Good Place* and got halfway through an episode when Martin came back.

"Well, it's like I said, Shay and Gerard have organised it with a solicitor so I should only have to pay a small amount or nothing, and on Friday I'll be represented, brought before a judge, and I'm to have some cash on me to offer up as a charitable donation. All going well by Friday afternoon I can start making things up to you and start planning our wedding."

"Mmm, good luck with that," said John. "Do you mind if I finish the episode?"

"No, of course not," lied Martin.

Wednesday and Thursday

The next day, while waiting by the kettle, Martin was pulled out of his swirling thoughts by the smell of tobacco and Tom coming in.

"Well, ya alright? Any update?"

"Yeah Tom," said Martin, peering around the empty staff room. "I'm to go before a judge on Friday."

"That soon!"

"Yeah, looks like it'll be taken care of without too much hassle. I have to go and look sorry for myself and probably get a slap on the wrist by way of making a charitable donation."

"That's great! Are you nervous."

"Yeah, I'm all nerves these days. I still don't want to talk about it. Maybe after work on Friday if it all goes well, till then I just wish I could put it out of mind…. I never thought I'd be one to get a microchip implanted in my brain, but if they found a way to compartmentalise and shut down worries until they were actually useful and relevant I'd go for it. That's the technology I'd choose."

"What?"

"Never mind," said Martin.

"Well, if you want a change in topic I've got one for you—do you eat figs?" Martin blinked, he looked at Tom for the first time that morning as he slowly replied:

"I guess I eat figs… sometimes, why?"

"Ah-ha!" said Tom, "because figs aren't vegan."

"What?"

"Figs aren't vegan" beamed Tom, "to pollinate, they have to attract a specific species of wasp that crawls inside the fig, lays its eggs, and then dies within the fig. So wasps die to make figs, and that's another thing truly militant vegans can't eat!"

"Th-that's not an argument against veganism though! That's just you looking for more justification to do the wrong thing."

"So are you going to stop eating figs?" Tom smiled.

"I'll look into it," mumbled Martin. He finished making his tea and went onto the computer, printed what he needed, and ran upstairs to read up on wasps and figs. Tom smiled, glad that Martin had finally installed himself with such an easy button to press.

As his students started arriving at the class Martin sighed and took out his dairy. In a minute he wrote a haiku:

Fig. In enters wasp
Male or female—life and death
Can vegans eat figs?

And with the question safely saved Martin was able to let go and focus on the class at hand. His quote of the day was: "Be the change you want to see in the world," by Gandhi. "Now," he started, after their morning routine was finished, "we've looked at the famine, we've looked at emigration, now it's time to skip forward to 1916." And so Martin gave an account of the 1916 uprising. He focused on the key figures who would feature in the film on Friday, the fact that it was timed to take advantage of England being preoccupied with WW1, the fact that many of the Irish who took part received their military training from serving in the English army, and the fact that many regular Irish people, at that time, didn't support the movement for independence. This last point caused the most confusion as his students asked *why*?

"Going back to WW1," Martin tried to explain, "you need to imagine that 200,000 Irish men were fighting as part of the English army. Now they did this for all sorts of reasons, but the most obvious one is that for most of them the English army was the greatest opportunity to earn some decent money and support their families. So approximately 200,000 relatively poor families in Ireland were being financially supported by the sacrifices of their children, many of whom died or were seriously injured during the war. At the same time, you have a much smaller number of Irish nationalists who refused to take part in the first world war and instead looked to take advantage of it to give England as much grief as possible, which probably seemed disrespectful to those families.

To make it worse, while England had a steady supply of home-produced guns, Irish nationalists had to acquire guns wherever they could get them, which often meant working directly with the Germans—either buying their guns for high prices or trying to reduce the cost by promising the Germans that these guns would be pointed against England.

"Also, on a more basic level, I think most Irish people were afraid of change. We had been ruled by England for so long that the thought of independence must have been frightening, especially during a time when the largest countries were tearing each other apart, and there were some Irish people who strongly identified with being a part of the British empire, Oscar Wilde being a great example. Oscar Wilde was born shortly after the famine, his mother was an outspoken Irish nationalist, and yet, Oscar Wilde, at least as a young man, loved the British empire. He saw it as being a sort of spiritual successor to the ancient Greek and Roman empires, and he loved it. Finally, we also need to remember that since the uprising took place mostly in inner-city Dublin, most of those killed in the Rising were civilians. In fact, people who had or wanted nothing to do with the Rising ended up suffering the most, including many children."

Martin then took the students through a slideshow of the places and spaces were the Rising took place, followed by the monuments built to commemorate 1916 and the ensuing war of independence.

On Thursday Martin went out of his way to avoid Tom (despite wanting to get to the bottom of the fig argument). The fact was that he was struggling and failing to pull his mind away from his approaching day in court. At this range, his mind was so overshadowed by the upcoming event that he only felt 'himself' during his morning class when, listening to BBC's one minute news summary as a warmer, he found himself having to explain to the class what the news presenter might have meant when she said that: "[North] America is threatening Russia with a raft of new sanctions."

'A *raft* of sanctions' panicked Martin as his mind scrambled to come up with an explanation as the students asked him to explain it. He fumbled an improvised explanation of the term, telling his class that a 'raft of sanctions' possibly goes back to Ireland and England's wooden days of trees, boats and rivers, and the possibility of warring tribes using rafts to deliver messages about trade, wars or tributary terms, but then, he couldn't imagine how anyone in North America could float a raft of sanctions all the way to Russia. And what were the sanctions to look like? He desperately drew on the whiteboard a stick figure floating on a sea of squiggles on a stick-twig raft laden down with oversized envelopes complete with an arrow to show that these particular envelopes contained 'sanctions,' but then he felt he also had to draw another stick figure waiting at port for the sanctions to come in, and in the end he gave it up and erased the board while mumbling: *"no, forget it, we don't use that term, only mad British people must use it."* R—A—F—T. The students were lost but amused, and Martin was frustrated that this strange turn of phrase wasted the first 15 minutes of his class. He skipped the quote and moved onto to the Irish civil war and the reconciliation between Ireland and England.

"Now, for the most part," Martin tried to summarise, "the relationship between Ireland and England is made up of Irish tolerance and British ignorance, as most British students only learn about their empirical highlights and not the consequences. But there's been exceptions. Two members of the *Beatles* wrote songs about Ireland, John Lennon and Yoko Ono singing about our miserable history because of the English, and Paul McCartney actually made a song about how Northern Ireland should be 'given back to the Irish,' but, the biggest moment of our reconciliation came in 2011, when, thanks mostly to our then president Mary McAleese, Queen Elizabeth the second came to Ireland as the first reigning British monarch to make a state visit to our independent country.

"And, to be fair to the Queen, she humbled herself while she was here. She, like Obama, made a point of addressing us in Gaelic-Irish, a language that her great-great-great-grandmother, Queen Victoria, helped to destroy in this country, but Elizabeth didn't speak Irish to humiliate us, she spoke it as sign of respect."

"Do you speak Irish teacher?" One of the students interrupted to ask.

"No," said Martin, "We're made to learn Irish in primary and secondary school, so I just really grew up to hate it as subject. I know it's a bad excuse, but I really hated learning Irish in school."

"And do you hate the English?" Asked another.

"No, of course not," smiled Martin, "sure my favourite teacher was from England, and in ways I can't explain I wouldn't be *here* now if it weren't for him. And as I've been trying to show, our history is long and very complicated. For example, I, like so many other Irish people, have a job because my ancestors were forced to adopt this language as our own, and to be fair, the Irish have had a lot of fun with the English language. For example, we took the 'e' out of 'Jesus' to make 'Jaysus,' and instead we've put an 'e' into such words as fuck and shit to make the more polite feck and shite, not to mention putting a random 'e' into whiskey to annoy the Scots. And anyway, even this idea of 'my ancestors' isn't simple, as I've English blood in my family, or, as we tend to say it, I've a Protestant streak in my family. There are many Irish people who have English blood and vice versa, especially in places like Dublin, Liverpool and London. I think most people would agree that we have a good relationship between the two countries, and when I mentioned before that English people tend to be ignorant of Ireland and our shared history, we should remember that we're just another tiny chapter in the long history of their unbelievably massive empire."

"What about Northern Ireland?" Asked another.

"Ah," sighed Martin, "that brings is back to the madness of Eamon de Valera, the Treaty, Northern Ireland and the Irish civil war."

Court Day

On Friday Martin woke from a nervous sleep and got dressed in his most sensible clothes: his black school-boy shoes, black slacks, a white long-sleeved lucky shirt and a sensible black jumper. In the time he had to kill before having to go to work he wrote in his diary the events of the last few days and then he tried to write a prepared speech in case he had to present himself before the judge, but he found that he couldn't write a speech in which he sounded either sorry or respecting of the laws which had brought him to this point. All he could do was prepare himself to apologise and promise that it wouldn't happen again, which he felt he could say with enough false conviction to qualify him for some degree of sympathy. He got through his morning class as calmly as possible, enjoying for the unknown time watching *Michael Collins*, finding anger and comfort in reflecting on those Irish men and women who suffered so much for what they believed in. The film finished too close to 12:00 for Martin's liking, but he did what he could to address the usual questions and confusion that came from the end of it:

"Yes," agreed Martin, "it's horrible, and to make it worse, Eamon de Valera continued leading our country for the next 40-odd years. During that time he controlled our media, he censored any controversial book or film in this country, he handed over the responsibility of our education system to the Catholic church, which had a particularly disgusting impact for the women of this country. In short, he made our country one of the most sexist and conservative countries in Europe, and, in the end, he did absolutely nothing to support Northern Ireland's road to independence. In general, he was a scumbag, a hypocrite, and, undeniably, one of the most professional and successful politicians in history.

"And like all the great scumbags of political history, he wanted nothing more than to bring us *back,* in his case, back to what Ireland was before England's influence, and it was a disaster. For decades and decades Ireland was a wretchedly poor and tyrannically ruled country. The poverty was, in some ways,

English policy, as the English government retaliated against our freedom by launching a long and severe trade war, not too different to how the U.S. government continues to treat Cuba. But the trade war ended, Eamon De Valera eventually died, and Ireland started to become a rich country from the 1990s due to help from the EU, foreign investment and jobs. Ireland became a controversial tax-haven, and, with our low corporation tax, white skin and now native-English speaking skills, we've attracted some of the biggest tech-giants from the U.S. here. But we'll finish on this point: let me say right now that any politician, of any country or time, that focuses their campaign on going *backwards* should be shot. Now, I'm sorry."

Martin looked at his watch—12:02, "but I really need everyone to leave! Write a review for homework, we'll follow up any questions on Monday, and visit the *Garden of Remembrance* during the weekend, and have a good one!" He quietly passed his teacher's folder to Frankie who wished him luck and then he ran out of the school as fast as he could.

Martin ran up and down the road like a lunatic until he managed to pick up a taxi.

"Where to, pal?" The taxi driver asked, a 50-odd year old male Dubliner.

"The criminal court," returned Martin, "soon as possible." His pulse was beginning to slow as his mind worked out that he would get there with plenty of time.

"Sure boss, heading back to work, are ya?" The taxi man asked as he eyed up the young man sitting behind him.

"No... I got caught with some weed on me," Martin smiled, already liking the taxi-driver for confusing his circumstances.

"You're joking, how much did they catch you with?"

"Ah, about 4 grams worth," mumbled Martin. The driver didn't reply, and Martin felt a change in the air. After an awkward silence Martin repeated:

"Yeah... a lot of bloody fuss just for 4 grams."

"4 GRAMS!" Shouted the driver, "I thought you said 4 grand. The fucking pricks, I've smoked 4 grams in one blunt and still did an honest day's work, and they're dragging you to court for that! The bastards!" The taxi driver was now outraged, and for the rest of the journey he pointed out every dodgy looking character to Martin and said something along the lines of—"You see that junkie there, he's there every day selling crack, just look at him, and they picked YOU up… Look, that lad on the bike, he's out there every day delivering drugs with a spliff hanging out of his mouth, and they picked YOU up? …You see that lad there? He's out there every day with a bag of gear on him, and the guards never bother him, and they picked *you* up!"

Martin didn't know what to say to all this, and he was afraid to ask how the taxi driver knew every drug dealer from O' Connell Bridge to the Phoenix Park. Martin only smiled, shook his head in disbelief, and gave other particulars of his arrest. When they got near the court the taxi driver turned around to say a word:

"Now, you listen to me son, if you go in there, and you don't get called up before they break for lunch, don't you leave, okay, or if you have to leave, present yourself to the Gardai behind the counter and tell them that you were there and for them to notify it. Otherwise they can send a warrant out for your arrest for missing court, and they'll pick you up where you live or where you work. So don't leave until those bastards know you've been in there, do you hear me?" Martin nearly cried for all the fatherly affection he had towards this man.

"Yes, thank you," he said, giving a fiver with the fare and getting out full of the driver's well-wishes and 'good luck to ya pal' and 'you'll be grand sure,' and 'they might have picked you up, but I'll eat my licence if a judge ever convicts the likes of *you.*'

Martin stood for a moment outside the criminal court, a building he had often passed without a second glance. Now, looking at it, he felt that the building, with its build-up of stairs, glass and steel, with its wide staircase leading to a bottle-necked throat of an entrance and overarching roof, that it gave him the impression of the court as some carnivorous animal lazily swallowing up all those who walked in, swallowing all except those who *worked* within, for *they* weren't food, no, not yet, but rather they became the living stomach of the beast, the stomach and the teeth.

They, in their very employment, necessitated the building and the mycelium-like police who scoured for victims on Dublin's streets. And yes, they also began to look like teeth, designed to pick and bite the humanity from those being pulled within. Some teeth were sharper than others, swallowing whole decades off of those walking in, other teeth were dull and soft, but functioned as the teeth of ruminates, chewing and spitting out and chewing again. Martin swallowed some grass sweetened air, tinged as it was from Phoenix Park just beyond, and prayed to meet with a dull soft tooth of a judge.

As he approached the entrance he saw an airport-style bag scanner and metal detector. He was asked by the stand-by security if he had his card with him, Martin muttered that he didn't work in the building and so he was directed instead to take off his coat and bag and place them in a tray. When he got through the security he saw a large open stage of confusion filled with interesting characters and easy-going guards. He wasn't long wandering around before he saw Gerard, who smiled and approached him.

"Good, you're here, let's get you in quick." He led Martin directly to a counter lined up with people waiting. Gerard skipped the queue with Martin in tow and spoke directly to the woman who was handling it.

"Sarah, got a quick one here, possession of hash, I promised he'd get back to work before his boss finds out he's gone, I know his uncle, can you sort us out?" With an eye roll Gerard was handed some sheets and given some details, then he led Martin to a quieter part of the room.

"Did you ring that number for a solicitor?"

"Yeah, there's meant to be someone here called Luke to help me out."

"Luke's gone, you missed him." Gerard looked around. "There's one I know, he works for the same firm, he'll sort us out." Gerard walked up to a solicitor who was engaged with another client. This client was a skinny nervous man in his mid to late thirties who scrunched himself in and squirmed so much that the scene took Martin back to primary school and waiting outside the principal's office. The solicitor looked stupid as he was wearing a curly white wig and a long black gown despite having a big bushy dark brown beard. There was a woman to the side of them who was doing the talking for the client.

"Right, this is a serious case, but I think we have a good chance here to escape a conviction," said the solicitor.

"Tony," Gerard cut in.

"Ah Gerard, I'll be with you in a sec."

"Nobody was hurt during the robbery so that'll stand to us, plus, you were only using a fake gun." The woman, talking for the young man, added "and be sure to mention that he has kept mostly out of trouble all this year, and his father passed away only last month."

"Right," said Tony the solicitor, "Father passed away last month, good, I'll be sure to mention that."

"Yes," continued the woman, "he's been really trying to turn his life around, and he's so close, but this has been a hard time with his father passing, and we can't let this incident put him back along the path to being a hardened criminal."

"Yes," said Tony, "absolutely."

"Tony," Gerard tried to cut in again.

"I'll be with you in a moment Gerard, I promise." Gerard turned to Martin and gave a long sigh. "So," said Gerard, "What did you say you work as?"

"I'm an English language teacher," said Martin.

Gerard whistled and winked, "Plenty of fine looking Brazilians in those schools, I'm sure you had yer way a few, huh?"

"No," said Martin.

"Right, right," said Gerard, "I forgot you're not into girls, but there must be plenty of gay Brazilians to choose from, Dublin seems to be riddled with them, what's that about anyway, eh?"

Martin blinked a few times and replied: "they've got a homophobic ass of a president. But I don't sleep with any of them because I'm engaged." Gerard shrugged and turned back to the solicitor, he was dying for a cigarette and he wanted more than ever to get this Martin character as far from him as possible. Since his arrest Martin had gone from a young, possibly teenaged, cheeky and out-of-his head drug dealer who enjoyed lying to the Gardai, to a convenient mark to get him and his partner off the streets on Halloween, then Gerard began to see him as a sorry-looking sympathetic idiot who was unlucky and stupid, and then the final blow came that his brother was not only a guard, but was known for being a sound guard! 'For fuck's sake' thought Gerard, 'let this be over today.'

"TONY," he tried again, louder than ever. Tony finally broke free from that criminal to deal with this one, the former he knew to be a no-hoper complete with an overbearing social worker, and the new one seemed like the kind of fish out of water that get thrown back to the sea on account of their purity (rather than any effort on his part). Gerard explained the situation:

"Tony, this is Martin, caught with 3 grams on him, I'm going to tell the judge it was 2 grams and that he was completely compliant, no complaints from me, I want to get him out of here fast, no fuss, he was talking to Luke yesterday."

"Ok," said Tony, "2 grams of what?"

"Weed," said Gerard, losing patience, "I picked him up, spliff in hand, and the feckin eejit tried to pass it off as a cigarette, but you're not to tell the judge that. I want him in and out."

"And is he working?"

"Yes," said Martin quickly, not wanting to be muted like the other, "English language teacher, recently engaged, mortgage to pay."

"Good, good," said Tony, nodding approvingly. "Excellent, anything else?"

"My job's gardai-vetted," said Martin.

"Good Christ," said Tony, "I'm not getting into that in there. Do you have any cash on you?"

"€200 quid," said Martin.

"Good, right, you'll get summoned after him," indicating to his other client "We'll go in now, find somewhere and sit down, when you're called stand where he stands, look sad and sorry, let me do the talking and we'll try and get you in and out before they break for lunch." Tony indicated to the two of them to enter the court, and the 5 of them did so. Gerard indicated to Martin a place to sit as he hung back to have a quick word with Tony.

"Look," he whispered to Tony "his brother's a guard, and he told us too late and he's a fuckin' eejit. Can you do this one on the house for me?"

"Well," said Tony in a low voice, "You'll have to talk to Luke about that."

"I tried but he was busy, listen, after what I'm going to say to this judge you won't have to lift a finger for him, in and out… I'll owe you one."

"Alright," said Tony, noting a favour away in his mind, courts are run on such.

Martin looked around him. There was a young man standing to be judged, his solicitor went through the details as follows:

"Your honour, my client here was found by the Gardai after just buying a small quantity of cannabis, and while he was taken in, his 6 friends, your honour, essentially got off *scot-free*. My client is a college student your honour, a hard worker with his whole life ahead of him, and, I believe, you will not see him here again. He has €100 on him which, he has told me, he would like to offer up as a charitable donation—and I suggest this to you now your honour." The judge let him finish before agreeing to the donation, a decision he had made well before it was offered. This was followed by another young man on a cannabis possession charge, and another, and another. Martin couldn't believe it, 'they're all in the exact same boat as me, what a stupid fucking country' he thought. But 3 young men who were sitting in a row across from him did look to be a different breed, they were so easy-going, thought Martin, that they must be regulars. Martin sat there and looked around. There seemed to be no women being tried, just young men, although there were a number of female guards and solicitors in the room.

Martin couldn't believe that the judge was wearing a wig and that the room and his seat were arranged so that he was towering above everyone, 'looking down on us' he thought, 'there he is, sitting above us and with a legion of henchmen gathered around him, and there's no way this judge has never broken a law—hell, I bet he eats animals.' Right then Martin wanted nothing more than to pull the judge down from his high chair and give him a good beating, in fact, it was the first time in Martin's adult life that he fantasised about beating someone to a pulp. He wanted to beat the judge for every stupid law he helped enforce now and past, he wanted to beat him for his case, for that of Oscar Wilde, for the assassination of Michael Collins, for all the crimes the Catholic church were allowed to get away with, for all the money squandered and stolen by Bertie, for Mathew Broderick escaping prison, for the taxi-driver who knew too much, for everyone who was *lawful*ly but nonsensically arrested.

He wanted to beat the judge until he heard the words 'no conviction' ring out loud and clear, and as his mind was running wild he saw Mr Scrunchy himself go up before the judge. Here their solicitor really went for it, he urged the judge by what sounded like sheer begging to consider all the circumstances and look favourably on this man who was 'so very close to turning his life around,' he mentioned that his client was mourning the death of his father, that he had stayed out of trouble for most of the year bar this incident, and that his client had a social worker who was willing to speak on his behalf. The judge, half listening, glanced down at some papers before him, and when Tony was finished, feeling quite proud of himself, the judge asked him:

"Do you realise, *Tony*, that your client is currently on bail for an armed robbery he committed in May?"

"No, your honour" Tony stammered, "I was not aware of that," he said, half turning to look at Mr Scrunchy, who looked as if he were trying to disappear within himself. Martin looked at him and wondered about Mr Scrunchy's life; his autonomy, the choices he must have faced, or the lack thereof. 'Conviction or not' thought Martin, 'Mr Scrunchy has already been shaped by our courts, I doubt he will ever stand up straight and steady again, if ever he did.'

"I ask, your honour, that we can reschedule this trail so that I may discuss this with my client."

"Yes," said the judge, "it *will* be rescheduled for 2 weeks' time, by which time I expect you know *all* the facts in this case," he said this as he gave Tony a hard look for wasting his time. Tony then told the judge that it was another of his clients who was next, and Martin got up and stood where poor Mr Scrunchy had stood moments before, looking as sorry for himself as he could. Martin, by contrast, stood looking more contemplative than anything. The judge saw a young man he wouldn't put past twenty looking mostly at the floor, but allowing his eyes to make quick surveys of himself and his surroundings. He checked the timer before him, only a few minutes until lunch, 'thank god' he thought. Gerard was called to give the circumstances of the arrest.

"Your honour, I caught this young man smoking cannabis in town last Thursday night. I asked if he had any drugs on him, he told me that he had in fact a small bag, he was brought back to the station and found with just over a gram of cannabis on him, I must say, he was respectful and compliant the whole time, and we've had no trouble with him, and we don't expect to have trouble with him again in the future."

"1 gram," said the judge with a laugh, "I would have thought that amount to be outside your jurisdiction *Gerard*." Gerard nodded absently, 'I fucking hate that kid' he thought. The solicitor gave a few more favourable details, but then shocked Martin by saying "my client has €200 with him in cash that he would like to offer up as a donation." 'What an asshole' thought Martin, 'why didn't he say I only had €100 on me!' The judge accepted the offer presented to him and then broke the court for lunch, stepping down from his high-step and leaving the room by his own private back exit rather than walk among those who bore the weight of his tired everyday judgements. Gerard came up to Martin.

"You can give me the money, I'll have to wait until after lunch to formally give it on your behalf."

"Thanks," mumbled Martin as he wrestled his wallet from his back pocket. He took out the 4 €50 notes and passed them to Gerard who counted them out.

"Thank you," repeated Martin as they made their way out of the court and back into the large open room. He checked his watch, he still had 25 minutes to get back to work. He turned and thanked Tony, despite losing more money than he needed to.

"You were very lucky," said Tony "to escape a conviction after breaking the law like that," Martin could see Gerard rolling his eyes crossly at Tony behind his back.

"Yeah," said Martin, "sure… what charity does the money go to anyway?" He asked.

"It goes into the one box," said Tony "and the charity changes every week." 'Yeah, right,' thought Martin. "And … how much do I owe you," he asked Tony.

"Nothing," he replied, "I have it sorted with Gerard, you're very lucky, sure, I probably didn't have to say anything anyway after Gerard's statement." 'I wish you had said nothing' thought Martin.

"Well, thanks, and thanks Gardai. So, is that it then, can I go back to work?"

"Yes," said Gerard. "no conviction, go, and hopefully I'll never see you again."

"That's the plan. Thanks again," said Martin as he left, he was in too much of a hurry to make sense of it all, but once he was on a bus he messaged John: 'Done and dusted, out of court, heading back to work, just had to pay a €200 "donation," talk later x,' then he took out his diary and wrote: *got off, no conviction, it's all madness. I'm only down €200 instead of €2,000 so shouldn't complain I guess, but, what a joke, we need to legalise it.* John messaged back— 'That's great!' with a series x's and smiles. Martin quickly messaged his mother and brother and arrived back to the school with 5 minutes to spare, he went into the staffroom, made himself a quick cup of tea, grabbed a Scrabble board from the games closet and headed up to grab his folder. He entered the class just as the fire-alarm of a bell went off and he beamed a smile at the one early student. 'Ah' he thought, 'I'm back!' Despite missing lunch he chatted away to the students as they came in and felt in general in a far better mood, and when Frankie popped his head in during the break to see how it went Martin's smile and nod said it all.

"So will you go for one after work?" Frankie asked.

"Yeah man, just the one, why not."

Friday

Settled with their beers settling they sat, and Martin smiled and thought again 'I'm glad to be back.' Among the 5 occupied seats in *The Black Sheep* he gave his workmates an animated account of his arrest and earlier release, finishing it all with a sigh of "madness."

"Well, it's a story," laughed Frankie, and his comment fell like music to Martin's ears.

"But," said Tom, "I'm sure that you gave a false name when the guards first stopped us."

"Why would I do that" grumbled Martin.

"Well… it's what I heard dude."

"Well anyway," said Martin, "it's over and done with, all that stress and drama for 2 minutes before a judge and €200 out of my pocket. Goddamn, we need to legalise it."

"So you'll be voting for the Greens?" Frankie asked.

"NO!" thumped Martin, "I can't stand the Green Party, shower of hypocrites. They call themselves the Green Party but they don't promote veganism, what a joke," he sighed.

"Not vegan shit again," said Des.

"Here! Here!" Tom said.

"Alright," said Martin, "but a day's coming when it'll be impossible to be taken seriously as an environmentalist, animal lover, nutritionist or even a doctor if you don't at least support a plant-based diet."

"Bullshit," said Des.

"Yeah," said Frankie, "we're omnivores, meat's good for us pal, and I fucking hate when vegans think they get a monopoly on loving animals."

"Red meat's carcinogenic, it increases your risk of cancer, so just like we once had doctors who smoked and recommended smoking, we now have doctors who eat red meat, but I'm telling you, a doctor that is at least unaware of the risks of eating meat will one day be as rare as a doctor who's unaware of the risks of smoking. Also, yes, vegans do get a monopoly on loving animals," said Martin to a chorus of eye-roles and protests. "Look," he continued, "to say you love animals while paying someone to breed, torture and slaughter them on your behalf, that would be like saying 'I'm not a racist or homophobe' while giving your money to the Ku Klux Klan and supporting gay-conversation therapy. If actions speak louder than words than any animal-lover who isn't a vegan is kidding themselves."

"Fuck that," said Ian, "I've a dog, I love my dog, I walk it, feed it, look after it, I make sacrifices, that's an animal I love without kidding anyone."

"Fine," said Martin, "but owning a dog isn't the same kind of sacrifice as being a vegan, because you directly see and feel the benefits of owning a dog, but a real sacrifice is doing something without any expectation of a return. That's a sacrifice. So I can honestly say I love animals more now than when I wasn't vegan, if actions speak louder than words then it's a fact—even if you find it an inconvenient fact—that vegans objectively love animals more than non-vegans."

"Fine," mumbled Ian, "I love dogs more than cows then."

"Man, you're not even vegan," laughed Tom, "you eat figs!"

"I'm still looking into that," mumbled Martin.

"Well I'm going to the jacks," said Tom.

"Anyway," said Martin trying to recover the conversation, "forget about veganism then, the point I was trying to make was that I know weed will be legalised someday, but if you were in court seeing the amount of weed possession charges being brought forward, the sheer waste of time of it, maybe you'd feel as impatient as I am. To be honest, I don't know why we don't go with the Portuguese model and decriminalise the possession of all drugs."

"They should do that," said Ian. "Why don't they do that?"

"Cause they're lazy," Martin replied, "they still haven't ended sex segregation in schools. To be honest, we need a whole new political system, what we have now is absolute madness."

"What we have now is better than most countries," said Frankie.

"Yeah bruh, you have no idea," said Des, "if all drugs were decriminalised in Ireland then Dublin would become a loonie-bin, the entire city would be destroyed in a weekend."

"Maybe," laughed Martin.

"And we'd be riddled with drug-tourists," said Frankie.

"Well we're already riddled with drug tourists," countered Martin, "the first thing that greets someone arriving into Dublin airport is an advertisement for the *Guinness Brewery*, and the second is an ad for *Jameson's Distillery*, and, come on, our pubs are probably our biggest draw for tourists, just look at *Temple Bar*, Ireland is full of drug-tourism. Plus, drug laws at the moment, they're just laws against poor people. When's the last time a rich person got sent to prison over drugs? Rich people go to rehab, *we* go to jail, how's that fair?"

"It isn't," said Ian, "It's bullshit."

"And as for our politics," continued Martin. "How is it, for example, that our minister of health can become our minister for transport, and vice versa, and half the time they don't even want the job? You need like 8 years of training to become a doctor but no medical training to be the minister of health? I mean, I get how Leo was our minister of health at one point, but why was he ever our minister for transport, tourism and sport, has anyone ever seen Leo on a bus?"

"You hate Leo," said Frankie.

"Fuck Leo," said Ian.

"No, I don't hate him," continued Martin, "in fact, he's without question the best Taoiseach we've had in my voting lifetime, and possibly my lifetime period."

"No way," said Ian. "EU scum."

"Who would you put above him?" asked Martin, "out of all the Taoiseach's you can remember in your lifetime, who would you put above Leo Varadkar?" After an embarrassing silence Martin, satisfied, continued:

"The problem with Leo is that at one point he seemed to be leaning towards supporting legalisation, but then he backtracked, and, even more telling, he dragged his foot for years before supporting same-sex marriage and that's despite the fact that he's openly gay. I feel like Leo means well, and he'll go down in history as one of our best, but he's too nervous about rocking the boat and losing voters to bring about the change we need, and the only answer for it is jury-duty politics."

"What's that?" Ian asked.

"It's politics run like jury duty," said Martin, "imagine receiving a letter or email saying, basically, you have been appointed to serve in the government for a six months to two year period, you'll be paid €50,000 a year plus whatever pay difference might exist between your main job and this one, and you serve in government for that time and then you're done, imagine it, no need to worry about rocking the vote, no need to appeal to voters or corporations, imagine it."

"It sounds messy bru," said Des.

"Messier than what we have now? Look, the way things are now, we have ministers for transport who have never taken public transport! We have ministers of healthcare who have private health insurance! And we have ministers of education who send their own kids to private schools. The fact that we have so-called public servants in charge of our public healthcare, transport and schools but who use private healthcare, transport and schools is insanity. We have set ourselves up to be taken advantage of."

"So you'd have everyone serve a term," said Frankie, "even prisoners and bums?" (Martin nodded), "whether they want the job or not?"

"Exactly," said Martin, "how else do you think our prisons will ever improve unless a prisoner or ex prisoner is able to have his or her say? How else will the homeless crisis be improved if not by putting a bum in charge?"

"You're a looney Martin," said Des.

Martin took a breath and replied "…I'm just wired, I've been on edge all week over court and now I'm high on adrenaline."

"Do you want a smoke?" Tom asked, "might calm you down."

"Go fuck yourself pal," laughed Martin, "I'll smoke at home."

Finishing his beer Martin made his exit and walked home. John was there already and in the middle of watching *The Good Place* on Netflix. Martin, in a good mood and with a Guinness-parched tongue, hung up his coat and entered with: "Well, are ya alright?"

John paused the TV, turned to Martin and answered: "Yeah, you alright?"

"Yeah," said Martin, feeling a little underwhelmed by this greeting.

"I've only ten minutes left," said John, "do you mind waiting till I've finished it before we talk?"

"No, work away," Martin felt obliged to say. He sat on his hands, unsure what to do with himself, before pulling out his iPad and sat staring at the Wiki search bar. After another 2 awkward minutes he got up to go to the kitchen. "Do you want a tea or coffee?" He asked.

"No thanks."

'For fuck's sake' thought Martin in a huff while waiting for the kettle, 'episodes of *The Good Place* are only 20 minutes long anyway!'

Martin sat down with his coffee, feeling too buzzed for his usual cup of tea, and when the episode was over John switched the TV to some background music and turned to him. "Now, tell me everything," he said. "Starting with the last time you made yourself a coffee!" Martin looked in surprise at his cup and saw bits of soy milk curd floating in his drink because he hadn't bothered using the barista oat milk, he only shrugged and said:

"The coffee's fine, you can't actually taste the curds, it just looks a bit gross."

"You used the wrong milk," said John.

"Whatever," said Martin, "it tastes fine."

"What would you know," laughed John, "you don't drink coffee." Martin, shocked, took his cup, took a long, long noisy si-I-i-I-i-I-i-I-i-I-i-I-i-I-i-I-i-I-i-I-i-I-i-p! Put it down and said "do you not call that drinkin' coffee?"

"No," said John. "I don't."

"Well, this is coffee, and I'm drinking it" huffed Martin.

"Wrongly," laughed John, "anyway, so, how'd you get on in court then?"

"Grand," said Martin.

"Grand?"

"Yeah. Grand. Like I said. In. Out. €200 out of pocket, back in time for work."

"That's good... is that it?"

"Y-yeah," said Martin, "Well, I had it better in my head when I arrived, when it was fresh, I guess waiting about to tell you has taken the excitement out, that and having my coffee criticised. You know... I don't make coffee for *you* to judge but for *me* to drink."

John glared at Martin: "Well," he said, "I guess I do feel a bit distanced from you. Here I am having to lie to everyone as they swamp me with congrats for our engagement, and you haven't been much craic lately, not that I blamed you, until you started turning your arrest into a funny story to tell your family and friends while I'm having to keep everything to myself, but then, you're still not good craic with me when I can't even make a joke about your coffee or finish an episode without being attacked for it."

"I'm not stopping you from telling anyone," muttered Martin. A silence grew between them that threatened to erupt until Martin suddenly got up and said "look, I'm sorry, it's been a stressful few days, today included, despite getting off, and my mind's still settling down. I'm sorry, I get you were joking about the coffee... After all that, I think I'll go upstairs and role a smoke."

"Sure," said John. "accuse me of not wanting to talk and then walk away."

"Yeah, I'm sorry, I didn't mean to accuse you, just... let me cool down before I do any more damage and we can talk in a bit."

"Sure," said John, "and you didn't have to get so upset, if I didn't finish my episode I would have been thinking of it instead of being able to listen to you."

"Ok," said Martin.

"And if it bothered you could have said."

"Sure," said Martin. He turned, left and closed the door tenderly behind him. He headed upstairs with his coffee, taking the steps two at a time, entered their bedroom and stuck on Yoko Ono's *Between my head and the Sky* (*The Sun is Down! Beat*les that!), and began rolling himself a small spliff, his first since Halloween. He smoked a few drags half-out of their bedroom window and smiled at the passing thought of passing through. Putting out his spliff early he tried to read a page or two of Walt Whitman but found himself unable to immerse, so he took out his diary instead:

My CD player, weed, my book. I feel like I'm picking up ancient artifacts after the few days I've had. And now, I think I'm fighting with John!

Yes. My ship-wreck John has come to port
And dumped his cargo on my shores.

One package read 'I've distanced myself from you.'
But he brought the solvent when I would have preferred some glue
And from depression it's hard to know what to do.

His ship-wreck's come many times before
Normally because I've drawn it to my port
With some stupid signal, my lighthouse seems to have come with a faulty bulb
Conveying mixed messages
Or just misunderstood

But not this time

I can't read,
I have Walt Whitman's poetry by my side

But I can't find him, I don't feel him anywhere
I've read a few pages and absorbed nothing, it seems I cannot read poetry while
I'm depressed, my thoughts cannot fly. I can see Walt Whitman like Peter Pan,
beckoning me to take his hand, but my thoughts cannot fly.

My mind lately has become a prison with a ship-wreck serving as my quarters,
my thoughts are too heavy to escape my cranium,
and they float unwanted in my head—becoming stagnant and putrid

I've been tossed by depression, for surely depression comes in waves.

Martin sighed and lit up his spliff again. Between the smoke and the space for his mind to untangle he began loosening up. Staring at the moon he laughed to think of its future inhabitants, and he gave them a wave. When the smoke was finished he crushed it into a tissue and threw it in the bin. He then read, more successfully this time, a few more pages of Walt Whitman before picking up his diary again.

Actually, Whitman's hand extends once more towards me in the form of 'To You,'
I half-heartedly take it and begin to float,
And I leave John's ship wreck to repair itself, as I must repair mine.
Relationships, do they really get easier with time?

(Yoko Ono's music is nuts!)

"I'm sticking on a pizza and chips" Shouted John. "Be down in 20 if you want any."
"Thanks," shouted Martin.

Yes

I was, or I am, spinning into misery, startled by how easy and comfortable it is. John joked that I don't drink coffee, because I drank a cup where the soy milk curdled, leaving bits of white floating around in the cup. In my distracted state I thought the curds interesting to watch, and when I drank the coffee I couldn't taste any substance, nothing solid. I drank it with my eyes closed and noticed that it really made no difference, it only looked strange, but it freaked him out, or enough to slag me anyway. Anyway, I told him of course I drink coffee sometimes but he jokingly and arbitrarily declared that I don't. I told him that he can't say I don't drink coffee while I'm drinking coffee, so he did, his competitive side being goaded. I told him that I don't drink coffee for him, I was growing increasingly irritated by the whole thing until he declared that I don't have to get upset. Of course I don't have to!

No one has to do anything, and I don't want to get upset over something so stupid. But we're both idiots. His back goes against the wall about getting the last word in and teasing and teasing, and sometimes I can act like he expects and shrug it off and join in, take the slag and have a laugh, but sometimes I can only be myself, oversensitive, and then he puts it on me that it's my fault for being upset. He rarely picks up the pieces he's left smash. But the whole thing is so stupid. And my cd player is beginning to skip, and I know the cd I put in looks perfect, no visible scratches, and if that cd player starts to annoy me I might lose it and fuck it out the window! Why do I feel miserable? I escaped the conviction, I put that behind me, so why does the misery linger? I haven't felt depressed in so long before this goddamn arrest, and that's over now. So why is it so hard to escape it?

I can see clearly ways out (meditate, write, cycle, listen to an album with my eyes closed), but I'm reluctant to take them. Why are we such idiots? I should be writing, working on a new stand-up set or story, but I feel lethargic and cross, and I haven't been able to write anything decent in ages. I got to calm down and find a way out. Our brains our such a muddle, such a puzzle. How easily we can upset each other.

Martin sighed and put is diary down, he slurped the rest of the coffee and headed down to the kitchen to leave his cup by the sink and to check the tide, but after a little more back-and-forth he came back upstairs gasping for air. He continued writing:

I went downstairs. He asked if I was mad at him. I told him of course not, but I am upset, even though I know I shouldn't be. I told him that when he told me I don't have to be upset it ticked me off, of course I don't have to get upset, but who chooses to get upset? I said that he upset me and why not apologise for it? Mistake! He got, in my opinion, aggressive, raising his voice and telling me that

I was going around huffing and puffing, sulking and now demanding an apology, and I told him that I felt like he was being a prick. Mistake!! I told him that I know he isn't a prick, that when I feel like he's being a prick what's really happening is that I'm in asshole mode and I'm projecting out to him and interpreting his actions as being prickish, as I'm telling him all this he's telling me I'm being closed off because of my body language, then he starts to mimic me—(only him and my brother ever mimic and caricature me like that, and I hate it).

He asks me what I want? What do I want? Well, I wanted him to apologise for upsetting me, whether he meant to or not, but in the end I told him that I'm just looking to kiss and make up, but he says I need to give him a moment to process everything, so I left the room to give him time to process, wondering if that will do any good? It's true anyway that I'm feeling better. Did I unload my misery onto him? Did I pass the parcel? Will he pass it back? Relationships can become so twisted. We barely understand our own feelings and actions, and yet, we assume with such certainty the feelings and actions of others, and its projection, and it bites us in the ass every time. He grew up in an environment that communicates through sarcasm, and in a family that shares his love of sarcasm and caustic jokes, and I grew up oversensitive to criticism, and not ok with someone criticising how I drink my coffee!

Madness. Relationships are like trying to merge 2 different environments; one devoid of oxygen where those animals have grown without it and feel oxygen to be poisonous, and another environment with oxygen which considers all else to be poisonous. Relationships are a game of adaption, of give and take. If you're lucky, you find that you can both grow in a way you couldn't on your own, if you're unlucky, one or both of you will cease growing, become stunted, misshapen and bitter. Humans are weird. But at least it gives me something to think and write about. It's our first proper fight in ages so either way not too bad.

"PIZZA'S READY," shouted John.

Martin, closing his diary with a sigh, carried it with him down the stairs. He threw that silent witness of himself on the couch. The table was set and ready and John was laying the food on the plates.

"You're cooking next, right?" John asked, his tone seeming fairly neutral to Martin's troubleshooting ears. "Yeah," he replied.

"Then," continued John, "can you do us a salad? Feel like our eating's been all over the place these last few days."

"Sure," said Martin. John brought the plates to the table with a thanks from Martin.

"Well," said John, "I suppose now we can start planning our wedding?"

"Of course," said Martin.

"For a start, no more arrests," said John.

"Never again," said Martin, "I'm sorry," he sighed.

"Well," said John, "I'll be lying if I said I'm going to let it go so easily… It's not that I want to give you grief, I don't, but, yeah, I'm a bit upset over the whole thing. I'm sorry, alright? I'm mad, and your coffee looked disgusting by the way, but, I'm sorry about that too."

"Sure," said Martin, "thanks, I'm sorry too."

"But," said John, grinding in the salt as Martin took the vinegar, "you can't get arrested like that again, and more importantly, you can't keep things like that from me again, understand?" Martin nodded. He brushed shoulders with John and the two of them smiled shyly at each other. They finished their dinner and the night continued on until it was time for bed and Martin wrote his last entry for the night:

After dinner and just before bed I asked John to dance with me, it started after the two of us finished watching the My Neighbours the Yamadas *and we were discussing the film and the madness of it all, eventually I stuck on Louis Armstrong's live version of* C'est Ci Bon *and I asked if he wanted to dance, but while also stressing that I've no follow-through, when he gave an initial 'no' I repeated that it was probably for the best since I had no follow-through whatsoever, he must have felt sorry for me because after 20-30 seconds of me standing and stretching like a dog locked out in the rain he got up, I put the song back to the start and the two of us gave it a shot. He had to teach me how to lead because I'm a little taller and I guess he's a traditionalist when it comes to dancing, but it was nice, I kept going in to kiss him was the only problem, 'dancing's for dancing' he said, I'm not so sure, but it was nice. Well, anyway, dancing may be for dancing, but bed, all kinds of things can happen in bed…*

You Can't Escape Shakespeare

'All's well that ends well' thought Martin the Martian to the 'I' in Martin. Yes. 'All's well that ends well' I thought to myself as I sat waiting for good old Mark to show and share a pint with me in one of our old watering holes. And so I sat and sipped, rolled a smoke and read a bit until Mark finally bustled in with—

"Well Martie, what's the craic?" with a pat on the back.

"Same old," I said as I put away my book, glasses, pen and diary while Mark got us a couple of drinks. "Cheers," we said with a clink.

"What are you reading?" He asked. "It looks big enough."

"It's a collection of Shakespeare," I said.

"Shakespeare!" said Mark, "you can't escape the Shakespeare lads! Who said that?"

"Watchem, I remember."

"So, what made you pick up Shakespeare then?"

"Well, after Walt Whitman I randomly picked up *The Sea, the Sea* by Iris Murdoch. I kept passing her plaque at the Basin and wondering who she was so when I found one of her books I went for it, have you read anything by her?"

"No," said Mark. "I think she was mentioned in college once, one of our Anglo-Irish writers, but I never read anything."

"She wasn't Anglo-Irish, if anything she was Irish-English or English-Irish, anyone who claims she was only one or the other is doing her a disservice, and to claim her as Anglo-Irish doesn't make sense when you look at her heritage."

"Fair enough," said Mark, "she's worth reading then?"

"Yes, so much so I'm rather angry I never heard of her before. *The Sea, the Sea* is a phenomenal book. Masterclass. Just when I think I'm about ready to get something published I read a book like that that puts me in my place! Anyway, she included a rant on Shakespeare and so I thought it time to give him a read, only this collection is a bit bulky for carrying around."

"Have you ever heard of a Kindle," Mark laughed.

"Well, I don't read Kindle books for two reasons: the first is that reading anything that looks online takes me back to college reading, and I've had enough of that for a while, the second is that they're disappointing—I mean, if I were to read an Ann Rice or Stephen King book digitally I would want the book to take advantage of the format, you know? I would want digital spiders racing across the page, I would want digital blood dripping from the murder scenes. I'd want the sound and graphics of rain hitting the page when a character is walking out in rough weather, or if a character were to disappear I'd want to have their names erased from the text.

"Imagine what could be done with something like *Lord of the Rings*? Like, if every time Frodo put on the ring his name all but disappeared, or when goblins drew near the text would shine like his sword. With eye-tracking software who knows what could be done. But no, when it comes to digital books our imaginations haven't caught up with the technology yet and it puts me off them. A book is a book. The reader knows that the writer's tools are limited and so I can't ask for these things and I don't miss them, only, I *do* wish more contemporary books would include the odd illustration, it's a nice touch in *The Hobbit*, and I used to love coming across them in Charles Dickens and Jane Austen."

"Fair enough," said Mark. "Anyway, shall we get to it then?" He asked. I nodded. Here's the part I hate, despite doing my best to pretend otherwise.

"It's not a bad story at all" went Mark, "but, you don't come across as very sympathetic in it, and the way it ended… well, it was a bit anticlimactic."

"Anticlimatic! They bloody arrested me!"

"Yes, but, imagine if Oscar Wilde was let off the hook like your 'Martin' did, well, we would never have got *The Ballad of Reading Gaol*, would we?"

I nearly choked on my pint. The trouble with giving your work to friends to proof-read is learning to hold your tongue, which is no easy lesson to learn. I snowballed back:

"Well, first of all, if I'm expected to write anything with *The Ballad of Reading Gaol* as my yardstick I'll be dead before I ever get to publish, and speaking of dead, it's not like everything Wilde wrote was as good as *that*. Have you read the rest of his poems? I'll tell you now, don't bother, because, besides *Panthea* and *Roses and Rue* they're shit, they've aged terribly, terribly! Unless you happen to know the name and symbolic meaning of every bloody plant and weed on top of knowing your ancient classics inside out, even then, even then!

all he does is lament the past and complain about the present—and talk about a West Brit!

"If Ireland decided to ignore Iris Murdoch because she spent most of her time in England, then Oscar Wild should have been completely forgotten about on this island! The way he writes about the British empire, you have to read it to believe it. Plus, with respect to *Panthea*, Walt Whitman said it better. No. *The Ballad of Reading Gaol*, as far as I can recall, was the last thing Oscar Wilde ever wrote, the last thing he ever wrote! And I'm still trying to get my writing off the ground for fuck's sake. And you want to measure me to that? Also, so what if I come across as unsympathetic? No Irish person ever gained sympathy through their work, least not from their own people."

Mark replied: "Well, if the reader can't sympathise with you as a protagonist, never mind as a writer, then any message you're trying to get across will fall by the wayside, and it's clear you're making a push for legalisation at least."

"*Because weed should be legalised,*" I thumped. "And when it is legalised, the Irish State owe me 10 grams! Look, the Martin in the text doesn't have to be sympathetic," I said, trying to calm myself. I could see I was one more outburst away from Mark laughing in my face. "and yes, I want to see weed legalised in Ireland, and mushrooms too while we're at it, and they will be, with or without me, but it's the writing that has to come first. And those things regarding the arrest happened to me as they happened in the book—whatever else I made up."

"But it *is* a story," Mark replied, "so can't you give yourself a conviction in the story and see where it takes you? It might make a full book out of your short story, and give it a bit more drama."

"No," I said. "I've changed plenty, but the absurdity of the arrest already seems stranger than fiction, and I don't want to mess with that. Plus, I wasn't convicted, so I wouldn't know how to write about it. As Oscar Wilde said so well:

For he who lives more lives than one
More deaths than one must die.

"I didn't get a conviction, but I came close and it scared the shit out of me, and for a short while the idea of it twisted my brain inside out, and that's all I feel qualified to write about."

"Okay," said Mark. "But I'm sure if Oscar were here he'd tell you; a writer *should* be able to live more lives than one because a writer only has to suffer a *fictional* death, not a real one."

"Okay" I moaned, he had a point.

"Have you read Kafka by the way? *The Trail*? It has a similar theme of someone being arrested and going through a mad sort of system."

I shook my head, groaned and said, "I got halfway through *The Trail*, I couldn't finish it, none of the characters made sense to me, the writing was ugly, I don't get the hype. It reads like the worst possible combination of *Alice in Wonderland* and *1984.* ." I stared at my pint and felt a bit desperate and continued: "I'm sorry Mark, it's just… I didn't have Oscar Wilde or Kafka in mind when I wrote it, if anything, I might have been leaning a little into Coetzee and Albert Camus, but even that's probably wishful thinking."

"*The Life and Times of Michael K*, what a fucking book that was," said Mark.

"Yes. I'll drink to that."

Clink. Drink.

"I liked the diary extracts," Mark continued.

"Well," I said, "I'll thank my sister for that. I wouldn't mind doing a little for diaries what Walt Whitman does for poetry. I always have a problem when a book's supposedly written from one point of view but the proteginist's reasons for writing a book are completely unsaid, and their supposed audience is a dry god. With a diary, its reason for existence is embedded in its format. That's the first and lasting impulse of a diary—to exist. Their endings are predictable—the incapacitation of their creators. Their value always *remains to be seen*. They are our most endearing confessions of a wish to live on, even if it has to be as ghosts made up out of ink and paper. All this makes diaries honest in such a way that they test *our* honesty, our honesty towards ourselves. And there's another dangerous edge to a diary, besides their endings—the gaps."

"I suppose" Mark said. "But it sounds like special pleading to look for merit over the gaps."

"I suppose, but the cleverest thing about a diary is that there's no authority that can dictate what it can or can't be. Anything you create can be read as a line from your diary. Oscar Wilde's collected poems read very much like a diary."

"How so?"

"Well, I felt like I could pinpoint the moment when Wilde read Whitman, I could feel it in how his poetry changed. I don't think anyone can read Walt Whitman without becoming a little more of a poet, or a better poet in Oscar's case. Just like how you can't read Virginia Woolf without becoming a better writer."

"Well then," said Mark, "that's all I got. Although the pacing seems a little all over the place, and, of course, if you're serious about getting it published you'll have to change the names."

"I've been avoiding that" I groaned, "bloody names… We barely have a say about the names were given, or the nicknames we'll be stuck with, and yet I'm to invest all this detail into naming a character. If I could have it all my own way, then the name of 'Martin' would be replaced by the name of whoever bought the book, let the name on their bank-card be inserted into the text, that's the way Kindle books should do it. *Names*. But your probably right about the pacing, the problem is I want the passing to be a little off, like that whole week had been, but maybe I'm not pulling it off right" I sulked.

"You take criticism well," Mark laughed. I grinned and sipped my Guinness.

"What was George Orwell's real name?" He asked.

"I can't remember now, something Clemens I think, Stephen maybe."

"Well," laughed Mark, "if you can't remember his real name then fair fucks to him for changing it! Anyway," he continued, "I still think you should re-think having your protagonist-doppelganger getting off with the conviction, but," he shrugged "sure it's your story, the rest is just grammar, typos and the odd comment." Mark finished by handing me back my first printed draft. I took this odd tumour of myself with a sigh and put it away with a dread I tried to hide, for I forbode reading through it all again with my self-critical self, where now Mark's surgical red pen would be bound to be found cutting into my clunky clumsy style. "Thanks," I smiled.

"Do you think this is the one to finally get published?" Mark smiled.

"Ah sure, hopefully. If not, it'll always be hobby. Anything that keeps me off video games and YouTube is good enough, even if it doesn't make me money, it's like free therapy."

"Well, good luck with it. So, any other news?" Mark asked politely.

"Well" I started, "No, I'm grand, I'm starting to feel a little in the doghouse with John, the thing is" I sipped, "he was very supportive, loving and helpful when I broke the story to him, but now that things have settled down I'm starting to feel him venting. But, all in all, we're in a good place. Looking forward to the wedding. ."

"Mmm," said Mark, noting the smoke I had rolled. "He didn't ask you to stop smoking though?"

"No… but I can't be such a feckin eejit anymore, Still, he doesn't mind me smoking the odd one now and then, especially after a stand-up gig when I need a come-down. Speaking off, I'm doing stand-up next week, need to get back into it, if you're around?"

"I might be, yeah. Any new material?"

"No, it's been a while, I've polished up my first stand-up routine and want to do it again, it's been so long it almost feels fresh again."

"Fair enough, I'll let you know."

"Sure…, what about yourself, any news, reading anything decent, you know, besides my masterpiece here?" Mark grinned from ear to ear.

"Clodagh got a book recently, *Everyday Sexism* by Laura Bates."

I nodded, it was always a good sign when Mark memorised an author's name. "Well?"

"So the book mostly deals with everyday sexism, of course, but it also talks about *unconscious gender bias*, how we unconsciously favour talking to, and engaging with, the work of people who are the same sex as us."

"Ok" I nodded.

"And" continued Mark, "our education didn't help. In college they mostly had us read books written by men, and primary and secondary school was probably worse."

"Not to mention segregated" I mumbled.

"And apparently the bias is much stronger in boys and men, and you can see why." I nodded, although in this one respect social anthropology wasn't the worst.

"Well" said Mark. "I read the book anyway, and I thought to myself, how can I correct an unconscious bias, assuming I even have one?"

"Consciously, I'd presume."

"Right, so since I've read the book, I've forced a condition on myself: for now on, for every book or new movie I see, at least every second one of them must have been written or directed by a woman."

"Okay, so you're reading books and watching films 50-50, 50% percent produced by men, and 50% produced by women."

"Exactly."

And how's that going?"

"It's a little too early to tell" smiled Mark. "But so far, it feels like a gamechanger. I've already started to notice things. For example, my birthday and Christmas pile up of books are nearly all written by men, whether given by my family, you, or even Clodagh." I sipped my beer, trying to remember what book I had given Mark for his birthday.

"And" continued Mark, "I went back over everything I had read, everything that I had kept track of anyway,"

"And?"

"and, over the last 3 years, 82% of everything I've read was written by a man, and films were even worse. I was consuming an even worse representation of gender then what's in the Irish political system." I shivered.

"I'm surprised it's as bad as that" I said.

"Me too, that's why they call it an *un*conscious bias. So now I'm reading *In a cafe and other stories* by Mary Lavin, and before that it was *The Wig my Father Wore* by Anne Enright. And both of them have been fantastic. I haven't been reading so well since I discovered the adult section in the library" Mark smiled.

"I'm surprised" I said. "I never would have thought of you leaning towards feminism."

"It's more than feminism" said Mark, "it's about taking control of my own education. About no longer denying myself the best of what's out there. Think about it. Take the classics, for example, for so long women couldn't vote and couldn't access mainstream education like men could. So this unconscious bias to favour male writers has been compounded throughout history, and unless I'm going crazy, it seems male-written books that are deemed 'great' are often mediocre, and women-written books that have been deemed 'good' are some of the best things I've ever read. I'm telling you, I haven't been reading so well, so consistently well, …, ever. And all the books written by men that I still want to read, not only are they not going anywhere, but I can be more selective about them, so that *their* quality has also gone up. The last bad book I read was *The Boy in the Striped Pyjamas*, and that feels like years ago."

"Really" I said, "I agree that it wasn't great, but you should read *The Heart's Invisible Furies*. I couldn't get over the difference. In fact, I'll make a note to give it to you."

"Hold your horses" Mark laughed. "I still haven't read the last one you got me. But yeah, I'm very happy. I haven't read a gamechanger in some time."

"Those are normally the kind of books I get from my sister" I smiled. "Is *Everyday Sexism* up for grabs then?" Mark reached into his bag and produced it like a magic trick.

"For when you finally escape from Shakespeare" he laughed.

"Speaking of escape, do you mind?"

"Go ahead" Mark nodded, "I need to message my missus anyway." I gave him a twenty to buy the next round and went out the back.

It was out there that I saw him, looking older, smaller and even sterner than I remember. He was sitting slouched and scrunched-in like a comma, but with a gasp I would eventually see him for the full stop he was. Yes, my beginning, my end, my old English teacher, face-to-face again. I saw him sitting and staring into his pint and my first thought was to walk back in the way I came. Yes. I wanted to bolt, and there he was. And as I stood staring the poetry of it hit me. My first instinct wasn't to buy him a pint. No, the first thing I felt was superior. But, as I stood and stared, I realised that I was as much as his equal as I could stomach. Sighing, I lit my smoke and walked up to him:

"Well. Mr Mulch, I guess you don't remember me? You were my English teacher up to 3rd year, before... well, how's it going?" He looked at me for a long time before answering, the smoke of his cigarette screening between us.

"Yes. I think I remember you, Martin?" I nodded, genuinely impressed, and he continued. "Yes, you haven't changed."

"It's a blessing and a curse," I said. "I'm teaching English to adults, and the amount of times I've bumped into an ex-student and forgotten their names and everything about them, you must have a very good memory for it."

He shrugged: "You were also in my class the year I got arrested, that's been a hard time to forget," he said into his pint.

"Yeah, I can imagine," I said, "I got arrested too this year, believe it or not, no conviction though, thank god."

Mr Mulch looked at me but said nothing, so I continued: "For smoking this if you can believe it, arrested over a bit of hash," Mr Mulch put his hand out and I passed it to him mechanically, he took an almighty long drag before offering it back.

"Take a second," I offered and he did, much like the first. I took it back, not wanting it anymore, but not wanting to seem rude.

"Did you ever teach adults," I asked. He shook his head. "Well, it's fun but frustrating. They're mostly Brazilians, and while I love them, a lot of them are glued to their phones, I mean obsessed, and they look at me like I've two heads when I lecture them about it, and, for the most part, I've come to realise that Brazilians read very little, either *Harry Potter* or some get-rich-quick shit, or nothing at all seems to be the norm. Although they have some very famous writers, it's exceptional to find a Brazilian who enjoys reading, and that drags on me a bit." Mr Mulch looked as if he wasn't listening, so, smiling, I tried one that normally got a laugh.

"Of course" I continued, "adults also come with more baggage, like, for their last test I got them to write about the best and worst holiday they ever had, so one of my students wrote about a holiday where his wife had to be rushed to hospital where she was tested positive for breast cancer, and what am I meant to do with that? He's a pre-int. student, the page was littered with mistakes, including using 'boob' for 'breast' and a misspelling of cancer. How are you supposed to correct something like that then?"

"You think only adults have baggage," Mr Mulch scoffed. "I learnt a long time ago—correct the mistakes, just the mistakes, and they'll soon stop bringing you their baggage. You have no idea the things I've read, and from children. Once I had a child write 2-3 pages about how his mother was hitting him and his dad, so I called in the mother to have a word and after a bloody bad time of it it turned out the kid had been grounded the week before and was lying through her teeth, and who knows which of them was telling the truth," Mr Mulch stared off to space before continuing, "…just correct the grammar."

"Mmm," I said, at a loss. "That's mad… anyway, I'm still enjoying teaching, even if it's a drag sometimes."

"Give it another 30 years," Mr Mulch said, "you'll know the meaning of drag then."

"Well," I said, "for all my moaning it's the only job I seem to enjoy—getting to know interesting people all day long… but I definitely think teaching adults must help." He nodded, but barely, and I started to feel that he would sooner have left my company than take much more of it. Still, he lit another cigarette and finished his beer as I stayed standing awkwardly. I couldn't take it anymore. He looked as miserable as ever, only older and shabbier. I hadn't it in me to ask what he was up to now, fired or not fired he could only have been retired. But that's not fair I suppose, for all I know he could have been writing poems and prose. But no, whatever it was he was up to these days I could only feel sorry for him. His comments about being affected by the essays of his students spoke volumes about his misery. In numbing himself against exposure to personal writing he became a numbing agent, slowly cutting and stunting *our* development. No. no matter what sob-stories or downright depressing things await me as a teacher, I'll never be one to focus only on 'English without mistakes.'

I sighed inaudibly, wished him luck and headed back in. Sitting down beside Mark I told him our old English teacher was out the back.

"Which one?" Mark asked. "Did you get to tell Watchem that you're finally reading Shakespeare again!"

"No, no, not Watchem, the other one."

"The auld rascal," beamed Mark. "He's here! Outside?"

"Yes. The one *I'll* become if I'm not careful," I said. "The one I might have been if I got that bloody conviction," I shivered and sipped my pint as Mark caught my drift and started to laugh. I touched wood, sighed, and told the barwoman to put on another Guinness for the gentleman outside.

"Are you related to the grumpy git?" she asked.

"No, even worse, he used to be my English teacher."

[18/01/2020]

On my journey home I reflected on the words of Mr Mulch and his insight into his 'English without mistake' approach, and I felt even more sorry for him, and all the students he's had, for surely the point in learning any language is to learn how to express yourself, whether through lies or the truth. If we're not learning to express ourselves then what's the point?

*I also reflected on something that Alan Watts once drew my attention to: We have a will we can direct, at least with some feeling of autonomy, and we use that will to re-collect and re-member the past, but just how much of that process is conscious? We love nothing more than to lose our conscious selves in a process in which we feel we have mastered, or that we're happy has mastered us. Like dancing, which, for me, masters me. The music masters me, and moves me, to where I do not know nor care, but it's the closest I get to a feeling of divinity, of feeling myself absorbed, ab*solved.

Reading is similar, but for want of movement and absolute abandon it isn't quite as liberating, not in a dizzying sense, but reading helps me to see beyond myself. In fact, reading is a form of getting to know myself, as the thoughts of other perspectives and lived experiences are given space to be absorbed or rejected, but at least entertained.... Writing is a funny one. Writing is like trying to put a harness on my thoughts, and then using thoughts in order to order thoughts! But I suppose the ordering is about making it accessible, fluent, directing the flow, like a river as opposed to an ocean. Yes. That's it, writing is trying to make a river out of an ocean.

Yes, that's good. Anyway, too much me, me me! Mark said he liked what I've written, so what else can I write? Maybe I need to revisit some of my old half-finished poems and stories.

Well, another thing. Isn't it curious that 'me' is 'em' backwords. Only 'em' is not as serious and obnoxious as 'me,' so I would write it: The flipside of 'me!' is 'em?' Or it's backwards for Shakespeare's quote: "The empty vessel makes the loudest sound." Anyway, this has been me! In all of my em? This has been me as I've moved through my diary as well as my unpublished poems and prose. And if you're out there, regardless of being separated by time and space, if you're out there—then your company's appreciated, so thank you, and remember, if Charles Swindoll's idea is to be taken at face value, that "life is 10% what happens to you and 90% how you react to it." Then reflecting on how you react to life is a very powerful thing indeed.

And who knows, maybe I'll be reading your reflections next.

Another One for the Road: Stand-Up Set 1-h

My name's Martin Penny and this is my first stand-up comedy routine.

Normally people sitting at the front are afraid of been picked on by the comedians, but it's getting puked on you lot need to worry about. My head's spinning, my hands are sweating, and I have to last at least 7 minutes again. Haven't heard that one in a while.

The open-mic virgin feeling is legit.

Not like those other bullshit feel-like-a-virgin moments people like to throw out there. Like 'oh, you're a yoga-virgin? You poor dear'. Fuck off, 'Yoga-virgin', that's a bit of stretch.

A nice girl I know actually called me a 'burrito virgin' once.

And she even offered to bring me into town and buy me my first Boojum so that we could pop my burrito cherry.

And she banged on and on until I asked her – 'what the fuck do eating burritos have to do with sex?', 'Well', she says, 'with what burritos can do to your arsehole, they're actually pretty similar to anal sex.
I had to stop her there when she said that to me, it was all a bit much, especially as this was coming from my sister.

No, I have to say, doing stand-up comedy is more terrifying than sex. My partner insisted on us having sex last night, he thought it would help calm me down, but it made me feel worse, because after 30 seconds of pumping and coming it hit me – stand-up is nothing like sex, if I bomb it here I can't lick my way out of this one.

I did consider it, about licking out all members of the audience if I bombed. My idea was to imagine you all naked, your genitals covered in Ben & Jerry's vegan Fish Food ice-cream, And then never doing stand-up again, but knowing, in my heart, that I made a whole bunch of people cum just for me.

But I never tested to see how many head and rims jobs I can give in one night, and I'm no politician. No, seriously, if I was to find out how much head I could give in the one go, I'd rather practise at a funeral, they always have low expectations and at least one stiff member.

For those here not Irish, I'll let you in on a secret, the Irish are great at licking and giving head, we can lick the literal fuck out of any dick, arse or pussy.

Sure we practise every year with the Blarney stone.

(If you haven't visited the Blarney Stone yet then type it into Google Images and you'll see what I'm talking about, if you have visited the Blarney Stone then good luck with the herpes).

No, no, I'm only messing, the real reason why the Irish are great at oral sex is that after the pubs are shut and the off-licences are closed, and you've had ten pints of Guinness, you'll lick anything that has a bit of moisture to it.

That's how most Irish couples meet, at a point of utter dehydration, our tongues drawn towards anything half-wet.

Anyway, I haven't bombed so far, so no head tonight.

Another reason why stand-up is harder than sex is because no one but my therapist and partner expected me to do stand-up, and people can react very weirdly towards you when you do the unexpected.

I'll give you an example:

So my mammy always encouraged me to learn how to dress myself. You know, she taught me to button my own shirts and pull up my own pants, luckily, just before I hit puberty, or I could have taken her eye out.

But, when I decided to spend one night, just one night! dressed as a woman, my mother called me a pervert!

She asked *why* I was dressing up as a woman – and I told her, look mam, it's just for a fancy dress party, you know, it's just for a bit craic.
She wouldn't hear of it, she says: why don't you go as something normal then, like Sadam Huesain, or Barrack Obama'. Because, apparently, it's better to go to a fancy dress as a terrorist, or worse, a terrorist *and* in black face, then it is to wear high heels and a sexy skirt.

I'll be honest with you, I think my mam was just jealous that, unlike her, I could actually fit into my sister's clothes.

I made that skirt look good baby!
Only my mam was so jealous that she ran me out of the house screaming that I was a pervert, which really really hurt, because that was the first time I ever had to run in high heels.

My dad is the same. When I got my first girlfriend my dad said: 'Son, just relax, take your time, and sure, if it doesn't go well, try her again in an hour or two'. Which seemed good advice, a little bit rapey maybe, but, you know, he meant well.

When I brought my first boyfriend home my dad said: 'Son, it must be well over a couple of hours, why don't you try those lovely girls again!'

When I started playing football it was the same, my dad was full of encouragement, but when I told my dad that I'll be doing stand-up for the first time, he told me: 'Son, I never would have thought of you as a comedian, sure compared to the rest of the family, you're not that funny'. Now, I never wanted my dad to get cancer before he said that to me, but the good news is, when my dad gets cancer now, at least one of us will be ready for it.

And both of my parents expected me to follow in our proud family tradition, going back to our earliest ancestors, of being functioning alcoholics, my mam encourages me to have a few glasses of wine with every meal, my dad encourages me to have a few whiskeys after every meal, so that between the two of them, I'm normally drunk by brunch. But when I started smoking weed a few years back, boy were they pissed! I mean, they're *always* pissed, but you know what I mean.

My mam thinks weed is destroying my memories – but last month my dad spilled a full pint of Guinness all over her phone. She lost over 500 hundred photographs, a dozen contacts, emails, passwords, you name it, so as far as I'm concerned, alcohol has destroyed far more of her memories than weed will ever take from me. Because when someone spills their weed on my phone, I don't panic or cry, I just laugh and get high.

Anyway, I'll tell you one true story before I go. The story of my manky ingrown toenail. Which is the reason why we don't do food up here!

First of all, fuck ingrown toenails.

Now, I handled my first ingrown nail like Irishmen handle most things, I ignored it, waited until it was life or death, and then I showed it to my mammy. My mam's first comment is that the nail must have made a u-turn at my socks. But then, just as useless, she insists on me showing it to my grandmother. Now I have my dotery 90 year old granny saying: '*I have a cure for that – you need to make a poultice*'.

I never heard of a poultice before, I just thought granny was seeing ghosts again.

Instead, she made me fill a sock with white bread, instead of my usual white sauce filling. And then I had to throw this bread-filled sock into a pot of boiling tea, and then I had to wrap this boiling, soggy sock around my infected toe, and leave it on for 4 hours.

I was still rushed to the emergency hospital, with the only difference being that when I got there, I somehow had to explain to my doctor why my gangrene toe smelled like soggy bread and Barry's tea.

That wasn't the first time my granny fucked me over either, oh no, the two of us go way back.
On my 10th birthday she promised she'd get me a donkey.

Now, I'm from the North-side of Dublin, so I was used to the idea of children getting horses as gifts.

And while a donkey's no horse – boy I was excited. I was so excited for me donkey that I told all my friends that, come Monday, they'd better keep an eye out for a lad coming to school on his very own donkey.

Of course, my granny, the bitch, didn't get me a donkey, she got a donation, on my behalf, to rescue a donkey, probably rescued from its previous North-Sider owners.

As a 10 year old, this present of a donkey that I didn't have physical access to was beyond *all* my powers of understanding. All I knew was, only one ass showed up to school on Monday, and I only have one pair of legs.

I called my granny a lying bitch, so she called me an ungrateful asshole. She said she got me the rescued donkey to help teach me to love and respect all animals. But when, years later, I take the love of animals she tried to teach me to heart and decided to go vegan, she called me a stupid prick, and an asshole.

So remember, you can be an alcoholic, animal-abusing womanizer who knows how to dress yourself conservatively, and everyone will love you. But if you go off-script, and become a cross-dressing, stand-up comedian vegan stoner who dates as many men as you do women, you'll be called a prick by your granny, unfunny by your dad and a pervert by your mam.

But you can all call me whatever you like, as long as you call me back!

My name's Martin Penny and you've been a magic audience, thank you very much and goodnight.

If I Can Have an Afterword with You

Let my name stand among those who are willing to bear ridicule and reproach for the truth's sake, and so earn some right to rejoice when the victory is won.
Louisa May Alcott.

Dear Reader,

The following afterword is a Q & A based on common questions I often get asked for being a vegan. I hope you take this opportunity to learn what it's all about. Or at the very least, take this opportunity to know your enemy, because vegans aren't going away.

Question: So what is veganism?

Veganism is an idea, outlook or worldview that seeks to end or reduce all abusive treatment towards animals as much as is practically possible. It also seeks to end the commodification of all animals. Veganism is not a religion. I almost wish it was, because then we would be afforded tax breaks and protection from discrimination. But, more to the point, you can be vegan and Muslim, Christian, Jedi, agnostic or atheist. And veganism is not a diet. A vegan's diet is known as a plant-based diet, but veganism also incorporates such things as the clothes we wear, the sports we follow, the cosmetics we use and the pets we keep.

So, veganism is an ethical or moral stance against unnecessary animal abuse. It is not about individual health, diet or even the environment. Veganism is about valuing and respecting the life of all animals to the point that we abstain from causing them unnecessary harm and cruelty. Once we do that everything else falls naturally into place

Question: Why did you go vegan?

I believe that everyone is, to some degree, already vegan. For me, 'going vegan' wasn't about learning to love animals—I've loved animals for as long as I can remember, 'going vegan' was more about becoming aware, even allowing myself to become aware, that my actions were not lining up with my values and beliefs. Just about every parent would stop their child from kicking a random dog on the street. I 'went vegan' when I accepted the idea that to pay someone to abuse animals on my behalf is just as wrong as being cruel towards animals directly. The mad thing is, it took me nearly 3 decades to 'go vegan.' Why did it take me so long for my actions to match my words? The next question I'm often asked will help us to understand.

Question: I have no problem with vegans—but why are they so annoying and pushy, why can't they just let me eat what I want to eat?

It feels strange to say it, but I've actually never dealt with a pushy vegan. Also, if you happen to work in an industry that requires you to commodify and exploit animals, then I sympathise with you sincerely. My own livelihood has never been affected by veganism, so I cannot imagine what animal farmers, bee keepers, fisherfolk etc. must go through when confronted by it. But I've come to believe that veganism, like everything good, is best spread by honest education, and on that note, here are the main reasons why vegans tend to be pushy:

1) Vegans are people who believe that any person or industry which commodifies animals is inherently oppressive and exploitative, and that, in any system of oppression, it is the voice of the oppressed that we should listen to, not the voice of the oppressors. Whether it's racism, sexism or homophobia, what we need to remember is that every system of oppression operates by: 1) silencing or dismissing the voice of the oppressed, 2) declaring that it is the voice of the oppressors which should matter, and, as a consequence, 3) the oppressors dictate the terms and conditions of the oppression.

Vegans are pushy because we are trying to give, or to amplify, the voice of animals, and their voices have not only been silenced, but are often perversely twisted to glorify and promote their own abuse. Dairy products are particularly notorious for this, but a lot of chicken, pig, cow and fish packaging is the same.

This idea that 'happy cows produce happy milk' is, biologically speaking, fucking stupid. It's akin to saying that happy child labour produce happy (I)phones and clothes, or that happy ejaculations produce happy people. One step towards veganism is to realise that all such labels and marketing is directed to manipulate us, the potential consumers. Labels are not, and never were, for the benefit of animals. In fact, it's a form of double-speak so invasive that even George Orwell couldn't see it. So we're pushy because we would like everyone to stop for a moment and consider the victims of these industries and what they go through.

2) We're pushy because the full truth behind these industries is supressed. For animals such as cows, pigs, sheep and especially goats, that is, very vocal animals, their voices are literally silenced by thick concrete walls, gag-laws and secrecy. I heard the sound of a dying pig for the first time in Vietnam. Dying pigs can be extremely loud and it was an unforgettable experience, but, unless you work in a slaughterhouse, you will never hear that sound in Ireland or most countries, despite the fact that it's our money that pays for these pigs to be killed, and it's happening every single day.

Also, farms may not be hard to access, but slaughterhouses are. In Ireland, for example, I have seen the outside of countless farms driving from A to B, but I've never driven past anything that I could identify as a slaughterhouse. When I was a child in primary school I was taken with my class to a farm, and I remember sitting in a large circle with my fellow students and having a baby chick being passed around to each of us, I remembered holding that little yellow chick and thinking what a tragedy it would be if I were to drop and injure it, and yet, death for human consumption is the reason why animal farming exists, and male chicks are killed when they are are less than a day old in the egg industry anyway. But that side of farming was completely absent from the whole farm experience, and, while it would have been objectively far more educational, no school has ever gone to a slaughterhouse as part of a school trip (at the very least, schools need to be encouraged to bring their students to visit animal sanctuaries, not animal farms. Animal sanctuaries provide information, animal farms only provide propaganda).

Indeed, slaughterhouse footage is often obtained, but it has never been freely released to the public. In order to get the full truth out there, sometimes we simply have to push—but access to the full story shouldn't be illegal, it should be freely available, if the truth isn't worth pushing for, what is? And if schools don't wish to traumatise children by bringing them to slaughterhouses, why don't they bring children to animal sanctuaries instead? Farms love to pretend that they are animal sanctuaries, but it's PR nonsense. Farms, by their nature, only care for animals up to the point that slaughtering them is most profitable, which in reality means sending their animals to be killed while they are little more than babies.

3) We're pushy because, for so long, these industries have had things completely their own way. As a non-vegan, you have a every right to complain about how annoying vegans are, but as a vegan, I am incredibly sad and angry that some of my tax money, some of the very money I've earned in writing this book, is going towards our horse-racing industry. Why should the money I've earned be used to abuse horses against my (and their) wishes? Not to mention the amount of subsidies our government gives to our fishing, dairy and meat industries. There is no 'vegan-lobby' that I know of existing in any country, so until we have the money to play our politicians around the moral chessboard like these other industries do, we'll have to be pushy.

Since going vegan I feel I'm owed a tax rebate and an apology for the fact that some of my money is still being used to fund and subsidise animal abuse. Just imagine being a lesbian (if you aren't one already) and finding out that your country gives tax breaks and legal protection to the largest homophobic and sexist organisation on the planet. (actually, the Irish government does do that, yes, Catholic Church, I'm talking to you. But since the Catholic Church turns a blind eye on child abuse, what hope do we have that they'll care for non-human animals? And if there are any good Christians reading this, then remember that: 'thou shall not kill').

4) We're pushy because most vegans have researched plant nutrition to make sure it was safe before changing our diet. Most of us know how to thrive on a plant-based diet, but, more than that, our research has shown us that eating meat, fish and dairy is bad for us. The only logical reason we have for eating them in this day and age is taste. Any source I give is liable to be dismissed as biased, so

please, do your own research, see how eating meat has proven to be bad for your heart and cholesterol, how it increases the risk of several types of cancer, how fish in the oceans are filled with ever-increasing amounts of mercury and microplastics, how eating meat is associated with an increased risk of type 2 diabetes and how meat and dairy are major causes of obesity. Please just consider the fact that dairy is nature's baby-growth formula, and, unlike human breastmilk, which is designed for the extremely slow development of human babies, cows' milk is designed to turn a baby cow into a full-sized adult cow in less than 1 year.

So, if you want to lose weight, why not consider a plant-based alternative? Also, why is it weird for an adult to drink human breastmilk, but it's considered normal for adults to drink the breastmilk of the mothers of another species? As Ed Winters put it, biologically speaking—we 'need' cow's milk as much as we need dogs' milk or dolphin milk.

5) We're pushy because these industries, often with funding and support from our governments, have been allowed and even encouraged to advertised to us for decades. They have spent lifetimes and billions trying to influence us to eat meat, fish and dairy. These are the same foods which are fed to us from the time we're babies, when we have absolutely no idea of what is happening, and before we even have the cognitive ability to consent. Just think, by the time we learn how to say things like—'the pig says oink,' 'the chicken says cluck' and 'the cow says moo,' he have already been hand-fed the flesh of these animals.

Just let that sink in—most of us grow up eating cows, pigs and chickens before we even know what cows, pigs and chickens are. And so it's no wonder we get defensive about eating them, as not only do most of us hate the idea of being in the wrong, but, to a certain extent, we were born in the wrong, just like our parents before us. For an atheist like myself, my past of eating animals is as close to a concept of 'original sin' that I'll ever understand. And so we'll be pushy until, like cigarettes, these industries are no longer allowed to push ads on us.

Because, let's face it, if it weren't for those ads and such an upbringing then I think everyone would no sooner kick a dog on the street than they would pay someone to cut the throat of a pig. Both are forms of physical abuse towards highly intelligent animals, both are unjustifiable, but only one is criticised by the media and mainstream society. Why? If, like me, you would never kick a dog on the street then perhaps you should be vegan. Or think of it this way—would it be acceptable to pay people to kick dogs for amusement? If not, why is it acceptable to pay people to slit the throats of pigs for our taste?

6) We're pushy because, and please research this for yourself if you don't believe me, veganism is the single greatest thing we can do to reduce our impact on the environment (barring suicide). If you want to 'do your bit' for the environment then you simply have to consider going vegan, or at least looking into a plant-based diet. David Attenborough, although it took him a very, very, very, very, VERY long to get there, says the same thing, and Jane Goodall, Melanie Joy, Greta Thornburg and Mr Rogers are/were all vegans. Legends, I would sit at their table any day!

7) Vegans are pushy because there would be minimal, next to zero risk of another zoological virus in a vegan world. People say, 'my actions don't affect you, so let me eat what I want!' forgetting that, time and time again, this has been proven false. I really really wish that your diet had no power to affect me, but it does, not just me, but everyone. Sick of Covid? Go vegan. Worried about antibiotic-resistant diseases? Go vegan! Farm animals are by far the biggest consumers of antibiotics in the world and industrial farms are the greatest source of zoological viruses, and if you think Covid's bad? Just wait for the next so-called 'Spanish' Flu.

8) Vegans are often pushy because most of us feel pretty guilty about our past. What makes non-veganism feel so criminal is that most people say that they love animals and most people say that they are against animal abuse, and yet, most people eat other animals and so pay people to abuse other animals on their behalf. Going vegan is like waking up from a hypnotic state or a cult; we feel guilty for what we have contributed to in the past, we want to wake up everyone around us, and, in the silenced background, billions to trillions of animals are still being tortured and killed every year, every month, every day.

9) Finally, I think the main reason why I'm a pushy vegan, personally, is because I've been disappointed by how easy going vegan has been. Before going vegan I imagined veganism as some life-changing, pleasure-destroying process that would somehow make my life worse and ruin food forever, and now I'm vegan and my life is, for the most part, better. I get to eat more while worrying

even less about weight gain, I feel less tired, I'm always ready for the dancefloor after a meal, my hey-fever symptoms have improved (due to my body producing less mucus), my grocery shopping is cheaper, my cooking has been reinvigorated, and, (just between us), my lifelong problems with constipation are long finished. When people say things to me like 'I'm proud of you for going vegan' or 'oh I could never go vegan' I really have to take a breath to stop myself from screaming how goddamn easy it's been.

Vegans aren't heroes or saints, all we've done is made some adjustments in our lives and now we carry on like everyone else. I'm not saying going vegan is or will be easy for everyone, but it's been so ridiculously easy for me that it feels maddening that veganism is held to be something difficult, extreme, or an 'out-there' lifestyle. And it's even more ridiculous to think that we vegans have a right to some sort of a moral high-ground. No longer allowing your money to go towards paying for animals to be abused shouldn't make me a good or moral person. I feel like a child who's finally been taught that there are better ways of having fun than kicking my brother or pouring salt on slugs.

So going vegan has felt trivial. Don't get me wrong, it's been wonderful, but it has not been difficult. As I'm writing this I'm halfway through a packet of biscuits on my second cup of tea, my life hasn't changed, only now I use oatmilk and look for chocolate digestives that don't use dairy, (or oreos, or Tesco's super-cheap double-bourbon creams). Easy. Tonight, for dinner, I'm having chips, mushy peas and a battered fish substitute. Easy. Tomorrow I'm cooking an aubergine and chickpea curry with rice and naan, full of lime and chili, delicious and unbeatably healthy. The only difficult thing about being vegan is wondering why it took us so long and how can we get others to give it a try. So I guess I'm pushy because sometimes we need a little push, and, to be honest, I often wish someone had of been pushy towards me.

Question: But haven't we evolved to eat meat?

Yes and no, but mostly no.
1) Scientifically – We are, by far, more evolved to eat plants than we are to eat meat. I mean, humans are omnivores. It's in the name! We have the eyesight of fruit-pickers. Most carnivores, and especially those that hunt, have various forms of black-and-white vision designed to track movement. Whereas humans have evolved to see colour so that our ancestors could judge whether some fruit

or leaves were ripe enough to risk picking and eating. Our teeth, despite common misconceptions, have evolved to strip and tear at fruit and to grind-down plants. Our lower jaws can move from side-to-side, the jaws of carnivores can't. The power in our bite is absolutely puny compared to other meat-eating animals, and if you think our incisors and canines are designed to eat meat, then please take a moment to google which animals have the largest incisors or canines, you'll be surprised. Even our intestines are designed to digest food slowly, whereas the intestines of carnivores are short to allow meat to be processed quickly before it has time to rot in the gut.

2) Morally – Just because we can do something doesn't mean we should, just like Jurassic Park, just because we can make endless sequels doesn't mean it's a good idea, Goldblum be damned. Or think of it this way—evolution has determined our bodies, but it has never determined what we do with those bodies. Our long limbs and grasping hands have evolved over the years for tree-climbing, but climbing trees is just another choice. Or take our legs; obviously they've evolved for walking, but we don't criticise people on buses, planes, boats or wheelchairs.

3) Common sense – we have no innate killer instinct. Hunting is something that has to be taught, it doesn't come naturally to us. Just think how much children, even toddlers, love cute animals. Or think back to the last time you saw a baby duck or a three-legged dog, did you lick your lips and feel hungry? Or did your heart melt a little? When you read or watched Golem eating his wriggling fish raw did you salivate or feel disgusted? Personally, I don't know anyone who has ever felt hungry while watching a living animal, especially a dying animal. Or just look into slaughterhouse workers and what they go through. There's a reason why slaughterhouse workers, in Ireland and all other industrialised countries, are mostly if not entirely made up of immigrants—nobody sane enjoys killing innocent animals as their 9-5, it's an abusive, humanity-destroying job. Slaughterhouse workers have been shown to suffer from high rates of addiction, abusive relationships, depression and suicides. If a lion got to spend 8 hours a day killing sheep it would feel like a superhero, do you think you would feel like a superhero for killing sheep 8 hours a day?

4) Finally, what really frustrates me about using 'evolution' to justify eating meat is that evolution is being used to justify stagnation, as if evolution were a cul-de-sac, used to justify where we are instead of being used to point to where we should be going. Would it not make more sense for us to move/evolve towards veganism? A way of living that's not only healthier for you as an individual, but healthier for us as a species?

Question: But our ancestors ate meat, and if it wasn't wrong for them, why is it wrong for us?

Context is key here. Imagine for a second that you needed a couple teeth removed and you went to a dentist, now, imagine if the dentist told you that she operates a Neolithic-style dentistry where she only uses the tools and equipment that our ancestors had access to. So she ties you to a chair, she blocks her own ears so that the sounds of your screams don't interrupt her work, and then, without any sanitisation or anaesthetic, she removes your rotting teeth. If you survived such an operation you would, I hope, seek to have her arrested for torturing you, but, if you were actually in Neolithic times, then, as bad as it is, you must accept that she did everything she could to treat you well. Neolithic-style dentistry, even early-to-mid 20th century-style dentistry, would be criminal in today's context. Similarly, when we have the choice to live rich, fulfilling and full lives without abusing animals, especially for our food and clothing, then to do otherwise is wrong, regardless of what our ancestors used to do.

Also, please consider the fact that in no other context do people concern themselves about their ancestors when making decisions. You likely didn't think about your ancestors when deciding your last holiday destination, or when you bought a car, or when you watched your last film or read your last book. The 'ancestors' argument, like the 'but lions eat meat' argument, are unique in that they are only used against veganism, because in any other context they fall apart for the nonsense that they are. To date—no lawyer has ever used 'but lions rape each other!' to defend a client from a charge of sexual violence, or 'our ancestors had slaves' to justify mistreating staff, or 'but our ancestors didn't even allow women to vote!' to justify sexual harassment.

Question: But don't plants matter too? And if so, is it not as wrong to eat plants as it is to eat animals?

1) Scientifically speaking, it is not believed that plants feel pain. They lack anything resembling a brain that would allow them to process pain and they lack a nervous system. Don't get me wrong, plants are amazing, but it's hard to feel pain without a brain. And more to the point—since plants can't move it doesn't make sense that they would have evolved to feel pain. Imagine a tree on fire, or slowly being eaten by insects, or being chopped down, because the plant cannot avoid what is happening it makes no sense that it would have evolved to feel pain. We feel pain because we can usually do something about it, plants can't.

2) Also, if you're really concerned about how much pain plants feel, then by all rights you should care even more for the pain of animals, which have been fine-tuned to feel pain to help in their survival. So, you should be vegan.

3) And, in the end, while vegans eat more plants directly, less plants are used in a vegan diet. This is because, for every animal that is eaten, that animal had to be fed up to the point of slaughter. Just think how many plants a perpetually pregnant cow or pig must eat compared to a human? So if you want to reduce how much plants suffer—you should be vegan.

Question: Well, if I don't care about (non-human) animals, why should I bother going vegan?

Being non-vegan goes beyond not caring about other animals, being non-vegan means that, to judge from the actions which your money goes towards paying for, you vehemently hate non-human animals. You hate them so much that not only do you wish for them to be abused, sexually violated, tortured and killed, but, for some odd reason, you wish for them to be forcibly bred into existence so that their suffering is never-ending. Which is pretty sick when you think about it. This is what I meant in my poem about non-veganism being worse than the holocaust, because the holocaust was intended to completely wipe out those groups of people that Nazi Germany found to be inferior, which was beyond awful, but the holocaust was intended to actually end, whereas there is no end point in non-veganism, it is a never ending system of abuse. Meat and dairy farms are the closest we'll ever get to a literal hell on earth. If, however, you do truly hate, and I mean really hate, (non-human) animals, then that still doesn't negate the other terrible side effects of eating animal products I've already mentioned.

Also, as many vegans before me have pointed out, isn't it odd that we regard the torturing of animals to be the greatest indicator of someone growing up to become a serial killer, and yet we pay for animals to be tortured and have been raised to see this as normal? This is why many of us believe that if children can be taught from birth that no animal should be mistreated or considered property, then this in itself will go a long way to helping children to see that all people are equal too, because, if we cannot discriminate by species, we have even less reason to do so by skin tone, sexuality, gender, ability etc.

Questions: I'm a moral subjectivist, (which means I believe that every individual has the right to determine their own moral code). Therefore, while I respect vegans and their decisions, I believe they have no right to tell me what to do. Can you not agree to even that?

Moral subjectivism is built on the false premiss that morals are self-determined rather than taught to us. For the record, no human can fully self-determine their own morals because all self-determining has to be built upon a foundation of how we have been raised and what we have been taught. Or as Alan Watts would say—the involuntary growth of the human brain and body is the foundation upon which all voluntary decisions are based. In the same way, all of our 'self-determined' morals rest upon morals we have been implicitly and explicitly taught. So how can 'moral subjectivism' make sense in a world where people are trying their hardest to control our thinking and influence our decisions?

In the end, many children are raised to be racist, religiously prejudiced, homophobic and/or sexist, and most of them will grow up to 'self-determine' to be racist, religiously prejudiced, homophobic and/or sexist. I don't want to live in a world where that process is respected under the banner of 'moral subjectivism,' I want to live in a world where those people can be better educated, for their sake and ours.

This is why veganism has been growing with the rise of social media. For the first time, generations are being brought up with access to information which is not controlled and censored by their physical environment. I hate to say it, but when it comes to morals; humans are sponges, not self-determining free-thinkers.

On the other hand, veganism follows the most basic standard of ethics, that is, the effort to minimise harm and suffering as much as is feasibly possible. Why take something so simple and twist it into something for every individual to self-determine when every year there are mass-shooters who self-determine their right to kill others? Or if I got a group together and we determined to burn down your property, I'm sure that you would appeal to the law to protect you, and the law has always followed either popular morals or those set by dictators, and so 'moral subjectivism' is a philosophy of privilege as the law currently protects you (in theory), so that you can be a moral subjectivist (on paper). But if you were a victim of an oppressive system, are you telling me that you wouldn't fight for laws and rights to protect you? Are you telling me that you wouldn't fight or wish for a more 'objective' moral system?

Finally, moral subjectivism, which values the rights of the individual above all else, should not be used to justify mistreating other individuals because they belong to a different species, it's pretty hypocritical. Moral subjectivists should be vegan.

Question: Can it not be argued that other animals, such as cows, pigs, sheep, chickens and fish, lack the cognitive abilities to understand life and death, or oppression in general, and so, if they cannot understand oppression, then they cannot be oppressed?

For the record, I've received many variations of this argument, but never from a cognitive scientist or someone with any background to suggest that they are an authority on what capabilities other animals have. Regardless, this is a silly argument, for even if it were true, we would never allow for the mistreatment of a human in a coma or the mistreatment of a human with a severe mental illness, and, in fact, it was because of the protection and respect given to each of *us* at *our* most vulnerable and stupid stage that allowed us to grow and develop in the first place. And just because a baby has no concept of 'what is fire?' Does not mean that they'll stick their hand in it twice. Feeling pain and wanting to avoid pain doesn't require a high degree of intelligence. And intelligence is generally not a measure used to justify how we treat people (instead we use money—which is sick and is slowly killing us as a species, but one problem at a time I guess), why should it be different for animals? In fact, it isn't. Pigs are at least as smart as dogs.

And even if you're determined to discount animals which cannot be proven to be self-aware, you should understand that all animals suffer from these industries. For most people, a line is drawn at, say, elephants, chimpanzees and dolphins as having enough mental capacity to justify our respect, but animal-derived products are the No. 1 cause of wild habitat loss. So no matter what animal you love or hate, all (us included) suffer from these industries. For example: no tuna is 100% dolphin safe, and even if it could be, the fact that dolphins have to compete with us for their food puts them at risk, and the plastic from fishing puts whales at risk. And remember, the vast majority of humankind's worse diseases can be directly linked to animal agriculture (MERS, Swine flu, the Spanish flu, bird flu, smallpox, covid, to name a few), so you cannot deny that non-vegan practises affect all life on this planet, intelligent and otherwise.

Question: Can we not move towards more ethical forms of meat production—such as free-roaming grass-fed/finished livestock? Afterall, if we didn't breed these animals, they wouldn't even exist!

There are only 3 sources of meat I can think of which would adhere to veganism: roadkill, meat acquired through dumpster-diving (although this is debatable within vegan communities), and lab-grown meat. Everything else is an effort to placate our conscience. Even if you have the greatest treated grass-fed cows, all you have to do is compare the age at which they're slaughtered to their natural lifespan—that difference is cruelty, and, as I've said, veganism is a moving away from the commodification of all animals. We believe we have no right to treat other living animals as property.

And yes, if we didn't raise them to exploit them then these animals wouldn't exist, or at least they would only exist in much smaller numbers. But that's not a bad thing. First, existing to be exploited is a poor existence, second, the land used to graze cattle, or the land used to grow the vegetables to feed to farm animals, should be rewilded, so that instead of having these human-engineered animals dominating our landscape we would go back to having local and wild animals instead, we would have greater biodiversity, a healthier environment, cleaner rivers, lakes and oceans, and a country-side that no longer smells like shit everywhere you go.

People like to say 'but eating meat is natural,' well, at the moment, humans make up 34% of land-mammal biomass, our pets around 1%, wild animals 4%, and our livestock/farm animals? 61%. So, our so-called 'natural' consumption of meat has pushed the truly natural animals to extinction. Also, world hunger in the face of these statistics is a myth. Like with capitalism, our problems arise not through a lack of resources, but at how those resources are distributed. How can we justify giving water, medical attention, food and land to livestock while we neglect to give these things to members of our own species? We must go vegan.

And for anyone who's not convinced—imagine if you woke up tomorrow and, for whatever reason, you found the taste of animal-derived products disgusting. Would you still argue that we should continue breeding these animals into existence if you no longer enjoyed how they tasted?

Question: What do you eat every day and do you take any supplements?

For breakfast I normally eat cereal or porridge with oatmilk, or toast with a butter substitute, jam and peanut butter, or toast with a vegan pesto and some fried tomatoes, or toast with a banana and peanut butter, or toast with a crushed avocado and a squeeze of lemon, or a bagel. At the weekends I'll normally treat myself to a full Irish (vegan) fry, consisting of vegan sausages, rashers, black and white pudding, grilled tomatoes, mushrooms and toast, or I might do vegan French toast with fruit and maple syrup, or a fruit bowl topped with a vegan yogurt and granola.

For lunch it's normally a sandwich, or a bagel, or noodles, or a salad or more toast with hummus, washed down with tea and bickies. At the weekend I might walk down to Bear Lemon and treat myself to one of their delicious cakes.

For dinner I normally cook a stir-fry with veg and tofu, or a pizza, or burger and chips, or a salad, or pasta, or a curry, or a broth or soup with chunky bread and croutons, or my partner might make a pasta-bake or a vegan shepherd's pie or a vegan Irish stew. Honestly, most of your favourite dishes have vegan alternatives, and while it can take a little time to find the perfect alternative to chicken wings, for example, once you've found it then you have it forever. Switching to a plant-based diet is about making a series of small adjustments, and you can make those adjustments at your own pace, all at once or one at a time. I think one of the biggest steps towards veganism is simply finding an alternative milk that you enjoy. If you can give up dairy milk for a month then you'll lose the taste for it altogether and realise how easy the rest of it can be. And vegans still get to enjoy such guilty pleasures as: caffeine, chocolate, sweets, cannabis and alcohol.

As for supplements—I take a B12 supplement most days and in the winter months I'll take the odd vitamin D supplement as well. B12 deficiency is scary because it can cause severe and even permanent damage to the brain and nervous system and it can take months or years before a deficiency is felt and you get diagnosed with it. For the record—B12 does not come from animals, but comes from soil and water bacteria. Some water-plants have been shown to contain high amounts of B12, so, if you do your research, you *may* be able to get by without a supplement, but I'm not a doctor or nutritionist, and if you want my advice— take a supplement. You can also obtain B12 via animals if those animals are getting it in the first place, but why not get your B12 directly rather than through an animal? I've known 2 non-vegans who have been diagnosed with a B12 deficiency, so this isn't just a vegan problem.

Question: What's the point of 'going vegan' if a plant-based diet still contributes to animal suffering, such as the killing of countless insects, birds and small mammals in crop farming?

First, remember that the majority of our crops are grown to feed farm animals, so by going vegan we are greatly reducing the overall deaths caused by crop farming. For example, more than 75% of all soy is grown to feed farm animals (mostly chickens in this case) and just 7% is used to feed humans directly. (Most of the rest is used for biofuel or cooking oil production). So if you want to reduce crop deaths – go vegan. Second, veganism isn't perfect. A nice way to think about it is this—there's a difference between murder and manslaughter, and vegans don't claim for a second that we can rid the world of manslaughter through veganism (although we can greatly reduce the manslaughter of non-human animals), so, while animals are killed unintentionally through plant farming, that doesn't mean that we shouldn't work towards ending the intentional murder of animals. Afterall, thousands of humans are killed in car-crash collisions, but that wouldn't excuse me from intentionally running down my neighbours and critics. As we work towards better farming practises in general, the most important thing to address is the ending of the purposeful breeding, commodification, cruelty and murder of animals.

Question: No honey… really?

While you might encounter the odd 'vegan' who eats honey—it can only be through a lack of education that they do so. The fact is—consuming honey is bad for bees and is a leading cause to the death of native bee populations. Whenever you read or hear some news about bee populations dying off, what they don't tell you is that it is local/native bee populations and varieties which are going extinct—not the commercially used honey bee. In fact, commercial honey bee populations have been increasing each and every year along with the increasing demand for honey. These bees are over-bred and over-worked, and they compete with local native populations, often outperforming them by sheer numbers and often spreading diseases to them. The more honey we consume, the more native bee species will become extinct. If you truly want to save the bees—then you have to stop consuming honey. And there are plenty of delicious honey substitutes available. Maple syrup anyone? Goes great with vegan pancakes.

Question: I agree that the fishing industry and industrialised animal farming are terrible, but I can avoid these things without being vegan, so why bother?

Veganism is a consumer-led movement. The less fish you eat, the less fish are caught, and the more fish alternatives are made available for everyone. This is also true for farmed-fish, as most farmed-fish species are carnivorous, you actually need to catch wild fish to feed to farmed salmon. Veganism is also the most powerful way we can affect the world around us. If you're against the idea of over-fishing then how do you tackle this problem? You can complain or campaign to your government, which seems very ineffective! Or, you can take what power you have into your own hands. What I would love people to understand is that, unlike veganism, the meat, dairy and fishing industries have been, for decades, producer-led industries.

These industries have been able to advertise lies and propaganda to us, our parents and our grandparents, and in most countries they are state-subsidised, which means some of our tax money goes towards keeping these industries afloat and keep the cost of their 'products' down. Veganism doesn't have the luxury of state/government subsidies, and if vegans started spreading false information through tv or on the internet we'd be called out immediately, instead, we need to realise our power as consumers and boycott non-vegan products out of existence.

In terms of sustainability, I'll assume for a moment that I'm talking to someone who only eats fish that they've caught and animals that they've killed/hunted. Even if this is so, it's not sustainable. When a bear kills a deer in a forest, the bear eats what it can, then comes the scavengers, then the birds, then the insects, the fungi, and ultimately the nutrients are absorbed into the soil for the plants. Does a bear shit in the woods? Yes, as part of a healthy ecosystem. The deer, even dead, never leaves the ecosystem which gave it life and sustained it's growth in the first place. But when a hunter kills a deer, she removes the body of the deer from the environment that created it, this results in a net-loss to that ecosystem. The same is true of fishing, we are removing fish from the rivers, lakes and oceans and we are giving nothing positive in return to replace what we've taken from those ecosystems. Imagine if someone was constantly invading your house, helping themselves to the contents of your fridge, and *not* replacing anything, that's hunting and fishing in a nutshell. Hunters may argue that their hunting licences pay towards the preservation of a hunting range, but we can protect nature and wildlife *without* demanding such a blood sacrifice. Would you rather live in the world of *The Hunger Games*, where the state demands an annual blood sacrifice of one person from each district or community, or would you rather not? Why should we enforce Hunger-Games logic on nature?

Question: But what about the farmers, the fisherfolk, the beekeepers, what will they do?

Personally, I see this as being the most difficult challenge in the vegan movement, but the first thing to realise is that as our preferences shift away from animal-derived products to vegan products so too will the job market shift. We don't want to destroy people's jobs, we want people in these industries to change their jobs. And it would be extremely useful to have the support of our governments to make this an easy shift for those working in these industries. For one, our governments should redirect all current subsidies and tax-breaks to help farmers transition to plant-based farming or re-wilding initiatives. But I have little faith in governments. In the short term, I think veganism, as a movement, needs to take this task into our own hands—meaning that vegans should work with people within these industries to help them find alternative jobs, even if it means providing them with the money needed to retrain and transition.

Basically—we need to embarrass our governments into doing what they should have been doing for decades. Because I, for one, am sick of hearing governments around the world pay lip-service to tackling global warming. They have failed up to now and they will more than likely to continue to fail. So the vegan community needs to go above and beyond and do the heavy lifting until our governments wake up and join us, and that means helping animal farmers, bee-keepers, fisherfolk and the rest to transition to other jobs as we continue undermining the demand for their products.

Question: a) Isn't veganism a form of privilege? And b) why are white male vegans dominating the vegan movement?

a) Veganism is not a form of privilege, but b) privilege does exist within the vegan movement.

a) Veganism is not a form of privilege—non-veganism is. The simple fact is that we can feed more people using less land, water and resources on a plant-based diet than on a non-plant-based diet. Domesticated farm animals generally outnumber humans by a factor of 10, meaning that animals, numbering roughly ten times the amount of humans, are being fed, sheltered, medically treated and watered at any given time. A dairy cow needs roughly 150 litres of fresh water every day, every single day. World hunger and water-shortages become sick jokes when you go vegan. Also, vegans are not asking people who need to eat or subsist on animals to survive to go vegan, we're asking that, for those of us with the ability to go vegan: to go vegan! And that, in turn, will make it easier for everyone else by bringing down the costs of vegan products and increasing their variety, as well as by changing how our governments give subsidies and tax-breaks.

And, in the end, the value of other animals should not be determined by us. Their own intrinsic value should be recognised. What makes eating animals such a privilege is that these animals cannot give their consent to be eaten or exploited, they are innocent. What can be more 'privileged' than deciding how to treat other animals without any concern for their wants and needs?

b) But white male privilege is real and it's in everything and it's everywhere. This includes, of course, the vegan movement. The weird thing is, I've seen white male vegans such as Ed Winters and Joey Carbstrong being questioned on this issue on shows such as *Good Morning Britain*, but it's actually pretty disgusting to blame the guest for a problem perpetuated by the host. If the host of any platform is concerned about white male privilege (and they should be) then it is up to that host to invite non-white, non-male guests onto their platforms.

And speaking as a white male, I'm not surprised that white men are coming to dominate the vegan movement, it is, literally, our white-male privilege that has allowed this to happen. White men generally have more free time, are generally given more opportunities to speak out, and we generally have less problems and off-point criticism to deal with. And you can hate that, I certainly hate it, I hate homophobia, I hate sexism, I hate discrimination, I hate that people are treated differently for things we have no say over, but veganism isn't about the messengers, you can nit-pick us, criticise us, dismiss us, hate us as much as you want, but you cannot fault the message: we need to stop abusing non-human animals, and we need to do it now. There's a reason why mainstream media prefers to attack vegans rather than veganism. To attack veganism is to advocate for animal abuse, or for the 'freedom to abuse animals for profit'. But veganism has never been about the vegans, the people, it has been, and will continue to be, about ending unnecessary abuse of all animals. So the good news is – if you hate self-righteous and smug vegans, well, in a vegan world, there won't be any 'outspoken' vegans left.

One last question:

I'll end by making one thing clear—veganism is not a position which should be defended. We defend veganism because, so far, vegans are in the minority and veganism in general is often poorly understood, but if veganism is the avoidance of animal abuse, then why should *that* be defended? In other words, non-vegan practises require actions: raising animals, feeding them, watering them, keeping them, medically treating them, and, ultimately, prematurely killing them, these are all actions, and it is actions which should be justified, not abstinence. We would never think to ask someone: 'Hey, why are you not abusing dogs today, what's wrong with you?' Similarly, we shouldn't be asking: 'hey, why are you not paying someone to abuse animals on your behalf?'

In the end, eating meat, when it isn't necessary, is a sick pleasure. The taste gives you pleasure, the sickening processes that went into giving you that pleasure is ignored. The fact that the processes are kept hidden certainly helps, but imagine if some woman or man grabbed a random pigeon or dog off the street and started trying to eat it, you would likely say—'that person is sick, they need help.' The only legitimately good excuse that exists for eating meat—ignorance—is disappearing. So, I must finish by asking, if you aren't already: ***Why aren't you vegan yet?***

Printed in Great Britain
by Amazon